for

Joan

Chuck
F
C

In the Gentle Blue Light of the Dog Star

A personal narrative

by

Chuck Farritor

ISBN 0-7414-5565-X

Edited by Jeanne Walker of JBW Copyediting

Cover art "Sandhills by Starlight" by Nebraska artist, Connie Leavitt

Glass-plate Homestead picture courtesy of Nebraska State Historical Society. Photo by Soloman D. Butcher

Newsprint copy of the 1949 Blizzard photo by A P World Wide Photos, picture is an orphan. (A P cannot find it in their files.)

Published by:

INFINITY
PUBLISHING.COM
1094 New DeHaven Street, Suite 100
West Conshohocken, PA 19428-2713
Info@buybooksontheweb.com
www.buybooksontheweb.com
Toll-free (877) BUY BOOK
Local Phone (610) 941-9999
Fax (610) 941-9959

Printed in the United States of America

Published September 2009

For Muriel

After 60 years, she is still my girl!

Acknowledgments

I'm indebted to the good folks at the San Dimas Writers Workshop for a long ton of advice and help, and to my wife Muriel, who rescued many a passage from my mostly incomprehensible notes scratched in #2 pencil on a lined, usually axel-grease-smeared, legal yellow pad. I must mention the always-willing friends who helped me, especially Ron and Edwin Bartunek and Norm Bortscheller, not to understand (that is not possible) but to deal with the constantly changing realities imbedded in the infernal machine with which I must work – my computer. It is admittedly light-years ahead of a #2 pencil and yellow pad, but I know full well, that machine has a hard Machiavellian heart. His name is Hal. I expect, Hal to, any day now, throw me into space.

The folks at Infinity Publishing were generous with advice that always made good sense. Cathleen, Timothy and Mark were a steady and fair wind on my sail. Invaluable editing was done by Saundra Sheffer. The final editing and formatting was done by the wonderfully skilled Jeanne Walker. The cover art "Sandhills by Starlight" is by Nebraska artist Connie Leavitt.

Grandmother Annie's Dog Star played a silent hand as did Miss Mae Jacobs. I must tell you about Miss Jacobs. Born in a sod house in the nineteenth century, the daughter of a Nebraska pioneer family, she became the classic "old maid country schoolteacher." To call her that is akin to calling a priceless diamond a rock. She loved the English language and taught its wonders to a generation or two of kids who came to her high school. She put a monkey on my back by telling me, "You have to write." It took awhile to get a fix on what she meant by that.

Table of Contents

Foreword

This is the remarkable story of one man and one family, yet is also the story of America. This book prompts us to remember our more complete selves. Herein we are quietly reminded that life is a collection of priceless moments, "as a doe and her fawn silently watch," a landless American family arrives at a broad green valley. That valley will soon belong to them, and the doe and her fawn will be their near neighbors. At its root, Uncle Chuck's book is a collection of his stories...but in that, it is so much more.

Stories are the sinews that connect our souls – as individuals, as families, and as a nation. They are the contours of our country and the colors that enrich the canvas of our lives. They give meaning through experiencing the gentle song of the cottonwood trees, light morning air made thick with the aromas of fresh-brewed coffee and frying bacon, the gleam and texture of wet raingear, the reassuring bite of a shot of Irish whiskey, love for the night sky and the comforting brilliance of a single blue star.

The brutal action and heart-wrenching pain that comes to this young cowboy-turned-sailor-then-builder will sneak up on you as it does on him. His lifeline is his faith and his love of family, the sky, the land and the sea.

These are stories of a strong pioneering people, tales of surviving a long, deadly drought on a once fair land and near death in a cold, gray Korean sea. The stories are never told as an exertion. The great effort of this work is to always treat daily life as a gift, never a struggle. In their telling, these stories, set in the past, are always about our future. And as such, they offer light as giving as the kerosene lantern that burned night and day to ward off the mind-warping terror that is brought on by continued exposure to around-the-clock darkness in a snowdrift-buried sod house on a blizzard-swept prairie. There is comfort in knowing that our lives are connected across the generations, and as Americans and as family, there is reassurance in knowing that we are heir to this power source. Simply put, these often sad but always uplifting stories give us strength as they whisper ever so softly, "God love you," as Uncle Chuck has so often quietly whispered to me while kissing my cheek.

– Scott Kleeb
Clean-energy entrepreneur and former history professor
Hastings, Nebraska

Preface

In the Gentle Blue Light of the Dog Star

Each of these stories can stand alone but each story is an integral part of the whole. The first story is of my grandparents. Their story was told at greater length in my book titled *Buffalo Grass and Tall Corn.* That book, now long out of print, can be seen occasionally on the Internet where it is being offered for sale, used, at prices as much as twenty times over the price marked on the cover!

In the beginning of the family's American experience, three Ferriter brothers, Michael, James and John, came from County Kerry in southwest Erin. They were fleeing the ongoing economic disaster that was British-occupied Ireland. They landed in America at the port of Boston, circa 1834. Desperately seeking work, they found their way to the coal mines in Pennsylvania. It's easy to see why they hated the darkness and foul air in the mines; in Ireland they had fished the clean blue seas and farmed the green land, always in pure open air.

Of the three brothers, it is John who is my great-grandfather. At age fifty-four John volunteered to fight in a company of cavalry in Abe Lincoln's army. Apparently he was willing to accept the risks of war to escape working in the mines.

John's great-great-granddaughter, Michele Farritor McMurray, has extensively researched John's life and times. She will tell Great-Grandfather John's story when the time is right for her. I know it will be told with love and an informed understanding of those extraordinarily troubled times for our country and for our family.

John Farritor's descendents have always questioned and speculated on the change in the spelling of the family name. In Ireland the English language spelling of the name was and is "Ferriter." In areas where the ancient "Irish" language is spoken it is spelled "Feiritear." In Ireland John's family spoke and were schooled only in "Irish" (scholars call the language Gaelic).

When John and his brothers came to America, they learned to speak American English but they could not read or write in that tongue. The first indication of a change in the spelling of the name was in a "Petition to the Honorable Court of Common Pleas in and for the County of Tioga, State of Pennsylvania. The Petitioner will henceforth support the Constitution of the United States and further will absolutely and entirely renounce all foreign sovereignties whatever and most particularly the Queen of Great Britain. Whereupon, on motion, the Court will admit John Faritor to the rights of Citizenship to the United States and to the Commonwealth of Pennsylvania." Note the new imaginative spelling of John's last name. It's possible that the clerk of the court simply spelled the name as John pronounced it. His American name became "John Faritor." It's anyone's guess when the third "r" that we use was added. John's signature does not appear anywhere on his petition for citizenship. That very simple but important document is dated September 16, 1845. It is written in a clear flowing hand, probably that of the clerk of the court.

The information on the near annihilation of the great Pawnee nation at the hands of the Sioux came from research done by Shawn Farritor. See his forthcoming book titled *End of the Pawnee Star Light.*

Grandmother Annie's small hardwood rocker, mentioned in Story One and Story Six, was passed around within the family so that it rocked and comforted many of Annie's grand and great grandchildren. Eventually, showing its years, it found its way to Annie's great grandson, Shane Farritor. Shane is an engineering professor at the University of Nebraska, but in his spare time, he is also a skilled woodworker. Shane has restored Annie's little hardwood rocker to its original beauty. It is now rocking and comforting Shane and his wife Tracy's children. There is no reason to doubt that, in its renewed life, it will rock and comfort many more of Annie's progeny.

The autobiographical stories are told in the third person. Names of ships and most small towns have been changed, as have all nonfamily personal names. The resources are not available to me to get the permissions necessary to do otherwise. Family, public, and historical names have been used as faithfully as I know how.

This lowly storyteller would be pleased to be told that you, the reader, found hidden, here and there in these lines, minute traces of Pierce Feiritear's poetry. That distinction would make it worth the risk of being hanged by the bloody Brit Queen. (You will learn of Pierce Feiritear's poetry and hanging in Story One.)

– Charles F. (Chuck) Farritor
Claremont, California

Story One

A Time for Growing

The whispering grasses were there in the valley to greet them. The tall grasses, bending and rippling in the soft prairie wind, flooded freely across the valley in a dozen shades of green. The teams had strained valiantly against their collars as they struggled to pull a heavily loaded wagon up out of a canyon. This was the last of many canyons the family riding on that wagon had followed or crossed on their journey to their new home.

Robert Garret Farritor (Bob), his wife Anna (Annie) and their family had packed up and left their rented house in the coal mining country of southern Illinois. They came west by train with all of their possessions carefully packed in a railway boxcar. Those possessions included a disassembled Studebaker freight wagon, all of their household furniture, goods, clothes, bedding, and a few precious books and pictures plus a single-bottom "grasshopper" plow. One item of note was a small hardwood rocking chair upon which Annie rocked her babies.

On a warm spring day in 1879, the westbound Union Pacific train let the family and their boxcar off at Wood River, Nebraska. After they unloaded the boxcar, the family's next task was to reassemble the freight wagon. That done, acting on advice from the man he had hired as a "land-locator," Bob went to the lumber and hardware dealer in the village to buy material to shore the walls of the 20-foot-deep well he would have to dig in order to survive on his claim. They trusted and prayed that good water would, indeed, be found no more than 20 feet deep in the new land. They understood all too clearly that many things, including survival itself, depended on that trust and those prayers.

Bob Farritor had dreamed and saved for most of his adult life to make possible an escape from his life as a coal miner. Most of all, he didn't want his sons to have to go into the mines with him. The federal government and the railroads were advertising free land newly available in the West. Last year Bob had traveled alone to the tall-grass country in the new state of Nebraska to locate and file a claim for land under the terms of the national Homestead Act. The family was now on its way to "prove up" on that claim by building a home and living on the claim for a prescribed number of years.

At the lumber yard Bob also bought a 1-0 x 3-0 glazed window with frame, four dozen slim lodge poles, and two 2-8 x 7-0 wooden doors with frames and hardware. They loaded their worldly goods into the wagon on top of the newly purchased building materials.

In the village they bought a milk cow with a baby calf at her side plus two teams of horses with collars and tack. Bob was advised that his heavily loaded wagon would be too much for a single team to pull. This was certainly true, as most of the trek to their claim would be across country where no roads existed. The man who sold them the cow gave Annie a young female dog. He said, "Mrs. Farritor, you're gonna need a friend ta talk to. This little lady'll understand ever thang ya tell her. If ya listen close, she may, from time to time, give ya some good advice too."

At last ready to move out, Bob and Annie sat on the spring-seat that fitted atop the front end of the wagon box. Baby Robb had to make room for Annie's new dog. She rested between Bob and Annie with her head in Annie's lap. The two older children, Jennie eight and Mary seven, and the baby calf hung on for dear life high atop the heavy load.

The box on their Studebaker freight wagon was fitted with overhead hoops. These hoops supported light canvas sheeting designed to protect the wagon and its load from rain. This feature gave all such equipped wagons the familiar names of "covered wagon" or "prairie schooner." When not needed, the canvas cover was stowed away.

Bob had never before driven a tandem hitch (one team ahead of the other). This method gave better access through broken country and onto narrow bridges. With plenty of advice from well-meaning townsfolk, Bob managed to get safely out of the village of Wood River. Once out on the trail, he learned quickly. Most of his learning came from the horses. Bob had long experience with the horses and donkeys that spent their whole lives deep in the coal mines. He knew that, given half a chance, the animals will do the right thing. The driver need only be smart enough to give them that chance.

At sundown, they made camp on a meadow by a small creek. The children and the baby calf were happy to get down off their scary perch atop the load. They began, at once, to romp and play on the soft grass of the meadow. At bedtime the calf would be safe tied near its mother, and the children were safe in their bedrolls under the wagon.

Bob and Annie Farritor, with their children, were realizing a long-nurtured dream; they were about to cross a financial and social chasm. They were to become landowners.

This, for any family, was a major step. This family had been landless since the 17th century, when the invading British had driven them off their land in Ireland.

In a decade-long defensive war, their several-generations-removed grandfather, Pierce Feiritear, (the Irish language spelling of their name), was able to keep the marauding Brits from taking over Corca Dhuibhne (the southwestern section of Ireland).

A many-faceted man, Pierce is acclaimed as one of the *Four Masters* (the classical poets of Ireland). A skilled harpist and balladeer, Pierce was also a scholar and swordsman of no ordinary kind.

A leader in the Irish Rebellion of 1641 against "The Stranger" (the British), he kept his small, well-trained army constantly on the move to attack and baffle the invading Brits. Pierce had three small, brass cannons. He was able to move those guns around so quickly that the invader thought he had a full battery of the lethal little weapons.

The family is indebted to literary historian Father Patrick Dineen for what they know of Pierce. Father Dineen published a book in 1903 telling of the death of Pierce Ferriter (the English spelling of his name) and Oliver Cromwell's rape of Ireland.

Unable to defeat Pierce in battle, Cromwell invited Pierce to a neutral area to discuss an armistice. Under a white flag of truce, Cromwell played his "Britt" card. He called up a battalion of his cavalry that he had secreted in a thick forest nearby. Pierce and his party put up a desperate fight, but outnumbered forty to one, they were overcome. Cromwell's men threw a rope over the limb of an oak tree, and before sundown on that tragic day, the infamous Britt, Cromwell, hanged the Irish poet/warrior, Pierce Feiritear. Cromwell's forces then put the sword to the surviving members of Pierce's party and promptly launched a full-scale attack on Pierce's castle, which stood on a promontory overlooking the North Atlantic just west of what is now the village of Ballyferriter. The castle was reduced to the rubble that remains there to this day. The site is frequently visited by people from near and far who know Pierce Feiritear to be a renowned forefather to them.

The members of the large Feiritear family, who did not die in that final battle or were not able to escape to Spain or

Normandy, became serfs under "The Stranger" on what was once their own land.

Back to the moment of Bob and Annie's arrival on their claim. The teams leaned valiantly into their collars as they struggled to pull the heavily loaded wagon out of the canyon and onto the ridge. A second team hooked to a light buckboard had climbed easily out of the canyon and stood waiting there for the heavily loaded wagon to come alongside. A bearded man with piercing black eyes, dressed in buckskin and wearing a wide-brimmed hat, sat on the spring-seat of that rig. A long, muzzle-loading rifle lay across his lap; his left arm was raised, pointing out toward the broad valley that lay before them. The teams were allowed to rest for a few minutes while Bob and Annie and their three children looked out over that grass-covered valley. They could not know it at that moment, but this valley, south of the Middle Loup River on the edge of the Nebraska Sandhills, would soon take on their name. It would become known as Farritor Valley.

From a knoll a hundred yards to their left, a doe and her fawn silently watched these newcomers in wide-eyed fascination. The mare on the lead team tossed her head to counter a nose fly; the doe and her fawn bounded away out of sight.

The broad valley, beautiful and benign in the warm sunshine, invited the family to come in. Affected but not beguiled by the beauty, Bob and Annie understood full well the dangers. They knew that to survive in this new land, they must immediately dig their well and, as the Indians had done before them, they must burrow into the earth to create a sanctuary from the killer storms that would come when the moon turned pale.

They picked a spot on the south side of a small hill in the center of the valley to unload all the materials from the wagon. Annie then set up housekeeping in the covered wagon.

Kaleb and Sarah, a couple living in a sod house beyond the east ridge of the valley, were there for them with advice and help. Kaleb was the tall man in buckskin who had led them to this place. He had been many things in his long life; at this point he was what he called a "land locator." He met people, as he had met Bob, at the trains from the east and offered, for a small fee, to guide them to lands to the north and west that were available for homesteading.

For many generations that area of central and north-central Nebraska had been Pawnee Indian land. Only recently the Pawnee nation had been all but destroyed by the Lakota and Brule Sioux. The Pawnee land was now available for homesteading by whites because the United States government had, in a political and military action, forced the surviving Pawnee to move to Indian Territory in Oklahoma and drove the marauding Sioux back to the Dakotas.

The winds were out of the north and turning cold when the family moved out of the covered wagon and into their now completed, warm dugout home. The south-facing wall, built of sod, included the door and window assemblies they had purchased in Wood River. The roof over the part of the dwelling that was not dug into the hill was well braced and sheeted with lodge poles. The lodge poles were then covered with several layers of sod. This combination would not be rainproof, but it would hold out the cold and snow.

The "big sky" that exists over the eastern-slope prairies left most newcomers in some degree of fear. The simple enormity of that sky could be overwhelming. Fortunately that fear was not a factor for Bob and Annie. That big sky was instead, for them, a source of wonderment. Fluffy white floaters in the brilliant blue vault would be replaced once or twice a week by rolling, black rain clouds. These fierce newcomers would frequently be touched here and there by entwined ribbons of white and yellow. Rolling claps of thunder would follow bolts of forked lightning that shot out of the dark clouds. The thunder and lightning were themselves things to be feared. Bob and Annie, however, accepted them without question because they seemed to be the signal for the precious rain to start falling. The cooling rain renewed the life-spirit in each plant, animal and being that it touched.

As the warm winds of summer began to fail, thousands of cranes, ducks and geese flew across the valley headed south. Their voices called out to all below who would hear them. "Come away with us to a new summer. Don't tarry! Winter's cold breath is due and it will kill all who would winter in the tall grass." Bob and Annie did not fly away; they would stay on in this new land.

The moon had turned pale and the first snow had fallen before the second dugout was completed. This second dugout, adjacent to their dwelling, would shelter their stock. They were as ready as they could be to face the winter storms.

Those storms formed as gray clouds on the northwest horizon. They then advanced in thickening layers across the sky. Eventually they blotted out the sun. Having conquered the sun, the storms felt free to have their way with the land below and all the creatures, large and small, that dwelt thereon.

Bob and Annie regretted the passing of summer and were apprehensive about the coming storms; however, they quietly anticipated the coming of winter. They had reason to hope that the winter sky in this great new land would approach the beauty of the winter sky over their ancestral Irish homeland.

The celebrated winter night sky over Ireland was the subject of many an Irish folktale and song. Family stories concerning the sky almost always dealt with the beauty and myths surrounding a brilliant blue star that rose each evening. The star Sirius didn't just rise like the moon or the other stars. It seemed instead always to fling itself into view. It would frequently first appear as a twinkling, rapidly changing kaleidoscope. It could show many colors, even sometimes a brilliant green. As it gained altitude, it would settle into its ancient, authentic blue-white mode.

The Irish were not the first people to treat Sirius with special reverence. Many peoples of early civilizations looked upon the bright sapphire star not only with reverence but also as a deity. Passageways in Egyptian pyramids were aligned to mark its highest nightly position. Sirius, the brightest star in Canis Major, has been known from antiquity as the Dog Star.

As the season changed, the Dog Star did, indeed, show himself. Each evening, as they watched, he would leap into view to greet them in all of his colorful, vested glory. Annie's mother, before her, had loved the stars in the night skies. She had often advised her children, "If you love the stars in the night skies; you'll not be afraid of the darkness." Perhaps the Dog Star's familiar presence in the sky was proof to Annie that her God had followed her to this remote new land with its strange Indian name.

Other than cash money, the one item most needed for further building on their homestead was pine poles and cedar logs. Bob recruited a bachelor named Tom Terrell to go with him on a log hunt. He had been told that old growth cedar and pine could be found in draws running off the Dismal River away to the northwest; the Dismal was the headwater of the nearby Middle Loup. Tom, a horse-soldier veteran of the Indian wars, always carried a Spencer rifle in a boot on his saddle. Men who had survived, but barely, with a single shot weapon, loved the Spencer. It was comparatively small and light, and it was said of that rifle, "Ya c'n load it on Sundee an' shoot it all week."

Bob asked Tom to leave his horse, saddle and rifle in Annie's care. Bob knew they were going into a land of heavily armed cattlemen. He figured it was safer to go there unarmed since he could not possibly match the arms of the men who were there.

The Sandhills land to the north and west was mostly federal "open-range country." Various cattle interests who grazed stock there claimed absolute proprietary rights to the land they were using. The cattlemen didn't give a tinker's dam about the cedar or pine trees in the draws, it was just that they wanted no trespassing on their grasslands. For good reason they considered any stranger to be a threat to their stock. Shooting and butchering "slow elk" (the poacher's name for range cattle) was a recognized industry on the prairie.

Bob and Tom traveled north from Farritor Valley across Victoria Creek and then north and west to the bank of the Middle Loup. There they turned left, traveling upstream on the south bank of that river. They were traveling with two teams and two wagons. The boxes had been removed from the wagons so the logs and poles could be loaded directly on each wagon's bolsters. Bob was heading for an area where the grass and water were "owned" by a cattleman he knew personally. The way he had gotten to know this man is a story in itself.

Ivory Prentise Olive (I P) had come to the Nebraska Sandhills from Southwest Texas. He came with a herd of wild cattle to sell. These were indeed wild cattle. I P, as he was called, and his brothers had caught them up in a land as wild as the stock they gathered. The seventeenth century Spanish empire builders were long gone, but descendants of the cattle they had brought with them from Spain had survived. The cattle had grown strong and wild in the river marshes and table grasslands of Mexico and the American Southwest.

I P liked what he saw in this north country. He decided not to sell his herd. He would stay on in Nebraska to build an empire of his own. One day he was moving a herd from his spread on the South Loup River to his "River Ranch" on the Dismal. They stopped to overnight near Victoria Creek. After watering at the creek they moved the herd onto a grassy flat west of the creek. There they put them into a "go-around." Most of the cowboy crew would bed down in a camp near the creek but two of their mates would spend the night in the saddle. They would ride around and around the herd to keep it settled through the night. The cowboys often sang quietly as they rode. Their songs were usually made up as they went along using standard melodies that they all knew.

Go ta sleep li'l doggie, sleep lak' ah stone.

It's y'r good fortune an' also ma own.

I P's River Ranch, will be 'r new home.

Come ah ti yi yi yipee, yae yipee yae.

Come ah ti yi yi yipee yae.

The singing kept them from falling asleep in their saddles, and the cattle seemed to like the sounds they made. A few would low softly in answer to the cowboy's voice as he rode slowly by in the moonless night.

Before I P bedded down at the camp by the creek, he decided to pay a visit to the Victoria Creek Postmaster. This man was known locally as Judge Mathews. The Judge's headquarters consisted of two cedar-log cabins on the east bank of the creek. (The well-preserved cabins can be seen, just as he built them, in what is now Nebraska's Victoria Springs State Park.) The Judge had named his little settlement New Helena after Helena in Virginia, the community from which he came. This was the spot where the mail riders delivered and picked up what little mail circulated through this part of the country. The Judge had no mail for I P, but near one of his cabins he had a crabapple tree and the tree was loaded with fruit. As was his way, I P helped himself. He filled his "ten-gallon" hat with the borrowed fruit. In the failing light he couldn't see that most of the apples were green. He ate a passel of them on his way back to camp.

After a couple of hours of fitful sleep, I P awoke with a ten-gallon pain in his gut. He was convinced that he was about to die. He hollered for his men to saddle up and go find a doctor. He shouted, "Gawd damit, ah' need ah Saw Bones ta' either fix me or ta' dee'clare me daid!"

His foremen quickly sent men off into the night. One of them galloped away in the darkness to the postmaster's cabin. He had to fire three or four shots into the night sky to get the Judge awake. Once awake, the Judge expressed extreme displeasure at the disturbance. Hidden in among the profanity, the cowboy found the message that there was no doctor within 40 miles, but Bob Farritor seemed always to have some Irish whiskey on hand. That was the only "med'cine" that the Judge knew about. "There's a trail to Bob's place, it's in a valley off to the east and south." The man also got the message that if he went into Bob's place shooting, he'd likely get shot out of his saddle.

The cowboy spurred his horse to a dangerous dead-run in the dark. He rode over several low hills into Farritor Valley. At

Bob's place, two dogs met him well away from the dugout. There was nothing much he could do but call out in the night for Bob. He did so while trying to calm his spooked horse. The dogs, leaping to bite the rider's legs, were far more than the cowpony wanted to deal with. With his mount leaping and spinning in fright, the rider's shout went out, "Halloo Bob Farritor! Judge Mathews sent me."

A tall figure holding a shotgun emerged from the shadows near the dugout. After hearing the man's story, Bob called off the dogs and asked the cowboy to wait up a minute. He went back inside and came out with a lighted coal oil lantern, a jug of whiskey and a pint-sized flask. With a man as sick as Olive was reported to be, he figured he'd best send along a full flask of whiskey. He filled the flask and started to hand it to the rider, but then looking at the agitated cowboy in the light of his lantern, he decided he needed to take some precautions. Holding the lantern high and looking the cowboy in the eye, he said, "Young man, if I was to ask you to take a good belt of whiskey from my jug, could I know for sure ya' won't drink up y'r boss's med'cine before ya' c'n get it to 'im?"

The cowboy said. "If ya' was to let me do that, Mister Bob, there jus' ain't no way in hell thet ah'd drink up the boss's med'cine. Ya' got ma' word on thet." The cowboy rested the jug on his bent right arm and took a heavy belt of its contents. He handed the jug back, took the flask from Bob's outstretched hand and then vanished into the night. His horse's shod hoofs could be heard pounding the trail over the low hills back to Victoria Creek. Bob shook his head as he returned his shotgun to its pegs on the wall and the jug to its safe place on a high shelf. He hoped the deal would hold.

The deal held. The cowboy slid his lathered mount to a stop at the encampment by the creek. He leaped from the saddle and gave his suffering boss the flask of medicine. I P removed the cap, sniffed the contents and downed the whiskey. A contented smile crossed his face; he then laid back in his blanket and slept like a baby.

A week or so later I P and one of his foremen, Fred Fisher, rode into Bob's valley. Bob was at the well, drawing water. He invited them to dismount and water their horses. When they did so, he handed them each a cup of fresh water from his well. The cattlemen squatted on their heels to enjoy the cool drink and to roll a cigarette. I P told Bob who they were and said, "Bob, I cum ta thank ya fer the "med'cine" ya sent to me t'other night when I was feelin' poorly. It fixed me up good an' I'm 'preciative of ya' neighborliness. When a man shows a kindness ta me or one ah my men I expect ta repay 'im fer what 'es done. Tell ya what Bob, I'll have my boys brand up and drop off a hunnert head of bred cows fer ya. If y'all don't have a brand workin' yet, my smithie will make one up fer ya. It's plain ta see thet some good breeding stock is jus' what y'r needin' here to get ya goin' good in this country. On our way across y'r valley, Fred and me noted all of them patches of four-foot high big bluestem grass, and we've tasted the good water from your well. Yes sir, them cows'd do fine here in y'r care."

Bob studied the ground ahead of his boots for a long minute. Then he looked into the cattlemen's eyes and said, "Mr. Olive, I appreciate y'r stopping by fer a visit, I have ta tell ya though, I can't accept y'r generous offer of the stock. Ya' see, Mr. Olive, I'm resolved to be beholden ta no man. What I would like, Mr. Olive, is y'r friendship. That would be an even greater value to me then the breedin' stock."

I P stood up, took Bob's hand and said, "Bob Farritor, I cain't recollect when I've been prouder ta accept a deal. And Bob, my father's name is Mr. Olive, I P is what I'm called by ma' friends. I'd be honored if'n yu'd call me thet." He retrieved the empty whiskey flask from his saddlebag and handed it to Bob.

The two cattlemen swung onto their mounts and galloped away to the southeast. Bob took the flask to the dugout. He wanted to reassure Annie. He knew that she, surrounded by her children, had been standing at a gun port in the door of the dugout holding the shotgun on the heavily armed visitors. There were only two of them and she had two shells in the double-barreled gun.

They made good time. Sundown of the second day found Bob and Tom in the area on the Dismal where Bob expected to find the trees he was looking for. Fresh-brewed coffee on their campfire was sending out its inviting vapor when two horsemen hailed them and then rode up to the campsite. It was Fred Fisher and one of the "River Ranch" cowboys. They had drawn their weapons and were holding them on the strangers. Bob reminded Mr. Fisher that they had met at the well in Farritor Valley and explained what he was up to. He then invited the newcomers to have a cup of coffee. The cowboys put away their guns, Fred declined the invite, then said that the ranch house was only a couple of miles away and they needed to get along or they'd miss out on supper. He said further, "Ya know Bob, now that ya've made camp here, ya may's well stay where ya are fer this night, but tomarree' night an' as long as y'r on River Ranch, I P ain't gonna hear tell of ya sleepin' under y'r wagon. No sir, he'll want ya' in fer supper, and you and y'r man'l throw y'r bedrolls on cots in the bunkhouse."

The next day they got an early start on the log hunt. After they warmed the cool morning air with the thick aroma of fresh coffee and fried bacon, they found trees just the size Bob was looking for. By sundown they had fully loaded the wagon Tom was driving. They tied the load down well and drove both wagons across the unmarked, rolling prairie in the direction Fred Fisher had taken the evening before.

They found the ranch headquarters on a rise on the south bank of the Dismal. Nestled in a stand of pine trees, it overlooked the east-flowing river and the endless stretch of grass-covered Sandhills that lay beyond. I P himself was at the stock gate to welcome them. "Turn y'r teams over ta' my man there, e'll feed an' water 'em an' put 'em up fer the night." Bob said, "I P, this young fellow is Tom Terrell, he was kind enough ta' come along ta' help me with wrestlin' them cedar logs."

I P responded, "Any friend of yours, Bob, is welcome here on River Ranch. Y'all kin' wash up at the pump there and then come on in; we'll be sittin' down ta' a beans and steak supper, pronto."

They quickly washed up and entered the 60-foot-long sod house. Bob guessed there were at least 25 cowboys at that supper table. They were all talking and joking and having a good time; they spoke mostly in an unmistakably slow Texican drawl.

The small windows in the thick sod walls allowed little light to enter the room. Several lit, coal-oil lanterns hanging from the rafter ties cast a warm, yellow light on the long cedar-plank table. The food was good and plentiful. After the meal they all continued to sit at the table, talking and picking their teeth with wooden toothpicks. The store-bought toothpicks were in a tin cup that was passed around the table. After a while, the cowboys got up, went outside and gathered in a circle on the grass in front of their bunkhouse. They were sitting cross-legged, rolling and smoking cigarettes, again joking and telling stories. One strummed softly on a battered old guitar.

Only I P, his two foremen, Fred Fisher and Jim Stockham, and the two guests were left at the table. After Jim Kelly, the black cowboy cook, cleared the supper dishes away, Fred got a jug of whiskey and passed it around.

I P invited everyone to gather at his end of the table. He broke out a deck of cards and said, "Let's play a few hands of draw poker to pass the evening." Bob declined; he knew this was no place to get into a poker game. Tom Terrell could not be dissuaded. He asked for cards and I P dealt him a hand.

Lady Luck seemed to be with Tom; he drew some winning hands right off. Feeling good about things he took a belt of whiskey each time the jug was passed. After an hour or so Tom's luck seemed to desert him but he kept asking for cards and drinks from the jug of whiskey. Eventually he had lost all of his money.

Suddenly he jumped up and stuck his finger in I P's face. "You gawd-dammed cheatin' little Reb, I saw ya dealin' off the bottom of thet deck!" I P said not a word. When he stood up, the pistol that had jumped into his hand was pointed at Tom's belly. The hammer was back and Tom Terrell was about to die.

As quickly as I P drew the pistol, Bob placed his hand on I P's gun arm. Bob said, "I P, don't kill my friend. He's drunk too much whiskey. Let me take 'im off y'r ranch an' out'a y'r sight right now."

After a month-long moment, I P eased the hammer down and dropped the gun back into its holster. He turned to Bob and said, "This fool'll live ta' walk out ah here only 'cause ya've ax'ed me fer 'is life. Ya' haf'ta know though 'es ah' dead man. Ah'll kill 'em the next time ah' see 'em, whether he's carryin' a gun or not."

By lantern light, Fred Fisher and Jim Stockham helped Bob get one of Bob's teams harnessed and hooked onto the loaded wagon. They got an ashen Tom Terrell up onto the load with orders to travel all night to get off of River Ranch. Bob divided their stores and described the spot where Tom was to make camp and wait for him to catch up with the second load of logs.

Bob slept in the bunkhouse. I P's cowboys were respectfully quiet in his presence. They had never before seen anyone with the guts to try to change I P's mind about anything. They knew I P as a loose cannon. The smart thing to do was to let him do whatever it was he wanted to do. "Thet quick gun of his'n gives him 'rats' that a man with a slower gun ain't got."

At daylight, Bob resumed his task of cutting cedar logs. Near sundown, a couple of I P's cowboys showed up to help him load the wagon. Bob thanked the cowboys for their help and asked them to thank I P again for his hospitality. He drove all night under a full moon to get to the spot where Tom was supposed to be camped. Tom was not there.

Tom had "seen the elephant." Fear of a gut-shot death had caused him to keep moving. A week later, when Bob got his heavily loaded wagon home, he found the loaded wagon Tom had been driving standing in the yard. Bob learned from Annie that Tom had gotten off the wagon, unharnessed the exhausted team, put them safely in the corral and then saddled his horse, checked the load in his Spencer rifle and rode away without saying a word, except to say, "Bob's okay, he'll be along directly." They never saw the young bachelor again. Rumor had it that Tom Terrell had gone to Montana.

Bob regretted that he had not had a chance to talk to Tom. He wanted to let him know that he too had seen I P deal off the bottom of the deck. Bob would've reminded Tom that, drunk or sober, you can only afford to be right if you're on the high ground and have the bigger gun. Without those two things, being dead-right can lead to being just dead.

Bob now knew where he could get all the logs he would need. It was the lack of cash money that was most hurtful. As their herd grew, the need for water would quickly outstrip the family's ability to draw the required water from the well by hand. They had to somehow buy a windmill.

After discussing the issue with Annie, it was agreed that Bob would go back to work in the Illinois coal mines during the winter months to get the cash they needed to further develop their homestead. Bob knew that Kaleb would keep Annie and the children supplied with game for the table and that she had on hand plenty of stored shelled corn for flour and meal.

For the stock, he had large stacks of prairie-hay near the sod barn. Fuel for the stove consisted of plenty of stored cow chips plus corncobs. Three drums of coal oil should be enough to keep the lanterns lit through the long winter evenings. Annie would keep the days and nights safe with Bob's shotgun. She and the children were not completely alone. Sarah and Annie had become fast friends. Lord knows, a woman surrounded by only miles of grass needed another woman to talk to. The comfort found in talking to a dog, no matter how wise and understanding that dog is, had often come up short.

Annie also knew that beyond the strength given her by her God, there was that presence in each night's sky that was her quiet source of reassurance, her celestial friend the Dog Star.

The plan worked well. With the money Bob earned working the winter months in the mines, they had been able to purchase the lumber they were going to need to build the roof of their planned sod house, plus the desperately needed windmill and stock tank.

Bob was anxious to get his family out of the dugout and into a regular sod house. He was able to do this with the help of

18

John Graham, his father-in-law. John was a skilled carpenter and a structural engineer (sans sheepskin). He was responsible for designing and placing the shoring in the coal mine in which he worked. John came with Bob on the train from Illinois to spend the summer months of 1881. Working long hours each day and with help from neighbors, they were able to get the sod house and new sod barn built. Both were all above ground with wood-framed gable roofs.

The winter of 1881-1882 was to be a winter unlike anything they had seen before. Busy with the task of moving the family into the new sod house, Bob was late getting away. It was the day after Christmas before he caught the train to go work in the mines.

New Year's Day brought a heavy snowstorm and as January wore on, it kept snowing daily. The family watched in growing alarm as storm after storm piled the snow higher and higher around them. Annie decided to keep all of the livestock she could in the sod barn, carrying hay and water to them daily. It broke her heart to know that all the animals she couldn't fit into the barn would surely die in the storms.

Annie had a guide rope strung from the house to the well, to the haystack and to the sod barn. The enormous quantity of snow eventually began drifting over the buildings. Annie kept the children digging at the snow. It was important to keep it away from selected windows so some daylight could get into the house. It was a constant struggle to keep the door from freezing shut. They knew that the front door had to be left open a crack to allow air in for them to breathe and for the stove to keep working properly. Eventually the pump at the well froze up. They now had to get water for themselves and the stock by melting snow in the washtub on the stove.

There came a time when daylight from the windows was completely blocked by ice and snow. Annie found that she had to keep the lanterns lit around the clock. Without the lantern light, the constant darkness was a source of terror for the children and the same was true for the animals in the barn. As the weeks of confinement became months, even with the lanterns lit, moments of panic among the children and the livestock became more and more frequent. The phenomenon is a very real and dangerous fact of life and possible death.

Early on, Annie had the children dig a deep hole in the floor of one bedroom to use for a sanitation pit. The dirt from the digging was kept in a pile nearby. It was there to be sprinkled over each new deposit. A page from an old "Monkey Ward" catalog served as the final touch to each depositor's daily "job."

In the barn, the efforts toward keeping it clean got to be more than the children could handle. The animals had to simply get used to standing or lying in their waste. The milk-cow was the exception; Annie insisted she be kept clean. Annie knew that the cow's milk was critical for keeping the children and herself well. All the more important because she had begun to realize that she had a new life, a new baby, growing within her.

Bob's brother, Jim, had homesteaded with his family in the upper New Helena valley a few miles over a range of hills to the southwest. Jim had not yet built a sod house so they were still in their dugout. The snow had drifted over it completely. Jim was in Illinois for the winter, working in the mines with Bob. When their supply of coal oil gave out, the deadly phenomenon resulting from extended exposure to total darkness was taking a heavy toll on his family. Wintering with Jim's family was his brother-in-law Tom Sullivan and his wife. They were recent arrivals from Ireland.

In desperation, Tom, a strong and healthy young man, decided to strike out afoot to the northeast to try to make it to Bob and Annie's place, hoping to find extra fuel oil there.

The familiar contours of the land were completely altered by the deep snowdrifts, making Tom's task an extremely dangerous one. Once he left Jim's place, he was alone on a vast sea of white. At any moment the wind could rise and lift the fine snow into the air, causing the horizon to disappear. If that happened Tom would be lost.

The weather held clear and the wind stayed calm. When he topped the ridge looking into Bob's valley, Tom was at first at a loss to know where the dwelling was. When he got down on the valley floor he could see a faint showing of steam against the sky. It was rising above the area where the soddie and sod barn were located.

Annie and the children were astonished and delighted to see Uncle Tom come trudging in. He was, of course, exhausted and covered with ice and frost. Annie fixed Tom a hot meal. After he had rested a bit he helped the children clean out the sod barn.

They decided it would be dangerous for him to try to return home that day. Darkness would surely catch him before he reached safety, and that could be fatal. They made a bed for him in the living room. The next day they made up a packet of cans of coal oil and bags of corn meal. He dragged the lot away on a wooden sled that Bob had made for the children. The good weather held long enough for him to get back to Jim's place safely.

When darkness fell that first day, with Tom not home, his family was sure they had lost him. Tom had surely looked death in the eye. In doing so he had rescued his and Jim's family from the certain madness that around-the-clock darkness holds for those who are exposed to it for too long.

The mail rider came only once that winter. He brought a letter from Bob and news that a teenage neighbor girl had died painfully of a ruptured appendix. Her body was stored in a snow-bank and would be buried when the ground thawed in the spring.

When Bob arrived home in April, he was proud of the way his family had fought off disaster. He, however, understood a devastating truth; had the door frozen shut, had Annie gotten sick, had any one of a dozen possible things happened, he would surely have lost his family. He would not leave them alone again.

When that deadly winter had at last given way to spring, the abundant moisture from the melting snows gave life to a lush carpet of prairie grasses. As the warm spring sun had its way with the deep snow drifts, a great tragedy came to light on the plains.

Thousands of cattle, along with wild deer and elk, had taken shelter in the east/west draws. As the drifted snow melted, these animals were found standing side by side just as they had stood during the storms. They had stood as they were found, taking small advantage of each other's body heat. The snow had drifted around them in ever-increasing depths until it had finally suffocated and frozen them where they stood.

There was, however, much proof that the storms had not killed everything on the land. The expanses of new grasses were accented here and there by bright Joseph's-Coat patches of wild flowers and now in the warm sunshine, surviving wild horses, deer and elk, along with domestic horses and cattle, grazed freely on the lush prairie.

Annie had been aware during the winter storms that a new life was stirring in her body. Now in the spring, the gentle prairie winds made the tall grasses dip and flow along the green hillsides. The new baby seemed to move in her body with a rhythm not unlike the motion of the grasses in the soft spring winds. The baby came in September. It was a boy;

they named him Francis Morris. He was the first "Farritor" and very likely the first white child born in Farritor Valley.

A few weeks after Frank was born, word came that a mission priest was coming to a settlement downstream on the Middle Loup River. The settlement was grandly called Loup City. There were three other children in the New Helena area who had not been baptized. It was arranged that a teamster named Paddy Kilfoil would take these children with their mothers to receive the sacrament. Paddy set out on the journey with his freight wagon loaded with this unique and very precious cargo.

There was never any question about Paddy's bravery. If there had been, his taking on this task would surely have laid it to rest. The trip went well, considering the possibilities for trouble. When they got to the ford over the river near their destination, Paddy decided that it would be wise to set the mothers and babies out on the bank and take them over the river, one mother and baby at a time. The first three trips went famously. The last trip was with Annie and Frank. This time Murphy's Law prevailed. Their good luck ran out at midstream, the river at that spot was not deep enough for the wagon to be floating free. The wheels were bumping along on the bottom. Suddenly the wheels on the upstream side dropped into a hole while the ones on the downstream side hit a bump. The water rushed into the wagon box and the force of the flowing river turned the wagon over.

As they were flipped into the water, Paddy grabbed the baby out of Annie's arms. He had assumed responsibility for the baby, but Annie and the horses were on their own. As they crossed the first sandbar, Annie heard Paddy shout, "Fear fer naught Annie, I've already baptized the baby!"

Well down river from the ford, they all managed to get out on the far bank. The only casualty was Annie's purple-ribboned hat. It was last seen dipping and spinning as though it were out on a lark of its own. It seemed to wave goodbye to them as it spun around the bend far down stream! Just to be safe, the mission priest baptized Frank again, conditionally.

The decade of the eighties brought prosperity to Bob and Annie in their valley. The dangerous but life-giving heavy snow and rainfall of the period combined with the richness of the soil made for a bumper crop of newborn calves, oats, corn and prairie hay. Their sod house now had a wooden floor in the living room and kitchen area and a store-bought window for each room. There was a bedroom for the boys and another for the girls, with yet another for Bob and Annie and the new baby. There always seemed to be a new baby. They continued to build. They built roofed cribs and granaries to store the harvested crops. The fine Halliday windmill stood atop its 35-foot wooden tower over a new deeper well. The prairie wind saw to it that the large wooden stock tank was always full to overflowing with the cool clear water. The water overflowing from the wooden stock tank was guided onto Annie's fenced vegetable garden.

The wooden floor in the living room and kitchen of the sod house made it a popular place for the neighbors to gather for dancing parties. It's possible that Bob's reputation as a man who usually had some Irish whisky on hand went a long way toward guaranteeing a good turnout for those parties!

At best, there was room for no more than five or six couples on the floor at one time. At most gatherings there would be several more couples than that on hand. Annie kept a tight rein on the quantity of whiskey allowed. No one, however, was ever heard to complain that it had been a dull party.

There was one partygoer over whom Annie had little control. He was an old ex-Union soldier who lived in a dugout over on Kaleb and Sarah's claim. He loved to do Irish jigs. The energy set free in those jigs would raise dust from the wooden floor and rattle the rafters. His name was Patrick Kelly. It was said of Pat that as a professional soldier he had fought under five flags. His only regret was his years of service under the flag of the bloody British Queen. Patrick came to know that his father, in his struggle to feed the rest of his family, had literally sold him at sixteen years of age to a British army recruiting sergeant. After killing his quota of lesser people in India for the Queen, she released him and he promptly fled her domain.

Living with Pat in his dugout was a large female bullsnake. She was not his pet. Snakes, like cats, really belong to no one but themselves. Because she grew fat preying on others smaller than herself, he called her "Queen Victoria." The snake, not being a student of history, didn't seem to mind the name at all.

Annie's standard control system of limiting liquor use at the dancing parties was to require all hands to surrender their jugs and flasks to her at the door. To beat that ploy, old Pat would, as did several others, stash his jug somewhere out by the windmill.

Late in the evening of one such occasion, Pat didn't return to the party from one of his visits to his stash. The next morning when Bob went out to start his chores he found Pat's hat on a post by the stock tank. This was a concern to Bob because he knew that Pat never went anywhere without his hat. It was in fact always the last thing he took off when he went to bed and the first thing he put on when he got up. Bob's concern led him to grab Pat's hat and start walking along the path that led across the valley and over the ridge to the canyon where Pat's dugout was located. As he hurried along, anxious for Pat's wellbeing, he was further surprised to find Pat's coat lying on the dew-wet grass by the path. Farther up ahead, he could see what looked like Pat's shirt. By the time he got near the east ridge of the valley, he had passed Pat's pants and long johns. Then low and behold, over the ridge came Kelly with not a stitch of clothes on. When Pat saw Bob holding his hat, he said, "Faith and beggora, Bob, and would ye be so kind as to hand me the hat yr' a holdin' so's I c'n go about gathering up ta clothes tat I was required ta trow off in ta unusual heat tat came upon me last evenin'? The bloody Queen must'a tinkered wit tat new jug of spirits. Tat jug was a strange one sure enough. Faith, it made me body, all over, as hot as ah stove lid!"

With the new dawn casting a pink glow on his bare behind, he took his hat, placed it squarely on his head and proceeded along the path to reclaim his clothes. The expression on his face was that of a man on a mission. Bob was speechless but relieved and happy that his friend Pat was truly himself on this fine morning.

The hills and canyons that surrounded Bob and Annie's Valley were host to a unique breed of wild horse. Most were the usual Roman-nosed, broom-tailed mustang. Some, however, showed the influence of a finer heritage. These had the long legs, deep chest and square face of the ancient Andalusia breed of horse brought to the New World by the Spanish conquistadors. Despite endless cross-breeding, that Andalusian blood somehow continued to show in some of these marvelous wild animals.

These small bands of wild horses were certainly a wise and hardy lot. They had survived the worst of drought, wolves and countless terrible blizzards, but they were now going out of existence due to a less deadly but an otherwise quite effective circumstance. They were being caught up by the cattlemen who were breaking them to the saddle.

Bob and Annie's first-born daughter, Jennie, saw and fell in love with a tall, deep-chested colt. The gray colt ran with a band in the canyons to the south of their valley. The family had no fast horses like those ridden by the cattlemen that were able to head off and corral the wild horses.

Jennie had her own plan to make the gray colt her own. It's likely she heard of the method from the Indian families who, from time to time, trailed by like lost souls through a land that was once free to them. The Indian visitors had come to know that Bob and Annie would share what food they had. They never stayed long. The families knew they had to keep moving; there was always a patrol of United States Cavalry close on their trail. They knew the troopers would herd them back to the accursed Reservation.

Jennie began shadowing the band of wild horses on foot. She spent every moment that could be spared from her chores out in the canyons with them. Eventually they accepted her presence to the point where she could stand among them. It wasn't long after that when she could pet the gray. He was surprisingly gentle and receptive to her touch.

The band frequented a box canyon where, especially on hot afternoons, they would literally disappear into the wild plum and chokecherry brush. On one such occasion, Jennie was able to separate the colt from the rest of the band and maneuver him into a small wood-railed pen her dad had helped her build. Jennie became the gray's only source of food and water. It was only a matter of days before he obviously enjoyed having her comb his mane and tail, and again only a few days before she was sitting on his back and sliding a bridle over his ears and a bit into his mouth.

It was a proud day for the whole family when Jennie rode her handsome gray colt out of the canyon and over into the valley. He was soon converted to gelding status, and the next time Bob came back from Wood River with supplies, he brought a present for Jennie and her gray – a well-used but well-cared-for leather saddle. Befitting the fact that Jennie was fast becoming a young lady, it was a type known as a sidesaddle. Jennie named her gray "Captain." They learned quickly from each other. Soon Jennie could herd cattle, keeping pace with any horseman in the county. Captain helped her catch and train other wild mustangs to be used by the family.

Two years after Frank was born, a blonde, blue-eyed girl arrived. She was named after Bob's mother, an ancient Irish name, Honora (Nora). Then they welcomed their third son and named him William (Will). Then again a fourth son Michael, named for the great uncle who came from Ireland in 1834 with their Grandfather John Ferriter. In 1892 their last-born child was delivered. They named this healthy, red-haired girl, Alice. Thus they had four sons and four daughters. All of the Nebraska-born children were born right there in their sod home. There was no doctor to tend any of the births. The neighborhood women looked after each other as their families grew.

Solomon D. Butcher, the self-proclaimed "photographer of the plains," came into the valley in 1890. The picture he took of Bob's place shows a clean, active, well-equipped operation with handsome and healthy horses, cattle and people.

In the center of Butcher's picture, Jennie is proudly holding her gray gelding. The picture is in black and white but the sky is obviously the bright blue one that Bob left the coal mines to find.

It seems that nothing survived those years without a struggle. That remarkable picture of Bob's place was no exception. Mr. Solomon Butcher was something of a celebrity in his time. When he came into the Valley with his camera, he put up at Bob's place for most of a fortnight while he traveled to the neighboring homesteads and ranches taking and selling his pictures. His wagon was heavily loaded with glass plates, chemicals and other tools of his trade so he traveled with a three-horse hitch. These horses had celebrity-size appetites, as did Mr. Butcher. The visiting photographer held off taking the picture of Bob's place until he had pretty well covered the pocket east of Victoria Creek, south of the Middle Loup River and north of Bob's place. When the day dawned for the "Farritor" picture to be made, there was no wind and the sun was screened by high, thin clouds.

Butcher declared that conditions were perfect for the picture. He was very particular as to just how he wanted everything and everyone placed. After considerable ordering about, he at last seemed to have things the way he wanted them. Annie, however, who had a thousand and one things to do in the house, was missing. Shouts from everyone in the line brought her running. She had baby Michael on her hip and was wearing her best dress. In the rush of the moment she forgot to take off her large flour-sack apron. Unfortunately that apron kept Annie's pretty dress from having its image recorded for posterity.

Mr. Butcher had them standing on the buffalo grass just north of the windmill. Annie's fenced vegetable garden could be seen in the near background. The older girls at the end of the line were holding their saddle horses as they stood among several head of browsing cattle. The new sod house and sod barn were in the background. Teams of harnessed horses and several pieces of haying and cultivating equipment stood in the yard. Bob and Annie had indeed accomplished a great deal in little more than a decade in their Valley.

The actual shoot went off without a hitch, except as Frank, the eight-year-old boy with the blurred face in the picture, explained later, "A horsefly was botherin' me so I had to move my head some."

Early the next morning the boys had Mr. Butcher's horses hitched to his wagon ready for his departure; Annie had packed a basket-lunch for him to take on the road. The whole family, anxious for the unveiling of the picture, had gathered near the photography wagon.

After much thumping and boot scraping within the covered wagon, Mr. Butcher, at last, appeared at the rear flap. He climbed over the endgate and hopped down onto the grass. With the large, still wet, photograph in his hands, he handed the picture to Annie and moved on to hand the invoice for his work to Bob.

The family was absolutely delighted with the picture. There were squeals of approval from the girls. The boys too were excited and happy. Frank liked it. His blurred face gave him another story to tell!

Bob, however, was feeling a bit put upon. He couldn't see any credit on the invoice for all the hay and oats the photographer's horses had eaten over the past two weeks. To bring that matter to Mr. Butcher's attention, he said, "Mr. Butcher, it's been our pleasure to keep and feed you and your horses, but you see, I sell hay and oats same as you sell pictures. Could it be that you jus' plum forgot to give me some credit for what yr' stock et off me?"

Having had no previous experience with the temperament of an "artist," what happened next put the family into shock. Mr. Butcher grabbed the picture out of Annie's hands and tore it in two. He threw the pieces down at Bob's feet and then turned and leaped onto the spring-seat of his wagon. When he slapped the horses with the reins, they lunged into their collars, and as the large-wheeled wagon reeled away, he shouted back over his shoulder, "Bob Farritor, no one'll ever see y'r damn picture. I'm go'na break the plate!" Bob launched a shot of spit after the departing photographer and his well-fed horses. He then quietly and carefully picked up the pieces of his family's picture. The next time he went to Wood River, he had a shop there fit the pieces together as best they could. They then made a green tinted copy of it. That copy with the rip showing unobtrusively across it hung proudly on Bob and Annie's living room wall. Bob didn't expect to see "the artist" again and he wasn't disappointed.

Mr. Butcher never came back to get a negotiated portion of his money. A copy of Butcher's picture hangs on the wall of most of Bob and Annie's descendents to this day.

A lifetime after Mr. Butcher grabbed the wet print from Annie's hand, ripped that picture in two, and fled the scene, a grandson of Bob's, the author of this narrative, was convinced that Mr. Butcher would never destroy the glass plate of one of his best pictures.

The "Butcher Collection of Plates" was by that time in the hands of the Nebraska State Historical Society. A painstaking search by the author and others eventually located the beautifully intact glass plate. Mr. Butcher had petulantly removed the Farritor name and filed the plate under the name "A Prairie Homestead." The following picture is a copy made from that unbroken glass plate, not a copy of the repaired print Mr. Butcher tore in two. Beautiful prints from that original glass plate are available from "The Nebraska State Historical Society" at the University of Nebraska, Lincoln.

All was well for Bob and Annie in their Valley. Bob was able to increase his holdings by taking over neighboring homesteads that had been abandoned. The folks on those homesteads had "seen the elephant and skedaddled." This was a term describing the actions of folks who for any of several reasons had given up. In some cases the husband or wife had died. Others left because of an unreasoning fear of the sound of the incessant prairie wind or the fearful enormity of the sky, or perhaps the wild threat coming out of the roiling black and yellow clouds during the summer electrical storms. These folks were unable to see the beauty in the sky that Annie saw and loved.

The Robert G. Farritor Homestead, Custer County Nebraska, circa 1890
Left to right: Mary, Jennie with Captain, Robert J., Frank, Will, Nora, Annie holding Michael, and Robert G.
This print is made from the "unbroken" glass plate, which is now in the hands of The Nebraska State Historical Society.

– Photo by Solomon D. Butcher

A significant weather change occurred on the eastern slope prairies in the early 1890s. The winters became mild and snowless and the summers became extremely hot and devoid of any rain. The heavy clouds that built up in the sky from time to time produced only violent electrical storms, more violent by far than any they had seen before. The fresh prairie winds had changed to what were called "Furnace Winds." These winds blew a hot blast daily from the southwest. They were a more passive phenomenon but one equally as frightening as the electrical storms.

The result of crop failure for a homesteader was immediate. Most had no reserves to fall back on, and Bob and Annie were no different. Without a harvest each fall, their animals and family would go hungry. They began butchering their stock, pickling and canning all they could find containers for. Frank, with his older brother Robb, kept the remaining stock alive by herding them daily in the hills and canyons. In those canyons, the stock would feed on clumps of natural grasses that were somehow surviving in spite of the terrible drought.

The term, "The Gay 90s" is familiar to everyone. The remarkable thing is that for all its fame, it describes the actions and lifestyle of a very limited number of people.

The nation was in great trouble. There was a panic on Wall Street and hundreds of banks across the country failed, including the bank that held the young State of Nebraska's general funds.

The decade of the "90s" on the eastern slope prairies was far from being a time of gaiety; it was instead a time of hunger and despair. The "elephant" ran amuck and Bob and his family saw him. He was the color of hunger and death. Not one to contemplate options for long, Bob made a decision. From his cattlemen friends he had heard stories of the possibilities of raising fruit and vegetables in southeast

Texas. The soil was rich and there was always plenty of rain. He would go there.

Preparations for making the long trip got underway immediately. A squatter was found to hold down the homestead. Bob had two wagons and bought another. He equipped them with good brakes, a water barrel and the prairie schooner-type canvas top that provided protection from the sun and inclement weather. A spring-seat located toward the front of each wagon was wide enough to seat a child and two adults. Bob and Annie would ride in their surrey pulled by Bob's handsome team of gray mules. As preparations for leaving became complete, everyone began to feel the pains of leave-taking. In spite of the terrible change in the weather, they were all deeply attached to their Valley. They had watched in disbelief as other families had loaded their wagons and left...now the unthinkable was happening to them.

The dreaded morning of departure came. The sun had not yet topped the east rim of the valley but it was already evident that it would be another hot, dry day. Bob cracked his long buggy whip and the several teams took up the slack in their tugs. There was a sound of quiet sobbing. The tears were stillborn, dried by the rising hot southwest wind. Little puffs of dust lifted around the hooves of the teams and the moving wheels as the wagon train got underway.

It was sixteen-year-old Robb's task to open the stock gate. He watched with his heart filled with fear and sadness as the big team of gray mules drew the surrey through the gate. His father was driving. His mother and his sister Jennie also rode in the surrey. Next in line was wagon number one, drawn by a team of mares named Gert and Giddy. They were driven by Mary, with Nora and five-year-old Michael as helpers. Twelve-year-old Frank drove the second wagon. It was being pulled by a big black team of mules named Tip and Coaly. Robb would ride with Frank. Together those lads were to join a daily, six-year-long battle with Tip and Coaly. That team of mules would prove to be as durable as they were mean. They would pull that same wagon back through that gate when the trip was done, and an eighteen-year-old Frank would be driving. The third and last covered wagon through the gate was drawn by a mismatched team of mules driven by a neighbor boy named Joe Hickman. Joe was sweet on Jennie and had gotten permission to go along on the trip. It was Annie's doing that Jennie was in the surrey with her, and Joe was as far away as she could arrange to place him. Will was riding with Joe.

A small remuda brought up the rear, which was made up of Jennie's "Captain," a spare team of mules and three milk cows. A young Sandhills cowboy named Orry Webb hazed this group along. Bob didn't ask Orry why he wanted to go on the trip but he agreed to his request readily because of Orry's skill with his Spencer rifle. That rifle, when not in Orry's hands, rested quietly in its scabbard on his worn but well-cared-for saddle. His mount was a quick and wiry buckskin mare.

Robb closed the barbed-wire stock gate and then ran to catch up to the second wagon in line. He joined Frank on the spring-seat behind Tip and Coaly.

Bob headed his lead mules across the hills to join the oft-traveled road to Wood River and Grand Island down on the Platte River. Grand Island was the first city that the children had ever seen. The national depression, the other half of what had driven them from their valley, was evident here. Men who should have been working were standing on street corners, and many stores were boarded up. Bob and Annie's children were disappointed at seeing the Platte; they expected to see a broad, rolling river. What they saw was a wide expanse of mostly dry sand. Due to the drought, the river was flowing only in its aquifer.

They moved smartly south from Grand Island to the state line, and they made good time as they crossed the flatlands of Kansas. When they crossed into Oklahoma the trail got considerably rougher.

Each night on the trail Orry Webb would pitch his bedroll out away from the camp with the hobbled stock. The stock would be safe out there with Orry and his rifle. The family in camp would be safe with Bob and his shotgun. Before bedtime, they'd all gather around the fire to tell each other stories. When the storytelling was done, Annie led them in prayers, her multiple prayers and Glory-be-to-Gods would be asking for a safe passage through the night and a good day on the morrow.

Later, snug in their bedrolls, Robb and Frank often launched skyward some prayers of their own. They usually asked their Lord if outlaws could come in the night to steal Tip and Coaly. From what they had heard about the Missouri border outlaws, it sounded like they would be good and proper company for that ornery pair of mules. If Coaly reached over and bit one of those guys, he'd probably get shot between the eyes. Then maybe Tip would kick that outlaw on the side of the head for what he had done to Coaly. Then for certain, another outlaw would shoot Tip. Nothing proper like that could happen unless Tip and Coaly got stolen!

Nearing the South Canadian River, they were joined by a young man riding a jet-black gelding. His chaps, hat and shirt matched the color of his horse. He wore a big six-gun in a black leather holster that hung low on his right leg. He asked Bob if he could ride along with them down to the Red River. Bob said it'd be all right. He probably welcomed a friendly gun.

The next morning, the young man tossed his tack onto Robb and Frank's wagon and turned his mount loose with the remuda. Explaining to Bob that he wanted to rest his big gelding; he joined Robb and Frank on their spring-seat. The big fellow told the boys stories all day long. The stories were mostly about hold-up men and horse thieves. He said those men were as "mean and wanton as rabid dogs." There was one young outlaw that he especially liked to talk about. He said that young fellow's name was the "Oklahoma Kid." That kid was tough but much different from the cutthroat outlaws with whom he rode.

In camp that night he told the family some of those same stories. All this talk about outlaws made Bob nervous. He decided it'd be best if he posted a guard on the camp. Robb was to keep watch with the shotgun in a clump of bushes a short distance from the camp. Orry was to sleep light in his bedroll out among the stock.

While Robb was on watch, he got to thinking about the stories the young stranger had told. It occurred to him that the rider's horse, out in the remuda, looked a lot like the one the young man said belonged to the "Oklahoma Kid."

When his dad came to relieve him at 2 a.m., Robb mentioned this possibility. Bob had his whole watch to stew on the subject, and stew he did. With the first light of dawn, Bob went over to where the young stranger was sleeping in his bedroll. He poked the sleeping man with the business end of his shotgun and said, "Young feller, I wish ya' only well, but it's probably best thet, after breakfast, you saddle up an' ride out on y'r own. The young man said, "Yes'r Mr. Bob." He put two fingers to his lips to send a shrill whistle into the morning air. His black gelding moved out of the remuda and came toward his master as quickly as he could with the night-hobble limiting his steps.

Before he left, the young man sat at ease astride his handsome mount, his big gun secure in its black holster. He thanked Bob and Annie for their hospitality and threw a kiss toward Jennie and Mary. Waving his black hat in the air, he touched his spurs to the gelding. The rested charger was eager to run and in a few moments they were out of sight. The family never saw either of them again.

While Robb and Frank were doing daily battle with Tip and Coaly, Mary, Nora and Michael were daily lavishing love and care on their team of mares. Mary drove them with never a whip in hand. Nora kept their tails and coats curried daily. Little Michael did what he could to show them that he loved them. The mares were soon in trouble. After a lifetime of drinking the cool, sweet water from the deep well in their valley, each day they now had to drink from a different creek, river or pond. This, or something unknown, seemed to be putting them off their feed. On the road, they were usually exhausted by midday. Bob eventually found it necessary to replace them on Mary's wagon with the extra team of mules.

They crossed the Canadian River into Indian Territory. The country was increasingly harder to get through with its steep canyons, washouts, thick stands of trees and the like. At one point they found a rope across the trail. Two armed Indians stopped them. One of the two said to Bob, "Traveler, it'll cost ya' 25 cents a wagon an 25 cents fer-yr remuda ta use this trail." The heavy toll charge did nothing to improve the road.

On one clear morning Orry's saddled mare and the remuda kept pace near Frank and Rob's wagon. The big cowboy was on the spring-seat with the boys, telling them stories. With the sun about four hands high, Orry spotted a rafter of tame turkeys up ahead near the trail. As the wide-eyed boys looked on, Orry broke out the fishing line he kept coiled inside his hat. (This harks back to a trick known to every Irishman since the days when Cromwell's occupying roundheads rejoiced in the orders to kill any Irishman seen with fishing gear in hand. The Stranger's King claimed to own all of the fish in the streams and the native Irish were not allowed to fish for them.) Orry removed the hook and spaced three kernels of corn on the line. Whistling the buckskin mare alongside, he slid off the wagon into the saddle. Dropping behind the remuda he let the line play out behind him. The corn on the line bounced along on the red clay of the trail. Soon one of the fine turkey hens spotted the dancing kernels and rushed over to gobble them down; then without hesitation she began to trot dutifully along behind the cowboy. Orry slowly shortened the line.

Two little Indian boys, whose job it was to herd their family's grazing turkeys, were on station about 30 yards away. They were flabbergasted when they saw one of their hens following and never seeming to take her eyes off this red-haired cowboy! When the invisible line got short, Orry leaned down from his saddle and took the hen gently in his arms. As he did so, he spotted the two bug-eyed Indian kids. He galloped his mare over to where the kids were standing. Doffing his wide-brimmed hat he grinned at them and said, "I haf 'ta tell you boys, this lady turkey fell plum in love with me. Ta' do the right thang by her, I jus' had ta' take her in my arms and carry her away. Now aint that jus' 'bout the way you boys would see it?"

The kids nodded in ready agreement. With a farewell doff of his hat, Orry touched a spur to the mare; she bounded away after the little wagon train. The turkey hen never looked back. Snuggled under the arm of her new master, she seemed eager to see what exciting thing would happen next. That exciting thing was of course dinner for the family on the next Sabbath.

A few days later they crossed the Red River on a toll bridge; the toll charge was a dollar for each wagon and 50 cents for the surrey. There was no charge for the remuda; Bob was relieved at that because he had no more money. He would've had to ask Orry to swim the remuda across the fast flowing river.

They made camp in a clump of trees on the Texas bank of the river. As they were setting up camp, they watched a three-wagon train approaching from the south. The northbound outfit circled and camped nearby. The family was gathered around the camp-stove when a thin, haggard-looking man from the other wagons came calling. He asked of Bob, "Friend, where' ya headed?"

Bob replied, "Welcome to our circle, Stranger, have a seat. We're headed on down Houston way, lookin' fer a place where it still knows how ta' rain."

The stranger, without sitting down, said to Bob, "I'm a preacher so's I'm used ta tellin' folks what not to do. Let me tell ya' Friend, tamarree mornin', put the tongue on tother end o yr' wagons an recross thet river. These Texacans'll spot ya' as ah Yankee even bafore ya' open y'r haid. They despise ya an' they'll see to it ya'll forever only suck a hind tit. Wust of all they'll hut cha chillins. The Lord is my Shepherd but he led me astray when he brung me into this land. I know now, iffen I had two spreads, one in Hell an t'other in Texas, I'd rent out cheap the Texas spread an live on the one in Hell."

The stranger turned without another word and walked back through the gathering dusk to his wagons. The air around the camp was so heavy the rest of that evening that the mosquitoes had to walk to make their rounds. Annie's prayer session included a passel of extra Our Fathers, Hail Marys and Glory-be-to-Gods.

The next morning at first light the two families broke camp, one headed north across the bridge and the other one south toward a place where they'd been told it still knew how to rain. Late afternoon that same day Gert and Giddy would die.

The four teams of mules were moving along at 20 to 25 miles a day. That pace was faster than the two mares, Gert and Giddy, could keep even as they moved freely in the remuda. Bob and Orry Webb had made the hard decision. Michael had Jennie's gray tied to Mary's wagon. He loved Captain as he loved Girt and Giddy. Michael, Mary and Nora were talking about what that hollow-eyed preacher had said. No extra prayers could make them forget that the Texicans had hurt his children.

Orry let the remuda drop out of sight behind the wagons so he could do alone what every horseman must be prepared to do. He ended the state of misery that the gentle mares were in with a well-placed rifle bullet for each. He left them there in a plum-brush thicket for the coyotes to clear away. That evening Bob had to tell Michael, Mary and Nora of the loss of their beloved mares. Wagon number one had suffered its first deaths.

The mules continued to make good time and were soon passing through the city of Dallas. Several tall buildings were strung along the hard-surfaced main street. Like the much smaller city of Grand Island, there seemed to be little activity and a lot of closed stores. When they saw that the Trinity River had little more water in it than they had seen in the Platte, they began to realize that some part of the drought and most of the national depression had followed them from Nebraska.

Traveling south of Dallas they were passing endless fields of cotton and were curious at seeing hundreds of black people working in the fields. Seeing blacks in great numbers like this surprised them. The family had only seen four other black people in their lives. That was Mr. Jim Kelly and the three other black cowboys who had come north with IP Olive. They were shocked at the way the Texicans treated the blacks.

41

As Bob went along, he asked everyone about the possibility of renting land. It soon became clear that none of the good flatland was available to him. As they came into a small town south of Waco, Bob spotted an old guy sitting on the front porch of his house. Bob signaled for a rest stop while he and Robb went over to talk to the gentleman.

The man seemed friendly enough, but that was not too surprising considering he was about four fingers down on a half-gallon bottle of red wine. Bob accepted when the man asked him to sit a while and wet his whistle. Turned out the man had a hill place to rent out. He told Bob, "T'is no good ta go on down ta Houston, too damn hot an' sticky down thar, they got mosquitoes big as crows." He fed Bob some more wine and continued selling him on the good life in Calvert, Texas.

Bob sent Robb back to the wagons to tell Joe and Orry to find a spot to make camp. They made camp in a vacant field not far from the man's house. The next morning, Bob and Robb picked up the landowner in Bob's surrey. The man seemed reasonably sober and quite friendly. They proceeded out of town to see the hill farm.

Time had run out and no one knew it better than Bob. He was out of money and it was getting past time to get a crop in the ground for the season. They rented the man's hill-farm, two thirds of the crop would be theirs and one third would be delivered to the land owner.

The land was a succession of small hills on which the soil was thin and badly eroded. The fields were only partially cleared of pine stumps. The house was a three-room shack that sat on posts about two feet off the ground. As they approached the house, there were black faces peering out of every window and door. From under the house several more were sharing space with three half-starved-looking dogs.

The boys could clean out the shack and live in it while they worked the land but it was clear there wasn't room for the family to live there. When he got back to town, Bob went looking for a place for the family to live. On the main street of the town he found a building for rent that was an old two-story, wood-frame hotel. Facing the street on the first floor there was space for a public dining room. After consulting with Annie and the girls, it was decided that they could live in the hotel and rent out the spare rooms. They concluded that running the dining room would be not unlike feeding 30 or so hungry men at haying time. They thought they could do it.

After the family moved in, there were only three rooms left for them to rent out. The dining room was large and well-located on the main street of the town. The "Farritor Dining Room" quickly became a busy and successful establishment. The customers, mostly working men, seemed delighted with Annie's good cooking and especially pleased with being waited on at a table by two pretty Yankee girls. They even got used to Bob's house rule that there would be no guns in the dining room. All of their guns and gun belts had to be hung on the wall just inside the door where there were hooks on the wall for that purpose.

The town marshal, being a bachelor, ate three meals a day in the dining room. His gun was the only exception to the "no guns" rule. The marshal proudly wore his wide-brimmed felt hat, his star and his gun as he ate his meals. He appreciated the good food, but it was fairly obvious that a secondary goal of his was to make time with one of those pretty waitresses. He made no progress on that mission but to his credit he never stopped trying.

Annie saw to it that Frank, Will, Nora and Michael were enrolled in public school, which began an experience fraught with danger for the boys. The old saw, "boys will be boys," hardly covered the situation existing on the streets of Calvert, Texas, in 1894.

As soon as the Yankee kids appeared on the street headed for school, they drew a crowd. The crowd of school kids would include four or more older bully types and a few adult spectators. To the locals it was a game, a game where the rules were subject to change. Usually the bullies would promote a fight between Frank or Will and other kids their size. The Yankee kids were never allowed to win the fight. If the local kid was getting the worst of it, the bullies would take over and "bump" the new kid. They would grab his hands and feet and lift him spread-eagled in the air, face up, as high as they could lift him and then drop him, bumping his Yankee ass on the ground.

Three or four bumps would make a kid throw up. This, of course, was the goal of that game. On other days, another mode of entertainment would kick in, which was called "dog pile." The Yankee kids (or dogs) would be held on the ground spread-eagled face up and then every kid in town would pile on. The weight on the Yankee kid's stomach would usually make him throw up, which again was the goal. A perverse delight seemed to exist among the local bullies and the spectators in seeing Yankee kids cry and throw up.

With the prospect each day of having to fight and get bumped or dog-piled all the way to school and all the way back home, it is certainly questionable whether they learned anything in school. After a few days of this, Bob took the town marshal aside and said, "Marshal Kirby, I don't have ta tell you what's happenin' ta my kids on their way ta school ever' day. I'm afraid one of 'ems gonna get hurt bad."

The marshal said, "Bob, I regret it all, but aint a damn thang I can do about it. Them folks thinks they got a right an a duty to pick on Yankees. If I was to say somthin' to em, that very night I'd be visited by folks wearin' white sheets an ridin' tall horses. I'd be lucky if all they did ta me was horse whip me half ta death, an Bob, don't you say nothin' to em. Bein' a Catholic an a Yankee, they'd hurt you bad. Best thang is ta jest move on to where folks don't thank like thet."

Annie kept Nora at home, and Bob took the boys out to the hill farm where he hoped they'd be safer. The boys were delighted at this turn of events. Orry Webb taught them everything there was to know about hook and line fishing and about his Spencer rifle. They each, even little Michael, became crack shots with that gun. They could easily bag a rabbit for supper at 30 yards.

The skinny dogs that were living under the house when Bob and Robb first saw the place stayed on when the black family left. The dogs were happy to have the young boys come to live with them. Those big white guys that had moved in earlier just weren't much fun at all.

Frank, Will and Michael spent most of their days running with the dogs on the surrounding scrub-pine covered hills and fishing in the nearby creek. The young hunters transformed the diet for Joe, Robb and Orry. The god-awful flapjack and black coffee diet that they were on suddenly became protein rich with fried rabbit, carp and catfish.

The drought wasn't as bad as they had seen in Nebraska but it rained sparingly on that hill farm that summer. They had planted peas, beans and corn. They knew that prospects were slim for a decent crop, considering the drought and the fact that the soil was so poor. These sad prospects did not deter Robb, Orry and Joe from putting in long days of hard work to try to make a good thing happen.

With the Dining Room a roaring success, Bob began to put away some money. He looked at that saved money as being their ticket out of Texas. Both he and Annie were deeply concerned that the children were not in school and they knew that the boys were not necessarily safe from being harmed while they were out alone up there in those piney hills.

They didn't know about the lads' skill with that Spencer rifle. Orry Webb had made it very clear to the boys there was danger in the piney hills and the real danger came not from four-legged animals. A two-legged stranger was not to be considered a friend. He was to be kept at a safe distance with the Spencer. Orry told them, "If thangs get scary, three quick shots in the dirt'll bring me and Joe on the run. And Frank, I want you to be the one totein' the rifle, if a man is comin' at any one of you, you'll know the guy is a rabid polecat. Don't wait, shoot him right 'tween the eyes. If there's two or more of 'em, shoot the closest one first then aim good and keep shootin'." Frank understood what Orry was saying. It was up to him to kill anyone who would harm him, Will or Michael.

Bob and Annie were resolved that in spite of the success with the Dining Room, they should load up and re-cross the Red River as soon as they could. "We must get out of this place where folks wantonly hurt children." The prophecy from the hollow-eyed preacher had to lie heavily on their hearts.

Come fall, when they totaled up their savings from the Dining Room and sold the meager crop from the season's work on the hill farm, they understood clearly that they had not enough to make their escape from Calvert. They would have to trust in the Lord to keep the children safe for another year.

The year 1895 in Calvert, Texas, for this Yankee family was even tougher than 1894. Frank had to draw down on one man who cornered the three boys in a piney draw. Orry had instructed Frank well. The guy's intentions became clear when he grabbed Will. Frank dropped to one knee, threw a shell into the chamber and leveled the Spencer rifle at the guy's forehead. Frank had started the skilled process of squeezing the trigger when the guy let go of Will, then broke and ran. He may be running still; they never saw him again.

The Dining Room continued to be busy, but due to the drought, the cost of food supplies had gone sky high. This made profits slimmer than in 1894. The crop off the hill farm was again meager. When it was in and divided, with one-third delivered to the landlord, they set about getting their little wagon train in shape for the exodus. Traveling in winter would be hard, but they felt a compelling urgency.

The family gathered at the hotel Dining Room for their Thanksgiving dinner. Frank and Joe Hickman were sitting on a bench in front of the hotel when a beefy man in a flat black hat and a black, knee-length, broadcloth coat came pounding down the street in a buckboard, whipping his lathered team as he drove. At the last minute he seemed to decide to stop at the Farritor Dining Room. He reined the team in sharply and hopped out of the buckboard. Frank jumped up thinking the team wasn't going to get stopped and would run right over him and Joe.

The beefy man tossed the reins in Frank's direction and said, "Boy, watch this team!" then marched importantly into the Dining Room. Frank started to pick up the reins but Joe signaled for him to do nothing. The mistreated team moved nervously from side to side and then moved the buckboard backward. As they did so, they turned and were now looking down the street. The next move they made was to break into a run with the buckboard bouncing along behind them. They ran to an intersection where a side road ran over a bridge across a creek. For unknown reasons they turned sharply and pounded across the bridge to go up the hill road and out of town. It so happened that the narrow bridge was already occupied.

A large, handsome black lady with a full-length, flower-patterned skirt and a matching head-kerchief was escorting a raft of small black children across the bridge; they were midway on the span. The sight and sound of the team pounding toward them caused the lady and the children to jump off the side of the bridge into the creek.

All of this commotion brought several folks running out of the Dining Room. The beefy man was among them. He promptly screamed at Frank, "Damn you, kid, I tol' you ta watch thet team."

Joe Hickman stepped in front of Frank, and towering over the beefy little man, he said, "Back off, mister. You spit when ya talk an' I don' wan'cha spittin' on my holiday shirt. We, prob'ly, more than you, are sorry bout the lady and the children have'n ta jump in the creek but, I didn't hear ya offer ta pay the lad fer watchin' y'r team. Guess what, shorty, you've got us all watchin' 'em for free. Look at 'em go! Way they're a goin', they'll be in another county by sundown." The beefy man ignored Joe's remarks. He spun on his heel and with his team and buggy rapidly leaving the county, he stomped back into the Dining Room where he glumly finished eating his Thanksgiving Day dinner.

The next day, the town marshal and the tired, working men who came to eat at the Farritor Dining Room on the main street in Calvert, Texas, found it no longer a comfort to them. The good food smells were gone, as were the small pleasures gained by being waited on at the table by the two Yankee girls, Mary and Jennie...they with their pretty faces and kind ways.

The resident dogs under the three-room shack on the hill farm would wait uneasily for the landlord from Calvert to bring their next housemates. The dogs would miss the three little boys who were so kind to them.

The tongues of the wagons were now pointed north as the hollow-eyed preacher had recommended. The sun, as it rose on their right each morning, always found the family already on the road. There was no longer any spirit of being on a quest. The mood in the little wagon train was instead fearful and apprehensive. They missed the milk from the cows. The cows had developed problems with their feet and legs on the way south, so they had been butchered and fed to the customers at the Dining Room.

Cold, rainy days on the road added a misery that they hadn't felt on the trip south. Unlike on the trip south, they were now unable to pick greens on the side of the road or "borrow" fresh vegetables from gardens they passed. Again, unlike the southbound trip, it was a rare day when Orry's rifle or Bob's shotgun could find a bird or a rabbit to provide the family with fresh meat. On some days, heavy wind and rain plus the deep mud on the trails made it difficult to make more than eight or ten miles. By December 24, they had made it only to the Dallas area. The lack of summer grass for nighttime grazing for the stock plus the unplanned extra days on the road were bringing about a financial crisis. They'd spent more money on grain to feed the animals than they had planned. This was money they had figured would be there to buy food for the family.

The daily meals of salt pork and water gravy that they were eating day after day were causing health problems for everyone, especially the children. In their camp on Christmas Eve, just before time for evening prayers, Annie, near to weeping, said aloud to herself, "My Lord in heaven, how can this be? Only a few years ago in our Valley, I was bakin' bread and pumpkin pies along with a big turkey. I had nuts an' apples an' so many good things for my family's Christmas dinner. Tomorrow we will have none of that!"

Orry Webb, who did not pray but was always there to kneel with the family while they prayed, spoke up, "Mother Farritor, I warn't at yr table in those days so's I don't know bout all o' thet. But I want ya' ta' know thet your Lord'll see to it ya got a turkey fer yr family tamarree."

Annie turned to Orry and said, "You're a good man, Orry Webb, but how can that be?" Without hesitation, Orry said, "Cut off a chunk o' thet salt pork an' I'll trade it fer a big turkey hen. With a prayer in her eyes, Annie cut Orry a chunk of the ill-tasting fat pork.

Orry and Joe Hickman got together near Joe's wagon. Joe asked, "Orry, how the hell ya' go'na make good ohn what-cha promised Mother?" Orry said, "We passed a prosperous lookin' place back down the road ah ways. I saw four hen turkeys a sittin' on a wagon in the front yard. I figure they'll be roostin' thar for the night. I also seen three dogs a lay'n on the front porch. Let's see if'n we c'n talk them dogs out ah' one o' them turkeys."

They trotted back down the road in the gathering dusk to the place where the turkeys were roosting. When they reached the place, they could see the family through the front window, eating supper. There was a bright lamp hanging over their supper table so there was a good chance they couldn't see anything that might go on in the front yard. The wagon Orry had seen was there and sure enough, there were not four but five fine hens roosting on it. Orry laughed and whispered, "Mother's Lord is sure 'nuf at work here. He put thet fifth hen there jus' fer her!" Orry cut the chunk of salt pork in three and then got down on his hunkers to crawl under the wagon, holding up the three pieces of pork for the dogs to see. See it they did; they bounded off the porch and ran right up to Orry. They each collected a piece of pork and ran off into the trees. Joe couldn't figure why they didn't once bark. He guessed that Orry had charmed them into silence.

Orry stood up and silently clamped one hand around the neck of the biggest hen and with his arm around her body he dropped down again behind the wagon. It all happened so silently; Joe figured that hen got stolen before she or her four friends could even wake up. In a matter of minutes they were back at camp with their prize. They buried the feathers and hung the dressed hen from a high tree limb to chill overnight.

Christmas Day dawned bright, clear and cold. The rising sun found them already underway. They took the road up onto the rise where Fort Worth sits. The village of Fort Worth was mostly mud streets and wood-plank sidewalks. They had hoped to find a priest there so they could go to mass. There was none, so they moved beyond the town to make camp. The camp stove was set up first thing so Annie could get her turkey dinner started. Bob sent Joe and Robb into the village to buy some milk and a loaf of bread.

Their Christmas dinner was not the baked apple, dried nuts and pumpkin pie feast that Annie had been tearfully lamenting last evening. It was, however, considerably better than what they had been eating the past five weeks on the trail.

Orry Webb had made the deal of the century: He'd traded a chunk of salt-pork for a fine turkey hen and in the bargain, he gave three errant dogs a Christmas present they'd not soon forget.

North of Fort Worth the wagon train was moving through an area that looked much like the Nebraska Sandhills, except that instead of cedar trees, there were stands of white pine and post oak scattered over the ridges and in the draws. Toward the end of a long day they came to a town called Sunset. As they entered the town, there was an extra sign that couldn't be missed. The sign read, "No Niggers Allowed in Sunset after Sundown."

They stopped at the town pump to water their horses and fill their water barrels. They then quickly moved on through to the north edge of town where they stopped for the night. Bob issued orders, "No one is to go into town." With the stock hobbled securely in a meadow, the family bedded down.

In the middle of the night everyone in camp came wide-awake at the sound of a dozen gunshots. Bob passed the word in the dark, "Prob'ly jus' ah gunfight in the saloon. Go back ta' sleep."

In the darkness, little Will, with near panic in his voice, asked of his big brother, "Are they comin' over here Frank? In the dark we sure 'nuff look a lot like black folks!"

Frank reached over and patted Will, "Go back ta' sleep Will. Ever thang'll be ah'right come mornin'." The words were confident, but Frank's voice clearly echoed Will's fear. Will, quietly cried himself back to sleep.

Frank knew that his grandfather had fought in Abe Lincoln's army to put an end to the nonsense of Southern white folks pickin' on black folks. He was glad Will didn't ask about that because he wouldn't know how to answer him.

The next morning they were on the trail to the north before sunup. A few days later they crossed the Red River on a ferry several miles west of the bridge over which they had entered Texas. The man at the ferry accepted Bob's last two dollars as payment in full for moving the whole outfit across the river. The money they had saved in two years of working the hill farm and running the Farritor Dining Room was gone. It had, however, thanks be to God, gotten the family out of Texas!

After crossing into Oklahoma, they came to a town called Duncan. In camp there was no hay or grain to feed the stock and the children were hungry. All of the men went looking for work, any kind of work. The national depression that had caused so many stores to be closed in Grand Island and Dallas was showing its face here in Duncan. There was no work to be found. There were idle men standing on every downtown street corner.

Orry and Joe spotted some unguarded piles of shelled corn. After dark they went back to that place carrying empty feedbags. They worked most of the night carrying filled bags back to camp. Before sunup they had fed the animals and the wagon train was again on the road to the North. Robb and Jennie worked the whole day grinding corn in wagon number two. Annie would use the finely ground corn for corn-meal flapjacks and mush.

Later they came to know that the man who owned those piles of corn became a millionaire and twice Governor of Oklahoma. His fortune came not from the corn. He would discover that under his corn fields lay an ocean of oil!

Robb, Frank and Will hadn't said anything to their folks, but for several days they had been feeling very weak and had been spitting out blood from bleeding gums. Scurvy, the age-old killer of travelers, was a silent passenger in each wagon of the train.

A tragic and lamentable fact of life and death is that, at this same time, there were thousands of other poor folk, both Mexican and black, who were surviving successfully on their culture's diet of rice and beans. The Farritor family, adhering to their northern European culture diet of meat and potatoes, was in deep trouble when neither of those foods were to be had.

The stolen corn unquestionably staved off disaster for the family. The problem with the bleeding gums eased and they all began feeling better; all except little Michael.

With the roads now dry, Bob was urging the mules on at 25 miles a day. The remuda existed no more. The only horses left were Orry's buckskin mare and Jennie's gray. The buckskin mare never strayed far from wagon number three where Orry was riding with Joe Hickman.

Michael was abed in wagon number one. Annie joined Mary and Nora at his bedside. They were doing what they could to comfort the boy. Michael had developed severe pains in his arms and legs. Jennie's gray kept pace near the wagon where he knew his little friend Michael lay ill. The weather held good, and they reached the town of Norman where they'd been told they could find a doctor.

They made camp in a vacant field on the outskirts of town. Bob and Annie went into town seeking help. A Dr. Robinson agreed to come to their camp. The good doctor was appalled at what he found. When he was told that they had no money, it didn't seem to make any difference. He told Bob to send a man to the store in town to get two crates of oranges. He gave Joe Hickman, who would drive the surrey on the errand, a note instructing Mr. Mayhad, the shopkeeper, to put the crates of oranges on his, Dr. Robinson's, bill. When Joe returned with the fruit, the doctor instructed everyone in the camp to eat at least three oranges immediately. To Annie, he said, "I don't have to tell you that Michael is a very sick boy. Please warm a cup of water, put in a tablespoon of sugar, and squeeze an orange into it, then spoon-feed the boy very slowly. I'll give him something to relieve the pain in his legs." To Bob he said, "Send your man back to the store with this note to get two more crates of oranges. Have all of your people eat an orange in the morning and another at bedtime each day until they're gone."

Before he left, Dr. Robinson said to Bob, "I can only imagine what you people've been through. I can tell you this, you've come now to a good place. The people here in Norman will help you through your time of trouble. Plan to stay here 'til you're all well again." Bob didn't know it at that moment, but they would stay among the good people of Norman for most of four years.

The introduction of citrus juices into their diet made everyone begin to show real improvement, again, all except Michael. The laudanum that the doctor gave him eased his pain and allowed him to rest quietly through the night and the next day. At sundown of that next day, February 6, 1897, Bob and Annie's fourth-born son, blonde, blue-eyed little Michael, died. Dr. Robinson and his mother were at his bedside. The rest of the family surrounded the wagon in which he lay. Wagon number one had suffered its third death.

There were many families of Irish decent in Norman, Oklahoma. Dr. Robinson saw to it that the word got out about the new family in town who was in great trouble. The family's grief was lessened by an outpouring of goodwill from the townspeople of Norman and the nearby town of Purcell in Indian Territory.

Bob and Annie were reeling from the shock of Michael's death but they had to somehow deal with the fact of it. How and where could they bury their son?

One of the families who had come to their camp bearing gifts, the Sullivan family, came to their aid and helped them to buy a family plot in the Catholic cemetery at Norman. Little Michael was laid to rest in the strange, red earth of Oklahoma.

The Sullivan family helped them also to find good land to rent. Bob and the boys started immediately to prepare the land for winter wheat. The fine house on the place was large enough to accommodate the whole family.

The stalwart Sandhills cowboy, Orry Webb, had been an ever-present source of strength to the family on their trip. The family had first come to know Orry at one of Bob and Annie's sod-house dancing parties. Orry had brought a neighbor girl to the party. He had danced mostly with his date and properly saw her home. But when he met and danced with Mary at the party, he knew at once that this happy, brown-haired girl with the sparkling blue eyes was the girl for whom he'd been searching. From the first meeting he knew that he was in love with her but he spoke of this love to no one. Unknown to Bob, this was the reason Orry had asked permission to come with the family on the trip.

Mary was aware of the shy cowboy's love, and she certainly loved him, but only as a brother. Realizing that she had an obligation to be fair to him, Mary quietly explained to Orry that she had long ago pledged herself to her God. She had wanted to be a nun as long as she could remember.

The thought of this lovely, happy girl becoming a nun was a prospect completely foreign to Orry. Orphaned as a small child, he was raised by nuns at an orphanage in Chicago. He remembered the nuns in that orphanage as being grim and straight-lipped. They always smelled of the lye soap with which they washed everything, including, frequently, the mouths of most of the boys his age. He couldn't picture this beautiful, caring girl being in the company of the kind of nuns that had raised him.

Apparently, here in this winter of sadness, Orry had come to grips with the facts of his situation. In a moment when they were alone, he spoke to Annie, "Mrs. Farritor, I figer you know by now I love yr daughter, Mary. I unnerstand now, it'll all come ta nought. I know I've drawn ta an inside straight an' lost. It's long past time ta throw in ma' cards. Ya've been' like a mother ta me. I'm thankin' ya with all ma heart. Now I must tell ya, I'll be leavin' yr table today." On the heels of losing Michael, the prospect of Orry's leaving the family had Annie in tears.

Later that sad day Orry saddled his buckskin mare, dropped his Spencer rifle into its scabbard and made his cavalry bedroll secure in its place on the cantle. With never-before-seen tears in his blue eyes, he said goodbye by hugging each sobbing member of the family. He shook Bob's hand, then threw his arms around him. The two men stood in a long silent embrace without speaking. He came to Mary last; silent tears were streaming down their cheeks as the shy cowboy and the would-be-nun stood holding each other close. It was then that they kissed for the first and last time. When he released her, he turned and swung into the saddle. His buckskin mare, without being spurred, broke into a run toward the hills to the west. Mary walked slowly in the direction Orry had taken. She stopped under a tree some distance from the house. There she knelt in prayer until darkness fell.

Like the handsome young outlaw who rode away from their camp over on the South Canadian River, the family never saw the handsome young cowboy, Orry Webb, again.

Joe Hickman, too, left the fold that winter; he went home to Nebraska to see his family. The railroads didn't run north and south, so he rode home on one of the mismatched mules from wagon number three.

It rained at just the right times during the season so their wheat crop was a good one. They were able to pay off all their debts. Jennie and Mary were again working as waitresses, this time in the dining room at the railroad section-house. Their bright smiles brought tips aplenty. Annie felt better about letting them work in that place because no one there wore guns. Jennie met a man named Frank Abby; he was an older guy and said to be quite well off. Frank was smitten and wanted Jennie to marry him. Jennie held him at bay for reasons known only to her.

During the next winter, Bob and Annie, with the team of gray mules on the surrey, made a trip home to their Valley. They needed to make an assessment of the situation there.

The family got word that Bob and Annie would be coming back to Norman in February and Joe Hickman would be coming with them. Apparently Joe and Annie had smoked a pipe of peace.

The Sullivan family planned a party to welcome Bob and Annie back. It was to be a grand affair. Two fiddlers would provide music and there would be a caller for square dancing. To attend the affair, Robb took a bath and put on a clean white shirt. He cleaned his boots and added a string necktie because for the first time in his life he was going to ask a girl to dance who was not his sister.

Frank Abby brought Jennie to the dance. To his dismay, when Jennie danced with the newly returned Joe Hickman, it was obvious to everyone, even to Frank Abby, that Jennie and Joe were in love.

Robb and Frank were confirmed in the Catholic faith at a little red church on a hill in Purcell, Indian Territory. It was there that Will and Nora received their first holy communion, and it was there that Joe and Jennie were married.

The wheat and barley crop was again good. Christmas of 1898 was a happy one. The members of the family were all in good health. Annie had all of the things she needed to prepare a grand Christmas dinner.

With Jennie married and the family doing well, Mary approached her parents again with the long-delayed request that she be allowed to join the nursing "Sisters of Mercy" at their convent in Kansas City. Arrangements were made that she would make the journey to Kansas City in February of the new year.

The new year brought with it first a terrible sickness. It spread like a prairie fire. The pestilence was called "black measles." Joe and Robb got it, as did Frank and Will. Jennie and her parents were spared but both Nora and Mary got it and were overwhelmed by it.

February came on with extremely cold weather. The boys stayed in bed in their unheated room with the blinds on the windows kept lowered to protect their eyes. They each had a cup of milk, which of course was frozen. They would suck on a chip of this frozen milk and then occasionally take a sip of "Chamberlain's Cough Syrup." When they ran out of "Chamberlain's," they'd take a sip of kerosene. It was said there was very little difference. That was pretty much the extent of their medicine.

The boys were completely miserable. It's possible that sucking on the ice milk and the cold in the room helped to control their dangerously high temperatures. They, for whatever reason, were able to endure until their measles came out. When that occurred the worst was over for them.

Mary and Nora, abed in a heated room, were given pretty much the same medicine that the boys took; however, the girls went into double pneumonia. Dr. West from Purcell was called and he called in Dr. Robinson from Norman who, of course, the family knew. On the night of February 22, 1899, the gentle child, Nora, with a brutally high fever, went into a series of violent convulsions and did not survive that terrifying ordeal.

Nora was dead. With the earth still raw on the grave of the son they had lost, Bob and Annie were now faced with having to bury a daughter. Nora was buried in the family's plot at the cemetery in Norman alongside her little brother Michael. Wagon number one had suffered its fourth death.

Mary was growing weaker and weaker. The many friends that she had made in Norman and Purcell came and went at the house as that lovely girl fought for her life.

On the night of February 27, 1899, the date she was to leave for Kansas City to start her training to become a nursing nun, a host of her friends were gathered in the house and in the chill of the front yard to keep a vigil of life for Mary. The moonless sky was filled with cold indifferent stars. Only the family's faithful friend the Dog Star looked with deep compassion on what was happening below.

The long cold night became early morning. Mary, though barely able to speak, continued to pray. Just before sunrise she focused her eyes on the picture of the child Jesus that hung on the bedroom wall. That small picture had hung on her bedroom wall in the sod house in their Valley and on the inner side of the canvas cover of wagon number one.

As the night sky paled in the east, Mary's voice became more faint and her breathing ever more shallow. Then her voice was stilled and her breathing stopped. In that same instant the sun rose over the hills to the east. Its first rays found their way into the window of Mary's room. The picture of the Christ child was bathed in golden sunlight. Mary's face, in death, became radiant in the reflected light, and a warm glow filled the room.

Everyone present was stunned by the power and beauty of the moment. The silence was broken by the attending priest who, in a voice that broke, said, "My dear God, we know you've seen fit to take this girl, your child, directly home. We doubt not that she is with you this day in paradise."

Mary was buried beside her sister Nora and her precious brother Michael. These three travelers had come from afar and would not return to their beloved native Valley. They would instead become one with the red earth of Oklahoma. Michael, Nora and Mary had joined their beloved mares, Girt and Giddy, in death. The covered wagon itself was now all that was left of wagon number one that had bravely taken its place in the line of the wagon train on that sad, dry morning when the family left their Valley.

There is little question that it was only the strength endemic in Annie that brought the family through such a terrible time of loss. The crop of 1899 was a good one, but Bob and the boys harvested without the joy that had always been theirs when they brought forth food from the earth.

The decision had probably been made the morning Mary died; however, it wasn't until fall that Bob announced that they would be going home to their Valley. The family received the news with great expectation. Any regrets over having to leave the children's graves and the task of saying goodbye to their good friends in Norman and Purcell were eased by the joy in the prospect of going home.

Before they left, Bob was able to pay all of his bills and buy a handsome stone marker for the graves of the children. There was cash aplenty to finance the trip home. The wagon train that formed was much different from the one that left the Valley in 1894. Without the remuda and with five strong, well-fed teams of mules, the wagon train was easily able to travel at 30 miles a day. Bob, with Annie and Alice as his passengers, led off in the surrey behind his faithful team of grays. For safekeeping on the road, Bob's money was in the false bottom of a double-bottomed toolbox. That box was bolted securely to the floor of the surrey.

Robb followed with the old wagon number one. It was now heavily loaded with new tools and disassembled equipment that they had purchased in Norman. The wagon was being pulled by a double team of mules. The teams were hitched in tandem so they would fit on narrow roads and bridges. Robb was now a fully grown young man, quite capable of handling those two teams of mules on the road.

Frank followed in wagon number two. As on the trip south, he was driving Tip and Coaly. Those ornery mules had not changed. They, like Frank, had just gotten six years older. The feud between the lad and that ornery pair of mules was still alive and well. Little Will had signed onto the feud. He had taken over Robb's old duties, helping Frank with wagon number two.

Bringing up the rear in the third covered wagon pulled by a strong new team of mules was Mr. and Mrs. Joseph Hickman. A new young family, Joe and Jennie were the embodiment of renewal.

Captain kept pace near the last wagon. An old horse now, he was the family's one luxury, a pet. It was somehow very important to everyone, especially Jennie, that they get the beloved old gray back to his native hills and canyons.

Christmas found them at a small town in Kansas where they all enjoyed a sumptuous Christmas dinner at a small hotel dining room, much like the one they had run in Calvert, Texas. Annie, Alice and Jennie were lovely in dresses and hats they had bought from a fancy ready-to-wear store in Norman. Bob and the boys sported broadcloth suits, white shirts with string-ties and new broad-brimmed felt hats. They had outfitted in an equally fine ready-to-wear store for men.

Back on the road after the holiday the weather held clear and cold. As the mules drew them quickly along, the wagons provided a rough ride over the portions of the road that were marked with frozen ruts. The spring-seats provided some relief from the bumps in the road. Flannel-lined buffalo and cow-skin robes on their laps and around their feet kept them reasonably warm.

They crossed into Nebraska on New Year's Day, the first day of a brand new century. When they came to the Platte River, they knew things had changed for the better. When they last saw it, the Platte was showing only its wide sandy bottom. Now it was flowing strong, wide and free, except for eddy-pockets near the banks, which were frozen over by the winter cold.

The city of Grand Island was bustling with commerce. The national economic depression had apparently died with the drought.

On their second entry into their Valley, the doe and her fawn of a quarter century before were not there to greet them, and the tall grasses were not flowing in the spring wind. This time, the Valley was covered by a welcome, fifteen-inch blanket of snow.

That blanket of snow would convert to moisture for planting in the spring. There was an air in the Valley that could be felt, an air of boundless optimism that reflected the feelings held by the family on coming home.

Jennie left her beloved Captain to live out his life among the familiar hills and canyons of the home place. Joe and Jennie took up land in the Sandhills near where I P Olive's River Ranch had been in the early days. They would raise their family there. Their great story is a story that must be told on another day....

On the home place, Bob now had three strong, young sons to help him. These were young men who loved the land and who saw the grand new twentieth century they had come into as being loaded with promise. They would embrace that promise and make it their own. Forged and tempered in the crucible of the drought and the depression of the 1890s, the strength of the spirit that Bob and these young men brought home with them would see them through.

They acquired more land and built a fine new home for the family. They bought the handsome, two-story, four-bedroom house by mail order. It came to them from Wisconsin in railway boxcars. It had two chimneys, three lightning rods, some stained glass and etched windows and lots of gingerbread. They off-loaded the material from boxcars into the wagons that had made the trip to Texas. They then hauled it the nine miles from the railroad siding to their Valley. The parts were mostly precut. They hired a carpenter to supervise; however, Bob and the boys did most of the work in building the house. They built it near the well, east of the old sod house, almost on the very spot where they had stood to have their picture taken back in 1890.

The first picture they hung on the living room wall of their new house was the green-tinted copy made from the tatters of the picture taken and then destroyed by Mr. Butcher. The sod house in that picture became a bunkhouse for the hired men who came each spring and fall to help with the branding, haying and harvesting.

On an acre of their land, near the east rim of their valley, they and the neighbors built a wood-frame, one-room schoolhouse. Frank, Will and Alice and all of the neighboring children would crack their McGuffey's Readers there. Bob and Annie's grandchildren would also go through eight grades at that school. The grandchildren would go on to high schools and some of them to the Teachers College at Kearney and others to the University at Lincoln.

The precious rains had returned. The land in their Valley responded year after year with bumper crops of corn, oats and prairie hay. Each year, carloads of corn-fed hogs and grass-fat steers were shipped by rail to the markets in Omaha and Sioux City. It was, indeed, a time for growing.

The federal government had declared the homestead lands to be free. All who survived on that free land knew that those lands were not free. It took danger-filled years of hard work, strength of body, steadfastness of mind and, in most cases, great and tragic personal loss to buy that land. Bob and Annie and their children bought the land in their Valley and they had sure enough paid a considerable price.

---Postscript---

In the first year of the new century, on the twenty-seventh of February, a lone rider on a buckskin mare came to kneel at a grave in Oklahoma. He seemed not to pray but knelt silently for a time in the chill of the winter's day. The aged cemetery caretaker made note of the visit. Eventually the caretaker's son replaced him in the task of caring for the graves. The son too made note of the tall man, now riding a sorrel horse, who came in February each year to kneel at a grave near a large, weathered, stone marker.

As the caretaker's son aged, so did the tall visitor. There came a year when the aging caretaker made note that the lone rider did not come to kneel at the grave of the young woman who rested there with her siblings. He guessed that the lone rider had died.

From that time on, it was the Dog Star alone, with its gentle blue light, who kept watch over the graves for the family.

On a trip to visit one of his daughters, Michele, and her family in Bay City, Texas, Edward L. Farritor, the third son of Frank (the eight-year-old boy with the blurred face in the "Butcher" picture), searched for and found the graves of Bob and Annie's children who died on the family's ill-fated trip "to find a place where it still knows how to rain."

The aging caretaker of the cemetery at Norman, Oklahoma, was much relieved to be able to tell someone the story of the lone rider's long, quiet vigil at the three graves near the large, weathered stone.

- * -

Story Two

Kaleb and Sarah

Sarah wore a straw and calico sunbonnet that framed and shaded her face. She was a tiny lady. As a lad of seven, the boy could look level into her clear blue eyes. His dad told a story about those blue eyes, there were many stories about Grandpa's friends, Kaleb and Sarah.

When she was a young lady, Sarah could spot a prairie-chicken in the foot-high grass at 100 yards. When she leveled her muzzle-loaded rifle on to it, she saw it turning on a spit for supper. Her husband, Kaleb, standing beside her, leaning on his own long rifle and dressed in deerskins, would get on his horse to go fetch the bird.

Kaleb was a beardless boy when the Confederacy writhed and died. He felt only relief when the end came. General Grant allowed him to keep Thumper, the horse on which his father had sent him off to war. His father and the handsome bay gelding on which he had ridden away to the war had not survived. They were killed by Yankee cannon fire at Fleetwood, west of Brandy Station.

The war was done, and the seemingly endless days and nights in the saddle were over. As ordered by the Yankees, Kaleb stacked his worn saber and carbine and then went home to Sarah. Their homeland was, for them, too deeply scarred with the graves of their kin and other reminders of the war for them to stay there. Together they rode Thumper away to the West. Thumper would never be free of the war. He would ever carry with him the terror and pain of it. He had a jagged piece of metal from an exploding canister shell lodged near his heart. Only death would deliver Thumper from the incessant pain caused by that scrap of shrapnel.

Kaleb's cavalry bedroll, folded behind the cantle of his saddle, was Sarah's daytime seat and their shared retreat each night. Thumper led their pack mule and carried Kaleb and Sarah through many seasons and across hundreds of rivers, streams and ridges. They stopped when they reached the tall grass country near the three Loup Rivers in the young state of Nebraska.

French fur trappers named the rivers for the people they found there, *The Wolf People* (the Pawnee). One evening Kaleb and Sarah made camp on a grassy side-hill south of the Middle Loup River, east of Victoria Creek. Thumper made the decision for them to settle there; he died peacefully in his sleep. The searing flames and crashing shellfire that had haunted his sleep ceased that night, as did the gnawing pain in his chest. The war that he and Kaleb had fought was, at long last, now over for Thumper. Kaleb and Sarah had been looking for a sign. They would bury him on that hillside, then make their home there to tend his grave.

When the lad named Chuck first knew Sarah, she must have been in her late eighties. She and Kaleb lived in a sod house that stood on a grassy side-hill beyond the rim of his grandfather's valley. Most kids from the neighboring farms and ranches seemed to look down on "Thet ol' pair in the soddie" but the boy and his kid brother, Eddie, saw them in a special light. They often crossed the ridge to visit. If their mom knew they were going, she'd send along a Ball quart jar of home-canned beef or perhaps a jar of home-canned fruit.

On a windless day as they crossed the ridge on their pony, they'd see a thin column of white smoke from the cow-chip fueled fire in Sarah's kitchen stove. The smoke rose straight as an arrow from the chimney of their sod house until it became one with the faultless blue of the sky. In dry weather they had standing orders from their dad to pick two gunnysacks full of cow chips for Sarah.

On the Fourth of July and Christmas, the jar of canned beef became a basket. It would be full of good stuff, like fried chicken legs, a mincemeat pie, potato salad, and at Christmas time, a small chocolate-frosted cake in honor of Jesus's birthday. The basket would be tightly covered with an embroidered dishtowel. Sarah would pat their cheeks with her tiny hands and accept the food with grace.

Her once lovely young shoulders had, by that time, undergone a change. A hump had come onto her back. Whatever its cause, Sarah accepted the burden she had been assigned. She accepted it as repayment to the Lord for a lifetime of his wondrous gifts.

The two visiting lads always hoped she'd set out a treat of home-canned peaches or such on the newspaper-covered table. Awash in a clear, sweet syrup, the peaches were no different from those their Mom served, but they somehow became a gourmet's repast when served in that wondrous old sod house with two storybook old-timers making small talk with two young visitors from across the ridge and from another time.

In company manners mode, the boys slowly licked their spoons while their eyes devoured the atmosphere in the room. There was a round black hole in the thick, sod wall near one window. They knew it belonged to the bull snake that lived with them. He made himself useful in the night by feasting on any mouse or rat that might foolishly invade Kaleb and Sarah's turf. The tin stovepipe elbowed and was plastered securely into the side of the sod chimney. Blackened pots and pans hung on pegs on the once whitewashed wall behind the flat, four-lidded cook stove.

Two rifled muzzle-loaders rested on wooden pegs above the entry door. The time had long passed when those rifles were used daily as priceless tools of survival. The rifles had now collected a respectful extra patina of dust.

On cold days the boys would join Kaleb with their chairs drawn up side by side in front of the stove. Their stocking feet rested on the open oven door of the cook stove. Their damp boots would be nearby, warming and drying. Kaleb was not a storyteller like most of the men in the boys' family. They knew however that this old man's head was chock full of stories that should be told. It was exciting just to be near him as the old man sat in silence.

He did seem to want them to know about his horse, Thumper. The boys knew that Thumper had been buried long ago only a few feet from where they now sat. Kaleb seemed to regard Thumper not as a horse but as a good friend, a friend who had helped a boy soldier survive in a place and time where a great number of hardened men had failed to do so.

One cold winter day as they warmed their feet on the open oven door, they learned that on a long-ago, bright, spring morning, Kaleb and Thumper were thundering forward in a long line of other horses and riders. With sabers drawn they were charging across a debris-covered field that was ablaze with the fire and smoke of battle. They knew that each ball of smoke and fire they charged through was laden with deadly, flying pieces of lead and steel. Suddenly Thumper's front legs folded. As the great horse slid to earth, his young rider flew over his head into the rich, brown dirt of a Virginia farmer's field. Unhurt, the boy stood up and was surprised to find that his saber was still in his hand. Turning, he saw Thumper getting to his feet. Blood was oozing through the mud that covered his chest. The wounded horse was snorting and blowing, anxious to regain his place in the line of charging horses. As the lad quickly remounted, he knew that his friend Thumper had taken a missile that the god of war had aimed at Thumper's rider.

Two racks loaded with dog-eared books hung on the wall near the south window. The books had obviously been read and reread. Like the muzzle-loading rifles, they were now covered with a sheltering layer of dust. It was no longer necessary that these books be read. At this late stage of their lives, the contents of those books were now a part of who Kaleb and Sarah were.

On pegs in the wall over the door to the bedroom, looking slightly out of place with its expanse of rich hardwood and blued steel, was a modern Winchester shotgun. Very proud of it, Kaleb said he'd ordered it from the Monkey Ward catalog.

On late afternoons the sun streamed through the deep-set west window making a warm spot on the hard-packed earthen floor. Strongbow, their old shepherd dog, usually slept in that spot. He'd shift without awakening as the warm spot moved with the sun. Sometimes the bull snake came out to cuddle with him in the warm spot. The two of them seemed to be, if not simply good friends, then veteran comrades in the task of looking out for Kaleb and Sarah.

A slightly medicinal smell touched the room. The smell could be traced to a black bag on a bench by the entry door. Kaleb, with experience and love of animals his only *sheep-skin*, had become doctor to most of the animals in his part of Custer County; Sarah would often be there helping him. When advancing age kept them from hitching up their buckboard to go out on calls, the farmer or rancher in need would come to pick them up and take them to the patient. The patient could be a young mare in trouble dropping her foal or a herd of 100 or so bull calves due for branding, castration and vaccination.

Kaleb and Sarah would be in the dusty center of the action. She in her laced, high-topped shoes and her long-sleeved, ankle-length calico dress. The dress was covered and protected by a light canvas apron. Her face and blue eyes were always well shaded from the bright sun by her calico bonnet with its straw visor.

Kaleb, now dressed in broadcloth, stood tall and unbent under his wide-brimmed felt hat. Quick and intense above his long full beard, his black eyes missed nothing, The Winchester 12-gauge, the last resort cure for a terminal illness or injury to an animal, was always somewhere nearby.

The boys understood clearly from their folks that a great privilege had come their way in knowing Kaleb and Sarah. They were aware of the privilege in knowing, early on, that a few of life's travelers give much and ask for very little. The experience of knowing Sarah and her man made it mandatory for the boys to always want to cross the ridges that are always there to partition folks one from another. They'd pay no mind to those who would do otherwise.

Story Three

Where Stories are Told in the Sky

The boy and his pony faced into a sharp wind out of the northwest. The chill in the wind was trying its best to bite through his warm jacket. It was late on an October day on the edge of the Nebraska Sandhills. The trail they were on was an old one showing the dual tracks of countless wagons traveling one behind the other. Some of those wagons passed this way long ago. Up ahead, the dual tracks climbed a sandy-clay hill and disappeared over a ridge into the boy's home valley.

After school, on orders from his dad, the boy had ridden out to the hills to the south to check on the windmill that supplied water for the cattle pasturing there. Before the onset of winter, this stock would be brought in to winter closer to home. Now he and his pony were on their way to that home.

When he was alone with his pony, they talked in a language of their own. Sometimes his thoughts and words got beyond the pony's understanding. When that happened, the pony often cut out to play games on his own, games like snorting and shying at an imaginary spook behind a real trailside Indian Soap Weed. Suddenly that occurred. The shy wasn't sharp enough to throw the rider but definitely sharp enough to get his attention. To even the score, the boy came up with an idea that he knew would annoy the pony.

Reining in near a clump of wild plum, he jumped off and dropped the reins to the ground. He knew this would tie the well-trained cowpony as securely as if he were tied to a post. From a saddle bag he extracted his Buffalo Bill Spy Glass. To get that jewel, he'd sent eight Post Toasties box tops and

15 cents to a place with an exotic name, Battle Creek, Michigan. Only a few weeks later, Mr. Maroney, the man who delivered the mail to the box out on the county road, had carefully placed that prized instrument in the mailbox. Mr. Maroney knew it would be safe there until the young man who was the addressee could come to make it his own.

Carefully clutching the glass, the lad patted his pony on the neck and then ran to the top of a nearby low hill. Those once-drifting sand and clay hills rested quietly now beneath a thick mat of buffalo grass. Here and there tall patches of big-bluestem flourished; he dropped on his back in one of the patches. Suddenly he was in a quiet cocoon. The wind was held at bay by the tall bluestem, and the earth was warm on his back. In the profound silence of his warm nest he began to hear a low murmur. It was like the sound of people talking in another room. The sound was detached and haunting. The hair at the nape of his neck felt funny and goose bumps formed on his cheeks. He lay absolutely still; any movement could dispel the coming magic.

Far away in the northern sky appeared a majestic V formation of Sandhill Crane. He knew that most cranes had already flown south; this might be the last flight of the season! The travelers, as always, were talking as they flew, they were telling each other stories. The stories were old and laced with the wisdom of many millions of generations. The younger birds that had not made this trip before knew that in coming years others not yet living would depend on them to be the leaders on this annual journey of survival. They watched and listened carefully.

The formation passed directly over the boy's position on the low hill. With his glass he could see the perfectly delineated colors, bright red and black with gray on white; he marveled at the feeling of power in the colors. The boy knew those intricate colors could only have been painted by the skilled hand of God.

He felt the cranes looking directly at him. Lying there on his hilltop he got for one fleeting moment an insight into the perspective from which they were seeing him. They'd seen him before, probably last spring, but more than that, they saw him thousands of years ago. His skin was a different hue and his sheepskin coat was made from the skin of a wild animal. One thing was the same: they felt a boy's love coming up to them, and they spoke of it as they flew.

All too soon the sound of their voices quietly faded, and the formation blended into the gray clouds on the southern horizon. They would fly without rest until they saw the broad marshes along the Platte River. They knew those marshes as their age-old place to feed and rest before continuing their journey to the south.

When the boy retreated from his hilltop, his pony was glad to see him, and all was forgiven. The moment the lad placed his foot in the left stirrup the pony broke into a run. He was anxious to get to his warm stall in the great weathered barn that sprawled among tall cottonwood trees and sweet-smelling cedar.

As they galloped into the yard, the boy's father called out to him, "No work tomorrow or Sunday, Chuck, so move the horses in the corral out to the west canyon." His pony was disappointed at not getting to go directly to his warm stall, but the boy was delighted with the new task. He loved to watch the giant work horses and the nimble-footed cowponies as they frisked and played like children out of school when delivered to the quiet freedom of the remote west-canyon pasture.

Stars appeared in the darkening vault of the sky as he went about the rest of his evening chores. He glanced up to do his nightly search of the heavens. He spotted Polaris and then found the star he always looked for. His dad had told him that its name was Sirius, the Dog Star. He knew this remarkable blue star had long been a friend to the family and that it was a very special friend to his Grandmother Annie. When she came here with her husband onto what was then a vast sea of grass, that familiar blue star had been a comforting, connecting link to her past life. More than that, it somehow represented an assurance that her God had, in fact, come with her to this new land with its strange Indian name. This land called Nebraska had a beautiful big sky that was so big it frightened some folks.

Some of the lesser stars in the silent black sky seemed to be chinning themselves on what looked to be juvenile snow clouds. Those clouds would mature in December and January and would then transform the grass-covered hills that surrounded the valley with wind-blown drifts of snow.

When his chores were finished, he went into the house for supper. It was the fine old house his grandfather built to replace the dugout and the soddie that had sheltered the family through their dangerous early years on this prairie.

The large warm kitchen welcomed all who would come in from the cold. Its warmth was bathed in the soft golden light of two kerosene lamps. The wicks of the lamps were trimmed daily, and the thin glass globes were washed and polished with care. The lamps sat high on a shelf on the east wall of the large room. They rested on either side of the round white face of the old Seth Thomas clock. Grandfather Bob, on one of his annual trips to sell his grass-fattened steers, had purchased that clock at a fancy store in Omaha.

The boy's mom, who was busy bringing supper to the table, greeted him with, "Well, my laddie, how was your day at school?" He heard his mom, but he was thinking of those magnificent cranes. He was wondering what he could do to share with others his friendship with those beautiful travelers.

He answered the question with, "School was okay, Mom. Miss Maroney says I'm to ask you to help me with my long division." He hesitated and then continued, "Mom, do you ever lay on your back in the big-bluestem and watch the Sandhill cranes?"

His mom laughed, then said, "Bless ye, lad. I love the beauty of that thought, but I'm afraid I don't have time to do that. You know I'd like to. Sure and I would."

Later, with an acceptable amount of horseplay, the supper dishes were washed and wiped by the siblings whose turn it was to do that less-than-exciting chore. The dishes eventually found themselves clean, dry and safely back in the store-bought oak-wood cabinet that stood against the west wall. Meanwhile, his tall dad moved one of the lamps from the high clock-shelf down to the center of the kitchen table. The boy's arithmetic book and papers were waiting for him there. He knew he needed to get busy because his parents and older siblings would soon want to use that table to play "Pitch."

That card game usually got them all excited, and occasionally there would be raised voices and some serious banging on the table. The boy figured the table-banging was a required part of the game.

When his mother joined him at his homework, the lad said, "Mom, we know the Sandhill cranes are just about the wisest things in the whole wide world. I figure they got that way without knowing a thing about long division."

His mom laughed and replied in a voice that still had more than a trace of the lilt that came with her as a young girl from her Irish homeland. "Never mind yer stalling, Mr. Twister. We must get on with your studies or we'll both have to answer to Miss Maroney. And you can bet your life, those high-flying friends of yours won't be there to help us arg' our case. You know, sure enough, they'll be busy living it up on some fine wet marsh in a sun-blessed land far and away to the south." The boy's eyes widened behind his glasses and he was silent for a moment. He liked the picture his mom had just painted for his friends. He wondered if they'd tell him about it when they come by again next spring.

-✴-

Story Four

A Prairie Parable

Purple-green stands of big-bluestem, flat green mats of buffalo grass, and stretches of silvery wild-oat covered the rolling land on either side of the road. The road, a graveled state highway, wandered to the horizon east from Prairie Center. Scattered clumps of dark green cedars seemed to have been casually tossed onto the low hills and into the draws. Perhaps the seeds for those trees were tossed there by God's hand as he surveyed this range from the back of his winged horse.

On a long-ago Friday afternoon, bucking and swaying, a four-wheeled box trailer reluctantly followed behind Joe Maurer's 1929 Model A Ford, which was headed out of town to the east.

Above the road, behind the little rubber-tired train a small cloud of white dust hung aloft in the hot, still air. Joe was not pulling his usual load of prairie-hay or bought calves. This hot August afternoon his trailer was loaded with something much more active than bales of hay and infinitely more talkative than new calves.

This was Joe Maurer's turn to carry his own and the rest of the kids from the farms and ranches east of town; he was to carry them to and from Father Keller's Summer Catechism class at Saint Anselm's Church. By agreement among the parents, the long ride into town would be provided and shared by all. Each day the kids could expect to be riding in a different rig.

This afternoon on the way home two of the Farritor kids, Eddie ten and Chuck twelve, were sitting like everyone else on the floor of the trailer. The younger brother, Eddie, who was seated toward the front, found himself surrounded by a bunch of big kids. Chuck, seated toward the rear, was talking to one of his many cousins, and this was not an ordinary cousin. This one had auburn hair that bounced around her neck in mysterious ringlets. The ringlets were long enough to touch and caress her creamy white shoulders. This cousin's name was Peggy Williams. Most people in the family had blue or green eyes, but Peggy's eyes were different. Chuck found that looking into her big brown eyes was an experience not unlike the jolt he felt when he once sneaked a belt of his Uncle Rob's home-brewed liquor. Another thing, Peggy had a laugh that a guy could still hear in his head days after he had looked into those eyes.

The light cloud of dust that floated in the air behind the trailer changed to a darker color as Joe steered his little train off the graveled highway where that road turned to the south. He turned onto a dirt road that headed on to the east. Someone peering over the rim of the trailer-box called out, "Hey, Peg, you're next out. We're nearin' the bridge over Victoria Creek." Peggy gathered up her things as the trailer slowed to a stop. Just before she stood up to get out she turned to her cousin Chuck; the softness was gone from her big brown eyes. As she climbed out she said, "Those big guys up front are pickin' on your little brother."

When she was gone, a pocket of chilled air settled over him. How could a girl with those eyes have to be the one to tell him something that he very well knew but thought he might get away with pretending he didn't know? Further, why was there written somewhere in stone a dumb commandment that older brothers had to risk getting clobbered by big guys just because those big guys had a thing about picking on kids smaller than themselves? His body was inert, but his mind galloped like a frisky pony in the newly chilled air.

He'd been thinking that he wanted to ask Father Keller about some stuff. He knew very well he'd get no real answer from him. Same thing here; he knew you couldn't question that dumb rule that says, "Ya got'ta stick up fer' y'r little brother." The reason was probably written in stone someplace, just like the rule was.

He let his mind go blank, and the air grew warm again. It was only a few miles to the side road where he and Ed would be getting out. The trailer again slowed and stopped. He saw Eddie jump up and vault over the side like a young steer escaping a branding chute. Chuck's mind somehow blanked out. He found himself not climbing over the rear end-gate like he expected to do; instead he was climbing over the legs of the kids in the middle as he made his way to the front of the trailer. Some power beyond him was calling the play.

When he got to where the big kids were, his mind was still a blank. Not a word was spoken, and though he could hardly believe it, he started throwing punches at the first big kid he came to. The kid was actually a friend of his, but, damn it, that friend was keeping bad company. After landing a few good ones, Chuck jumped out of the trailer, ready to call it a day.

Walter Schultz, the kid he had smacked, took quick exception to being hit on the nose and ears; so he too jumped out of the trailer. Walter managed to land on the back of his escaping attacker. The two of them were soon rolling around in the fine gray dust of the county road.

In no time at all, a third party joined the battle; it was Joe Maurer's wife, Estelle. She jumped out of the Ford and began swinging her purse wildly. She danced in and out of the tiny cloud of dust being raised by the flailing ball of youthful heads, arms, and legs. As she danced, she screamed incomprehensible phrases in a mixture of heavily accented

English and probably correct, Low German, all the time continuing to swing that purse like a medieval mace.

It came to pass that on one of the revolutions of the swinging purse, as the boys rolled over and over in the dust, Walter went as limp as a cheap throw-rope in Chuck's arms. With his friend and adversary out of it, Chuck jumped up and, on his second try, made his escape from the scene. As he fled down the road to the south he could see his brother Eddie just disappearing over a rise 50 yards ahead of him. Eddie, too, was seriously high-tailing it for home.

There was no catechism class on Saturday. On Sunday morning all of the faithful were in their places at Saint Anselm's Church. They were there to hear Father Keller sing the prayers of the Holy Mass and Benediction. The priest's rich singing voice shaped the mysterious Latin words and phrases into a message of beauty that entertained and comforted all who came to hear.

Everyone in the parish just knew that it must please God a bunch to hear the Mass that was so beautifully offered to him each Sunday morning from this, His very own house on this wide Nebraska prairie.

The beautiful beige-brick, Italianate-design church was full of people as usual. Chuck and Eddie were there with their siblings and their mom and dad. Joe and Estelle Maurer were there with their kids. The large Schultz family was there; that family nearly filled a whole pew. This day, however, they were not all there. Walter was missing. Chuck wondered and worried some about that.

On Monday morning, to start the last week of Summer Catechism class, Ed Knoell came along in his big Ford truck to pick up the kids. The truck with its high stock-rack had been washed down, and there was a fluffy layer of oat straw on the floor. The truck hardly smelled of cattle manure at all.

The kids were being their usual noisy selves. Chuck and Eddie climbed aboard and sat on the floor in the clean-smelling oat straw. To their surprise, they saw Walter sitting quietly in a corner; he had a great blue lump on his forehead. No one was talking about it, but looking at the blue lump in amazement, Chuck and Eddie understood clearly that one of the things that Father Keller had taught them was indeed true. God sometimes finds a way to smite those amongst us who need to be smitten. Chuck went over and sat down beside his friend Walter. Neither of them knew how to say what needed to be said. With the other kids chattering all around them, they sat together in silence as the big Ford truck noisily covered the many miles to Saint Anselm's church.

It came to pass that Mrs. Maurer never admitted to having cold-cocked her neighbor's kid with the pint of home-brewed liquor that she had in her purse. Therefore, Chuck got full credit for creating the educational lump on Walter's forehead.

Growing up seemed to speed up after that summer. In what seemed like no time at all, two guys named Hitler and Mussolini went crazy in Europe, and the Japanese bombed Pearl Harbor. The result of all this for the people of Saint Anselm's was a great diaspora.

One of the results of that diaspora was that a grownup Chuck, in far-off Hawaii, would come to know another girl, a nurse at Queen's Hospital there, who came from a small eastern state called New Jersey. He knew her not in the biblical sense, but they did a lot of fun things together. They both loved those wonderful islands of bright sun, white sand, and blue seas. This new girl was not a cousin with long auburn ringlets and soft brown eyes. This girl had curly brown hair and blue-gray eyes. Strangely, it turned out that this girl's laugh, too, stayed in his head long after he looked into her eyes.

It came to pass that Chuck would learn that there are, indeed, many rules that are carved in stone. On the other hand, as he grew older Chuck came to know that there are many issues that were not dealt with at all in Father Keller's green Catechism Book. To resolve some of the really tough ones, he just had to do the best he could. He understood full well that God couldn't always send Estelle with her swinging mace to help him. He knew that he alone would have to wrestle those pesky issues to the ground in the fine dust of his life's many roads.

A host of summers have now come and gone. Indeed, gone too are most of the folks who played a role in the tiny drama that unfolded on the stage of that dusty road on that long-ago summer afternoon.

It came sadly to pass that also in the diaspora the Japanese would kill Chuck's good friend, Walter Schultz. This happened half a world away from Saint Anselm's. Walter and many other young Americans died while liberating an island called Leyte from its Japanese invader. From that day on Walter would forever be missing from the Schultz family pew at mass on Sunday mornings.

Walter would not know Father Keller's replacement, a new priest in a new time. A decision had been made by higher-ups that the new priest would not sing the beautiful Latin words and phrases as Father Keller always had. Father Miles would recite the holy prayers in English. The world of the church had gained provincial clarity but in so doing had lost a plethora of beauty and color.

There are some things that have not changed. The beautiful beige-brick church on that wide prairie still holds a cross high above its doorway. The cross and the high bell-tower are there to guide the faithful to the quiet space within the church's walls. On hot, still afternoons a white dust still rises behind vehicles traveling on the graveled state highways leading to the village and the church.

Much more sophisticated vehicles than Joe Maurer's 1929 Model A Ford now carry the children to the summer Catechism classes at Saint Anselm's Church. The dust that hung in the air behind Joe Maurer's four-wheeled trailer on that long-ago summer afternoon has long since settled back onto that graveled road. That road, however, still wanders to the horizon east from Prairie Center. It wanders there among the grasses and cedars that still paint the surrounding low hills with a dozen and more soft colors. There is something very special about those colors.

If you were to ask the kids in any Saint Anselm's Summer Catechism class about this, they would tell you true. "The gentle colors on those hills and in those draws were, sure enough, created in heaven. They came, most certainly, out of God's very own celestial color-mixing pots."

Anyone who would argue with that simple wisdom has clearly been adrift in the outer world for much too long.

-*-

Story Five

Tall Grass Warfare

Coach Radnicheck dreamed the thing up. It was early spring of 1942. At the close of the basketball season he invited Sandy Crossing High School over to Prairie Center High for an evening of the gentlemanly art of boxing. He announced that the Eighth Marquis of Queensbury's rules would be observed. No one but Coach "Rad" had any idea who that fellow was or knew about his rules.

Coach Rad had come to Prairie Center from down east near Lincoln where college professors and politicians hung out. As you probably know, there are really two Nebraskas. There's the rather crowded "down east" one and then there's the rest of the state. In that western section, horses and cows outnumber folks by a considerable margin. There are other differences as well. The coach wasn't at all aware of the fine tradition of warfare that had existed between the young bucks from Sandy Crossing and Prairie Center for all of remembered time.

It should be noted that these two Nebraska towns were quite evenly matched. They shared equally the big sky, the tall grass, and the prairie wind. Prairie Center, however, had a railroad and 53 kids in high school. Sandy Crossing had fewer kids and no railroad; what it did have was a river that ran through it. The kids from Prairie Center did sorely envy them that wonderful sandy-bottomed river!

To make ready for the boxing event, Coach Rad had a ring built in the center of the old gymnasium and had wooden plank seats assembled several tiers high all around, even up on the stage, which was logically planted at one end of the gym. At 50 cents a seat, he was obviously hoping for a financial bonanza.

On the afternoon of the appointed day, all the cows for miles around the town of Sandy Crossing were on their own. The cowboys and girls, their mothers and fathers and friends, along with their aunts and uncles and grandparents, had all packed up and gone to Prairie Center to support their lads at the Queensbury doin's. They got there early and packed the house.

The Prairie Center Volunteer Fire Chief declared the house full before the local folks could even get there. The locals mostly ended up milling around outside. They were wishing that they, too, had let their cows fend for themselves early. The coach had, sure enough, gotten his financial bonanza. And best of all, it was mostly "out-of-town" money!

There was no program. The boxing matches were arranged by drawing numbers from a hat in the various age and weight groups; not very scientific, but as far as anyone knew, there were no scientists anywhere in Custer County to pass judgment.

Coach Rad had wisely arranged to have referees come up from Broken Bow, the county seat. The refs were as surprised as the coach at the degree of electricity in the air and the intensity of the crowd, both crowds, the one in the gym and the one milling around in the schoolyard. The inside crowd managed to maintain a noise level well above that of the inside of an overturned tin washtub in a summer hailstorm. A win for a Sandy Crossing lad raised the din to a point where the vibrations in the old building caused a fine white mortar dust to drift away from its brick walls.

The excitement abroad in the place caused some inexplicable things to happen. Normally much too wise to be caught up in such foolishness, a senior student at Prairie Center named

Chuck became a participant. In a moment of enthusiastic insanity, he tossed his name into the hat, and as sure as sunrise will come, it got drawn.

Chuck made three decisions that night, two of them bad and one that was brilliantly good. The first mistake, of course, was dropping his name in the hat. The second mistake was the opponent he drew. It was a young cowboy named Buck Krieger. The brilliant move he made was in picking his corner man. He picked a good friend named Bates O'Leary (Batesy for short).

By the time their fight came up, the inside crowd had, with their breathing and their body heat, completely displaced the clean spring air in the gym. There being no air, it was necessary to breathe what was present, which was pretty much limited to the body heat, the fine white mortar dust, and the vibrating sounds that filled that space.

Very early in the first round it became quite clear to Chuck, and to the crowd, that Buck Krieger fully intended to knock his opponent's head off. During the break after the first round, Batesy assured Chuck that Krieger was missing most of his shots. He was swinging wildly and widely with both gloves. The news that Krieger was missing some shots was a complete surprise to Chuck. It was definitely the only good news he'd had in the past three minutes.

Batesy had further advice. He reminded Chuck that he had the reach on Krieger, so he was to work short left jabs to Krieger's face while bringing his right up inside, looking for the cowboy's unguarded chin. Near the end of the second round, a cut opened inside Chuck's nose. As they had all evening at the sight of Prairie Center blood, the Sandy Crossing folks responded with enthusiasm. The newly redoubled noise had the ceiling of the old gym figuratively warping and lifting, and the fine white mortar dust was putting on a show of its own. The inside crowd, looking forward to a knockout, was making so much noise that no one in the ring heard the bell signaling the end of round two. The battle continued in the center of the ring. Suddenly Chuck found Batesy in his face and found himself being steered to their corner.

The referee told Chuck later that at the height of the melee in the ring, while they were separating the fighters, Batesy landed a couple of really good shots on Krieger's chin. The referee apparently had no problem with that. He could see perfectly well that Chuck needed whatever help he could get.

In their corner Batesy went to work trying to stop the bleeding. Over the drumming, screaming crush of sound in the place, Chuck recognized Coach Rad's voice. The coach was shouting advice into his left ear, "Son, I think it'd be a good idea to stay away from him this last round. Just back-peddle some."

The coach's advice made Batesy mad as hell. The coach went back to his seat, and Batesy continued with the task of trying to seal off the bleeder. In the last seconds before the bell rang, the bleeding stopped. Batesy put his gels and gauze pads away and then grabbed Chuck's head in a vice-grip. He pressed his forehead against his fighter's forehead so tight their eyelashes were touching. Batsey's eyes were blazing and were projecting a message that was loud and clear. Mixed in with the sounds of a double-engine freight train passing through the gym, his words echoed what his eyes were saying. "We're not gonna run from that saddle tramp. No way. We're gonna keep your left in his face and keep working your right inside and up. If we connect just right, that bum'll land in the third row."

Coach Rad had given Chuck a lot of good advice over the past four years. Tempting as it was to go with the coach's plan, Chuck just couldn't do it. Batesy and he had too much invested in Buck Krieger to do any "back-peddling." The bell rang and Batesy let go of his fighter's head.

Through to the last bell, Chuck continued to follow Batesy's orders. Regrettably none of his right upper cuts landed just right, so Buck Krieger was cheated out of a trip to the third row. On the other hand, the Sandy Crossing folks and their fighter got their win, but they didn't get the knockout that they had felt sure was in their pocket.

It was not always apparent to the folks around Prairie Center, but they all knew there was another world beyond the big sky and the tall grass. In that outer world a great war was raging. When school was out that spring, Tom O'Leary, Batesy's father, who was a fine cattleman and a self-trained first-class machinist, moved his family to Chicago. There he felt he could contribute more directly in the war effort; he would work in a defense plant making parts for Sherman tanks. His foreman and hired men could tend the ranch until the war was over.

Totally by chance Chuck and Batesy met once again. They met in "The Crow's Nest," a beer bar on the Seattle waterfront. They got wonderfully smashed, bawled in each other's beer some and then parted again.

In the years after the war they lost track of each other. Not long ago, Chuck got word that Batesy had died surrounded by his wife and children up in Oregon. Chuck knew that surrounded by family or not, dying is a thing that you do all by yourself. When he got word of Batesy's death, Chuck prayed that at the moment of his death, Batesy found God's forehead pressed to his. Chuck knew that with God brushing eyelashes with him, Batesy would surely be guided to a way that would see him successfully through that ultimately final round.

Prairie Center still has its railroad, and that priceless river still flows through Sandy Crossing. However, in obedience to the unforgiving laws of progress, both high schools have been torn down. Their students were melded into a third, newer high school.

Be that as it may, just as sure as those heavy trains still roll and that wonderful river still flows, the young bucks from those two tall-grass towns will still find some way to keep their feud as alive and healthy as is the grass that still grows tall in the summer sun, the grass that daily dips and rolls its way to the horizon, guided there by the soft prairie winds.

Story Six

Eddie: Tall, Quiet, Wise and Brave

Bob and Annie Farritor brought their young family onto the ocean of grass that was Custer County, Nebraska, in the1870s. Amid dangerous and trying times they survived and in the end prospered. This story is about their grandson, Edward L., Ed or Eddie. Eddie was Frank's third son. You will remember Frank, the eight-year-old lad who in the family portrait on their homestead in 1890 had to move his head some because a horsefly was bothering him.

Bob and Annie would've been proud to hear these stories about their grandson Edward. They would've been pleased to know that the human quality called guts, of which they had demonstrated aplenty, would live on in the young Nebraskans who came after them.

One part of little Eddie's story goes like this: Ed and 17 other lads made up the Anselmo High School football squad. The year was 1943. America's defenses had been badly damaged in an attack two years earlier at Pearl Harbor by the Empire of Japan. Emperor Hirohito had aligned himself with Germany's Hitler and Italy's Mussolini. That unlikely trio was in the process of taking over the world. The peoples of the earth were locked in a death struggle with the would-be conquers and an end to the war was nowhere in sight.

Anselmo High had lost its coach to the war. Amid cries of anguish on all sides, the school board had decided to cancel the football season. Lloyd Chandler, the man who owned the drug and sundries store in town, went to the school board and said, "I'll coach the football team under these conditions: you pay me nothing and I quit the first time any one of you offers advice on how I'm to do the job." With some trepidation they handed him the keys to the sports locker room.

The boys' lockers and showers shared space in a basement room of the old high school with a huge fire-spitting coal furnace and a hulking boiler-tank that hissed and fumed alarmingly. At least three generations of Anselmo athletes knew that belching boiler well; they called it "big thunder."

Coach Chandler applied his own tough work ethic to this new task. He worked the team hard, and he was surprisingly football astute. He produced an array of interesting plays. He had several plays where his guards pulled to run interference for the ball-carrier. That tactic was not commonplace in those days. Bob and Annie's grandson, Ed and his good buddy, Gene Lewis, were the guards on both offense and defense.

Each Friday afternoon the Anselmo "Eagles," in their crimson and blue jerseys, took the field expecting to win one. Somehow it didn't happen. They managed to keep the scores respectable because on defense they were quick and durable.

The last game of the season was against the South Loup "Bears." South Loup High School had as its "Star" a senior they called "Bull Fiddle." Bull Fiddle, a giant of a lad, had run roughshod over every defense that the Bears had faced all season.

The Anselmo Eagles came to this season and this game without their "Star," a good friend of Ed's named Billy Jim English. A big and talented kid, Billy Jim had made the team his freshman year in high school. The summer after his starring sophomore year an ominous lump appeared on his forearm. Billy Jim's arm was quickly amputated, but too late. The demon in the lump had fled to other parts. With the leaping fury of a prairie fire, cancer swiftly and brutally consumed the life of Billy Jim English.

Game day at South Loup High dawned cloudy and cold; a stiff wind blew from the goal posts at the north end of the gridiron. Before the game, Coach Chandler spoke quietly to his team. "I want you lads to understand this: that north wind is our friend, and know this too, we're going to give these Bears a surprise here today. Our game plan is simple; at least three people will hit Bull Fiddle the moment he gets the ball. Remember, we hit him low and quick!"

"Hear me on one other thing. When we've got the ball, each one of you pretend, just for today, that Billy Jim is carrying the pigskin. To protect him, I want you to hit harder than you've ever hit before." There were tears on the cheeks of the pack of young Eagles who blew out of that room and out onto a winter-browned grass field.

The Bears won the coin toss. Right off, they felt that things were going their way. With the wind at their backs they elected to receive the ball. Their game plan, too, was simple. They planned to score quickly and often.

The Eagles lined up and kicked. It was a fine, squib kick that stayed under the wind. It bounced twice, then directly into the hands of a Bear lineman. The Bear found himself on his own 33-yard line looking close up at a pack of swooping, angry Eagles. He got hit hard, and the ball squirted loose. When the fur and feathers stopped flying from the battle that ensued, it was an Eagle that was covering the ball, and he was on the Bear nine-yard line.

On the first play from scrimmage the Eagle guards pulled to run interference. The fullback and quarterback followed the guards to the right; as they went past the right wingback, the quarterback slipped him the ball. The new ball carrier turned to the left. The Bear defense, following what they thought was the ball to the right, gave the right wingback an open field. Running to the left, he scored standing up.

On the try for the extra point, they set up for the kick but with the wind in mind, they pulled a "student body right." In the midst of a mob scene in the far right corner of the field, after a fumble and a recovery, the Eagle ball carrier got over the goal line for the extra point. The Bears were stunned.

The game settled down to a grim defensive battle, and the Eagles held their own. In the fourth quarter Bull Fiddle got loose once to score. On a short pass for the extra point the Bear receiver found himself looking at the back of a crimson and blue jersey. An Eagle had gotten in front of him to knock the pass down.

The team in crimson and blue welcomed the final whistle. The lads with the dried tear stains on their cheeks had won it! They knew they'd won it for Billy Jim, but they knew they'd won it for themselves, too.

With the war in Europe and the Pacific still raging, most of the lads in that football game went on to wear khaki or blue. In response to a curt letter of greetings from his Uncle Sam, Ed donned khaki. He graduated from "Killer's College" at Cannon Town, Texas (Fort Bliss Infantry Training Center). Ed soon earned a Combat Infantry Badge with the U.S. Tenth Army in the Pacific. In May of 1945 his infantry company was fighting its way across the shoulder of a mountain on the Japanese Island of Okinawa. One bright morning, Ed heard a thud behind him. He turned to see that an American white phosphorus grenade had landed near him. Ed's buddy shouted, "Look out, Ed! Some son-of-a-bitch thinks we're Tojo!" Ed had a momentary thought of picking the grenade up and throwing it toward the enemy, but suddenly his view of the grenade dissolved in a silent white flash!

The blast threw Ed onto his back. Try as he might, he could not see the bright morning sky. He could see nothing.

His buddy, who had escaped injury, didn't try to remove the rifle from Ed's white phosphorus-covered hands. He was able to get Ed to his feet and gently guide his, now blinded, friend to an aid station. The medics managed to separate Ed from his rifle after they had put the young infantryman into a drug-induced coma.

Days later aboard the hospital ship *Comfort,* an army general placed a brace of medals on Ed's pillow. Eddie could not see the visiting general or the medals; his face, neck, hands, arms and chest were covered with white gauze, and he was still in a coma.

The only area not burned on his face was his forehead. It had been protected by his G.I. helmet. Weeks later at an army hospital in Honolulu he was finally out of the coma. As the dressings over his eyes were being changed, he found that he could not close his eyes but he had not lost his eyesight. Bob and Annie's grandson Eddie suffered those grievous wounds when he was nineteen years old.

He would survive those hellish burns. At Beaumont General Hospital in Texas, in the skilled hands of U.S. Army doctors, he would undergo multiple skin grafts on his hands, arms, face, ears and eyelids. He would learn to live with incessant pain and a multitude of scars. He learned also to accept for all of his remaining days on earth, a nightly viewing of the silent movie of the exploding grenade. Eddie had inherited the guts to play and to fight with skill and honor, and he had inherited the strength to endure.

At home in Broken Bow, Nebraska, barely free of his bandages, this brave young American, who seemed never to acknowledge his pain or scars, met a pretty girl named Vicki. It was at a Saturday night dance. Vicki would come to be Ed's life-long friend and love. They married and raised four fine boys and three lovely girls.

Ed wasn't always tall. One of his brother Chuck's early memories of Eddie was at Saint Anselm's Cemetery. It was an unusually cold spring day. The sky was low with gray clouds. The grownups in the family and the community were burying their baby brother Joseph. Their big sister Anna Marie was holding Eddie in her arms to keep him warm. Chuck was holding tightly to a handful of the skirt of Anna Marie's warm coat.

They were watching their mom and dad who, with a host of other folks, were over near the pile of sandy dirt that would soon be Joseph's new coverlet. Their mom, Mary Ann, was sobbing and barely able to stand. Their Aunt Mary Knoell was holding her to keep her from falling. Most everyone was crying. Anna Marie's face was very pale, and her eyes and nose were red from crying. Eddie was looking at his mom and dad; he was crying too. He was a skinny little guy; his shock of brown hair was trying to escape from under his little kid's cap. It's not likely that either Chuck or Eddie understood about grief. Chuck felt like crying but only because he was afraid of what was happening to his mom and dad. They seemed always to be strong, but today they looked as afraid as any of the kids.

The kids understood full well that something awful had happened to their baby brother. Last Sunday afternoon they saw Joseph lying on their mom and dad's bed. He wasn't moving or making any sound. His face was very white, and there was a drop of blood under one nostril of his tiny nose. Their mom was looking down at her baby. She turned and went to the west window; her shoulders were shaking. Anna

Marie moved to her side and put an arm around their mom's waist. Anna Marie was crying, too.

Their dad was talking on the big, dark-wooden telephone that hung on the east wall in the kitchen. When he got off the phone, he came to the bedroom that was off the kitchen and picked Joseph up. Holding the tiny baby in his big arms, he carried Joseph to the rocking chair in the kitchen. His mother, Grandma Annie Farritor, and his wife, Mary Ann, had rocked all of their babies on that small hardwood chair. He sat down holding the silent baby. The chair began to rock slowly.

The only sounds in the room were the small sounds the chair was making on the pine floor of the kitchen. Their dad had tears running down his cheeks, but he was making no sound.

Sister Eileen came to take care of Eddie, who was fussing. When his diaper was changed, she picked Eddie up, then took Chuck's hand. She took her two little brothers outside to a bench by the "stone-house." (A large water storage tank sat atop a round, gray, cement-block building.) Sitting on the bench, Eileen held both boys closely as they watched the sun drop behind the hills to the west.

Their sister Lenore came out of the house and joined them. She was two years older than Chuck. Chuck didn't know whether she knew about Joseph being so quiet. Eileen didn't say anything about it, and Chuck was afraid to mention it.

Folks that the kids' dad had called on the telephone began arriving. One man arrived on a saddle horse and tied his mount to the hitching rack near the front gate. The rest parked their cars in the yard. They spoke quietly to each other, then went into the house. After the sun had set, Eileen picked Eddie up and took Chuck's hand. Lenore opened the door for Eileen as they went back into the house.

Aunt Emma and Father Keller took Joseph from his dad's arms and carried the silent baby to the north bedroom. Dr. Spivey arrived and was taken in to see the baby. In a few minutes he came out and quietly announced that Joseph was dead. Chuck didn't know for sure what that meant, but he knew it was something scary. The doctor then gave their mom some medicine and assisted her into her bedroom, which was off the kitchen. He soon came out and quietly closed the door. Chuck was seriously scared. Would the doctor now announce that their mom was dead, too?

As time passed, the kids got over losing Joseph. For their dad and mom, getting over that loss may have been something that never happened. Things were different in many ways; for one thing, Eddie was now the baby again. Chuck didn't know how Eddie felt about that, but it made Chuck love his little brother Eddie all the more.

As they grew bigger, there was one really scary summer when Eddie was probably five or six years old. He was always a skinny kid, but that summer he got thinner yet, and he had no energy. He got so weak that Chuck had to pull him around in their *Radio Flyer* coaster wagon. Their mom was really worried. There was talk around of a terrible thing called Polio. Their mom asked Dr. Spivey about it. Many frightening things probably went through the good doctor's mind, but what he said was, "I'm thinking, maybe that little devil ain't eating his vegetables. Stuff some spinach and carrots into him. If that don't do the trick, we can talk some more."

The doctor had guessed the truth. Eddie hated vegetables. Chuck knew that Eddie ate only bread, potatoes, meat and gravy. He was feeding his green vegetables to his dog "U-know," who wisely sat quietly under the table as the family ate. In a few weeks, with Mom riding close herd on Eddie's plate at mealtime, old U-know began to lose the pounds that

Eddie began to put on. Chuck no longer had to pull Eddie around in their coaster wagon.

A word about U-know. As the kids were growing up, they lived with several big dogs, not all at once but in succession. They came as puppies but soon grew really big. In that country, with the heavy frequency of snake bites and accidents involving larger animals, a dog's life was often short. The dogs seemed to all look alike and were all named U-know. When people asked about the dog's name, well, you know the routine. Their dogs were an Abbot and Costello joke, long before anyone ever heard of those guys.

Mr. Charlie Mohat, who delivered gasoline and tractor fuel to the farms and ranches out their way, had his truck vapor-lock on the county road some distance out from their house. When Eddie and Chuck saw him stopped out there, they ran out to see what was wrong. Mr. Mohat was leaning in over the old truck's engine. He turned to the boys and said, "If you lads'll get me a small bucket of cool water, that water just might get this old pile of junk goin' again." They did, and it did.

Early in the morning about a week later, the boys were still in bed when their mom came into their room holding a little bundle of fur. She said, "Mr. Mohat wants you boys to have this puppy." She handed it to Eddie. For both of them it was love at first sight. There was no question that it would be Eddie's dog. He called him Little-know.

A year or so later when the present big U-know died, Eddie's puppy became the new U-know. He would grow big just like the others. Big as he grew, he still insisted on lying across Eddie's feet as the boys slept in bed. More about Eddie's dog later.

Our mom was a hard worker and knew well how to delegate responsibility. Eddie was assigned to their sister Eileen for daily care, and Chuck was assigned to their sister Anna Marie. Chuck's caregiver complained frequently that Eddie was a good little boy who didn't get dirty as quickly as her charge did. Eileen responded to those complaints by smiling and hugging Eddie, Chuck quietly resolved to try to get a little less dirty while playing in the dirt. They both knew they were lucky that their mom had given them these two beautiful and loving girls to look out for them.

When Chuck and Eddie grew bigger, they were moved upstairs to the "boy's bedroom." There they joined their big brother John. Because Eddie had least seniority, he was stuck with the middle spot. John told them a story every night before they went to sleep. The story continued from night to night. The story was about John's imaginary adventures in the army. John didn't know about the Marine Corps yet, or the stories likely would've been wilder still. Eddie loved that serial adventure. They would be playing out in the ruins of their grandpa's old soddie, and Eddie would ask a specific question about the story of the night before. Or he would say, "I sure hope our big brother can get the best of that mean old Sergeant Kelly." Eddie was a serious fan of those nightly stories.

There were special hazards to sleeping in the middle. On more than one occasion, Chuck woke up with Eddie pounding on Chuck's chest and saying, "Dag-gone it, Chuck, you et too much watermelon, an' you wet the bed!" There were, of course, occasions when the tables would turn. Their mom, who grew up with three brothers, seemed to have inherited a system that dealt with all minor emergencies. To deal with this one, there was a light canvas sheet protecting the mattress and fresh cotton blankets on a shelf in the room. The standing orders were, "Get up, light a lamp, and change everything that needs changing. Be quick about it, and don't make a fuss that will wake other folks up." Their mom probably would've even had a system to handle mean ole Sergeant Kelly.

Uncle Will, who had lost his only son, took to Eddie. He liked to have Eddie ride with him as he worked the fields on his 1927 IHC tractor. Eddie sat on the axel-housing right beside one of the big, steel-lugged driver wheels. His feet rested securely on the idle power-take-off pulley. He tolerated the noise and the dust to be with his Uncle Will.

There was a scene that played out every night before bedtime in the kitchen of the house that Grandpa Bob built for his Annie. Just as Grandma Annie had done before her, Mary Ann led her family in evening prayers. See, if you will, six kids and their dad and mom, sometimes joined by a hired man or two, all kneeling at chairs scattered around the large room.

Sometimes at play, out of the blue, little Eddie would refer to one of the prayers that their mother, Mary Ann, had led her family through the night before. There was one that he especially liked. His love for the beauty in the words of that prayer tells much about the mind of that little boy. A printed version of the prayer can't catch the beauty or the lilt in the voice of their Irish-born mother as she led her family through this prayer:

Hail, Holy Queen, Mother of Mercy, our life, our sweetness and our hope. To thee do we cry, we poor banished children of Eve. To thee do we send up our sighs, mourning and weeping in this vale of tears. Turn then, most gracious advocate, thine eyes of mercy toward us. And after this our exile we pray, oh sweet Virgin Mary, that with your divine intercession we may, one day, be found worthy to see the face of God.

About the time Chuck was in high school, Eddie became Ed. He had, in fact, grown to be a strong, independent young man. Of course, in the family's heart he was still their little brother Eddie.

You were promised another story about Eddie's dog. U-know had grown to be an old dog by the time Ed went into the service. Mary Ann got it into her head that she had to keep that old dog alive until Eddie came safely home from the war. With a ton of tender loving care she managed to do just that. U-know survived for nearly twice the usual ranch-dog's lifespan. Of course, it helped that they had moved to Broken Bow away from most of the hazards that country dogs are called upon to deal with.

Old U-know liked living in town. He developed a route that he walked every day around his part of town. Mary Ann told of it this way, "Those two old codgers (her husband Frank and U-know) would cut out of here every day. Frank would go to see his friends at the pool hall. That old dog had several new friends, both canine and human, that he stopped to see each day." Those new friends, at least the human ones, reported to Mary Ann of looking forward each day to seeing the big old dog who had retired from his job out in the Sandhills.

No doubt U-know told each of his new friends about his good friend Eddie who had put on big shiny boots and a coat with brass buttons and then went away – to where, he didn't know.

Eddie's mom took it upon herself to remind the old dog daily that Eddie would be home any day now.

The first time Ed came home from Beaumont General Hospital on medical leave, he walked into the house in his coat with brass buttons. He was still heavily bandaged. When U-know was awakened from his afternoon nap, he hobbled over to sniff at Ed's knees. He probably couldn't, and didn't need to, see the heavy bandages.

After that one knee-sniff the old dog promptly laid down across Ed's big G.I.-booted feet. In old U-know's mind, his good friend Eddie had come home, and things were finally back to the way they used to be.

Eddie's good friend, U-know, died quietly before Ed came home from the hospital again on his next medical leave.

After a long life together, Ed lost his beautiful Vicki. His and their children's love and prayers could not protect Vicki from the cancer that came to take her from them.

One night, less than three years after Vicki's death, Ed did not see the nightly grenade explosion. He had, that day, gone to a quiet place where he could be with his God and his beloved Vicki. In the quiet haven to which he had gone, there is only love. Pain and memories of pain are not allowed there.

Under the big sky on a grassy hillside near their Ravenna, Nebraska, home, his family and a host of friends buried Ed alongside Vicki's grave. A bugle sounded softly on a near hillside. His aging veteran buddies saluted smartly and folded his flag gently.

★ ★ ★ ★ ★ ★ ★ ★ ★ ★

Story Seven

Carolina Night School

He usually avoided yard sales, but this Saturday morning, for no good reason, Chuck had followed the advice of a hand-painted sign that pointed off Indian Hill Boulevard onto Eighth Street. The sign that caught his eye extended the promise of valuable antiques. The tree-shaded front yard and driveway of the house at the end of the sign trail were covered with the usual assortment of yard-sale junk. It all looked pretty much like the same stuff that threatened to keep his cars out of his garage at home.

Going down the driveway on his way out, he spotted something that stopped him. A hardwood police truncheon stood in an old umbrella stand. The shiny butt-end of the truncheon seemed to glare at him. The leather thong that looped through a hole in the handle of the nightstick looked dry and hard. The thong's natural leather oils and the oils it had absorbed from a once gripping and sweating human hand had long since dried. As he bent to touch the nightstick, he realized that the hand he was extending was trembling and wet. It was wet with the kind of sweat that fear and anger produce. The fear and anger that surfaced for him this day was as viable and real as the suddenly remembered sound of a bone breaking. He couldn't touch the protruding end of the wooden stick.

Wiping his sweaty hand on his pant leg, he straightened up and stood for a moment on that elm-shaded driveway in a peaceful village 30 years and 3,000 miles from the time and place where he had been beaten by hardwood nightsticks like the one in that umbrella stand. Those handsome hardwood sticks had been wielded by cursing, sweating policemen. The uniforms they wore had his country's flag stitched to the upper sleeve.

On this pleasant summer morning he suddenly felt nauseous. He hoped no one was watching; he was sure he was going to lose his breakfast right there on that driveway. Damn that umbrella stand, damn the stick it contained, damn a memory that had the power to change his morning.

He managed to get back to his car without further incident. He turned his car's ignition key; the engine started quietly. The radio, tuned to an oldies station, came on with Jo Stafford softly singing "A Sunday Kind of Love." These quiet, familiar sounds brought his mind back to the present. He eased back in the leather seat and the sick feeling passed. To hell with that umbrella stand and its nightstick; he must work harder at keeping the past where it belongs.

The car moved smoothly away from the curb. In spite of his resolve, he found his mind wanting to return to that long ago night of pain. Surrounded and protected by the realities of his present life, he decided he could afford to indulge his mind the trip it seemed to want to take. He drove the few blocks to his own house, then pulled into the driveway and parked. With the radio playing softly, he eased back in his seat and closed his eyes.

Chuck was a deck sailor on the United States Army Transport *U.S.A.T. Hunter's Bend*. He was a smooth-faced lad. His ship, on the other hand, was a scarred veteran of service to her country. Few of her scars actually showed, most had been healed by skilled men with welding torches. She had come down the ways as a sparkling new cargo ship not all that long ago. Though the war was now over, her promise and duty was still to deliver stores and munitions to

America's fighting men wherever in the world they might be.

Ships age quickly in time of war. There are exceptions to that truism. In World War II, scores of star-crossed ships were not allowed the privilege of age at all. They, with their precious cargos and even more precious merchant marine crews, were sent to the bottom in their first few hours or days at sea. They were sent there by a skilled enemy who had his submarines laying in wait off America's coasts.

Like most of her sister ships, the *U.S.A.T. Hunter's Bend* had from time to time found the usual monotony of her duty at sea interrupted by moments of bounding terror. During those moments or hours, her life and the lives of the men who sailed on her were in great peril.

The *Hunter's Bend* felt pride and a pressing humility knowing that she had survived where others had not. One dark winter night off the coast of Greenland, a German submarine's torpedo slid past her stern and hit the small troop-carrier *U.S.A.T. Dorchester*.

The *Dorchester* in prewar years had been a small upscale, passenger steamer. She had graciously carried vacationers and honeymooners from New York to Bermuda and around the Caribbean.

All through the big band era, she had a reputation for great music, good food and happy times. Now all of that was behind her. With the outbreak of war, she had been called to serve her country. This night, bound for Greenland with a load of her country's young soldiers and airmen, she had been dealt a mortal blow by the enemy. She slipped beneath the waves in a matter of minutes. She went down with her crew of skilled merchant marine sailors and 1,000 of America's soldiers and airmen.

The *Hunter's Bend* could not stop to rescue the men who were struggling in the cold dark sea. It was required that she hold her course and speed; these orders were given and followed to maintain the integrity of the convoy and the safety of its remaining ships. Time of survival for a man in that cold water was so short that only a very few of those men were picked out of the water alive by the escorting U.S. Coast Guard cutters.

The sinking of the *Dorchester* gave the world the "Legend of the Four Chaplains." Two Protestant, one Catholic and one Jewish Chaplain each gave away his life jacket to soldiers who, because of the suddenness of the disaster, found themselves going over the side without life jackets. When last seen, the four Chaplains were quietly awaiting the inevitable. They were holding hands as they stood in a circle on the sharply sloping deck; their heads were bowed in silent prayer.

The *U.S.A.T. Hunter's Bend* remembered well each of the young Americans who had been injured or killed in her service. She wore these unhealed scars with a quiet dignity. She wore them as proudly as she wore her coat of paint, which was the quiet gray color of the sea at dawn. She had been delivering supplies to troops in the far west Pacific. Reassigned to the Atlantic, she would now be doing the same for the troops serving in Europe.

Coming in from Panama with her holds empty, she moved quietly into Charleston Harbor, her Plimsoll mark was riding well out of the water. Skirting the buoys off "Old Fort Sumter" she moved on up the Cooper River to her assigned berth.

Whatever the reason for his ship to be making this port of call, the young deck sailor named Chuck was excited to be in Charleston, South Carolina. An avid Civil War history buff, he couldn't quite believe he was going to get the opportunity to see and walk two more places with hallowed Civil War names, Fort Sumter and Battery Wagner.

Because the *Hunter's Bend* had spent the recent months in the Pacific, most of her present crew members were from the West Coast. Realizing the potential for his people to get into trouble in this most southern of southern cities, the skipper had a memo posted. The memo read in part, "DON'T BE FOOLED BY THE AMERICAN FLAGS ON THE FLAG POLES. SOUTH CAROLINA IS A COUNTRY FOREIGN TO YOU. 'JIM CROW' IS KING. YOU MUST OBEY THEIR JIM CROW LAWS TO THE LETTER. THERE IS NO ALTERNATIVE." The message was duly read but not fully understood by most of the young men to whom it was addressed.

Chuck tried to never go on liberty alone. Finding another crewmember with a bent for Civil War history wasn't easy. The interest had to be strong enough to withstand the jolt of the nine-dollar fee for the tour. The fee covered the cost of the guide, transportation and a brown-bag lunch. A black kid from Oakland, California, named Jimmy Call began to show some interest. His interest quickened when Chuck told him the tale of the fight at Battery Wagner. Incredibly, he had never heard the story before.

The story of the fight at Battery Wagner is the story of "The 54th Massachusetts." The 54th was a volunteer black regiment that had in defeat covered itself and the American infantry soldier with everlasting glory.

The day of their tour Chuck and Jimmy spent a lot of time in the back seat of buses and ferries, but they were enjoying an experience that any student of that history would cherish. The tour guide was knowledgeable but painfully free with the knowledge that the South had won the battle at both forts. One tourist from Ohio felt it necessary to interrupt at one point, "Mr. Tour Guide, I understand that after they lost the war, Mr. Jeff Davis and some of his friends donned their wives' dresses to hide from the Yankees. Now, ain't that the truth of it?" The tour guide chose not to answer the man from Ohio.

On a remote coastal sand dune, no guide was needed for Chuck to see and feel the stark drama of the history that had taken place there. He felt it as he stood on the top of the dune that was once the south wall of Battery Wagner. His mind created a vivid diorama of the awesome action that took place there on a sweltering July evening in 1863.

Spread out across the wide beach, a good part of a Union infantry regiment is charging the dune. The flag bearers are in the front echelon. One soldier carries the stars and stripes, and another carries the 54th's regimental colors. The long blue line moves silently forward on the wide cushion of the beach. The dark forms of the men fill the space from the low-tide edge of the restless Atlantic Ocean on their right to the high sand dunes on their left. In near regimental strength the line is several files deep.

As they march at the quick, the orange light from the setting sun is reflected forward from hundreds of fixed bayonets. The startling flecks of light are like as many tiny signal lamps gone mad. When the forward line starts firing, the angry orange muzzle blasts and the powder smoke immediately obscure the crisp detail of the line. No longer only a silent threat, the regiment is now a churning mass of charging, shouting human forms. They are coming forward out of a cloud of smoke that eerily has taken on the orange light of the setting sun. The forward blue-clad line thins as the fire from the battery takes its toll. From time to time they take whatever cover they can find or quickly dig, then up and forward again. The blue-coated regiment will not stop its charge. The closer they get, the more deadly is the fire from the rifles in the battery. Artillery and mortar fire from the battery sends men and parts of men in blue, flying into the air. The Union regiment still charges forward.

The final charge that crosses the dry moat and climbs the dune onto the outer wall of the fort is made by no more than two dozen "bluecoats." They are quickly overcome. With his final effort, the fourth man who has taken up the regimental flag as other bearers fell, jabs the base of the flagstaff into the sand on the wall of the fort. A puff of cool wind off the Atlantic lifts the flag. In the light of the muzzle blasts, the flag is seen to be torn to shreds.

The shattered but living, the wounded and the dead of the 54th Massachusetts, lie in the sand along the path of the charge. The sudden silence that falls when the firing stops bears testimony of foreboding. Cries of pain come out of the darkness. As the hours pass, there are fewer and fewer cries. Until dawn, the shadows of night will gently hide the enormity of the Union loss.

With tear-filled eyes, Chuck looked at the faces of the sightseeing tourists standing on the sand dune around him. He could see no indication on those faces that anyone had witnessed the battle as he had just seen it. He felt disappointment, but was proud that at least he, the great-grandson of an Irish immigrant who fought in Abe Lincoln's army, understood the measure of the tragedy that occurred here on that long-ago summer evening.

A new hot summer night had settled over the beautiful city of Charleston when the tour boat returned its exhausted passengers to Waterfront Park. The beautiful antebellum mansions that overlook the harbor lent a strong sense of cultural elegance to the scene. The heavenly scents of wisteria and magnolia softened the sultry night air.

The two sightseeing sailors had enough money left for their bus fare back to the ship, but no more. The fragrance of jasmine wafting over from the nearby White Point Gardens was great but not fulfilling enough to make them forget how hungry they were. The brown-bag lunch had been more brown-bag than lunch. They made their way quickly to the spot where they could catch a city bus back to their ship and food, real *Hunter's Bend* food. The bus took them along Meeting Street, under the beauty of its moss-laden old trees to the north edge of the city. There they were to transfer to another bus that would take them to the port area along the Cooper River. They found their second bus standing at the curb, the door ajar. They climbed in and sat down just behind the driver's seat. In the past, they'd found it wise to sit near the driver so they could talk to him about the location of their ship in the maze of piers on the riverfront. All harbor and riverfront piers seemed equally confusing. Tired as well as hungry, they dozed off while they waited for the driver to appear.

Sometime later the driver climbed aboard. The two dozing sailors came awake with a start. The driver was standing over his only two passengers, screaming at the top of his voice, "Nigras ta back the bus!"

They should've jumped up and ran to the rear. Instead Chuck said, "But, sir, we thought we needed to talk to you about where our ship is berthed."

Was it the shock of being awakened so sharply? Was it anger at the disgusting smell of beer coming from the flushed, spitting driver? Something had made the boy forget the skipper's warning. His remark and failure to quickly flee proved him to be a dumb kid with no understanding of the violent capabilities of those whose task it was to maintain the intricate structure of the system called "Jim Crow." He didn't understand that the slightest show of defiance had to be killed aborning.

The driver turned and vaulted into his seat. The old bus's engine came alive and it roared away from the curb. It careened around three or four corners, then screeched to a stop in front of a police station. Three policemen sat on chairs that had apparently been carried out of the station and placed on the grass in front of the building. One of them ran over to block the door of the bus. This foiled the two sailors' furtive attempt to escape into the night.

The driver, screaming unintelligibly, dashed into the station with the other two officers on his heels. In a matter of minutes the two officers came out and boarded the bus. They grabbed the two offenders by the feet as they sat now at the rear of the bus, and they dragged them out the door. The two sailors struggled to keep the backs of their heads from banging on the steps of the bus, the concrete curb, and the steps of the station. They were dragged quickly past the booking counter and on through a door at the rear of the booking room. They were dragged through a second door, a steel-barred door. They were left lying on their backs on the deck of what appeared to be the "colored drunk-tank." As they lay on the wet concrete, their pockets were quickly emptied. One officer grabbed the tiny silver cross and chain on Chuck's neck: also on the chain was a Star-of-David medal. That medal had been given to him for safekeeping by a shipmate who had been badly injured and was now in the Marine Hospital in Seattle. (It was an accepted fact that jewelry or precious keepsakes did not survive a hospital stay.) Chuck had promised to hold it for his friend. The officer gave a sharp yank on the silver chain, breaking the chain.

The police officers left with their prisoner's I.D. cards, Chuck's California driver's license, and the Star of David medal. As they left, the lock on the steel-barred door clicked with the despairing sound that only jail locks make. The two sailors stood up and looked around in disbelief. Jimmy said, "Holy Jesus, what'll the Skipper say when he gets wind of this?"

Chuck stooped to pick up the tiny silver cross that had fallen to the deck from the broken chain. He asked, "Why did that dumb son-of-a-bitch have to steal my silver chain and Sid's medal?" Blood was accumulating in the crease on the side of his neck where the sturdy chain had cut the skin before it broke. When the crease was full, the blood drained in crooked rivulets down his neck. He was completely unaware of the bleeding.

Drunk tanks are a study in incivility. Like this one, they are usually in a large concrete-floored room. The floor slopes from all sides to a large scupper in the center. The short fire hoses on racks at either end of the room are there for a purpose that has nothing to do with fighting fire. The inmates are contained in an iron cage. The walls of the cage are about five feet away from the walls of the room; thus the jailors can walk all the way around the cage.

The drunks do considerable throwing up as a consequence of their condition, and they are not allowed out to relieve themselves. The accumulated mess is occasionally washed into the large center drain by guards using one or both of the fire hoses. For entertainment the jailor manning the hose usually nails selected inmates to the barred wall with water from the high-pressure fire hose.

The eight or ten drunks in the cage seemed terrified at having a white man in the cage with them. They all rushed or crawled to the farthest wall of the enclosure.

Soon the outer door opened and the officers were back. While two of them stood with drawn weapons, an officer with short legs and a sweat-stained shirt opened the cage door and came inside. His nightstick was raised over his head. Looking up at the white sailor he said, "Hey, Jewboy, we see thet yo's fum Califo'nee. Thet tells us thet you ah queeah an this Nigra ya' got wit'ya is yo sweetie." The dark splotch under his upraised arm was emitting a wave of body odor that struck the white sailor's nose like a mailed fist. Breathless, but getting smarter, he said nothing.

The officer continued in a soft voice that seemed totally at odds with his ugly message. "We unnerstan', Califo'nee Jewboy, thet you don' know thet queeah Jews an Nigras gotta sit ta back the bus. It's a passel ah trouble fer us but we'll jus' hafta put you thoo some schoolin'. Now sit down an' poke yo feet out thoo them bahs. Be quick now les'n ya want me ta lay this stick up long side yo haid."

When Chuck did as he was told, the lock clicked again as the officer rejoined his fellows outside the cage. Taking a piece of small stuff that had been carefully looped over a hook on the outer wall, the short-legged officer secured the ends of the manila line around each of Chucks ankles as they protruded through the bars. With a sharp yank, the feet were lifted to a bar that ran horizontally about mid-height on the barred wall. Each ankle was securely tied in place there, leaving only the back of the sailor's head, shoulders and upper back resting on the concrete deck.

The officers had holstered their weapons; they each now drew their nightstick. There was momentary confusion as to which one would get first crack at teaching the "queer Jew" from California his lesson. The short-legged one with the heavy body odor won out. Without ceremony, he began striking the bottom of the sailor's feet with his club.

The sound of each blow on the thin leather soles of Chuck's dress shoes was a sharp crack like the sound of a rifle fired on a cold morning. The sound of the blows caused the occupants of the cage to cover their ears. Most made sounds that were not words, just primal cries and moans.

The beating victim, too, tried to distance himself from the scene. This thing that was happening just could not be happening! Chuck knew that Japanese and Germans beat Americans, sometimes to death. What made it possible for these Americans to be acting like the enemy? He listened to the sounds the other inmates were making. His mind tried to make a hymn or a prayer of those unworded sounds. Could the sounds be just that, without his having to make them so?

In his detached state, sounds were everything. Chuck heard each blow and the accompanying wheeze or grunt from each attacker as he delivered the blow. One of the blows brought a second sound. He had never heard a bone break before, but he knew that the new sound he heard was that sound.

After what seemed an eternity, the sounds stopped and the room was filled with a strange silence. The sweating officers disappeared through the door in the outer wall. Chuck lay unmoving, dreading the return of his tormentors. When he heard the door in the outer wall open again, he steeled himself for a resumption of the lesson. Instead, he found his ankles being untied. His legs fell to the deck. He now lay half in and half outside the barred wall.

Two of the officers came inside the tank while the short-legged one stood outside with his sidearm drawn. The two officers dragged Chuck away from the barred wall and flipped him over. With one on either side of him they picked him up by his shirt collar and the seat of his pants. As they did so, they were shouting accusations at him. They were accusing him of sinning against their God. In his innocence he didn't fully understand all of their charges. They carried him out through the booking room and threw him through the open front door of the station. He landed beyond the concrete steps in the grass of the front yard. The short-legged cop tossed the offenders' I.D. cards and Chuck's driver's license out the door. Jimmy, the kid from Oakland, was there. He was looking sick but he seemed otherwise unharmed.

"Jimmy, go get a taxi. Don't let the cabby know that we have no money." Jimmy picked up their cards then left on a dead run. Chuck turned himself over onto his back. As he lay in the grass, he felt utterly degraded and alone. He strained to adjust his eyes to the darkness. He wanted to be able to see the sky. After a while he found what he was looking for. His family's mentor, the Dog Star, was not in view, but his God had placed a golden-haired lass in the night sky. She was placed there to keep all lonely and injured sailors company. When he found the golden star Capella, he still felt degraded and in pain, but he was no longer alone. Chuck lay there for most of an hour in severe pain and total misery. As he lay there, groaning softly, life at the police station went on around him. The three officers, in great spirits, resumed their party on the lawn chairs. They managed to completely ignore the "queeah Jew" who lay in the grass nearby.

Jimmy had to run to a part of town where he could hail a black cab driver. When they arrived on the scene, the driver helped Jimmy get his friend into the cab. The sojourning officers in the lawn chairs seemed not to notice. The taxi took the sailors to the foot of their ship's gangway. The sailor on gangway watch helped Jimmy get Chuck aboard and into his sack. They then woke people up until they had gathered up enough money to pay the cab driver.

The watch officer woke the skipper. No bells rang or whistles sounded, but within minutes the crew of the *Hunter's Bend* was wide awake and making plans to go burn down that police station. The skipper put an end to that plan by placing the watch officer on the dock at the foot of the gangway with a sidearm. He then ordered all hands not on watch to get back in their sacks.

The good ship *Hunter's Bend* sailed away from that foreign port on the morning tide. The white sailor with the swollen black and blue feet stayed in his bunk until the ship reached its new home port, the Port of New York.

The trip up the East Coast was comparatively painless. The nearest thing the *Hunter's Bend* had to a medic was a ship's carpenter with a seemingly unlimited supply of Jamaican rum. The skipper ignored the alcoholic haze in the cabin when he visited the young sailor the first night out at sea. He said to Chuck, "I'm not going to remind you, Lad, that I warned you, but I must tell you this. Don't expect anything like justice to come of this. You were breaking their law. I don't dare even report the abuse. The congressman from that area and the two senators from that state are great friends of the service. To do our job we need the money that they have the power to withhold. I know it's lame advice, but I have to advise you to just forget that this thing happened."

Chuck stirred in the soft leather seat. On the car radio Helen O'Connell was softly caressing the words to the song "Someone to Watch Over Me." He rubbed his face. There were tears on his hands, and he understood why they were there. In his determination to block out the memory of that police beating, he had deprived himself all these many years of enjoying the memory of the friendships that existed among those wonderfully innocent young Americans on the *Hunter's Bend*. Those guys wanted to go burn down that police station for him! And while he lay helpless in his sack, they tended to him with food trays, bedpans, and ice packs for most of a week as their ship made its way to the port of New York.

After they had heard Chuck's story, the medics at the Marine Hospital outpatient clinic were incredulous at the good condition he was in. They needed only to put his broken foot into a walking cast. They no doubt marveled at the apparent healing powers of Jamaican rum! In their examination of him, the medics were, of course, looking at bone and tissue only. No attention was given to dealing with the state of his traumatized mind.

His wife waved as she drove onto the driveway. Her car was loaded with the fruits of her grocery-shopping trip. Getting out of his car, he lifted the hood and leaned in over the engine. He needed a moment to regain some composure before he could help her with the groceries. Chuck wondered momentarily if it would be fair to share the pain of this thing with her. After the groceries were carried into the kitchen, he got back into his car to put it in the garage. As he did so, he was still struggling with the question of whether he should tell his wife the story he had just relived. He decided that he could not. Was it not true that sharing pain only doubled it?

On his car radio, Peter, Paul and Mary were singing, "The Answer is Blowing in the Wind."

★ ★ ★ ★ ★ ★ ★ ★ ★ ★

Story Eight

A Love Story

Will Farritor was a storyteller. Family history and memories of Ireland that had been handed down through the family were Uncle Will's favorite subjects. His mystical and colorful stories were woven together from bits and pieces of history, myth, and magic. Sprinkled with shamrock-strewn meadows, besieged castles, fair maidens, skilled swordsmen, poets and brave but often-doomed heroes, his stories captivated all who heard them. In Uncle Will's stories the villain was always *The Stranger*. We knew *The Stranger* to be the British occupier of Ireland.

Will's broad-brimmed hat usually sat on the back of his head, allowing a profusion of dark wavy hair to tumble onto his forehead. His smiling blue eyes and friendly laugh cheered all who came near.

Born in the sod house his folks had built on a virgin prairie. Will was the third-born son of Robert Garrett and Anna (Annie) Graham Farritor.

From Will's stories the family came to know that in more than 600 years of invasions and occupations, the British did only cruel things to Ireland and its people. The Brit Queen's hirelings cut and carried away the native Irish forests, and with arrow and sword, they randomly killed the people.

The spirit of those who escaped the sword was systematically diminished and crushed by the Queen's administrators and scribes. The one good thing *The Stranger* did for the Irish was to expose them to the English language. The Irish writers and storytellers embraced *The Stranger's* tongue. Lovers of the written and spoken word, the Irish grew to love this versatile new language, much as they loved and respected Gaelic, their own ancient tongue.

The family's interest in cattle was lost on Will. He would have no truck with those remarkable animals on whose split hooves rode the wealth of the early West. Always an avid reader, Will poured over the Sunday edition of the "Omaha World Herald." (A fat roll of wondrous words and pictures, it arrived by mail each Wednesday.) He was especially drawn to the ads for the horseless carriages. For this young man in 1910, this new thing, the automobile, was clearly the path to the future.

A lovely, red-haired lass named Ruby Nolan heard and heeded Horace Greeley's well-known advice intended for young men: "Go West, young man, go West." Ruby packed up and traveled alone from Springfield, Massachusetts, to Nebraska in 1914. She was bright and better-educated than most of the folks she would come to know in her adopted state.

Ruby found work as the bookkeeper for a farm and ranch equipment supplier in Broken Bow, the county seat of Custer County. She became good friends with another pretty red-head whose name was Alice Farritor. On a weekend trip with Alice to Farritor Valley, Ruby met Alice's big brother Will. Everyone who spoke of the occasion agreed that it was love at first sight. Will and Ruby were married a few months later.

After a honeymoon in Omaha, they bought a green-painted bungalow and settled down in the village of Merna about 15 miles southwest of the home place. Merna was on the route of the Chicago, Burlington and Quincy Railroad.

A year later, a healthy red-haired boy was born to them; they named him Charles. Their circle of love seemed complete.

In 1916 they established an agency in Merna to sell and service Ford motor cars. The waiting room at "Farritor Ford" with its circle of old chairs around a wood-burning, potbellied stove became a mecca for the local "good old boys." They gathered regularly to get their Fords fixed, to tell stories and once in a while to swap a horse or two.

Will's business mushroomed. When the Great War in Europe was over, an unlimited supply of new Ford cars and trucks arrived in railroad boxcars from back east. Heady prosperity came to the town of Merna. It came with heavy loads of golden grain being delivered to its three towering grain elevators and herds of beef cattle that were trailed into town to be loaded onto railroad cars to be shipped to markets in Omaha and Sioux City. The prosperous 1920s took the small town of Merna and Will's little family into its velvet-clothed arms.

The folks on the home-place in the Valley were proudly bedazzled when, on Sundays, Will would bring his family out to visit. He'd be driving an expensive automobile. The one most remembered was a Buick, painted a bright red. In good weather, the Buick's handsome, cream-colored canvas top would be folded behind the rear seat. Will and each of his passengers wore long white dust-coats over their Sunday best. Brightly colored silk neck-scarves streamed on the wind. Saddled horses at the hitch rack spooked as the purring and gleaming red Buick swept into the yard.

The second-born son of Frank and Mary Ann, a lad named Chuck's first recollections of Will and Ruby are of a time late in the decade of the twenties. As a lad of five or six years, he remembered Aunt Ruby's special kind of beauty. Her dresses were soft and silky, usually accented with a long flowing sash. Her bright red hair was softly marcelled; her earrings and necklaces flashed and sparkled in any light.

A small but important item, a paper-thin crystal vase stood in the center of their dark-mahogany dining room table. On most days a single, long-stemmed yellow rose stood in that vase. How, in that time and place, Will was able to provide that fresh-cut rose is a mystery. The memory and mystery of that yellow rose seems symbolic of their quiet love and the separate uniqueness of their lives. At the time, understanding none of its significance, the country kids (Will and Ruby's nieces and nephews), with their well-earned reputation for accidentally breaking things, felt strangely intimidated in the presence of that oh-so-fragile-looking vase.

Chuck was invited to the birthday party that Aunt Ruby gave for his cousin, Leona Williams. Leona and he were the same age; their birthdays were only days apart. Alice Farritor Williams, the pretty girl who had introduced Will and Ruby, had died in childbirth. Uncle Ed Williams found it impossible to keep his family together. The children, all six of them, were "loaned" out to relative families. Will and Ruby took Leona in to raise as their own. Their circle was now even more complete.

The birthday-party table was set in the cool shade of their grassy side-yard. Colorful paper-streamers decorated the lower limbs of the trees. Most of the kids at the party were "town kids." Chuck didn't know any of them except Leona. She was too busy to play with him so he felt a bit lost. His big cousin, Charles, likewise had no time for a little country cousin also named Charles. His Aunt Ruby soon put him at ease. He vividly remembered how she looked on that day in her long white dress. Tiny green ribbons flowed from her hair and her dress had a long sash of the same bright color.

Leona got many nice presents. All the kids helped her blow out the five candles on her cake. That was the only real birthday party Chuck attended as a kid. He didn't need another; that one was good for a lifetime.

Leona's party was on September 20, 1929. In the next month the United States and the world would undergo a great trauma that would change everyone's lives. The stock market crash of October 1929 shattered the national economy and brought on a deep financial depression, one that most folks couldn't comprehend. How could something that happened on a street named Wall in far away New York City make the good times go away here in Nebraska?

A second monster accompanied the financial depression. A great drought quietly descended upon the land. It was reminiscent of the drought that had struck in the 1890s. This new drought, again coupled with a national depression, brought devastation to the land and the people. From Texas to the Dakotas, the precious summer rains and the winter snows simply went away. The severe drought became a physically depressing mantle that blanketed all of the eastern slope states.

On some days giant brown dust-clouds rolled across the sky, extending from horizon to horizon. The next morning the gray dirt of Nebraska would be colored a dull red by dirt that had blown in from Oklahoma and eastern Colorado. On other days swarming clouds of flying grasshoppers swooped in to scour the land. They stripped every plant of its foliage, all except a newly introduced noxious weed named Russian Thistle. This noxious weed was dubbed the "tumbling weed." It apparently needed little moisture to thrive and grew by the millions into three- or four-foot round inedible balls. They were constructed of thousands of prickly stickers; hungry stock would not go near them. When the wind broke them loose from the ground, they tumbled across the land, collecting at fence lines. They, pushed by the wind, often broke the fence posts over, destroying the fences and causing harm to the scattered stock.

The eternal optimism for "next year" died in the suffocating heat and dust. "It'll be better next year," is that intangible spirit-promise upon which all farmers, ranchers and the merchants who supply them operate. It would take a decade of "next years" for the rains to return and the hard times to pass.

Most of the farmers and ranchers in Nebraska survived this onslaught. They had more reserves to call on than their fathers possessed back in the 1890s. Then, too, the new president, Franklin Delano Roosevelt, came to their aid with meaningful programs of assistance. Low-cost feed and seed loans were made available to them to buy feed for their starving cattle. Free salt was provided for the stock and free fresh fruit was magically shipped in for the children. These commodities were distributed from trucks in the parking lot of the post office in Broken Bow. All, including adults, learned to eat "FDR" green pears from God knows where and free "FDR" grapefruit from Florida and California.

Also at no cost, they could get tree seedlings to replace the trees killed by the drought. They planted "shelter belts" by the thousands. Rows of pine, cedar, Russian olive, elm and cottonwood made up those protective rows. They were placed strategically on the land, attempting to break the prairie winds.

The effect of the economic crash on Will and Ruby's Ford dealership was traumatic. Before the crash, Will would often have the new cars sold before the invoice for them arrived. After the crash, things were different; cars and trucks came from the factory C.O.D. The dealer had to come up with cash before the railroad would let him have the product.

Equally devastating, Henry Ford began attempting to raise cash by sending obsolete and unordered spare parts to all of his dealers. He made it very clear that if these junk parts were not accepted and paid for, the dealer would get no more new cars. Uncle Will cut the unordered wooden floorboards up for firewood and threw the metal parts into a pile out back to gather rust. It is a sad fact that Mr. Ford managed to save his company by stealing from his friends, his dealers.

It became apparent that Will and Ruby's once thriving business was doomed. While under this unrelenting economic attack, Will and Ruby were struck a blow from a completely unexpected quarter. Their son Charles (they called him Chazie) had grown to be a fine lad and a good athlete. After winning all of the distance-running events in record times in his freshman year at Merna High School, the Coach predicted that Chazie would become the State Champion in long-distance running. His long legs, broad shoulders and deep chest allowed him to run with a champion's ease.

Chazie, the family and Merna High School were denied the promise of his being named the State Champ. On a hot afternoon in late August of 1932, a group of young people decided to go swimming at Victoria Creek. Chazie and seven of his friends were riding in an open-topped touring car. The driver failed to make a turn in the graveled road about halfway to their destination. All were thrown free except Chazie. When the car turned over he was pinned beneath it.

Diagnosed with a broken back, he was taken to a hospital in Omaha. Even the doctors in that big city could do nothing for him. They sent him home to die.

Chazie died a week later in his own room in the green-painted bungalow where he had lived all of his life. His sophomore class, which included his cousin, Chuck's older sister Anna Marie, were honorary pallbearers. At ten o'clock on a windless sunny morning in September they walked by two's out of the high school building in Merna. They walked across the street to St. Paul's Church. Few who attended would forget the overwhelming sadness of that day.

Uncle Will once said of this time of trial and death, "Thank God we had that precious child Leona with us. Without her, Ruby and I would've become lost in a pit of despair."

Will's inherited portion of the home place, two good 80-acre fields, had mostly lain fallow during the years he was in the automobile business. With the loss of his business, he returned to the land. Because of the ongoing drought, the land could not return bounty commensurate with the labor expended. However, Mary Ann, Chuck's mom, understood what he was doing. She said of Uncle Will, "After his great losses, his son and his business, he needs to work the land to get his strength back."

It was during this period that Chuck grew to know and love his Uncle Will, who always found time to talk to Chuck and his younger brother, Eddie. He told them a raft of wondrous things.

He loved sports. He told them of a great school called Notre Dame where a man with a funny-sounding name (Knute Rockne) taught strong, young men to play football. The name of the school was French and the coach was Norwegian but somehow the team was called "The Irish." The boys never questioned how all of that could be.

They learned of a great football-playing Indian named Jim Thorpe. They learned, too, what they had not learned in school, of the great natural and human tragedy that occurred when the white people killed off the buffalo. This action impoverished the Omaha, the Ponca, the Arapahoe, the Pawnee, and the Sioux. Starving, but defiant, remnants of most of those tribes fought a desperate 30-year war. In that war, over 60 percent of their people were killed. Eventually the survivors were forced to give up their freedom and accept life on "reservations." Chuck and Eddie felt very sad on hearing that story.

Uncle Will's favorite athlete was a big man with a baby-face. This man could knock a baseball out of the park almost anytime he wanted to. Folks who knew him called him "Babe." It was a comfort for the boys to learn that Mr. Ruth was a Yankee. They'd heard a lot of bad things about Confederates. Shucks, Confederates probably didn't know how to play a good American game like baseball anyhow!

On the hottest, driest days of the drought, Uncle Will spoke of the cool, emerald-green land from whence the family had come. The boys wondered what awful things the occupying British had done to drive our people far and away to the gray-brown place that Nebraska had become. When they asked him about it, he assured them that *The Stranger* had not killed off the buffalo in Ireland to drive our people out.

He seldom spoke of the terrible things *The Stranger* did. He instead spoke of the fair land, the deep rivers and the white-capped, blue seas. The boys knew their people had been fishermen on those blue seas and farmers on the green land.

He told of the "Wee People," the Leprechauns, who laugh and dance in the moonlight. The boys understood clearly that only people who believe they are there would ever catch a glimpse of them.

On successive visits to Ireland, Chuck looked for them far and near. He looked for them in the moonlit mists in the Hills of Wicklow above Clonmore where his mother, Mary Ann, was born. He looked for them in the spray of the Westward Sea where it pounds the Cliffs of Moher. He searched for them in the shadows at the rock houses left by an ancient people on the seaward side of the Mountains of Kerry. So far he's failed to see the "Wee People." However, there is no doubt that one day he will see them, just as his Uncle Will said he would.

When winter gripped the land, the neighbors made up crews to saw ice into blocks from protected ponds on Victoria Creek and trucked them to the participating farms and ranches. At each place they lowered the ice into a large square pit in the earth. The ice blocks were packed in sawdust or oat straw. The pit was covered with a wood-framed roof. They called the building an "icehouse." Three or four times a week during the next spring and summer a chunk of the ice was retrieved from the pit for use in the kitchen icebox. On Sundays a chunk of it might be used for making ice cream. This wonderful supply of ice lasted most families well into August or September.

One cold winter day, the "icing crew" was having their noon meal at Frank and Mary Ann's house. During the meal, one of the men told of a loaded truck that had broken an axle. They had commandeered Uncle Will's tractor. When they fired the tractor up, they found that it had little power. The tractor barely managed to pull the truck to the icehouse where it could be unloaded. During a moment of silence after the story, Chuck said in a voice as defiant as he could make it, "All that tractor needs is my Uncle Will on the seat." For reasons that he neither understood nor appreciated, his remark had them all roaring with laughter. They slapped their thighs and pounded the table. Chuck thought they had gone nuts. His mom later quietly told him he had done well defending Uncle Will and his tractor.

Will and Ruby continued to live in their green-painted bungalow and did their best to remain a part of their community. They, like most folks in those very hard times, made adjustments to fit the new realities. Each day during the growing season, Uncle Will drove his small Ford car out to the Valley to tend his land. Aunt Ruby gave piano lessons in her home and sold "beauty aids" door to door. They were both doing what they could to maintain a secure home for Leona.

The Great Depression affected Frank and Mary Ann's family in sometimes curious ways. One Saturday morning, the family went to Merna for supplies and to exchange the weekly "box of books" at that quiet place of wonder, the Brenizer Public Library. They, of course, went to Uncle Will's house first thing. When Uncle Will came home for lunch, he reported that "Doc Morrow" told him that he had one shot of vaccine left and someone could have it for free. From the green-painted bungalow, they climbed into the family Model A Ford and followed Uncle Will's Ford over to Dr. Morrow's office. The cars stopped in the shade of the trees on Central Street.

Uncle Will came over and beckoned for Chuck to follow him. He took the lad's hand and led him into the doctor's office. Chuck wondered aloud, "Why me?"

They walked through the waiting room into what seemed to be an inner sanctum of some kind. Dr. Morrow was there, dressed in a dark suit. He had a shock of white hair on his head but his mustache and eyebrows were as black as his suit. He stood in front of a sink with an enormous steel and glass thing in his hand. The thing had a point on one end that looked a lot like one tine of a pitchfork.

Dr. Morrow turned to the boy and asked, "Do you want this shot?" The boy said, "No, I don't want that ol' shot."

To the boy's great relief and astonishment, he said, "Okay," then turned to the sink and began taking the ugly glass and steel thing apart under a faucet of running water. The boy turned to his Uncle Will; he looked as surprised as the boy was relieved. He said, "Thanks Doc." They turned and walked out of that, suddenly less scary, inner sanctum.

Apparently Uncle Will felt it necessary to tell Frank what had happened. Since Frank was not accustomed to having a kid make that kind of decision, the news got him a bit upset.

Later when he'd cooled off, Chuck heard Uncle Will and him laughing at a joke that he didn't hear anyone tell. Whatever illness that shot was designed to protect Chuck from must have missed him on its own, just like the shot had.

Contrary to Mary Ann's prediction, the elixir of tending the land was not medicine strong enough to bring Uncle Will's strength back. As the years passed, he developed cardiac-asthma and eventually was not able to work at all.

With the outbreak of World War II, Aunt Ruby was offered a good job in a defense plant at her hometown of Springfield, Massachusetts. They made arrangements for Leona to finish high school at a Catholic boarding school in York, Nebraska.

One winter morning in 1942, Will and Ruby left their beloved town of Merna. They packed their things and took the train to their new home, an apartment in Springfield, Massachusetts. Together they had the strength to leave their green-painted bungalow with its lifetime of memories. Between them, they'd found the courage to reach out to catch a new ring on the carousel of life.

Aunt Ruby worked long hours at her job, helping to win the war. Uncle Will took charge in the apartment. He soon made it into a comfortable home for the two of them.

While on leave from a ship in New York harbor, Chuck took a bus north to Springfield to visit them. During that visit they treated each other and him in the same loving way that he had been treated at a long-ago birthday party where a lovely lady wore a long white dress with a bright green sash, a sash that matched the color of the tiny ribbons flowing from her lovely red hair. Aunt Ruby's hair was now edged and laced with white.

On their dark-mahogany dining room table, Chuck saw again the tall, paper-thin crystal vase with its single, long-stemmed yellow rose.

That visit was all too short. As they were saying goodbye, Uncle Will hugged his nephew and said, "Chuck, you'll one day find a girl to love. When you find her, never let a day pass without telling her that you love her."

A few years later, Uncle Will and Aunt Ruby traveled to Preakness, New Jersey. There they attended a wedding. The bride was the young lady that Uncle Will had promised Chuck he would one day find. She was a lovely young lady named Muriel Teeling.

At the big party that developed at Muriel's folk's house after the wedding, and after the newlyweds had left for South Florida and Havana on their honeymoon, Aunt Ruby played jazz piano to the delight of everyone and Uncle Will made friends as he always had with his stories and good humor.

A few months later, Muriel and Chuck drove up to Springfield to spend a weekend with them. They seemed content and comfortable in their retirement. That visit also was all too short. As they were leaving, Uncle Will took Chuck aside and, looking at his Muriel, he again told his nephew, "Chuck, you must tell her you love her every day." The young ex-sailor would not forget that gentle admonition.

Muriel and Chuck would be leaving the East Coast soon. They planned to make their home in California. Because of this, Chuck knew he would probably not see his Uncle Will again. It was a quiet but very painful goodbye.

Driving back to New Jersey through the beautiful Connecticut countryside Chuck stopped at a roadside flower stand. Without explanation he bought Muriel a single, long-stemmed yellow rose.

Uncle Will died in his sleep shortly thereafter. He died far from his native Valley but he died in good company. His God, his friends the "Wee People," and his Ruby were with him.

In time, Will, Ruby and Chazie were reunited. They rest together beneath a soft coverlet of buffalo grass near their beloved town of Merna.

Their circle was again made complete; Leona rejoined them. While her loving husband is still earthbound, God chose to send Leona on to be with Will, Ruby and Chazie. She is with them in their newly recreated, green-painted bungalow. This time their bungalow is located far away in a quiet realm of love and peace. There can be no doubt that Uncle Will has a garden there. Each day, for his Ruby, he cuts and places a long-stemmed, yellow rose in the tall, paper-thin vase that rests on their ethereal, dark-mahogany dining room table.

-*-

Story Nine

Eddie Boone

Wheelman Farritor paused at the door to Mr. Wilson's quarters. He hesitated for only a moment before he knocked firmly on the gray steel door. At one o'clock in the morning there was no immediate response from within. After a moment, he knocked again, harder. A sleep-clouded voice said, "One moment please." After another long moment the same voice said, "Come in." The young sailor opened the door and stepped inside. First Officer Wilson had gotten out of bed and was seated at his desk. He was in his pajamas and in an understandably sour mood. He peered through his eyebrows at his visitor and said, "Wheelman Farritor, this better be somethin' damned important."

The first officer of the *U.S.A.T. General McFall* received the news about Eddie in silence. He leaned forward with his elbows on his desk, the color draining slowly from his face. His normally suntanned face came near to matching the color of his navy-gray pajamas. The absolute silence in the room seemed to produce a sound of its own. After what seemed an eternity of that sound, Mr. Wilson bolted from his chair and shouted at the sailor standing in front of his desk. "That dogface son-of-a-bitch wants to drop an artillery shell on my desk, does he? If that bastard thinks my sailors are picking on his people, he don't know what hurt is 'till I go over there and bust his spleen!"

Mention of the artillery shell and the ruptured spleen came out of the report that Wheelman Farritor had made. Farritor was due back on watch at 0400 hours. His report was complete and he wanted to get away. He needed to take a shower and get some sleep. When he, at last, turned and fled, he left the first officer of the *McFall* with his eyes blazing. His arms were spread as he leaned over his desk, a position he seemed to have taken to protect the desk from the threatened incoming. A thought entered the escaping sailor's tired mind. Mr. Wilson is wound up way too tight. What he needs is a visit to Madam Kormarov's place.

Below decks in his quarters, Wheelman Farritor turned a fan on to move the hot night air. He stripped and took a shower to wash away the sweat and try to wash away the shock of this night. The stale sweat went down the drain, but the shock of what he'd just gone through clung to him untouched by the soap and hot water. He toweled, switched off the light, and with a fan blowing directly on him, lay naked on his sack hoping to go to sleep. Though bone tired, his eyes would not close.

Light from the moon reflecting off the water through an open porthole made mystical and threatening dark forms of the life jackets that nested in their racks on the white-painted overhead. His mind would not come to rest. Instead of sleep, there came sharply focused pictures of the events leading up to the tragedy that occurred in that Old Walled City stockade cell this night.

Able Seaman Farritor stretched his long body out on the mid-ship thwart of upper lifeboat number five. The foremast of his ship kindly cast its shadow across the spot on the seat where his head lay. He had decided to goof-off for the few minutes it would take for the shadow to move on. The blue sky he was gazing into was cloudless as it spread its unblemished arc over Elliott Bay. His ship, the army transport *U.S.A.T. General McFall*, was berthed at the Army Port of Embarkation on the Seattle waterfront. The chief bosun had assigned him the task of checking the equipment in the captain's gig and each of the ship's lifeboats. The job had to be completed and reports filed with the U.S. Coast Guard in the few days it would take for the *McFall* to take on her new load of troops and be ready to sail again. He'd asked the bosun to give him one helper, and he had struck a deal. If he got the job done early, he could have a free day ashore. A free day ashore would allow him some more time with a pretty girl named Ruth Ann.

The task with the lifeboats was not an easy one. First the heavy canvas cover had to be removed from each pair of nested boats. The set was then lowered outboard on their davits to the point where the nested pair hung one above the other. This made them both accessible for inspection and inventory. This equipment check is an annual U.S. Coast Guard requirement for all ships that fly the American flag. The understanding was that the lifeboat could not serve its function fully without each prescribed item being in place. Some of the items were a bit off the wall like a canvas bag of various-sized corks. There was no instruction with them; it was rumored they were to be used for plugging machine-gun bullet holes in the lifeboat's thin steel hull. If that be the case, planners of that item were obviously counting on the enemy to kindly make only nice round holes as they shot up the boat. Each boat's survival kit contained several wound bandage packets. These waxed-paper-wrapped packages contained pieces of clean cotton cloth. Most pieces were cut from the likes of someone's old winter long-johns. There were small bottles of iodine and single shots of morphine. The morphine device consisted of a needle attached to a thumbnail-sized rubber bag with the words "insert needle and squeeze" printed on it. Each device was sealed in a small waxed-paper envelope.

"Look alive, sailor!" The sharp command brought Seaman Farritor up and wide awake from his unplanned nap. The sun was in his eyes so he had a momentary problem seeing who had shouted the order. It was soon clear enough; a tall, muscular, red-haired sailor was grinning at him from the forward thwart of the boat. The grinning stranger said, "My name's Eddie Boone, my rate is Ordinary Seaman and I'm new aboard. The bosun sent me up here to give you a hand." He paused and then continued, "I want ya ta know right off, boss, I'm a screw-up. The bosun told me you're the guy who can keep me out of trouble. Can you do that?" The grin never seemed to fade from the newcomer's face. Somehow though, the grin didn't show in his blue eyes. There was a quiet sadness there that stayed no matter what he was saying.

The question he had asked was apparently a serious one, and his sad blue eyes were expecting an answer. Able Seaman Farritor chose not to be questioned. As a method of taking charge he said, "Okay Eddie, my name's Chuck. I've checked this set of boats so let's get them nested and covered so we can move on."

They set to work. The powerful wench motor lifted the large lifeboats back into their seagoing position. They were secured in place and the heavy canvas cover-tarps were soon back on the nested pair. The usual way of making conversation with a new guy was to ask, "Where ya' from?" Chuck asked that question.

Boone answered, "Shucks, boss, I'm from a little cowpoke town in Nebraska that you never heard of."

Chuck came back with, "Why not run it by me?

Boone said, "Okay, ever heard of Pawnee Creek?"

Returning Boone's grin, Chuck said, "Yah I've heard of it. It's a short day's ride on a good horse, north and west of another cowpoke town called Prairie Center, where I graduated high school."

Boone feigned astonishment; his grin went from ear to ear. "Well I'll be damned; do you mean to tell me I'm in the presence of ah real honest-to-God, high school graduate? I'll be double damned. You done good, boss!"

Boone's boss, rising to the bait, foolishly continued, "After I graduated high school I passed the tests to go into the Navy V-12 program, the one where they send you to college and teach you to fly? I went to Omaha and failed the physical exam so I was out of that program before I got in. At loose ends, I hitchhiked down to Lincoln and spent three months there trying to figure a way to afford to go to the university. When I went broke in Lincoln, I called a number I got off a poster at the train station. I soon found myself in the Merchant Marine. It was up to me to get myself either to New York or Seattle. I was able to catch a ride to Seattle. Once there I found myself being sent to school at Sheepshead Bay in New York state. I could afford their school, it was free. That school was teaching mostly country kids how to keep themselves alive and their ships afloat."

Boone chose to let all of that lie like a road-killed frog. What he said was, "You know what, boss? I walked to Prairie Center once't. It took me most of three days. I was pretty bummed out, and by the time I got there, a lot hungry. There was an old guy there, his name was Rube something. He treated me damn good."

This announcement brought a flash of memory to his listener. Chuck was flabbergasted and incredulous at this apparent re-crossing of two life paths. He was sure that he knew Boone, but he decided that he wanted to get to know this self-proclaimed screw-up a little better before owning up to anything.

Boone proved to be a good and smart worker; they finished the lifeboat checking and the Coast Guard reports ahead of time. The chief bosun's mate honored the agreement he had made and gave them both a free day ashore. This gave Able Seaman Farritor another chance to see Ruth Ann, a pretty girl whose family lived a ferryboat ride away over in

Bremerton. On this free night Ruth Ann and he would not be taking the Bremerton ferry to see the folks. There were too many exciting things for a sailor and his girl to do right there in Seattle.

The Farritor place lay in a valley well to the east of Prairie Center. It was too far to consider riding a horse to high school, and Chuck's dad wouldn't hear of a fourteen-year-old kid driving a car to town. To manage getting the kid's freshman year under his hat, it was arranged that he would stay in town with the Rube Anders family. Rube, when he was younger, had been the town's longtime constable and sometimes mayor. Millie was a crackerjack whist player and probably the best cook in the county. There was more; they'd raised a large family in their big old home over on the north edge of town. They'd seen most of their kids through Kearney State Teacher's College down on the Platte River.

Rube's five old milk-cows were still keeping several families in town supplied with fresh milk and cream. With the kids all grown and gone, and Rube's lumbago giving him fits, he was having a hard time keeping his contract with those folks. Chuck's mom heard of Rube's situation and committed her kid to help get that milk bottled and delivered. The deal was cinched when Chuck's older sister Anna Marie, who was working as a waitress while going to the Teacher's College down on the Platte, agreed to pitch in a dollar a week for board and care. In those days of national depression, that cash dollar was huge. Rube and Millie would feed and shelter the boy and see that he did his homework. They assured the boy's mom that there'd be enough chores and homework to keep the lad from hanging out with the out-of-work cowboys in the pool hall down on Center Street.

One afternoon shortly before Christmas, the boy got home from school and found a small pile of dirty old clothes on the floor of the Anders' back porch. There was a ragged jacket, a broken down pair of boots, a worn pair of jeans and a kid's old flannel shirt. In the kitchen, he saw an empty milk glass and an empty soup bowl on the table. He just had to ask, "Mrs. Anders, who undressed on the back porch?"

Mrs. Anders cooed, "Now be a good lad, go straight to your room and see to your homework. It'll soon be time to feed and milk the cows. Later on I'll tell you about the boy who came to our back door." As he went down the hallway on his way to his room, he caught a glimpse of a big, redheaded kid in the parlor. His hair was wet like he'd just gotten out of the bathtub. He was dressed in new boots and blue-jeans, and he was putting on a new green flannel shirt over a new white tee shirt. At supper in the dining room that evening, the new kid downed Mrs. Anders' great cooking with all the good manners of a hungry coyote. Not once did he look up or say a word.

They were just finishing supper when Rube got up to answer a knock on the door. It was a tall, red-haired lady. Rube escorted her to the parlor. He and Mrs. Anders soon joined the newcomer there. The boys were told to go to the kitchen and close the door. After a short conference among the adults, Rube came and asked the red-haired boy to join them. Though not invited, the second boy joined the movement to the parlor. It was obvious that the pretty, red-haired lady and Mrs. Anders had been crying. Rube's tradition of good manners led him to introduce the lady to the uninvited extra boy. She was the red-haired kid's Aunt Mary Louise. Everyone stood up. Aunt Mary Louise hugged the red-haired boy and kissed him on the forehead. Rube too hugged the boy then gave him a new plaid-lined, blue denim jacket. The kid put the jacket on and left with his Aunt Mary Louise. He hadn't spoken a word to anyone.

During the Christmas holidays, Chuck was finally told the red-haired kid's story. It was not Mrs. Anders, but his mom who eventually filled him in. Not surprisingly, because of the party phone line, his mom usually knew all about everything. Rural tradition of long standing required that somebody at each farm or ranch on the party-line listen in every time the phone rang. It was usually the lady of the house who became the appointed "listener." Mary Ann Farritor felt quite at home with that task.

The kid's name was Eddie Boone. He and his parents lived on a small ranch a few miles south of the Sandhill town of Pawnee Creek. Eddie's mother, Annie, had died of scarlet fever when the lad was twelve. Chuck's mom said, "You have to know, that was a terrible loss for that lad. His dad took the loss very hard too." But there was more. Just three days before he had stopped to beg for food at the Anders' back door, Eddie had come home from school to find his dad's horse frantically dashing back and forth at the outer gate to the corral. The gelding was dragging his bridle reins on the ground. A well-trained cowpony will not do that; reins on the ground should hold him as though he were tied to a stake. What could have made him forget his training like that? The boy quieted the animal, then removed its bridle and saddle and put the gelding in his stall in the barn. He got back on his own horse to ride out to see what he could find. In a draw only a short distance out, he found his father's body. It had been nearly decapitated by a blast from his own shotgun.

The fourteen-year-old boy couldn't make sense of the things that began happening in his head. There wasn't room for any new sorrow. He was already filled with all the sorrow he could hold from his mom's dying. Eddie got off his horse. He wanted to hug his dad but found that he couldn't touch him. The boy wanted to smash the gun that lay nearby in the winter-browned grass but couldn't touch it either. He was able to pick up the empty whiskey bottle that lay near the gun. He held the bottle for a moment, then threw it down on the gun. The bottle shattered and flew away in a hundred pieces. The handsome shotgun just lay there, arrogantly ignoring his rage.

A sharp cramp gripped, then rolled through his innards. He suddenly wanted to have his mom kiss his forehead like she always did when he was troubled. He wanted to hear her say again the lilting Gaelic words that told him how much she loved him. Eddie stood, frozen in place. His pony moved forward and touched his arm with its nose. After a while the boy turned away. Except for the bottle, he left what he had found as he had found it. His stomach was hurting and he wanted to cry, but somehow he couldn't do that. He felt as though he was going to throw up so he didn't get back in the saddle. On that bright, cold winter afternoon, he walked through a cloud of frightening darkness back to the corral and barn. His pony, his one constant, kept pace. The pony occasionally touched his arm and his back with its nose. After sitting for awhile on a bench by the barn, the boy dunked his head in the cold water of the stock tank, then got on his horse and rode to a neighbor's place to tell that neighbor where he would find his dad. Returning home, he turned the mortgaged horses loose with the mortgaged cattle on the mortgaged land. The saddles were left hanging on their pegs in the mortgaged barn.

When he had done all of the things he knew to do, he walked away across the hills toward the southeast. His pony walked with him until they came to the southern line-fence. They stopped at the fence and stood together. Eddie put his face in the pony's mane and at last found that he could cry. After several long minutes of sobbing, he caressed his pony's nose one last time. He then climbed through the fence and walked away.

The pony stood alone at the fence neighing softly. He held his position long after his young master had disappeared into the folds of the winter-brown, grass-covered hills. When the sun went down, the pony turned and quickly walked back to the corral. There he joined the other horses and cattle standing mutely in the gathering darkness. Most knew not what, but they knew something awful had happened. Eddie's pony and his dad's tall gelding knew, and they were very much afraid.

Eddie knew that his mother's sister lived some 50 miles away to the southeast in Broken Bow. With his mom, and now his dad dead, he didn't know what else to do but to walk in that direction. When it got dark, he dug his way into a haystack to make a place to spend the night. He cried for his mom most of the night. He worried about whether the neighbor had found his dad before the coyotes found him. And he worried about his pony. Would the banker just take him out and shoot him when he found that the pony sometimes stumbles and falls when he runs downhill? Much as he wanted to let that fence down and take the pony with him, he knew that he could not. The banker had his dad's word that all the stock would remain on the ranch. Nothing could be sold or moved without the banker's permission. When daylight came, he started walking again.

His worn boots were hurting his feet. He realized with a pain in his chest that he would never know if his dad had already bought and had hidden away to surprise him on Christmas morning the new pair of boots he had promised to get for him. About midday he came to another windmill and stock tank. The piping at the well was protected from freezing by a thick padding of oat straw. Eddie broke the ice on the stock-tank and held his breath while he drank his fill. He drank as some horses drink, with his nose and mouth thrust into the water. That technique allowed him to take in water that was free of the shredded and broken ice floating on the surface.

He kept moving. It was too cold to stop to rest. When the sun went down, he chose another haystack to create a place to sleep. It seemed to him that before he went to sleep, he cried the same tears he had cried the night before. He wanted his mom to again touch his forehead with her always-cool hand, and he wanted to feel his pony's soft nose on his cheek. Even scarier than his stomach ache was the hollow hurt in the upper part of his chest. It hurt the most when he thought of the pretty quilt his mom had made for his warm bed at home. He started out again at daylight. It was getting so he couldn't walk straight; he felt kind of dizzy. About midday he came to a paved highway that led into a town. He knocked on a back door to ask for food. Not all of his luck was bad; it was Rube and Millie's back door.

On the day the *McFall* sailed, Eddie Boone was late getting back from his free day ashore. He was so late that he almost missed the ship. The First Officer chewed him out and let it go at that. Not so easy for Chuck, Boone's hangover-pained eyes looked at him with that first day question again in them.

The chief bosun liked to pair people up and contract work to them. Remembering the successful lifeboat-checking job, he approached Chuck and Boone about painting the foremast and replacing the worn signal halyards. The schedule was simple: have the job completed before the ship reached Honolulu. Chuck examined the paint on the mast, which wasn't in really bad shape, just faded and dirty. There would be a minimum of chipping and red leading. He figured two guys should be able to do the job in three days or so. That would give them some free time to work on their ranchland-bred pitch skills. (Pitch is a card game somewhat akin to pinochle.) They would work those skills among hopefully unskilled but well-financed pigeons in the paint locker and the crew's wardroom. Cognizant of the financial possibilities, they took the job as offered.

Bound for the Philippines and Korea via Honolulu, the *McFall* sailed at noon. The weather was perfect as the Puget Sound Pilot debarked into the pilot-boat off Port Angeles on the Strait of Juan de Fuca. Puffy white clouds floated here and there in the blue September sky. At the top of the mainmast, the commission pennant stirred only occasionally in the still air. The *McFall's* engines were soon at full ahead as she headed up the Strait on a northwesterly course. She began to pitch a little on incoming sea swells. Those sea swells had probably originated in a storm far out on the North Pacific Ocean.

As the great gray ship swung to a southwesterly course after rounding Cape Flattery, the now heavy northwesterly swells came to her on her starboard beam. This caused her to heave and roll heavily as she lifted on the crest of the swell, then fell into the following trough. This sometimes violent motion brought an immediate end to the perfect day for all of those aboard who did not possess the immunity from seasickness that so-called sea legs provide. Boone was still badly hung over but he understood the need for them to get started on their project. Never mind the rough sea, bright dry weather is not a guaranteed commodity on this or any other part of the ocean. As soon as the ship was secured for sea, the bosun cut them loose so they could get busy gathering up the gear they'd need for their mast-painting job.

All of the work on the mast would be done from bosun's chairs, a deceptively simple device that had been handed down, with little change, from ancient seafarers. It was used for all ship's maintenance aloft or over the side. The chair consisted of a wooden board about ten inches by twenty inches. Lines passing through holes in each corner create a harness that allows the occupant a safe seat to work from. Simple rigging allows him to raise or lower himself as required to reach the work he is to do. To rig for the work on the forward mast, it would be necessary for a man to shinny up to the masthead. Normally Chuck would have palmed that job off onto his helper, but looking at Boone, he knew that today was not a good day for him to spend time at a masthead. Chuck had been to the top of masts before, but never with a ship pitching and rolling as this ship was doing this day. He was getting excited about the prospects for a fun time aloft. All ships' masts, of course, start at the keel but the visible base of the foremast on the *McFall's* was on the flying bridge above and aft of the navigation bridge. A steel ladder on the mast led only to the heavy yardarm located about halfway to the top. They had carried all the tackle and gear they would need up to the flying bridge and were making ready to move it up to the yardarm when the captain and the chief wheelman came up on the flying bridge; they were there to check on something or other with the signal flags. Observing the activity at the mast, the captain came over to where they were and said, "Are you sure you want to go up there today with this sea the way it is?"

Chuck answered, "Captain, sir, the bosun wants us to paint this mast. We need to take advantage of this dry weather while we have it. We'd sure enough appreciate it if you can find some smoother water tomorrow when we'll actually be red-leading and painting."

The skipper said, "There's a good possibility of that."

Chuck said, "We'll thank you for that, sir. Come to think of it, this ride I'm about to take here today would, if we could bottle it, sell for good money at Coney Island or the Pier at Santa Monica."

The captain smiled, then said, "I know that you know well what you're doing lad, but please be careful." What could the young sailor say? He certainly intended to be careful, just as he knew the skipper had been careful when, as a boy aloft in the rigging of a sailing ship, he had religiously clung to a lifeline with one hand as he dedicated the skill and strength of the other hand to the task he was expected to do for his ship. To the frosty-bearded chief wheelman, Chuck said, "Chief, wait'll you see the beautiful new material we've got to replace those ratty old signal halyards of yours." He paused a moment, then asked, "Chief do you play pitch?" He got a thumb's up response but no audible answer. Chuck grinned and turned to the ladder; he hadn't given up on the chief. He would try again; there had to be green aplenty in that old chief's deep pockets!

They moved the gear up to the yardarm and lashed it down securely. One item was a bag of clean rags. The rags were needed to wipe away the greasy salt-film that covers every exposed surface on the ship. The trip up any mast is memorable. Chuck had a feeling that today's climb would be especially so! Once, as a kid over at the Ray Chrissman ranch, he had foolishly slid off his pony onto the back of a 300-pound steer. Today, with the proper gear, he'd not be thrown off.

Climbing and wiping clean the mast above the yardarm was a slow process. The safety harness that fitted securely around his waist and under his rump had an extended member that encircled the mast. With the section of mast in front of him wiped clean of salt film, he clamped his legs around the mast as he moved the mast-encircling belt another foot or so higher. He repeated this process over and over again as he worked his way to the top of the mast.

The effort of the climb was all-consuming. Chuck had little awareness during the climb of the wild, multiple arcs that the mast was traveling. Reaching the top totally exhausted, he rested for a few moments against the small circumference of the upper mast to allow his strength to return. His rest period was interrupted by the realization that knots of soldiers on the main deck far below had apparently conquered their seasickness enough to watch his progress to the top. They were pointing and shouting to him.

He hoped he wouldn't do anything dumb that would give them the excitement that they were probably hoping for. He thought of an automobile accident he had seen as a kid. On the way home from Broken Bow, the family came upon the scene of an accident on Highway 2, just south of Merna. His dad told his older sister, who was driving, to pull over and stop. They recognized that the sedan involved in the accident belonged to a family they knew from Saint Anselm's church. The car was being driven by that family's nineteen-year-old daughter. In an inexplicable moment of inattention, she had driven into a bridge abutment. The pretty girl, along with a box of groceries, had been thrown partially through the windshield. A loaf of sliced, white bread had broken open and laid in position to catch and soak up her life's blood. The boy's father ordered his kids back into the car and instructed them not to look further. From the people who spilled out of every car that came along, the boy and his siblings learned a bit more than they wanted to know about human nature. The newly arriving people got out of their cars and ogled at the dead girl. The girl's long blonde hair tried its best to hide the blood-soaked loaf of bread. The people from the cars gawked as though this was the thing they had waited all week to see.

He fully intended to cheat the spectators, on the deck below, out of seeing the fall that each, perhaps, secretly hoped to witness.

Chuck had a length of small stuff hanging from his safety harness. Down on the yardarm, Boone made a tack-block fast to his end of that manila line. Chuck pulled on the line to draw the tack-block to himself. When he got it in hand, he made it fast to the starboard side pad-eye at the top of the mast by using a shackle and threaded pin.

Considerable care had to be taken not to drop anything. Even a shackle pin dropped from this height could kill a person on the main deck below. They repeated the tack-block process for the port side pad-eye at the top of the mast. Then Boone sent up the two three-quarter-inch manila lines that would be the primary rigging for the bosun's chairs. Chuck threaded one of the lines through each tack-block and sent the bitter ends back down to Boone. Today's part of the job was done! He again leaned against the mast for a few moments' rest. He would now allow himself the ride he had spoken to the captain about. With the workday behind him, he could let himself be a kid on a carnival ride at the County Fair. He started the ride by looking out to the horizon for the first time. That horizon was definitely on the move. Sometimes it was on a near mountain far above him; then it would be at the bottom of a terrifyingly deep canyon. The side-to-side motion of the mast would often be interrupted by a sharp change. The top of the mast would be yanked forward as the bow of the ship dropped into an errant trough in the pattern of sea swells, then be yanked aft as the ship climbed a suddenly appearing blue-green mountain of sea water. The horizon was, indeed, a much-traveled thing.

In the brilliant afternoon sunshine the sky and the sea each claimed their own shades of blue. The sky was a deep picture-postcard blue, while the sea boastfully showed off many shades of that color. Some of its blue mixed itself with green, some with the blue of the sky, some mysteriously with a deep purple or brown. All of the blues in the sea were constantly changing and being accented here and there by dancing whitecaps. The giant swells, marching across the 30-mile circle under his view, marched not in disciplined ranks. They, instead, constantly melded into and crossed each other. This was somehow accomplished without interrupting the powerful force of each swell's relentless drive toward the southeast.

Off to the east he could see a pod of California Gray Whales blowing and playing as they migrated southward. They would continue on their course until they reached the warm waters off Baja California. There in the warm waters of Scammon's Lagoon they would have their babies and spend the winter. The Grays have, for millions of years, made this annual voyage of migration, their course altered only occasionally by some earthly phenomena like a passing ice age.

A half-dozen schools of dolphin played in the great circle of ocean under his gaze. One school was happily doing escort duty at the bow of the *McFall*. It was as though they were eager to lead this strange giant fish to an exciting and secret place that only they knew of off to the southwest. He wondered if these extremely intelligent mammals had a name of their own for those sparkling jewels in the central Pacific, the Hawaiian Islands.

Looking down at the ship from his catbird perch, the true design for her stability was not evident. The tall steel pole he was on seemed to be stuck into the topside of a long floating log. On the heavy rolls, there seemed to be no reason at all for the mast to come to a stop instead of crashing on downward onto the restless sea. After the mysterious stop, it would laboriously start its climb back to vertical, then repeat the process to the opposite side.

Boone's shout broke the spell, "Boss, what the hell you doin' up there?" Chuck looked down to the yardarm. Boone was crouched against the mast, his safety belt straining with each roll or pitch that the ship made; he was a sorry sight. The look on his face today matched the always sad look in his eyes.

"O K., Eddie, I'm comin' down."

Down on the yardarm, Boone looked his partner in the eye and asked, "What the hell's ta see out there but cold sea water?"

Chuck cuffed Boone on the side of the head and said "I can't explain it to ya,' partner. Somehow your big Irish heart is missing its beauty appreciation gear." Boone gave him a vertical middle-digit-salute, then quickly climbed down the ladder on the mast to the flying bridge. With their equipment secured, they were free to knock off for the day.

The seas leveled off like the captain thought they would, and the good weather held. They finished the project in good time, and the goof-off days proved to be financially successful. Their pooled, more or less honest, "pitch" effort earned them a modest wad that would make possible a respectable liberty in Honolulu. The old chief wheelman circled the game in the crew's mess like a whiskered catfish sizing up a baited hook, then veered away without taking the bait. There would be other games; the bait would eventually work its magic. The old chief's deep pockets would finance liberties yet unplanned.

During the hours Chuck and Eddie spent in the bosun's chairs, they had plenty of time to talk. Boone was a great storyteller. He told colorful stories he'd heard from old cowboys around campfires. Those men wanted their stories to be heard and retold. They knew their stories were the only record of their lives. They knew, all too well, their lives and times were rapidly coming to an end. The country humor Eddie always used seldom obscured completely a line of depression that threaded its way through the stories he told of his own life. The remembered scene of his father's suicide somehow overpowered all the pleasant memories of his life. Even the loving memories he held of his mom lost their way behind the searing moments he stood with his pony looking at his dad's once handsome, now grossly shattered head.

Drink had always been, it seemed to Boone, a friend his dad could count on. When the day was cold a shot of whiskey would warm him up. If the day was hot, a beer would cool him down. It always seemed to be a part of the mix when good friends gathered. It was always there with the music and songs, strong laughter and good stories that gave color to their lives. The contents of the empty bottle that Eddie had cast down on the shotgun that killed his father had probably made it easier for his dad to do the thing he apparently had to do that day in that grassy draw.

Boone had sought the same relationship with drink that his father had seemed to enjoy; for him, though, it didn't work at all. Sure there was some fun in it, but he was getting sick of the web of trouble that drink seemed to always weave for him. He had started drinking in high school. That soon got him in trouble with his aunt and the school. Then Sheriff Baker got into the picture, and his troubles got serious. When the Japanese bombed Pearl Harbor, one of the sailors they killed was his mom's younger brother. Eddie's "Uncle Bill" was a sailor on the battleship *Arizona*. Eddie figured he had a score to settle. He begged his aunt to sign the papers that he needed for him to join the navy. When she eventually did, Eddie was soon out of school and out of Sheriff Baker's county. He survived boot camp at San Diego and was at sea on the aircraft carrier *Yorktown* when he quietly celebrated his eighteenth birthday.

On the Coral Sea, east of Australia, the enemy that had killed his uncle came looking for Seaman Second Class Eddie Boone. The Angel of Death came on the silver wings of Japanese dive-bombers. At the "general quarters" bell, ammunition passer Eddie Boone ran to his gun station. He had done this hundreds of times before, but this time it was clear that it was not a drill. Enemy planes, flashing their "meatball" insignia, dived and looped in the sky.

The gun was firing ammunition that he had passed when Petty Officer Stark relieved him. Stark sent Eddie to central stores to get a replacement part that the gun needed. That trip was an exercise right out of John Bunyan's tale of a Pilgrim's tough going. Every one of several ladders he had to descend automatically had a horde of officers and men trying to come up that ladder. Every passageway he tried to move in had those same, it seemed, officers and men running along it, of course in the direction opposite to his. When he got to central stores and had fought his way to the counter, the storekeeper advised him that his petty officer had to sign a requisition form to get the needed part. In the passageways and on the ladders that he had to renegotiate to get back to his gun, there, sure as hell, was that same horde of officers and men. There was no shouting or even conversation. Strangely, they were individually and collectively silent. Each one of those men was, in fact, silently coming to grips with the reality of war at sea. Until today "the enemy" was a ghost entity that someone else was fighting. This day the enemy had searched out and found, personally, each man on those ladders and in those passageways. Each man understood that the enemy was here to kill him. They now understood what they had been told, A warship at sea is a world all her own. She knows that one lucky enemy shot or one well placed bomb can cancel her existence as a fighting unit. The alternative to being a fighting unit is death in the sea.

When Boone got back to the gun with the requisition form in hand, he found Petty Officer Stark dead. Stark was lying on the deck a few feet from the gun. He had been dragged there and attended to by the medics. A wedge-shaped piece of steel was sticking out of his chest just over his heart. Blood formed a strange halo under his shoulders and around his head. The blood had turned dark. The medics had gone on to treat other wounded, those wounded whose blood still showed the red color of life. Stark's eyes were left gazing into the sky above the innocent and beautiful Coral Sea. Boone stuffed the requisition slip into his pocket, then knelt to gently close Stark's eyes.

When he resumed his place at the gun, he stood again in the spot where the Angel of Death had come looking for him. In his absence, an enemy dive-bomber had planted a bomb on the flight deck near the gun. The bomb sent scraps of metal flying in all directions. The bomb itself penetrated the flight deck, raising hell and killing people as it went. In its wake work crews were putting out fires and fixing things as best they could. The *Yorktown* managed to continue sending out and landing her planes around and over the holes in her flight deck. She was a tough and resourceful old lady.

One of the last enemy planes to come in whacked Boone on the forehead just below his helmet with a sharp piece of something. It sliced a gash five inches long clear to the bone. His eyes immediately filled with blood. The *Yorktown* and the Republic temporarily lost another ammunition passer.

In their after-the-battle dispatches, the enemy gloated that they had "Sunk the *Yorktown!*" The unsunken *"Lady" Yorktown* sped away to Pearl Harbor for succor. While welders, electricians, pipe fitters and painters were putting her back in shape, the surviving members of her crew took their splints and bandages ashore for some R&R. They repaired noisily to the beaches and the "Social Clubs" of Honolulu. Eddie Boone took his bandaged head ashore to seek the comforts to be had at "Rope Yarn Haven," the social club just a heaving-line throw from the gate at Pearl Harbor.

A few months later, and less than a thousand miles west of Hawaii, the *Yorktown* was again back in action. With the paint hardly dry on her earlier wounds, she again engaged the enemy, this time in the all-out battle for Midway Island. While continually launching and retrieving her planes, she took several serious hits from Japanese planes. Late in the day it was determined that this time, her wounds were mortal. Her planes were instructed to land on other American carriers, and the "abandon ship" order was passed. Her crew, those who could, went over the side.

Seaman Second Class Eddie Boone was a member of the salvage team left aboard to try to save her. They scattered below-decks, searching for wounded and fighting fires. To add to her troubles, the wounded *"Old Lady"* suddenly took two torpedoes from an enemy submarine. When the torpedoes struck, she seemed to leap in the air, then settle back into the water with an audible sigh. Minutes later the "all hands abandon ship" order was passed. The dying *"Lady"* would take any wounded the salvage crew hadn't found and all of her many dead to the bottom with her. Boone, carrying a seriously wounded sailor that he'd found, worked his way aft; there he joined the rest of the salvage crew sliding down lines into the water. Boone's size and strength allowed him to get the wounded man safely into the water and to keep him afloat until medics from a destroyer took him under their care.

It was a beautifully clear afternoon with the sea as smooth as glass. In a matter of minutes the survivors were safely out of the water and onto the decks of rescuing destroyers. The destroyers were, at the same time, maneuvering sharply as they looked for the enemy submarine. Most *Yorktowners* wept openly as they kept a deathwatch for their wounded ship. In the soft tropical twilight after a beautiful sunset, their gallant *"Lady"* died. Her ensign and signal flags were all still flying as she settled slowly and quietly to her new home on the floor of the Pacific Ocean.

The *Yorktown* survivors were given 30-day furloughs. All the talk among the crew was of "going home." Eddie Boone knew he couldn't go home; his home was the *"Yorktown."* The enemy had taken his home from him.

In "Frisco" he put on new dress blues, his campaign ribbons, his battle stars, his purple heart and the decoration he had received for saving that injured sailor's life. Then, because it seemed to be expected of him, he crowded aboard a train headed east.

Boone spent the trip to Nebraska bombed out on four bottles

of the costly but God-awful whisky he'd gotten from the shoeshine guy at the train station in Oakland. With yeoman effort and considerable relief the Union Pacific conductor got Eddie **Boone** awake and off his train at Grand Island. A military policeman, called by the conductor, steered Eddie aboard "Old Number Two" on the Chicago, Burlington & Quincy line. That train headed northwest from Grand Island. When it arrived in Broken Bow at four in the morning, the CB&Q conductor had to get help to get the decorated but totally passed-out sailor off his train. They loaded him onto a four-wheeled baggage cart. The Broken Bow station master, a Mr. Tom Ryan slid him off the baggage cart onto a counter in the baggage room and gently spread a blanket over him.

The station master figured someone would eventually show up to claim the big fellow. A handsome, decorated guy like that had to belong to someone! By noon the next day no one had come to claim him, and the visiting war hero had not yet come around. Tom Ryan turned the radio in the baggage room up very loud and, while the Andrews Sisters expounded loudly on the merits of "Rum and Coca Cola," Mr. Ryan did what he could to get his guest to start making plans to move on. The station master's son was with him. When the boy got a good look at the baggage room guest, he told his dad, "Hey, Dad, that's Eddie Boone. You remember him; before he left to join the navy he was a heck of a running back at Broken Bow High. His Aunt Mary used to teach school here, but she's gone now. She's teaching way over in Clay County. He may not know that. He's a really good guy, Dad!"

Eventually the loud music and black coffee had the desired effect. The big red-headed sailor came alive. The CB&Q station master let him know that he was welcome to sleep on the counter in the baggage room any time he wanted. A half dozen old army blankets made the spot quite comfortable. Mr. Ryan let him use the company phone to call his Aunt Mary. Mr. Ryan's son had guessed right; Boone didn't know that his Aunt Mary no longer lived in Broken Bow. His aunt sobbed when she heard his voice. She'd heard rumors that his ship had been lost. She daily awaited arrival of the telegram announcing Eddie's death. She recalled her, now-dead mother's sad ordeal waiting for word of her brother's death after the attack at Pearl Harbor. That perspective brought little comfort as she waited for word that she had lost Eddie.

Once he sobered up, Eddie Boone was not at loose ends for long. He found a host of eager listeners to his war stories at Frank's Beer & Pool Tavern. Old cowboys who were fighting the war by proxy from the back of a cowpony hung on his every word. Frank, too, fixed up a place for him to sleep. It was in a shed out back of the tavern. The otherwise homeless sailor began to enjoy his hero status in Broken Bow. Pretty girls, who in high school wouldn't give him the time of day, were now trying to catch his eye to invite him home with them to meet their folks.

With Eddie Boone, however, it seemed that nothing ever went right for very long. Eddie was soon in trouble again! He had beaten the crap out of the loud-mouthed, draft-dodging son of a friend of Sheriff Baker's. The sheriff gave the town's war hero a choice: either get out of the county or go to jail. Eddie caught a ride to North Platte with one of the regulars at Frank's place, a cattle trucker. Another trucker took him to Cheyenne. There his rides dried up. He sat on his sea-bag in the vestibule of a jam-packed chair-car as a westbound train took him home to the navy in San Francisco.

Big trouble in his next assignment landed Boone in the brig at Mare Island. He wouldn't elaborate on the details; he said only there'd been a fight with a jarhead Marine in a bar in Oakland. The marine, along with his bleeding jarheadedness, got a free ride in a meat wagon to a hospital.

After being in the brig for a couple of months, with Marine

guards beating on him regularly, he'd begun to think that he'd spend the rest of the war in that six-by-eight by eight-foot cell. Then one day a lawyer-type lieutenant came by and poked an envelope through the bars at him. It contained $250 and a "Convenience of the Government" discharge from the navy. Boone sat staring at the papers. He was stunned. First his parents, then his ship, and now the navy had been taken from him.

Boone was still sitting on his sack with the bad-news letter in his hand when a Shore Patrol ape came to the cell door to spring him. The knuckle-dragging ape told him to be ready to march in five minutes. He was thankful that it was to be a navy chaser that would close-order march him off the base, not one of the hated jarhead guards. Wouldn't you know? After all those months of being sheltered in a nice dry brig, the day they kicked him out it would be raining like a tall cow pissin' on a flat rock.

The Shore Patrol ape relaxed his "chin in" attitude when they passed through the front gate. He put his hand on Boone's shoulder. When Eddie turned to him, he reached out to shake the new civilian's hand and said, "Good luck, Boone. I know you earned those medals. Take care of them, and yourself." The ape then turned and was gone back through the gate. Standing there alone in the rain, Eddie was struck with a stark realization. He shouted out to no one but the falling rain and the gray morning, "God Damn it, Eddie Boone! You're all alone." The idea of no longer being in the United States Navy was a hard thing to grasp. He had lived with the idea that a navy sailor was who he was. Now who the hell was he?

A large city bus appeared out of the grayness of the day. The bus swished up to the curb in front of him; the sign over the windshield said "San Francisco." Boone had no plan to go there, but to get out of the rain he climbed aboard that bus. He fished a $20 bill out of the envelope the lawyer-type lieutenant had given him. When he gave it to the driver, the driver made a fuss that he had to make change. As the driver fumed, Eddie stood dripping rain water as he slowly and carefully checked the driver's count of the change. Before moving to the rear of the bus, he looked the driver in the eye and gave him a vertical middle-finger salute.

On a very wet morning a month later, again to get in out of the rain, Boone entered a bar in North Beach. The bartender eyed him as he climbed onto the end stool near the front door. The half-drowned newcomer slid something across the lacquered bar top and said in a barely audible voice, "I need some hair of the dog."

The bartender picked the object up, and even in the dim light quickly recognized it for what it was, and for what it should mean to its owner. It was a double bar of campaign ribbons. He counted the battle stars, noted the Purple Heart and the special decoration, then turned to the back bar to drop it into a lidless cigar box. There it joined some stubby pencils and an old comb. Without looking directly at the newcomer, the bartender said, "Okay, Pal, what'll it be?" The newcomer removed his headgear, a GI sailor's hat with the rim turned down. He shook the rainwater out of the hat and placed it on the stool next to him, clear notice that he wanted no company. His curly red hair was the hair of a schoolboy. The blue eyes in the face below the hair told of a sadness that no schoolboy should know.

A barely audible voice answered the bartender with a question, "How many boiler makers will they buy?"

The barkeep had already started to draw a beer but stopped and, looking his customer in the eye, said, "Look Pal, I'm beginnin' to rethink this whole damn thing." After a moment's pause, he finished drawing the beer and placed it on the counter in front of his customer. The bubbles rising in the clear golden liquid spoke comfortingly to the rain-soaked newcomer. They spoke to him in femme-fatale voices. The bartender next filled a shot glass from a whiskey bottle on the back bar, then placed the glass in the shadow of the foam-topped beer. "Drink up, Pal." The bartender turned away. He chose not to be watching as his shaky-handed customer, who looked like he hadn't eaten for a month, struggled to get the shot of whiskey down without spilling the precious liquid. When he heard the clack of the shot glass returning to the bar top the bartender turned again to his customer. After looking at the young man for some moments, he retrieved the campaign ribbons from the cigar box and said, "If you'll listen to some advice, I'll return these, and that drink is on the house."

Boone shrugged as he sat savoring the glass of beer. "That's sure as hell the best deal I've been offered lately." The hair-of-the-dog drink had done wonders for his voice. To himself Boone thought fat chance of this guy dumping anything on me that I haven't heard before.

The bartender leaned against the back bar and said, "Tell me about the special decoration."

Surprised, Boone sat in silence for a moment then said, "Not much to tell I got it serving on the *Yorktown*."

Someone at the other end of the bar wanted service. When he came back, the bartender stood quietly. He seemed to be deep in thought. This sad-eyed young man sitting on a barstool in front of him was one of many young Americans who brought their sad eyes to his place. He was thinking to himself, "I'm not smart enough to really help these troubled kids. Where the hell are the people with letters behind their names who should be helping them? Those bastards only talk to themselves or to each other." The barkeep's eyes were reluctant to return to the eyes of the big red-headed, sad-eyed child who sat before him. He pulled his eyes away from the nothingness of watching the bright colors change in the jukebox that stood against the far wall. Mentally snapping his fingers, he brought his eyes to bear on the eyes of his rain-soaked customer. He said, "You still haven't told me about that special decoration; there has'ta be a story there."

Looking into the golden prism of his half-empty glass of beer, Boone started talking as though to himself. "I was below decks, mostly in the dark looking for wounded. I had a good electric lantern, but it was findin' nothin' but dead men. In one of the machinery spaces where everyone was dead, blood mixed with water was about an inch deep on the deck. It looked like boardinghouse ketchup. About that time the '*Old Lady*' took another shot of some kind; she leaped in the air like she'd been goosed. When she came down, I was knocked flat on my face."

"Word came over the public address system: 'All hands abandon ship!' The ship was makin' sounds that I'd never heard before. She seemed to be tellin' herself that she was gonna die. I got to my feet, wiped the ketchup off the lens of my lantern and started running up ladders toward the main deck. Two decks up I heard a heavy bangin' sound. It was comin' from behind a watertight door that was securely battened down. It's a fool's move to open a door like that. That door could be secured for good reason. There could be gas or fire or God knows what behind it. Apparently my folks raised a fool because I opened that door. In that machinery space were two dead sailors and one tough son-of-a-bitch tryin' his best not to die. He was pounding on the deck with a 36-inch Stillson wrench. When he saw me, he said, 'Holy shit, sailor, you're a mess!' I guess the dunkin' I got in that ketchup showed. I could see that his left leg was pinned under a millin' machine that had jumped off its mount. I found a long piece of steel pipe that I could use as a pry-rod to lift that machine off the guy's leg. The leg was busted all to hell. I broke the heads off of two fire-axes, and with his and my shirts I wrapped his leg tight to those axe handles. Then I picked him up and hauled ass for the fantail.

161

I knew he was gonna be all right because he never stopped cussin' at me. In the water some medics took him off my hands. I never saw him again."

The words of the story had flowed into and through Boone's half-empty glass of beer. When the quiet words stopped, the newcomer downed the balance of the beer. His eyes moved to the campaign ribbons now lying on the bar top. He picked them up and returned them to his shirt pocket.

Still leaning against the back bar, the barkeep hadn't moved through the telling of the story. He shifted his weight now to his other foot and said, "Look, Sailor, I've changed my mind about the advice I was gonna lay on you. Seems to me that whatever problems you have'd be eased a good bit if you could jus' get your ass back to sea. My nephew's the chief cook on an army sea tug. He was telling me they're about to sail short-handed in their deck crew. I'll give you bus fare to Fort Mason where that sea tug's tied up. An' don't worry; they don't hire altar boys to man those ships. They use regular Merchant Marine sailors. Just show 'em your navy discharge papers, an' you're good for three hots a day an' a dry sack at night."

Boone was skeptical, but what the hell, why not check it out. With part of the donated bus fare he bought a cup of coffee at a corner stand, then walked and hitched over to Fort Mason which was in the shadow of the Golden Gate Bridge. On the way serious doubts began to build. Who the hell ever heard of the U.S. Army having a sea tug? When he came over the hill on Van Ness Avenue where he could see down into Fort Mason, he realized the army did indeed have a whole fleet of ships, and sure as hell he could see a sea tug or two.

He broke out his COG discharge and showed it to the M.P. at the gate, then asked about the sea tug job. After making a phone call, the M.P. sent him to a doctor and an army medic.

They thumped the scar on his forehead, then made him look at the ceiling while he stood on his heels, then his toes. In his emaciated condition he had trouble with that exercise. They x-rayed his chest and peered indiscriminately into all of his body orifices. When that and a bunch of other stuff were done, they left him sitting naked on a cold steel bench, wondering where his clothes were.

Ex-hungry orphan, ex-fugitive from Sheriff Baker, ex-navy ammunition passer, ex-decorated war hero, ex-brig bird, ex-beached drunk, now "Ordinary Seaman Eddie Boone of the U.S. Army Transportation Corps," sailed out through the Golden Gate that night on the U.S. Army LT. 076. The large tug "076" was towing a U.S. Navy machinery barge that was to be delivered to Dutch Harbor in the Aleutian Islands. The cook of the "076" had orders from his uncle to put some meat on Boone's ribs.

Like his shipmates, Chuck did not presume to plan beyond the next liberty. He held strongly, however, that the next liberty always deserved careful planning, especially one in Honolulu, undoubtedly the most beautiful place on earth.

The great beauty of Hawaii has always been beyond description and is a thing impossible not to feel as well as see. The Islands in the 1940s, when first experienced, left most visitors struck numb in wonder. The fragrance and softness of the air and the power of the colors gave multiple dimensions to the wonder. Given a chance, the pervasively gentle ambience of Hawaii would very quickly overcome any malaise that a visitor may have brought with him.

The *McFall* would be in port over the weekend so the day-watch deck crew could plan a Sunday ashore. After the brutal hangover Eddie had after his roaring alcoholic bout in Seattle and his continued spoken and unspoken pleas for help, Chuck had finally responded by dumping a ton of truth on him. One day, hanging side by side in bosun's chairs, Chuck said, "Eddie, you keep asking me for help. I can't help you. You're an alcoholic. The only cure for that sickness is, to stop drinking. There's only one guy in town that can make that happen. That guy is you!" Eddie's questioning sad blue eyes didn't change an iota as he weathered those words. He said nothing for several minutes, then he launched into an unrelated story.

The understanding that Chuck had with Eddie for their pitch-financed liberty in Honolulu was simple. They'd stay absolutely sober, and they would come back aboard together. This plan constituted considerable sacrifice for Chuck. There were a couple of colorful watering holes in town that he liked to frequent. It was no secret that the major attractions in those places were the libations served up by their pretty lady bartenders. Boone confessed that in all the times he had been in Hawaii he had never gotten past "Rope Yarn Haven," the big beer garden and social club just up the road from the gate at Pearl Harbor. The *McFall* tied up at a commercial pier in Honolulu, so they went nowhere near "Rope Yarn Haven."

Ashore, they walked past one of Chuck's hangouts, the "AY Bar" at the Alexander Young Hotel. He wanted to stop in to say hello, but he decided against it. There was another bar farther up the street that Chuck felt he had to show his friend Eddie. In that place there were pool and snooker tables plus art on the walls that should mitigate the risk of being in a bar for this pair, an unacknowledged alcoholic and his untrained mentor.

The owner of that bar had some sort of agreement with an alcoholic ex-sign painter from San Francisco. Rumor had it that they were boyhood friends in Mill Valley. The ex-sign painter was now living as a beach bum on some island in the South Pacific. He'd chosen his island well; he'd picked one that the Japanese didn't choose to occupy. The war had not been a problem for him at all. In spite of, or because of, his alcoholic affliction, the ex-sign painter had developed a method and a talent for painting fabulously exotic nudes on black velvet. His success was in his colors; the rich, flamboyant colors of the Islands. His colors ranged from the ultimately subtle to a super sparkling radiance. His work and technique would be much copied later, but these were originals. His ladies on velvet seemed to absolutely live and breathe in the expert lighting provided on the walls of that bar. The paintings were, of course, for sale. Few of the soldiers, sailors or marines who spent hours nursing beers in that bar were art lovers, but there is no question, they were all lovers of that art. Each painting had an expensive price tag on it. Some paintings had "sold" tags on them. The buyer's name was on the back of the tag. Some of those men would not be back to take possession of their purchase; the Angel of Death had seen to that. The painting, with its sold tag, would become a living memorial to the dead art patron.

Eddie Boone fell in love with one of the ladies. She hung in well-lighted glory on a wall near the third snooker table. Her presence made it very difficult for anyone, but especially Eddie, to concentrate on the game. Chuck beat him two games out of three. That meant Boone would buy supper. When it came time to leave, they, like most other patrons, backed out the front door. Visitors to that bar were always reluctant to leave. They each felt strangely protective of the lovely ladies who dwelt on those walls. It was not easy to leave those girls there to be visually pawed by others, other dogfaces, swab-jockeys or jarheads, guys who were totally unworthy.

Out on the street, even here in downtown Honolulu, Chuck became aware anew of Hawaii. The air was, as always, the breath of a thousand flowers. The sun warmed the two sailors as rain fell across the street; people walking there seemed oblivious to that falling rain. The coming sun would dry them out quickly.

Chuck rented a car from the guy in the Uncle Sam suit on upper Hotel Street. They folded the top down and tooled up beautiful Nuuanu Avenue, over the Pali, then down the Waimanalo Highway, around Makapuu Point and Diamond Head. They'd taken the long scenic route to the beach at Waikiki.

An old guy at Waikiki rented surfboards. He required first-timers to also rent and wear a life jacket. Boone was impatient with the life jacket rule; Chuck on the other hand always claimed first-timer status. The board tended to go on a trip of its own after a spill. The nearest land was 50 yards away, straight down. That lifejacket was a good friend to a dry-creek swimmer from Nebraska. If the life jacket spoke of nerd status, Chuck could handle it. The old guy also rented swim trunks. The pair beat him out of that two dollars. They had their swim trunks on, instead of skivvies, under their khaki pants.

A long paddle out from the beach, the surf broke in beautiful long cascades of tumbling white seawater. Once there, it was easy and exciting to catch and ride the small breakers. When the large ones came in, the smart neophytes let them pass. The dumb ones soon wished they had. None were so dumb that they couldn't see the wisdom in staying clear of the no-life-jacketed, dark- skinned locals. Those guys, some of them just little kids, eagerly caught and rode the big ones. They rode them with a strength and grace that was a thing of absolute beauty to see.

Back in their clothes after a fresh-water shower behind a canvas screen on the board-rental dock, they repaired to the bar at the Royal Hawaiian Hotel. They chose a table deep in the cool vastness of that storied place. The bar had a roof but somehow very few walls. Out through a tall grove of Royal Palms that stood on the seaward side of the hotel, they could see and hear the surf they'd been riding. The deck of the bar seemed to be at least an acre of smoothly waxed flat stones. Rattan tables were covered with a brightly colored batik. Cloth from those table covers would've made a thousand and more great aloha shirts.

The tropical forest of potted plants and trees in the bar made finding one's way to the men's room a sylvan odyssey. They hadn't long to wait for service. A willowy young woman in a sleek green sarong emerged from the potted forest and glided toward their table. A camellia-like red flower rode triumphantly on her left breast. Her lipstick exactly matched the color of that lucky flower. To this pair of Sandhill swab jockeys, she was a thing of startling beauty, not regal and aloof but real and touchable. They were both thinking, "Oh Lord, to be able to touch a reality like that!" When her golden slippers came to a stop at their table, her perfume seemed to emanate in rocking waves from the red flower that rested so smugly on the natural shelf her left breast provided. Chuck was thinking, any poet, sailor, warrior or fool would surely, with weapons carefully chosen, fight to the death to secure the shelf from which a perfume like that was launched!

Standing before them in her sarong and golden slippers, she gave them her very best waitress smile and asked, "What would you boys like?" The sailors burst out laughing.

Chuck recovered first to say, "Have mercy on us, girl! You've got to somehow rephrase that question."

Her pretty face lit up with a friendly girl-next-door smile, "Okay, I can do that. What delightful item from our menu can I get for you gentlemen?"

Chuck grinned and said, "Thank you for that. I must tell you. We're in the midst of a critical social experiment. What does your barkeep have in the way of a cool nonalcoholic drink?"

The answer came back, "It's just so lucky that you guys came here! We have the most beautiful and innocent Mai Tai in the Islands. Our creation is called the 'Gelded Barbarian.' You absolutely must try it!" While she waited for their decision, she tapped lightly on her order book with a long green pencil. Neither of her potential customers were musicians, but Chuck thought he could hear the strains of "A Sunday Kind of Love" in her pencil tapping.

Always to the point, Boone said, "If it's cold an' wet, I'll try it, and I'll buy one for my caretaker too."

The pretty waitress looked questioningly at the big redhead, then her mind chose to move on. She closed the sale with, "I must tell you guys, each one of our 'Barbarians' is a work of art so it'll take a few minutes." The idea of two sunburned, callous-handed swab jockeys ordering nonalcoholic drinks was enough to keep the girl-next-door smile on her face as she vanished into the potted jungle to place the order.

Chuck's idea that he was hearing the surf they were seeing out through the palm grove got blown out of the water by his partner in pitch crime. Boone noticed that the breaking surf they were seeing in the orange light of the now setting sun was not in sync with the sounds they were hearing. They were probably the only customers in the place to realize that the surf sounds were actually background sound in the soft Hawaiian music that seemed to float through the forest of potted plants.

Boone said, "You know what, College Boy?"

Chuck regretted once again having bragged about his brief exposure to higher learning. He decided to say, "Eddie, settin' in a place as beautiful as this, I'll answer to anything. What's on your mind?"

Boone, continued, "I haven't ever told this story while sober, but I'll try it." Leaning forward in his chair with his big grin in place, he said, "There was this harmless looking little guy sittn' on a bar stool. Each time he'd get a refill for his Martini he'd say, 'Get 'em Killer,' an' this little mouse would poke its nose out of his shirt pocket and take a sip of the Martini, then he would disappear back into the guy's shirt pocket. That went on all evening. Finally the bartender figured the guy'd had about enough, so he said, 'Friend, I'm cuttin' you off; go home now, an' come see us again soon.' The little guy began pounding on the bar with his fists then shouted, 'Damn you, Mr. Bartender, give me another Martini or I'll rip your face off and throw it at the ceiling fan.' The little mouse poked his head out of the guy's pocket and said, 'That goes for your God-damn cat too!'" Boone followed that with another story.

Chuck had begun to realize that he thought of this character, Eddie Boone, as a close personal friend. Very few men he sailed with made that cut. He knew that this growing friendship had a lot to do with that strange first meeting when they were lads in Prairie Center at Rube and Millie's supper table.

The girl with the lucky red flower and the golden slippers arrived back at their table bearing the Gelded Barbarians. The two drinks filled a large serving tray. Boone asked, "Do we get an instruction book with these beauties?"

The waitress said as she expertly swished the Barbarians onto the table in front of them, "Don't be silly, you're going to love these gentle giants!" Someone at another table was calling for her. The golden slippers carried her red flower, the special shelf on which it sat, and her stirring perfume away from them.

The drinks were contained in large, cut-glass, stemmed goblets. The goblets stood in a fancy crystal bowl of chipped ice. Each goblet was crowned by a host of colorful somethings. Boone's question regarding need for an instruction book actually made good sense. It turned out that all of the colorful somethings were edible. In the large goblet under that umbrella of color, exotically spiced coconut milk had been poured over shaved ice.

Chuck asked, "Boone, have you ever been served a drink before that came with a salad fork?" They followed the delightful Mai Tais with supper and coffee; it was all served to them by the pretty girl wearing the lucky red flower.

Chuck had agreed to stand the midnight-to-four quarter-deck watch for the Duty Watch Wheelman, so he had to cut out early. They took the short way downtown to return the rented Ford. Walking down Hotel Street on their way back to the ship, Boone said, "Damn, Chuck, we did have fun today, and I think I could develop a hankerin' for those Gelded Barbarians, but right now you'll have'ta go on ahead; I wan'na spend some more time with that pretty lady on black velvet." Chuck had a scolding answer ready to drop on his friend, but it was left unsaid. Boone had turned and disappeared into the happy Sunday night crowd on Hotel Street.

The Honolulu police carried Boone up the gangway just before the ship sailed at noon the next day. Chuck had to get in line behind the chief bosun and the first officer to chew Boone out. Eddie wouldn't look him in the eye. It was clear to Chuck that the pain in Eddie's eyes had a source much deeper than the ugly lump that had been created by a policeman's truncheon on the side of his head.

As the *McFall* steamed westward, the bosun kept them working as a team. Chuck tried to put out of his mind a very real fear that his friend Eddie was not just an ordinary drunk. Something deep in Eddie's head just wouldn't let him be. That dark something was a thing to be feared.

They kept working their less than totally honest pitch system on everyone they could. Boone wanted money to buy that lady on velvet over the third snooker table, and of course they needed money for liberty in Manila. Sadly, they lost out on the hoped-for opportunity to mine the deep pockets of the old chief wheelman. The chief had taken sick. Rumor had it that it was something very serious. In Manila, he would be transferred to the sickbay of another ship, a ship on its way back to the states. For one half of the team of pitch pirates, this sad development presented an opportunity. Chuck had been striking for a wheelman rating for months. With the old chief leaving the ship, the expectation was that one of the watch wheelmen would be promoted to chief. That would leave a watch wheelman's spot open. The senior member of the pitch-pirate team recognized this sad turn of events as his chance to press for the upgrade. He suspected that the old chief, who was a lot overweight, could be suffering from extremely high blood pressure. He hoped they'd get him into a hospital before a major stroke did him in.

There were no "social clubs" in Manila like in Honolulu. There were instead many "gardens," and many "flowers" for visitors to choose from in those lovely Gardens.

Tradition had it that, when the fires under the boilers of the *McFall* were banked and the rat guards were in place on the mooring lines, the off-watch crew would head for the many delights to be found at the Garden of the Purple Lotus. The honorable madam at the Purple Lotus was a cultured veteran of the Garden wars. In her younger days, she'd had to walk away from a lucrative Garden in Shanghai, after making a wrong decision about which warlord to pay homage to. Long before that, her forbears had, for similar reasons, fled Russia. Her name was Madam Kormarov. She dressed in tight-fitting, full-length gowns of black. Her jet-black hair was pulled straight back from her strong, high-cheek-boned face.

She always wore a black, Spanish-lace mantilla. That beautiful mantilla tried its best to hide an angry red scar on the soft white skin of her neck. She disclosed the history of that, certainly near-fatal, wound to no one.

Madam Kormarov entertained her "guests" by playing classical piano on a baby grand in the spacious, potted-palm studded parlor of her establishment. Her scantily clad girls were multi-talented; they danced, played parlor games and served beer and drinks to her guests at the many tables. While doing so, the girls "worked" the guests for the more lucrative activity carried out in the palm-frond decorated, bamboo stalls in the garden out back. When the work effort began to bear fruit, the waitress effort was abandoned. The girl would take her client by the hand, and like a sorority girl leading her date to the dance floor, she would lead her date to the delights to be found in the rear courtyard. First the client would join her in a sudsy, communal shower bath, after which she would expertly rub him dry with a fluffy white towel. Clad in clean white robes, they would then repair to her assigned cubicle. Her client would probably learn a new thing or two in that bamboo enclosure. The waltz and the samba were not on the list of things taught there.

Between movements of *Scheherazade,* Madam Komarov would swing around on her piano stool to hold court. She had to act alternately as an understanding counselor and hard-nosed boss to deal with the multitude of situations that ebbed and flowed through her establishment. She handled no money; others less gifted took care of that chore. She did handle a kill switch for the jukebox. When she wanted to play the piano, she'd hit that switch and immediately the music blaring from the jukebox would take a vow of silence. When she finished her musical offering, the jukebox would be freed from its vow and the likes of Helen O'Connell, Dick Haynes, Bea Wain, Hank Williams, Bing Crosby, The Mills Brothers and Tex Ritter would sing their songs to the guests. "Hit Parade Extras" would make even the potted palms want to dance. On this day with the jukebox newly blaring, Madam Komarov turned on her piano stool to find one of her girls on her knees before her. The girl's cheeks were wet with tears. The Madam put out her hands to cup the girl's pretty face, then spoke in Tagalog, the girl's native tongue, "Tell me Serena, my little mermaid, why the tears?"

The girl moved closer to lay her head on the housemother's lap for a moment, then she raised her head to say, "Please, Mother, will you help me? The tall, blue-eyed, American boy that has been with me these past two days has been taken away by the M.P.s. Dear Mother, he fought them and I fear for his life! I ask your permission to go to him."

Wiping the girl's tears away with her lace-trimmed handkerchief, Madam Komarov said, "May all the saints in heaven come to our aid, child. Can it be that I have not reminded you enough of our need to protect ourselves? We must, indeed, allow these young men to know our bodies but we must never allow them to know our hearts." She pulled the girl to her bosom and held her close. "I cannot break the house rules and allow you out on the street. No good could possibly come of that. You must forget this young American; I will pray with you for his well-being, then you must put him out of your mind."

The *McFall* rested uneasily at her pier. The captain had not broken sea watches for her stay in Manila. The hukbalahaps, a dangerous post World War II insurgent force, was trying to overthrow the US-backed Philippine government. A possibility of guerrilla action on the streets of the city existed. In the event of such action, all American ships in the port would slip their lines and move to an anchorage out in the harbor. The shattered hulls of half-submerged ships that littered the harbor made this a very dangerous maneuver, especially after dark.

Chuck, the newly promoted watch wheelman, was on the quarter-deck (at the top of gangway) standing his "four-to-eight" watch. A military policeman with a carbine slung on his shoulder, walked the pier at the bottom of the gangway. His tasks included checking the I.D. cards of all who came aboard.

One of the guys from the deck crew, looking a lot the worse for wear, came lurching up the gangway. Chuck asked him if he'd seen Eddie Boone. "No, Wheels, I ain't seen 'im, but I heard he got locked up after a brawl with about 20 M.P.s."

When the "eight-to-twelve" watch-wheelman came to relieve him, Chuck went to the first officer to get a note requesting that the military police release Boone. That always worked if the prisoner was in custody for only the usual charge of being "drunk in public." As he turned to leave the office, the first officer stopped Chuck with the question, "Farritor, what the hell're we gonna do with that boy? He just can't seem to stay out of trouble." When he got no answer, Mr. Wilcox continued, "Until we get back to sea, have Sergeant-at-Arms Kellerman put him in the brig for safe keeping. Remind 'Kell' to have plenty of help on hand before he tries it. And check out and wear a sidearm. Only drunks are safe on the streets here."

Chuck asked the M.P. at the bottom of the gangway how to go about finding a guy who's apparently been locked up.

The soldier said, "If he got picked up in the area around the Purple Lotus, chances are he's at the Old Walled City, M.P. Headquarters. Watch yourself around that place. The Huks have those folks as uneasy as a milk-cow with sore tits."

Chuck thanked him and moved on. When he got well up the pier, he turned to look back at his ship. She stood tall above the silent dark waters of Manila Bay. In the dim light of the new moon she looked like a still life painting of herself. The painting displayed a thousand shades of gray and black. 'Still life' was not really the right term. In the shadow-on-shadow scene, the thrusting line of her prow seemed to project a violent rush of stilled movement. He paused for several moments, committing this scene to memory, and then turned to the task of finding his friend. He knew he would find Eddie Boone in a different kind of shadow.

At the main gate, he steered clear of the hoard of pickpocket minions who kept watch night and day for returning sailors who looked drunk enough to be fleeced safely. He didn't have long to wait for a roaming taxi. The cab was a flamboyantly altered and painted ex U.S. Army Jeep. The cabbie, perhaps in recognition of the sidearm his passenger carried, drove slowly and carefully through the dark, pot-holed streets to the Military Police Headquarters. That headquarters turned out to be a series of Quonset huts spaced like circled wagons in a grassless open space near the ruins of the Old Walled City. The installation seemed to be grossly misplaced, adjacent as it was to the dusty seventeenth-century ruin. That quiet historic space seemed violated by the presence of the tin buildings, the unnatural roar of diesel generators and the rattle of modern arms. The area was glaringly lit by floodlights mounted on bare poles. There was no fence. Armed sentries walked posts on all sides of the installation.

The taxi stopped at the picket line. When Chuck climbed out, he found himself in a small group of native women. They were almost as one, crying and praying in Tagalog. A young girl stood silently apart from the women.

When Chuck passed, the girl put her hand on his arm and asked quietly in accented English, "Sir, are you from the *McFall*? Will you see Eddie Boone?"

Taken aback, he stopped to look more closely at the pretty girl. He said, "Yes, Ma'am. Yes, I'll see Eddie, if he's here."

The girl kept her hand on his arm. "My name is Serena, I love Eddie Boone. When you find him, please bring him to me. I will take him to my village. My family will help me to make him well. We will be married and I and our blue-eyed babies will forever keep him from being sad." Serena's words were more than a plea. They were a plan, a plan filled with hope and promise.

Serena's simple plan of love and peace took the tragedy of the life of his friend Eddie Boone to a place beyond where Chuck's mind had ever been before with the problem. Damn the thousand and one reasons that made Serena's plan impossible.

Wait a minute, could it be that he was the one guy that could make it happen? His mind toyed with the idea of bringing Eddie to Serena, then taking the two of them in his taxi to a place outside of the city where they could catch a bus to Serena's village. It could be, as Serena had promised, a place of renewal for his friend Eddie. He was shocked that he was entertaining such a move. He did not, however, drive the idea from his mind; he instead tucked it away in a spot where he could quickly find it again.

He showed his I.D. card to the waiting sentry. The sentry waved him on. He spoke quietly to Serena, then moved away from the pretty girl who had a plan for Eddie's future.

The Quonset huts were identified only by a large number painted on each. The number one building had the American flag hanging from a white-painted pole in front of it. The stars and stripes hung motionless in the hot night air. He headed for that building. The door in the end wall of the hut stood open to allow some night air to enter that tin oven. The sergeant-of-the-guard sat at a small desk just inside the door. An electric fan rotated tiredly from the top of a rusted olive-drab file cabinet against the wall. Chuck laid his I.D. card and the letter from his first officer on the sergeant's desk.

"Sergeant, I speak on behalf of my captain and my first officer. I'm here to request permission to escort Seaman Eddie Boone back aboard the *McFall* where he will be incarcerated. My captain hopes for a favorable consideration of this request." The sergeant's khaki uniform was sweat darkened and beads of sweat stood in relief on his forehead. He looked at the I.D. card, then read the letter. He looked up at the sailor and said, "We've got Boone here aw' right. I'll check with my O.D. about your request." He picked up the field-pack phone on his desk, turned the crank and spoke into it. After a moment he hung up, picked up the letter and the I.D. card, then after knocking lightly, opened and went through the door behind his desk. An angry voice could soon be heard through the closed door. The sergeant reappeared and sat down at his desk. He looked up, and in a curious mixing of realities said, "Hold your horses, Sailor." The heat in the room was brutal. Chuck held his position in front of the sergeant's desk. He could feel sweat running out of his hair down his cheeks and off his chin. He knew that his uniform shirt was becoming as sweat-soaked as the sergeant's.

Suddenly the door behind the sergeant was yanked open and an angry first lieutenant stormed through it. He came around the desk to face the bearer of the letter from the first officer of the *McFall*. Chuck turned a half left to face him. The officer of the day handed him his I.D. card and the letter, which had obviously been crumpled up and flattened out again. The O.D. moved in so close that his sweating, up-turned face nearly touched the chin of the bearer of the apparently offending letter. The lieutenant spoke in a barely controlled voice, "Sailor, I'm not going to tell you what you can do with that letter, though I'd like to! I will tell you this. If I had a howitzer in this company, I'd drop a shell on your first officer's desk. If I have my way, the man from your crew that we are holding will stay right where he is until Hell and Manila Bay freeze over. I've got two men in the hospital, one with a concussion, the other with a ruptured spleen. You can tell your captain and your first officer that Seaman Boone's ass belongs to me now." The sailor managed to answer in a level voice, "I understand your anger, sir. Would you grant me a personal favor? May I see the prisoner?" Without answering, the O.D. did an about-face and marched back into his office. The door slammed behind him. The murmur of the sergeant's wearily oscillating fan was now the only sound in the room. Chuck returned to his position facing the desk. He stood staring over the sergeant's head at the O.D.'s office door. After what seemed like a sweat-laced eon, the field-pack phone rang. The sergeant picked up the receiver and said, "Sir?" After a moment he said, "Yes, sir." He put the receiver back in its pouch and said, "The O.D.'s approved yer request ta see the prisoner. See the guard on duty in buildin' four."

The guard in building four sat on a folding chair just inside the open front door; an M-1 rifle lay across his lap. A field-pack phone rested on the deck near him. Chuck entered the building with his hands over his head. The guard stood up, his rifle pointed at the visitor's chest. He took the visitor's sidearm from its holster and without lowering his rifle, dropped to one knee to place the sidearm on the deck near his chair. "Face that wall, put your hands on the wall, then step back so's you're leanin' on your hands. Turn your face to the left." As the nervous young soldier frisked the visitor with his left hand, he kept the muzzle of the M-1 stuck in the visitor's left ear. His sweating young finger continued to grip the trigger. When he found no other weapon he stepped back and said, "The sergeant says you're here to see prisoner Boone. He's clear to the back on the left. You stay on that white line in the middle of the corridor. If you step off that white line toward any prisoner, I'll shoot your ass from right here where I sit. You got that straight?" Chuck said, "Calm down soldier, I hear you."

The Quonset hut was divided down the middle by a five-foot-wide corridor with barred cells on either side. The corridor walls and the locked doors to the cells were rusty iron bars; the walls between the cells were corrugated steel like the arched outer walls and ceiling of the hut itself. The concrete deck sloped from both sides to the center of the corridor then to a drain at the rear. The white line down the center was the only thing painted in the place. Everything else consisted of either rust-stained concrete, rusted iron or weathered galvanized steel. Chuck started the grim walk down the white line. Some cells were occupied by sleeping, moaning drunks, others by wide-awake, angry-eyed Filipino natives. He guessed that the natives were captured outlaw Huks. Internationally directed, these indigenous warriors had been very carefully led to believe that the Americans had cleverly replaced the hated Japanese as occupiers in their land.

Chuck could not have prepared himself for what he found when he got to the last cell on the left. His good friend Eddie Boone was hanging silently on the inside of the steel barred door. His webbed belt encircled his neck then led upward behind his head to the top bar of the door. The taut belt pressed his face against the bars. Eddie's lifeless blue eyes were strangely, genuinely at peace. They looked calmly back at his friend. That friend stood for a moment in shock then he turned and retraced his steps on the white line. When he got back to where the guard sat, he said without raising his voice, "Get your ass back there and cut my friend down." The guard jumped up and ran down the line to number eight left. He took one look, then shouted, "Son of a bitch! I didn't hear nothin'." He turned and ran back to his field-pack telephone. Eddie's friend walked back down the white line. Ignoring the threat that he'd be shot if he did so, he stepped off the white line to touch his friend. Through the bars he grasped Eddie's right hand in both of his. Badly swollen, there were very likely broken bones in the hand. In spite of the angry red swelling, the skin was cold. With his right, he reached up to touch his friend's forehead as Eddie's mom was wont to do. The warmth of life had not yet completely left his forehead. Chuck next felt for a pulse on the side of Eddie's neck. He found none and the skin, even in the heat of this night, was cold. It was clear that Eddie Boone had been dead for some time. He again touched Eddie's forehead, then let his hand brush gently downward to close the eyes that no longer showed their perennial sadness. Eddie's blue eyes were now at peace.

After several prayer-filled moments, Chuck turned and walked back up the white line toward the entrance. The guard was bent over his phone; his rifle lay unattended nearby. Eddie's friend stooped to retrieve the sidearm he'd surrendered, then went out of that place. He walked across the compound toward his waiting taxi.

Over at building one the American flag still hung motionless in the bright white light. In the building all hell was beginning to break loose. He found the girl, Serena, kneeling silently with her face in her hands near the praying women. He moved through the knot of women to kneel beside the girl. He said, "Serena, I must tell you that Eddie Boone was in that place, but he is no longer there." The girl dropped her hands to her chest to stare silently into the dust. "Look at me, Serena. I know Eddie would want me to see to your safety, please allow me to take you over to Madam Komarov's place, where she can look out for you." Without raising her eyes, the girl stood up and said simply, "Yes." He knew it was not necessary to tell her that Eddie Boone was dead.

At the noisy and happy Purple Lotus Gardens, they found Madam Komarov at her piano. When she saw them, she stopped playing and flipped the switch to the jukebox. Bea Wain began singing softly, "When the 'Deep Purple' falls over sleepy garden walls." Serena ran to the housemother and threw herself on her knees before her. She sobbed, "Dear Mother, my beautiful Eddie Boone is dead!" The housemother pulled the girl to her. She stroked Serena's long black hair, then kissed the top of the girl's head. Chuck understood clearly that there was nothing he could say that would make any difference. When he met Madam Komarov's eyes, he saluted, then turned slowly and retreated to the humid darkness of the street. There his taxi waited.

It was now past midnight. He had equipment to turn in and a heavy report to make. He'd have precious little time to sleep before he was due back on watch at 0400 hours.

At high noon of the new day, the *U.S.A.T. General McFall* threaded her way carefully out through the massive debris of a past death-struggle. In that historic Bay of Manila the silent, rusting shapes of steel protruding through the surface of the warm salt water served well to mark the place where many of the men who had once served those ships had died. The great gray ship *McFall* saw to getting her remaining people safely back to that one place of innocence, the open sea. She gently carried in the stillness of her morgue one of her least, but one of her own, a flawed but brave young man who had triumphed. That young man won all of his many battles, including the last one. In that last battle, he had summoned the towering strength he'd needed to reach the state of peace he'd been seeking. He'd reached that state with class and in a majestic and profound silence. Before the warmth of life had totally left him, a friend came to him to hold his hand and touch his forehead the way his mom used to do. The friend who would pray for him knew that Eddie Boone had fought well in this, his last battle. The friend knew that Eddie's final victory had somehow regained for him the peace that had forsaken him late one winter afternoon in a mortgaged grassy draw.

Story Ten

To a Grieving White Mountain

The night's darkness was quietly retreating from the bridge deck of the U.S. Army Transport *U.S.A.T. General Kincaid*. As the sun was about to emerge from the mists on the eastern horizon, two sailors left the wheelhouse and ran up the portside ladder to the flying bridge. They went immediately to the large canvas-covered steel tub that housed the signal flags. There they quickly assembled a string of flags, then moved to the rail where the signal halyards were made fast on belaying pins.

The four-to-eight watch wheelman hooked the topmost flag of the string to the snap on a yardarm halyard and tugged at the braided line, lifting the signal flags,into the soft morning air. This display would announce their ship's call letters to the Port Commander and to all the ships around the *Kincaid*. The other young man, Chuck Farritor, the chief wheelman, held the string of four signal flags, letting the flags slide through his hands one by one as the halyard pulled the string of flags up to the yardarm. The first rays of the sun lit the colorful flags as they fluttered quietly in the gentle morning breeze. The braided halyard holding the signal flags aloft was then carefully made fast to its belaying pin. The signal code flags joined the round black ball that was hanging on a far halyard. That large black ball advised the world that the *Kincaid* lay at anchor.

The two friends turned and walked to the portside railing of the flying bridge. There they would steal a quiet moment to contemplate the reality of their first morning as invaders in the Empire of Japan. The war with Japan was over. The *General Kincaid* had come up from the Philippines with a load of troops gleaned from combat *divisions* no longer needed there. The *Kincaid* would not have to again land her troops from the open sea onto a beach under enemy fire. This time she would wait her turn for space at a dock to allow her load of troops to go ashore in dry boots. They would quietly take up military occupation duties on this former enemy terrain.

The Japanese had a funny-looking little man they called Emperor Hirohito. The emperor, historically identified by his subjects as the "Son of Heaven," had lived in luxury and dozed at his post for decades while his people pillaged and raped their neighbors. He apparently awoke when the tables turned and his country and his people were systematically being destroyed by incendiary weapons and then, as last-resort convincers, two atomic bombs.

In his newly alert state, Hirohito had finally found the courage to properly do his job. He had defied the military-industrial dictatorship that ruled his country. That dictatorship had rejected the allied surrender terms. With newly found wisdom, the emperor had belatedly taken it upon himself to accept the terms that had been offered. These peace terms had been offered well before the atomic bombs were dropped. Besides being war criminals, the *"Son of Heaven"* and his military leaders had to be the world's champion slow learners. This harbor, Yokohama and its large anchorage located in central Japan, had served the Japanese navy well. It would now do the same for the allied occupiers.

The morning sun had now driven away all traces of the night and was quickly dissolving the morning mists. The watch wheelman responded to a call from the watch officer down on the bridge deck. He scampered down the ladder and was soon out of sight and back to work.

The young chief wheelman turned from the railing and walked to the weather-tight box where watch binoculars were kept. Selecting a pair he turned and walked toward the base of the foremast. Chuck had decided that the occasion called for an extension of his goof-off time.

At the foot of the mast, he paused and looked up the ladder to the yardarm. He would go up there for a better look around. Hanging the strap on the binocular around his neck, he began the long climb upward. This familiar action brought on a poignant memory.

He and his now-dead friend, Eddie Boone, had painted the mast and replaced the halyards on a mast exactly like this one. It was on a voyage from Seattle to Manila on the *U.S.A.T. General McFall*. The *McFall* was one of several sister ships to the *Kincaid*.

His memories of his friend were always selective; he chose to remember Eddie's quick wit, warm smile and funny stories. He chose not to think of Eddie's always sad blue eyes.

Perched on the yardarm of the *Kincaid*, the young chief trained his glass on the port city. As in the now defeated Germany, the allied bombers had spared selected seaports, facilities that would be needed for landing an occupying force.

Yokohama, Japan, one of those cities, stood more or less intact. It was a small city, made up mostly of two and three-story buildings. From his elevated vantage point, he could see beyond the port city to a vast plain of desolation. As far as the eye could see only masonry factory chimneys stood in an area where hundreds of thousands of people had once lived and worked. The homes and factories built of wood on that ancient plain were kindling for the hundreds of tons of incendiary bombs that fell from allied bombers out of many night skies.

Rail lines had been repaired and rebuilt by the Japanese war machine across this newly created desert. Steam trains could be seen puffing this way and that.

The colossal tragedy of the twentieth century was the transformation of the once proud Japanese people into an ugly pain-machine. This transformed people became bent on invasion and the subjugation of all their neighbors in the Western Pacific. The transformation was complete. The young Japanese, who were sent abroad to attack their neighbors, accomplished their tasks with great skill and a finely honed appetite for cruelty. With movie cameras recording the fun, young officers held competitions as to who, with his long-sword, could lop off the most heads of kneeling prisoners without breaking a sweat. Those beheaded prisoners were perhaps the lucky ones. The not-so-lucky would be subjected to years of beatings and starvation in slave labor camps until death or an allied victory could mercifully set them free.

The bestiality of the rapes of China, Korea, the Philippines and several countries in Southeast Asia were conspicuously ugly and for reasons yet unknown, the invading Japanese employed a special degree of hate and brutality on the American servicemen and civilians they captured when they invaded the Philippines.

History tells us that, given time, any military dictatorship will deliver itself and its people to destruction. That said, there is nothing to explain the rampant excesses of the Japanese people's behavior on their way to that fate.

The further question is whether the Japanese will be able to find peace by acknowledging those ugly excesses. History does not lend much hope. It tells us that a bully quickly moves on while his victim is locked forever in the pain that the bully has inflicted.

From his vantage point on the yardarm, the young chief could see past the fields of devastation. In the new morning sunshine, he looked wide-eyed at the single most beautiful white mountain he had ever seen. The mountain stood boldly in place yet it was surreal in form as it graced the blue morning sky. An errant morning mist had somehow resisted the sun. Perhaps it persisted there on ethereal instructions. That mist lay at the mountain's base making the white mountain appear to have somehow levitated from the earth.

The young chief had seen this mountain before. He'd seen it in the pages of an old National Geographic magazine. The black and white photo in the magazine had done its best to portray this extinct volcano's beauty. This morning this young American was looking at the mountain's true beauty through bright, clear binoculars that were perfected to spot marauding enemy submarines in the dark of night.

The young American's mind suddenly locked and his eyes were clouded by tears. He was experiencing a strange and unexpected insight. His mind had gone to a dimension with which he was totally unfamiliar. For a moment he felt a tiny fraction of the sorrow that this *White Mountain* was feeling over the tragedy that had befallen this ancient land, a land where, for far too long, mad fools had been given the helm.

The feeling that had come strangely to him came naturally to his grandfather's friends, the Plains Indians. The plains and eastern slope people, the Pawnee, the Omaha, the Ponca, and the Arapaho, had loved and revered the spirit of the *Coyote*, the *Wind*, and the *Big Sky*. The young chief wheelman somehow was inexplicably feeling a like reverence for this *Grieving White Mountain*.

He had no understanding of what had happened in his head but he knew that he had to somehow pass through this port city, take a steam train over that field of devastation, then journey through that heaven-placed mist. As his grandfather's friends would have done, he would make a pilgrimage to this beautiful *Grieving White Mountain*. He must further understand the strange new field of knowledge that he had come upon.

While kneeling at its foot, this young American would pray for the souls of the Japanese people and for the wellbeing of the people they had so grievously harmed. Then he would pray for himself and for his friend Eddie Boone. The Japanese had tried to kill Eddie Boone. Later, for reasons having nothing to do with the Japanese, Eddie found it necessary to end his own life. Yes, it would be well to pray to his God for his friend on the face of yonder beautiful *White Mountain*. Perhaps that mountain, in its spiritual wisdom, could help him to understand Eddie's torment, and this young American's grief at losing his friend.

The young chief's detached state of mind flipped to reality when his training made him aware of a signal lamp blinking from the port city. The lamp was addressing the *Kincaid.* The message advised her that one of the docked transports was finished with her unloading and was preparing to leave the dock. He spotted the transport through his glass. Three brief spurts of steam from the front of its smokestack indicated three short blasts from its whistle. This was the standard signal for, "I am preparing to get underway." The whistle blasts could not be heard at this distance, but the three spurts of released steam spoke clearly of her intent.

Down on the bridge-deck, the watch officer picked up on the signal and notified the captain. The young chief wheelman terminated his goof-off time on the yardarm. He quickly climbed down the mast to the flying bridge, returned the binoculars to their safe place, then ran down the ladder to the bridge deck. In the wheelhouse he took the dustcovers off the compass and the gyro repeater, then moved to his regularly assigned position behind the ship's handsome, hardwood steering wheel. The *Kincaid* would soon hoist anchor, and with the aid of a U.S. Army Transportation Corps tugboat, she would carefully move to the newly vacated space at the dock. The navy destroyer that had escorted the *Kincaid* up from the Philippines had been treading water, on guard duty, nearby. She had been watching for a possible enemy submarine whose commander was one of those Japanese who had not agreed to the surrender. The destroyer would see the *Kincaid* to her assigned dock, dip her colors to the *Kincaid*, then swiftly and quietly make her way to her next assignment.

There were several pressing reasons to quickly throw thousands of troops ashore on the Japanese Islands. The first need, of course, was to take possession of all their weapons of war. This would forestall any insurgent action by the thousands of hard-core militarists who, not having good sense, felt betrayed by the emperor's acceptance of the peace terms. A second need for a strong occupation force was to make it clear to the Russians that they were not to set a boot in Japan. They had already moved into Manchuria and Korea.

The Japanese surrender on September 2, 1945, caught the allies short of the massive numbers of troops needed for a full occupation of all the Japanese islands. The battle-hardened American and British troops in the recently defeated Germany were being sent home on 30-day furloughs before being shipped out to join in the effort to defeat Japan. With this reality in mind, the all-out invasion of the Japanese home islands was not to occur for another few months. The Japanese surrendered after the second atomic bomb was dropped. That drastic action cancelled the plans for an armed invasion, saving the lives of many thousands of men on both sides.

As each transport was unloaded, it left immediately for Europe or America to get more troops. The *Kincaid*, low on fuel and water, was dispatched to Guam for those staples, then on to Seattle. There, her new load of troops consisted mostly of youngsters just out of basic training accompanied by a few retreads from the war in Europe. To save fuel and precious time, the *Kincaid* navigated the shorter but often dreary, great-circle route through the North Pacific back to Yokohama.

During their second visit to Yokohama, for their whole three-day stay, the *Grieving White Mountain* was veiled in clouds. The morning they left, again for more troops, the clouds parted for a moment. The young chief was aware of an ancient Japanese legend claiming that, having seen the mountain on leaving, it was ordained he would safely return to see it again.

While maneuvering within the harbor on their third trip into Yokohama, the *Kincaid* struck an uncharted, submerged object. There was damage to her rudder. The decision was made to put her in for repairs at Sasebo, a nearby shipyard that had served the wartime Japanese fleet. Since the buildings at the shipyard were made of masonry and steel they had survived the fire bombs.

The *Kincaid* and her crew were happy to see a warning buoy placed over the sunken object, but the truth was, they welcomed this happening. They needed a rest.

There were, of course, those in the crew who were not so weary that they weren't eager to get ashore to do research among the legendary geisha girl population. There were certainly a few who knew of that ultimate love story, *Madam Butterfly*. Was it possible there existed a new such lovely lady waiting for another lonely American sailor?

To repair her rudder, the *Kincaid* would have to be lifted out of the water. With any luck at all, that work should give them at least a three-week break. On the third day in the shipyard, with the ship lifted in a dry dock, the view from the flying bridge was spectacular. It was easy to see the vast burned-out area, then see beyond that area the beautiful apparition in the sky, the *Grieving White Mountain*. The young chief was disappointed to find that when others looked at it they saw only the snow covered extinct volcano that the Japanese call "Fuji San."

Chuck was carefully laying plans for the pilgrimage he planned to make. He had discussed his commitment with the captain who had given permission but with a few conditions. The captain said, "I guess I did some pretty questionable things when I was a kid and I survived. With some luck you should survive this. You must take one other man with you. Choose him well. Remember, we'll be sorry to lose you, but if you're not back by the time we sail, you're to report to the U.S. Army Master of the Port for reassignment."

In his mind, the chief was sifting through the personalities of the men in the deck crew, searching for the right man to accompany him. He was looking for a man who was level-headed yet with some imagination and who could be talked into going.

After a week of sifting and talking, he came to know that the last requirement was the tough one. When he explained what he guessed he knew of the conditions of the trip, no one was interested in going. He decided to go back to the captain to ask if he would reconsider and let him go alone.

Climbing the ladders to the captain's quarters, just below the bridge, he was stopped by a kid that he knew from the steward's department. The lad said, "Chief, word's out that you're lookin' for someone to go with you to that yonder mountain. Chief, I'm your man."

The chief was flabbergasted. He knew the kid. The lad was called "Rappy," short for Arapahoe. The chief also knew the kid was plenty tough. He'd been in Rappy's corner when the young Indian had beaten a bigger guy in a boxing match on a Rope Yarn Sunday program. (Because sailors at sea work seven days, a tradition handed down from sailing ships declares a midweek half holiday for all who are not actually on watch. On some ships, Wednesday afternoon is set aside as Rope-Yarn Sunday.)

Faced with the need for an immediate decision, the chief found himself mentally going over his original list of requirements. Rappy had proven himself determined and level-headed when he won that tough Rope Yarn Sunday fight. By volunteering, Rappy eliminated the last requirement entirely. Damn! He had his man. The wonder is why the hell he hadn't thought of Rappy first thing. The chief knew that Rappy was the captain's dog-robber. Suddenly, in the face of a new realization, Chuck's jubilation came crashing down around him. The captain seemed willing to risk losing his chief wheelman but it was dammed unlikely he'd allow his personal steward to go wandering off into unknown mists. A chief wheelman could be replaced, but a good dog-robber was irreplaceable. Damn it! Some of what he was thinking must've shown on his face.

Rappy said, "Now Chief, let me talk to the captain. I believe he thinks enough of you that he may want me to go along to maybe increase the odds of gettin' your white ass back safe."

The chief thought to himself, "*Hot damn, this kid has a great backhanded way of kickin' ass. He is definitely my man!*" Again in high spirits, and eager to have the lad take his shot at convincing the captain, he said, "Okay, Rappy, ask your Coyote to go with you when you go in to see the Old Man."

The chief turned and was retracing his steps down the ladder. He was smiling to himself and thinking that with Rappy's

Coyote working the field it was a done deal. The captain didn't have a chance.

The repairs on the rudder were progressing well so there was need to get the pilgrimage underway. After the captain okayed Rappy's participation in the venture, he began taking an active interest in the plan. The captain insisted that they take no weapon and wear no uniform. Tanker jackets, dungarees, pea caps and G.I. boots would do the trick. They were each to take a first-aid kit, a bar of soap, a G.I. blanket, three rolls of toilet paper, two canteens of water and they were to leave immediately!

On a Sunday morning, the two sailors caught a ride on a U.S. Army truck to the Yokohama railway station. Their first face-to-face encounter with the former enemy was a lady in a white, flowered kimono. She had what looked like a small pillow strapped to her back. Her feet peeked out from under the kimono. They were clad in tiny white socks fitted with a slot between her tiny big toe and the rest of her toes. She wore equally tiny, wooden shoes. She was trotting along at a curiously, bouncing gait. The gait was reminiscent to the young pilgrims of the way a cowpony manages to walk with night hobbles on. The two young Americans glanced at each other and shared the thought, "Why the hell would a centuries old civilization require its women to wear equipment that kept them from walking properly?"

The little lady's bouncing gait brought her to the door of the railway station just a second before the two young pilgrims arrived. One of the young Americans attempted to reach around her to open the door for her. Suddenly realizing that two giants wearing backpacks were immediately behind her, she turned her face to them. Stark terror registered in her beautifully-slanted black eyes. Immediately, she managed to do two things all in one motion. She bowed from the waist and backed her wooden shoes quickly to the right, away from the door. She stood frozen in that submissive position.

Looking at the top of a beautifully coiffed head of jet black hair, the jaws of the two young offenders dropped in astonishment. They could only surmise that in this weird land there was something terribly wrong with opening a door for a lady.

The young Americans moved past her into the lobby of the train station. Their next exposure to the former enemy was with a tiny man wearing black-rimmed spectacles who sat behind the ticket counter. They were soon to learn that he spoke not a word of English. Furthermore, he kept bowing his head to the counter so actively that they feared for the safety of his eye glasses.

Rappy was quick to see the need for sign language. There was a map of central Japan on a near wall. Rappy ran to it and pointed to a prominently marked Mount Fujiyama. The little man immediately stopped his bird-like head-dipping and started consulting his schedules. In a minute or two he pushed a piece of paper across the worn, wooden counter. On the paper was a number, then the word Offuna, then another number. The pilgrims figured the numbers to be trains and they knew Offuna to be a city. They thanked the man. This sent him into another spell of head-dipping.

They carried the slip of paper across the room to a wall-mounted schedule board. On the board, sure enough, was the first number and behind it a time number, 0820. It was now 0810 hours. If a train came by in ten minutes, they could figure they'd scoped the thing out okay.

A sign above a corridor leading out of the room displayed some Japanese language characters and a drawing of a section of railroad tracks. That corridor, sure enough, led them to the tracks. In a few minutes, a train came puffing into the station. The engine of the train had a number on it that matched the first number on their slip of paper. Shucks, this pilgriming was a cinch!

When the train stopped, the lads climbed aboard confident that they would eventually see the city named Offuna. There they were to change to a train with a different number.

The train was not crowded so they were able to find seats well away from any natives. The locals ignored them completely. This was definitely fine with the strangers. They were not looking forward to another encounter like the one at the train station door. They kept wondering if that tiny lady was still frozen in place where they had left her.

The train headed off into the burned-out area. They were relieved that it seemed to indeed be heading inland toward the *White Mountain*. The two pilgrims settled in as best they could on the badly worn, very hard benches.

Chuck turned to his fellow traveler and said, "Rappy, I wan'na thank you and your Coyote for gettin' us launched on this trip."

The young Indian grinned and said, "When it's done, I hope you're still thankin' us." He continued, "Ya' know what, Chief, there's somethin' I been wantin' ta get off my chest. I guess you know every Indian kid is told ta watch for a *Vision*. I want you ta know, I've been watchin' for one all my life and none has ever come to me. How the hell do you, a white guy, come off having one?"

Chuck was taken aback. He had long known the importance of *Visions* to the plains Indians. A *Vision* was an insight into the spirit world or it could be advice from that world. He sat for a moment not knowing quite what to say. The word *"Vision"* was the sticker. He said, "Now wait a minute, Rappy, the feelin' that came to me regarding the *Grieving White Mountain* was just that, it was a feeling."

"Chief, you c'n call it what you want, but no matter what you call it, that was a *Vision*. *Visions* can be just something you see but mostly they're something you feel about something you see. Anyway, you've had a *Vision* and this Indian kid has not. That leaves me more than a little pissed."

Chuck lucked out; he didn't have to come up with an answer to that. A little man in a conductor's uniform had suddenly appeared in front of them. His uniform looked as tired and worn as the chair-car they were riding in.

The little man put his hands in the air as if he was being held up, then he bowed from the waist like the lady had done at the train station door. This time they were looking not at the top of a beautifully coiffed head of hair, they were looking at the top of a very worn uniform hat. When he returned to an upright position, the conductor's hands were still in the air. The pilgrims then got a look at his face. His eyes were small chunks of coal. They were set in a grim and hate-filled face. The face looked as though it were made of stone. Without speaking, he spun on his heel contemptuously and walked away.

The pilgrims looked at each other dumbfounded. On the positive side, with all social and political considerations aside, they assumed that the guy's crude action meant they'd not need a ticket. They pocketed the occupation script money they had in hand to pay for their fare.

Leaving Yokohama, the train moved slowly out through the vast area that had been devastated by the fire bombs. After a couple of hours, the smoke-stack-studded area of desolation gave way to tiny villages on green hillsides. Chuck knew when they arrived at Offuna. Again from the pages of that old National Geographic magazine, he recognized the giant figure of some probably very holy lady. That statue was the "set piece" for the town of Offuna. Quite coincidentally that tall, holy lady had witnessed thousands of war crimes performed under her very nose. One of the most deplorable slave labor camps for American and British prisoners of war was located just down the hill from where she stood so piously.

They climbed down from the train and went looking for a schedule board like the one that successfully got them out of Yokohama. They found the board and on it found the second train number on their slip of paper. Behind the train number was the time number, 1755 hours. It was now 1700 hours so they had most of an hour before their train was due. They decided to find a quiet spot to eat some of the food that one of the ship's cooks had prepared for them. They stopped in a tiny park across from the station. The native family, who was there quickly, gathered up their things and fled. The pilgrims ate sandwiches of crisply fried bacon with sliced pickles on rye bread and drank water from their canteens.

When they heard the sound of a train coming, they scampered back to the station platform. The train that came into the station did not have the number they were looking for. Checking their watches they realized that it was not yet 1755 hours. They decided to wait quietly for the train that carried the right number. They waited, then waited some more. After a while, they decided to go looking for a public restroom. The facility they found was indeed very public; it gave little privacy. There was time to memorize the Japanese characters for "male toilet area."

At 1840 hours, a very sad-looking little train chugged into the station. It had the number 999 on the engine. That was the number they were looking for so they moved to get aboard.

The pilgrims could see that most of the windows in the cars had no glass. They managed to find one car that had some window glass on one side. They climbed aboard and took a seat near one of the glazed windows. It became obvious that the natives were also inclined to choose a car with some window glass. The locals entered the car, then upon seeing the pilgrims their faces first registered astonishment, then changed to anger and fear. These folks, with their light-weight wooden shoes hanging on their big toes, were probably seeing the ugly round-eyed face of their new invader for the first time. They, of course, had seen them by the hundreds roaring past in G.I. trucks; however, to have two of them here on their train was too much. The young Americans were saddened by the reaction but could only sit quietly and try to look harmless. They were also busy hoping their tired-looking little train could actually make it to the *Grieving White Mountain.*

With considerable wheezing and puffing, the little train eventually moved out of Offuna. The sun had set, and through the cracked and battered window glass, a bright twilight was making the countryside look absolutely beautiful.

It would be a long night on the very hard seats of the car. They decided it was best to sleep one at a time. Rappy volunteered to take the first watch. Chuck decided that to avoid being tossed off the bench by the train's jerking and swaying, the best bet would be to stretch out on the worn wooden deck. Wrapped in his blanket and using his backpack as a pillow, he was soon fast asleep. His travel-mate got up and moved to one of the glassless windows. The long, bright twilight was fading into a moonlit night.

The train was climbing another grade so it was moving slowly with a minimum of jerking and swaying. As it wound its way through the tree-covered foothills, only occasionally the moonlit, *White Mountain* came into view. Each time he saw it, Rappy was reminded of the chief's Vision and his own puzzlement over why a white guy was chosen over an Indian lad to experience one. A further question was, why a Vision in this land so far from the land of the Big Sky? His people's homelands were where Visions are supposed to happen.

The train came out of the range of foothills and seemed relieved to be running along the floor of a valley. The moonlit *White Mountain* stood over this valley so starkly that Rappy could suddenly see a similarity with the way the Big Sky watches over the lands his people used to call home. Could it be that this land is not so different? Could it be that this land is loved by its people with the same simple love that his people had loved their homeland before it was taken from them?

Suddenly, Rappy felt the quiet presence of Coyote the spirit. Coyote told Rappy, "It was me who gave the Vision to the white boy. I figured that would be the surest trail to take to get you, Gray Cloud, on a quest to the *Grieving White Mountain*. This strange mountain and this land are wiser than its people; there is much to be learned here."

Coyote understood the need for a nickname but when he addressed Rappy, it was always with his given Indian name, Gray Cloud.

The young chief wheelman stirred and awakened. When he sat up, he reached for his canteen to freshen his mouth. He got to his feet and moved to an open window to spit the mouthwash out. The only light in the car was from the small amount of moonlight that could find its way in. He wondered momentarily where Rappy was, then saw him at his window. He called out over the rattle of the train, "Okay Rappy, make up your Pullman berth, I'll take the watch."

The young chief moved to Rappy's open window. He could see immediately why Rappy had set up shop there. Toward the front of the train the *Grieving White Mountain* stood boldly in the sky above low black hills.

The young Indian said, "Good night, Chief," then began creating his own place to rest.

Chuck spent his watch-hours gazing at the incredible moonlit painting in front of him. As the track twisted and turned, the painting of the mountain would sometimes go away but in his mind's eye it was always there. In the face of its beauty he had not forgotten what the *Grieving White Mountain* was doing for its people. At 0400 hours, he prodded Rappy awake, then returned to his backpack bed and fell immediately to sleep. He awoke with a start at 0530 hours. Rappy was sound asleep with his head on his arms at his window. All seemed well, so he let Rappy continue to sleep.

The little train had been stopping frequently at farming villages all through the night. It was curious that, for all the coming and going on the train, none of the people seemed to travel beyond the next village.

After sunup, the train stopped at a comparatively large village. The young pilgrims guessed that it would be stopped there long enough for them to seek out another "male toilet area." Mindful of the wisdom of not meeting anyone face-to-face, they grabbed their backpacks and dashed off the train. The toilet area they found was even less private than the one they'd used in Offuna. One thing they couldn't help notice was that most men didn't bother to go inside the enclosure at all. If they needed only to urinate, they matter-of-factly relieved themselves against the outer wall of the facility.

The pilgrims concluded that, all cultural peculiarities aside, the men seemed to be clearly expressing how they felt about a pretty dismal toilet area system. If this were in fact the case, their point seemed to be lost because the passing public paid no attention to them.

Thanking their stars for the captain's good advice about the toilet paper, they completed their mission in time to get back aboard their train before it started its wheezing and puffing routine, which meant that it was about to leave the station.

They managed to reclaim their seats by the glazed windows. It was beginning to be obvious, however, that out in this rural area, things on the train would be different today. The population seemed to be made up of only very old people and children. There were no middle-aged or young people.

The raw hostility toward the Americans so evident in the seaport areas was totally missing here. The young and the elderly seemed to be curious as to why these two giant, round-eyed young men should be way out here all alone. It was obvious that the natives wanted to ask questions, but none of them found the courage to do that. The two pilgrims concluded that the years of indoctrination by the military-industrial dictatorship had failed to reach these farming people. Perhaps these gentle folks had just ignored the dictatorship's message of hate.

The tired little train made all of its familiar noises and slowly moved out of the station. The pilgrims no longer had the car to themselves. The car was full of people and animals. There were fat pigs whose feet were tied to a pole. The poles were carried between two gentlemen of the soil. Each team carefully and gently laid its porker on the deck of the car then squatted beside it. One gentleman occasionally reached over to comfort his porker by scratching its ear. Other farmers, usually women, carried chickens. The chickens were tied, two or three in a bunch, by the legs. They were carried heads down. Like the pigs, the chickens were laid gently on the deck with their carriers squatting beside them. The people as well as the chickens looked with fascination at the young round-eyed pilgrims. The pigs were not impressed; they closed their eyes and tried to sleep.

Knowing more than a little about the cycle of rural life, the young Americans understood that these fat pigs and birds probably had been traded for or purchased and were being taken home to be slaughtered. Throughout the morning, other people and animals cycled through the car as the train stopped at villages.

The little train began again to labor mightily as it left the valley and climbed into another band of foothills. When it could be seen, the *Grieving White Mountain* looked very near.

Several times the little train ducked into dark tunnels. With the engine casting clouds of black soot and smoke into the open windows of the completely dark chair cars, everyone began to present a distinctly darker visage.

The fat porker population had long since debarked. They were replaced by an occasional goat on a leash and many more chickens. After a longer than usual tunnel, a rooster shook the soot off of his comb and crowed loudly as though greeting a new dawn.

The train was now running along the base of the *Grieving White Mountain*. The mysterious mists, visible from Yokohama, were wrapped in and around these low, tree-covered hills. They were providing a truly mystical air of protection for the *Grieving White Mountain*.

There was nothing to tell the pilgrims which stop would be best for them to get off the train. Rappy, with his skill for sign language, approached an old farmer wearing the usual pointed, straw hat. He bowed from his waist as he had seen the natives do then put his hands together at his chin in a praying mode. He then pointed to the mountain. The old man bowed in return. When he straightened up with some difficulty, his eyes showed clearly that he understood Rappy's question. The little man held up one of his knobby, worn hands. One crooked finger was extended. The pilgrims took this to mean they were to get off at the next stop. They assembled their packs and were ready to move out when the train slowed. The old man made a chicken-shooing motion toward the door. The young pilgrims bowed from the waist to the old man, then when the train stopped, they bounded out the door. The bent old man stood watching them. His hands were together at his chin in Rappy's praying motion.

The tired little train, number 999, moved off along the track with its usual puffs and rattles. When its sound was gone, the pilgrims felt a quick pang of regret at her leaving. She had somehow quickly become an old friend to them.

They looked at each other, then up at the beautiful mountain standing before and above them. It stood bold and serene in the clear blue sky. A small, white cloud stood guard at its tip.

This train stop was not really a town. A few tacky stores and eating places were apparently there only to meet the needs of holiday pilgrims who came to visit Fuji San. Today, two round-eyed lads seemed to be the only pilgrims present. The single street of the non-town was deserted.

They visited the, as usual, better-marked-than-ventilated "male toilet area," then took a well-worn trail upward through the evergreen forest. Rappy led the way at a rapid clip. Chuck suggested that it would be well to stop in a green spot and break out some of their take-along food. He had trouble getting his companion's attention. Rappy had slipped into a strange silent mood; it was impossible to get through to him. Eventually Chuck grabbed him by the shoulders and steered him to a fallen log where they could sit to eat. Chuck got busy building bacon and pickle sandwiches on pieces of rye bread. The bread was getting a little dry. He sprinkled water from his canteen on the bread so it wouldn't break apart. Rappy would not eat. He was instead sitting, looking upward at the *Grieving White Mountain* through the treetops.

Chuck said, "Rappy, you've got to eat something."

In a voice that Chuck didn't recognize, Rappy said, "My name is Gray Cloud. I will not eat today. We must hurry; I must be beyond the tree-line before sunset." He stood up and set out at a dog-trot up the steep trail. The young chief suspected that Coyote was setting the pace. He quickly put away the food things and ran to catch Gray Cloud.

At the upper edge of the evergreen forest, the trail led to a small open pagoda-roofed Shinto temple. The building was made completely of wood. The steps and floors were worn to the point where traffic-pattern paths could be seen in the wooden deck. It was all natural wood; nothing had ever been painted. A large darkly patinaed brass bell hung from the ridge-beam of the low roof. A heavy cedar log was suspended on ropes in a way that if the log were pulled back and let go it would strike the outer wall of the bell. This day the great bell was silent.

Coyote and Gray Cloud ignored the Shinto temple. They went to a spot where only the great *White Mountain* itself stood over them. Chuck, of course, couldn't see what Coyote was doing but he watched in wonder as Gray Cloud stripped to his waist and stood as in a trance with his strong brown arms upraised. The Indian boy's eyes were closed as he seemed to be staring at the sun, which was directly above the peak of the *Grieving White Mountain*. The small white cloud that usually stood guard at the peak was missing.

Gray Cloud was singing to the spirit of the mountain. He sang in a voice that only Coyote had heard before. As minutes passed, the sun moved behind the peak of the mountain, causing a startlingly radiant halo to form around the peak. Gray Cloud's song changed as the sun assumed this new position. An hour passed, then another. The sun was behind the mountain and the sharp chill of a strange twilight was making its way down the *Grieving White Mountain*.

When Gray Cloud's song ended, he opened his eyes, folded his arms across his chest, then dropped to his knees exhausted. His eyes were fixed on the mountain's peak.

During the second hour of Gray Cloud's song, Chuck had knelt to offer the prayers he had promised to say to his God and to the spirit of the Mountain. With Gray Cloud's acappella song as a background choir, Chuck spoke his simple prayers. First he prayed for the soul of his good friend Eddie Boone. Remembering Eddie's great tragedy, Chuck prayed for the wisdom to direct his own life away from such sorrow. Then, as promised, he prayed for victims of the Japanese long reign of terror. Last, here at this primal altar of sorrow, he prayed for the Japanese people. He prayed that they would find peace by asking for forgiveness from those they had so grievously harmed.

Chuck was sure that Coyote was with Rappy but he understood that it was up to him to see to the exhausted boy's welfare. He walked quietly over to where Rappy still knelt with his eyes still lifted to the mountain. Without speaking, Chuck proceeded to get his friend's shirt and tanker jacket back on to ward off the chill of the coming night. He then helped Rappy to his feet and together they retraced their steps down into the evergreen forest. Chuck spread their blankets in a sheltered spot. The two newly bonded brothers slept the cold night through. They cuddled spoon fashion to take advantage of each other's body heat just as they had done on cold winter nights with their fraternal brothers back home.

These two young men had shared an experience that was by any frame of reference "profound." Chuck was unsure just how the happening at the mountain had affected Rappy or whether the experience gave him his long-sought Vision. From a white kid's perspective, it had been that and more. He wished that Coyote would speak to him. He wanted to talk with him about the beauty of Gray Cloud's song. For

Chuck, the song had been mind-bending. No other thing in his life's experience could touch it.

The new morning's sun warmed the air in the mist-shrouded evergreen forest. Chuck rolled out to greet the new day. He changed socks, then put on his boots, after shaking them upside down to dislodge any homesteading critters.

Rappy was awake looking up into the low, green canopy. He spoke for the first time since his Gray Cloud's voice was stilled. He said in his familiar voice, "Chief, you have to get used to days like yesterday if ya' choose to hang out with Indians."

Chuck looked up from lacing his boots and said, "Rappy, that experience you had yesterday was a bell-ringer. It's gonna be damn hard for any Indian nowadays to top that! For now, Rappy, we've got'ta get movin', get your butt out of that sack. You must be hungry as a tree'd raccoon."

They ate the last of their food. It left them still hungry. They were careful to leave the spot in the forest as pristine as they had found it. Down at the railroad track, instead of more breakfast, they had some surprises coming.

They first visited the local, very public male toilet area with its resident near-lethal smells. Later when they stepped inside an eating place for breakfast, their senses were slammed by another god-awful odor. They staggered outside to try another place. It had the same foul odor, an unholy cross between rotten cabbage and long-dead fish. In this second place they managed to get the proprietor to step outside with them. They could in no way eat in his establishment, but they found that he spoke good English and wanted to talk. He spoke English words with little accent, and the words tumbled from the little man's ancient lips. He had spent five years at the University of California and had returned to Japan in 1924 to teach at a school of higher learning there. He and his wife had retired to this mountain in 1942. They had come here to try to escape complicity in their country's terrible wars of conquest.

The little professor had many questions he wanted to ask these pilgrims, but they got their questions in first. Their first question was, "When is the next train to Offuna?" The answer to that question put a damper on everything.

They were told that the train they came to the mountain on would not be back. It makes a loop and returns to Offuna another way.

They asked, "Where is the other leg of the loop? Can we walk there to catch the train again?"

The old Berkeley grad pointed to a range of hills and said, "If you go down that road and climb over those hills you might re-catch your train. Now you must come into my place and have breakfast with me. I like to speak American. It reminds me of my days as a young man in Strawberry Canyon. I was lonely but happy there. I wrote to my girlfriend almost daily. We were married when I came home. I have lost her now; she is with the ancestors."

The chief wheelman said, "Sir, we are saddened by your loss. We thank you for speaking English and we thank you for your kind offer of breakfast. We would appreciate it if you could fill our canteens with water, otherwise you must please excuse us. We must run to catch our train." When the canteens were filled, they bowed from the waist to their ancient Berkeley graduate friend then trotted off down the road toward the far hills and hopefully toward the other good friend they'd made, the tired little train number 999.

The "road" they were traveling was not really a road at all. It was the three or four-foot wide top of a dike between what they guessed to be winter fallow rice fields. The fields were not now flooded.

Their inevitable first encounter on the road with the former enemy came soon enough. They watched closely as the party approached. It was a party of five, walking single file. The man in the lead was not a farmer. He was dressed not at all like the working men they'd been seeing. He had a fancy black folded headgear and cream-colored pants. His dark-colored jacket like his hat had many folds and details. Many animals can puff up to make themselves look larger. This man's jacket and hat appeared to be designed to do that for him. With or without aid from his designer clothes, he was larger than the people in his wake. The pilgrims could not tell whether the followers were women or perhaps boys. The leader carried a heavy walking stick. They'd seen enough training films to be leery of that stick. They decided it would be prudent to defer to the fancy hat, designer coat and big stick. When they were about ten paces from the oncoming party, they moved as far to the side as the narrow road would allow, then bent from the waist toward the leader. It was not so deep a bow that they couldn't keep an eye on that big stick.

The gentleman must have been some sort of dignitary who expected to be deferred to. He eyed them disdainfully as he walked by. His followers, all women dressed in dark clothes, seemed not to see the round-eyed pilgrims at all.

So far, so good. They moved on at a dog trot. As the day wore on, there were more and more people on the road. Their deferential bow routine worked most of the time. Only once in a while, a bowing impasse would result. This most often happened when the oncoming party was led by a man in other than farmer's clothes. They learned by deduction that in these cases a curt nod of the head would draw a return curt nod and both parties could go on their way.

They were getting wiser but their growling stomachs were reminding them that they were hungry as hell.

The road widened as it moved into the range of hills. They began to pass two-wheeled carts loaded with farm produce. The carts were being pushed by three or four people. The pilgrims were making better time than the carts so they could check the cargo in each one as they passed by. They were looking for something that they could eat. For an agonizing time, they could see nothing that looked edible without having to be cooked.

The sun set behind them over the *Grieving White Mountain*. There was beauty in its setting but nothing to compare with the show it had put on for the pilgrims when they were on its shoulder.

Just before nightfall, they came upon a heavily loaded cart with a tarp over its cargo. Three people were struggling to keep the heavy load moving up the hill.

As they approached from the rear, Chuck peeked under the tarp. This was the cart they were looking for! It was loaded with wonderfully edible tangerines. A plan began to form in the young chief's head. The Pilgrims were hungry and these farmers obviously needed help with getting their product to market. Even with no way to speak to these folks, there had to be a way to make a deal. Chuck said to Rappy, "This cart is the one we've been looking for; it's loaded with tangerines. I'm gonna try signing with them. Whatever happens, don't let this rig get away back down the hill."

Chuck, hoping he could pull it off, grabbed a tangerine from under the tarp and moved up the trail ahead of the three pullers. He then turned and put his hands up motioning for them to stop. They did.

The pullers were, of course, sure that their load was being hijacked. As one, they tried to run away. The little towing harness they each wore stopped them short. As expected, the task of holding the cart from running back down the hill fell to Rappy. He grabbed and held one wheel; this turned the cart at ninety degrees to the slope. There it sat, motionless and safe.

It was now up to Chuck to sell the cart owners on his program. He definitely had their attention. The fear in their eyes easily matched the fear they had seen in the eyes of the lady in the flowered kimono in Yokohama. Chuck began alternately rubbing his stomach and pointing to his mouth then pointing to the tangerine he was holding in his hand. He held up five fingers then pointed to himself and Rappy.

The two women were still locked in fear but the man began to show signs of understanding. After a long moment, he got out of his harness, went to the cart and picked out ten specimen tangerines. He gave five to Rappy and five to the holdup man. He then got back into his harness and told the women to start pulling. The cart turned and resumed its laborious journey up the hill.

The pilgrims quickly ate three tangerines each and put the remaining fruit in their jacket pockets. Rappy said, "Let's give these folks a hand." They each chose a spot at the rear of the cart to begin pushing a load of tangerines to market.

The cart was making such good time up the hill that they began passing other carts plus individual men and women with enormous loads on their backs. The long twilight began to give way to the darkness of night.

The hill road was now lit only by starlight. Chuck looked to the high southern sky to find his family's friend, the "Dog Star." The blue giant was there as always. He was smiling approvingly on two young American sailors who, with survival in mind, had become farm laborers.

The moon had not yet appeared. Almost as a part of their clothing, each native wore a surgical type white mask over his or her nose and mouth (the pilgrims could only wonder what the hell the mask did except make it harder for them to breathe). As the young pilgrims looked back down the mountain road, those bobbing and weaving masks seemed to catch and reflect the starlight. The masks took on an eerie life of their own. In the darkness, they appeared as disembodied spirits that were dancing in a grimly silent conga-line where the drumbeats were silent and the lively beat of castanets was not permitted. The conga-line was dancing its way up the hill road in the labored wake of the tangerine cart.

The pullers and the pushers of the hundreds of carts, and most certainly the tangerine cart, became like soldiers on a long night march. The motion of putting one foot forward past the other became first automatic and then hypnotic. The motion became a thing apart from the puller's or pusher's conscious intent. Each motion was however, without notification, silently stealing strength from the puller's or pusher's body.

In the case of the two pilgrim pushers who had walked all day after only a meager breakfast, the reservoir where the strength was stored was fast becoming a hollow place. After three or four hours, perhaps only just in time, the strength needed to push the next foot forward became less demanding. Without knowing it, they had arrived at the top of the hill. The tangerine cart stopped on a level place at the crest just as the moon made a welcome appearance in the eastern sky. That moon would provide much-needed light for the downhill trek.

The three pullers exited their harness and set about building a tiny fire. In no time at all, the aroma of boiling-hot tea reached the pilgrims who were lying in the road behind the cart where they had collapsed when the cart stopped. A second pot on the tiny fire contained warming pre-boiled rice. One of the women left the fire to go to where the pilgrims lay. The look of fear was gone from her eyes; it had been replaced by a look of sincere respect. She aroused the prostrate pushers and motioned for them to follow her to the fire.

Each pilgrim's strength was quickly renewed by the strong tea served from a large tin cup that was passed around, then from several helpings of boiled rice served on a green broadleaf. After the final serving, when the rice-pot was empty, they ate their green broadleaf plates, as did their hosts. The pilgrims ate the two tangerines from their pockets for desert.

During the meal the man, showed a toothy grin and said as he pointed to himself, "Papa-San." Pointing to the older of the two women, he introduced "Mama-San." The pilgrims smiled and dipped their heads to Mama-San. There was no further conversation.

The fire was extinguished by smothering it with road dust. All unburned charcoal and wood were sifted from the dust and saved for the next cooking fire.

The tangerine cart was quickly made ready for the passage down the far side of the hill. Two of the harnesses were moved to the rear of the cart. The two women got into their harnesses and made ready to keep the cart from running away. The man tossed his not-to-be-used harness up on the cart. He then picked up the tongue of the cart and with a push from the women at the rear, the downhill portion of the trek began.

The pilgrims, knowing full well the weight of that load and seeing that there were no mechanical brakes, realized how dangerous this downhill trip would be. The young chief said, "Rappy, grab onto that tongue with Papa San. I'll use his harness at the rear. He grabbed the abandoned harness and made his way to the rear of the cart. The women were happy to see the big round-eyed kid come to share the labor of holding the cart back.

There were many sections of that downhill trek that were so steep that it was all that the five holders could do to keep the heavy cart from getting away.

There were wrecked carts all along those sections of the road. They bore bleak testimony to the very real danger of the passage. Each one of those wrecks no doubt caused death or serious injury to one or more holders. The pilgrims prayed that at least on this passage there would be no one hurt.

Dawn began to break in the eastern sky. At a turn of the road that provided a lookout over this new valley, the pilgrims could see a train puffing along its track. They hoped the train they were seeing was not their little friend the 999 train. If it were, they would surely miss it. There was no way to hurry. Safety required continued, very deliberate, progress down the hill. Eventually, they made the final drop and turn into the village that hosted the railroad track and the farmer's market to which they would deliver the tangerine cart.

The pilgrims could not but wonder why the man and the two women thought they could perform the task of delivering that tangerine cart to market. Why did they not know that the task was simply more than they could possibly handle? The wrecked carts on the side of the road offered assurance that other farmers frequently made like miscalculations.

On deeper reflection, each of the young Americans silently knew that their own people had many times taken on tasks that were too much for them. Somehow, through dumb luck or perhaps divine intervention, the tasks got done. Could it be that there is a rule about dangerous and impossible tasks? "That is how impossible tasks are supposed to get done."

The man and the two women were profuse in their thanks to the two young Americans. Papa-San gave them a bag of a dozen or so tangerines to take with them. The pilgrims bowed from the waist to their three new friends, then turned and hurried to the railway station to check out the "male toilet area" and the schedule board that would hopefully get them back to Yokohama before their ship sailed.

They walked past the usual open-air urinators and went behind the half wall to make their contribution to the local night-soil cause. Their next stop was the train station schedule board. Wonder of wonders!

Their tired little friend, train number 999, showed on the board. It was due at 1000 hours today. This was unbelievably good news. The two young Americans jumped up and down with joy. How the hell could that little old 999 train have planned it so well?

They had time to kill, so they wandered out of the station. They had a plentiful supply of tangerines but they were hungry for some more of that great boiled rice. There had to be some way that they could get some without having to go into one of those grossly smelly eating places. Being careful not to have a face-to-face confrontation with anyone, they moved out into the busy street. They were hoping they would find a street vendor with a rice pot. The people in this village seemed a little more sophisticated than the folks on the other side of the hill but they had pretty much the same attitude toward the invaders. They appeared not to be afraid, rather they watched the young Americans with side-long looks with simple curiosity showing on their faces.

It suddenly occurred to the pilgrims that Papa-San just might be good for another boiled rice hit. They returned to the farmer's market area hoping to find their tangerine-carting friends who should be there selling the fruit of their labors. The pilgrims turned a corner in the large and busy market and there before them was that infamous tangerine cart and their three friends. It was as though they had been gone a month. Papa-San and Mama-San grinned happily.

Rappy assumed the role of sign language spokesman. He pointed to ten o'clock on his watch, pointed to Chuck and himself, then made a choo-choo sound and a going-away motion. Not finished, he pulled some occupation script money out of his pocket and pointed to the family rice pot that was boiling over a tiny fire.

Mama-San immediately took charge of the situation. She motioned for Rappy to put his money back in his pocket, then motioned for them to sit down. In less than a minute, the pilgrims had in their hands a green broadleaf heaped with delicious boiled rice. They dipped their heads and thanked Mama-San. Beaming like a fairy godmother, Mama-San proceeded to line a paper bag with green broadleaves and with a large wooden spoon she ladled several helpings of drained boiled rice into it. The pilgrims figured they had died and gone to heaven! Recognizing a good thing, Papa-San squatted beside them and he too was served a helping of boiled rice. The three friends sat silently together while they ate their rice with a spoon. The spoon was made of the back of their thumb and a bent forefinger.

The pilgrims said goodbye again to the tangerine folks. Mama-San, seemed to want to hug them, as did Papa-San, but they did not. The pilgrims wanted to hug their friends and benefactors, but they did not.

As the pilgrims walked slowly toward the train station, they couldn't shake the feeling that somehow there was something missing here in this village. Rappy was the one who spotted the shortcoming. He exclaimed suddenly, "Well, son of a she-bear, do you know these folks don't have a view of the *Grieving White Mountain*!" The young chief wheelman turned and joined Rappy in looking to the west. Sure as hell! This village was tucked in so close to the hill they had come over that the lone *White Mountain* could not be seen. What a damn shame! They should either knock the hill down or move the village

Their minds were not allowed to dwell on that fact for long. A plaintive whistle sounded in the morning air. They recognized that apologetic and somewhat hesitant call. It had to be their friend 999! Though it was not yet ten o'clock, they moved quickly to the station. Could it be that she was actually running ahead of schedule?

She was doing just that. Perhaps she knew of their need to get back to Yokohama before their ship sailed. She came puffing and rattling into the station proudly displaying her 999 sign. Again looking for a car that had at least some window glass, they climbed aboard and found seats at a glazed window.

On this return leg of her voyage, 999 seemed to be carrying more people and fewer animals. Just as they had made that conclusion, a lady farmer came aboard with three bound chickens in each hand. She carefully laid them on the deck in front of the pilgrims and squatted among her flock. Neither she nor the chickens seemed to mind the round-eyed strangers.

Number 999 began her familiar noises preparatory to getting underway. The noises were again successful. She pulled triumphantly out of the station headed for Offuna.

The trip back to Offuna was pretty much a sequel to the trip out. The pilgrims were, however, much more comfortable in their skin. They saw no need for one to keep watch while the other slept. As the track twisted and turned, they were treated again to a hundred and more marvelous sunlit and moonlit portraits of the *Grieving White Mountain*. Chuck couldn't know whether Coyote was there with them, but Rappy was strangely silent as they shared those very real still life paintings of that special mountain.

There was again room on the deck for them to make up blanket and backpack beds. After their extreme exertion and loss of sleep in getting the tangerine cart over the hill, they were now free to sleep, and sleep they did.

Two lady farmers with a half dozen bound chickens came aboard and plopped on the deck near where they were sleeping. Luckily the chickens made enough fuss to awaken them in time for them to get off the train at Offuna.

The Offuna to Yokohama train ride was easy. They had perfected their technique of avoiding the people who seemed to enjoy despising them. And a different conductor ignored them completely.

Exiting the station at Yokohama, they were happy to find that the lady in the white flowered kimono was not frozen in place where they had last seen her.

While they waited to hitch a ride on a G.I. truck or jeep, they had time to examine a phenomenon, the old, black Japanese taxi cabs that were waiting for fares in front of the station. They were apparently powered by regular internal combustion engines. What was arresting about them was a large black box on the rear bumper. The box contained a charcoal burner, smoke stack and all. How the hell it worked to power the cab is anybody's guess. After awhile when no G.I. vehicle had come by, the pilgrims went over and asked a cab driver if he would take occupation script money. In accented English, he said he would. Their next question was,

216

"How much for two, to go to the *Kincaid* at Sasabo shipyard?"

He thought a moment then said, "Five dallah."

They piled into the ancient black motor car and in what seemed no time at all, they were at the gate to the shipyard in Sasabo. They could see the *Kincaid;* she looked great! She was out of dry dock and tied up at an outfitting pier. She was obviously about ready to go to sea. They had made it!

The pilgrims gave the cabbie twice the price he had asked; then running down the pier toward their ship, they looked at each other. They knew that few would believe their story and fewer still would understand it. They, themselves, had a lifetime to try to figure it out. The white kid, because he didn't have Coyote to help him, would never fully understand the incredible depth of their pilgrimage to the *Grieving White Mountain*; the mountain the Japanese people call Fuji San.

-*-

Story Eleven

Interlude

The Union Pacific Streamliner, *City of Omaha,* glided silently westward. Through the viewing windows of the train's club car, the rolling Nebraska prairies had disappeared. They were lost in a silent world of swirling whiteness. The heavily falling snow seemed to isolate each car from the others and from the sounds that normally filter upward from the wheels on the steel road.

The whirling, wind-borne snow that spun past the window was hypnotic and silently threatening. It struck the viewer as not unlike that of a standing cobra that makes soundless moves intended to prepare its victim for the silent death that is surely coming. The enormity of the threat that lurks in the velvety mouth of a cobra is dwarfed by the numbingly lethal threat wrapped in the churning white folds of the storm that had taken charge of the world beyond the window glass.

A line of cottonwood trees trace each bank of the Platte River. The river itself dictated the route chosen by the Union Pacific Railroad across western Nebraska. Through the swirling clouds of snow, those route-defining cottonwoods could be seen only occasionally. When they appeared, they were ghostly shadows that fled past the window like exorcised dark spirits.

The powerful *City of Omaha* seemed unaware of it, but the road she was traveling that morning had already begun its climb from Nebraska's broad prairies and rolling Sandhills to the high Plains and mountains of Wyoming.

The train's conductor entered the car and touched the arm of the young man who was sitting transfixed at the window. A cup of coffee, grown cold, was forgotten in his hand. Though he was in a business suit, in this land of winter, his suntanned features and crew-cut hair made the conductor suspect that he was a sailor. The sharp business suit he wore had been custom made at a shop on the Strand in Hong Kong. The conductor had business in mind so he was looking for expensive business suits.

The conductor asked of the young man, "What's your name, son?"

The young man turned from the window to look at him then answered, "It's Chuck Farritor, sir. Why do you ask?"

"Mr. Farritor, I want to thank you for traveling Union Pacific. It so happens that we have empty berths in the Pullman cars. I've come by to see if you'd like to upgrade to one."

For just $9 cash, the prosperous-appearing young man could have a Pullman berth for the run into Los Angeles. This would certainly be a good deal for the young fellow and, of course, a sweet deal for the conductor; cash leaves no trail and for that cash he had a special inner pocket in his uniform jacket.

Not as prosperous as he looked, the young sailor struggled for a moment before making the $9 decision. In a show of good judgment, he shook the man's hand and left therein a $10 bill. He then followed his investment aft to the high rent district where he was shown his Pullman berth.

He moved his gear from the chair car and had just settled into his new digs when the train slowed and stopped. After awhile it moved, then stopped again. It continued, fitfully starting and stopping until it eventually stopped completely.

Knowing that the bar in the club car is always the best place to find out what's going on, the sailor made his way to that place of refreshment and information. The bartender's name was Pete.

"Good morning, Pete, I'll have a black coffee." The hoped-for information came with the coffee.

Pete confided in his Chicago accent, "Word is, 'tween here and Cheyenne there's a train and a snow plow near buried in drifted snow. Lord help the poor souls on that train." The young sailor sipped the hot coffee while he absorbed that information, then Pete dropped the almost unbelievable news that, "Our train is standing on the mainline in front of the depot at North Platte, Nebraska an' we ain't goin' nowhere for a while."

It was indeed unbelievable that at high noon on this third day of January 1949, the imposing old depot at North Platte could not be seen at all. It was completely hidden behind a whirling curtain of white. "Pete, my name is Chuck, I'm a sailor. From what you're telling me, it sure sounds like I may miss my ship!"

The bartender expressed regret, then said, "They won't shoot ya' fer that." Then seemingly using better judgment, he said, "O' course ya' could get some hard time on a rock pile! Mind ya' now, a little time spent bustin' rocks could be character buildin'."

The young man grinned but offered no comment on any of that; he was mulling another thought. In light of this new information, he saw an immediate need to consolidate his claim to that now priceless Pullman berth. After asking around, he found that the porter for his Pullman car was a man named Winston. He found Winston and gave him the tip expected for the run into Los Angeles. He then made a deal with him. He, not Winston, would be responsible for making the bed and keeping his area policed for any nights beyond this one until they reached Los Angeles. Winston okayed the plan.

At lunchtime, the dining car was abuzz. The passengers were showing signs of unease but were calmed by the usual elegance of the setting in the car. In that place, good taste and tradition held fast. Brilliant white linens covered the tables. Each place was marked by a setting of heavy, brightly polished silverware and accented by an artfully folded, gold-colored, heavy linen napkin. Seemingly in direct defiance of the weather outside, a cut crystal vase in the center of each table proudly displayed a bouquet of fresh spring flowers.

The black steward and his waiters were dressed sharply in their dark uniforms. Their friendly faces above starched white shirts and black bowties assured the public they were ready to do everything possible to make each guest glad that he or she had come to this place for lunch. Chuck ordered a roast beef sandwich and a beer. The large very blond lady across the table from him asked for the chef's special, a "cattleman's cut steak with eggs," the steak to be rare and the eggs sunny side up. The young sailor was able to eat up and excuse himself before he had to witness the inglorious mixing in her plate of the red blood from the rare steak and the yolks from two nearly raw eggs.

The sailor was prepared for the weather outside. He had been home over the holidays visiting his folks, who had retired from the ranch and bought a house on South Jay Street in Broken Bow, Nebraska. Only a fool would venture into that country in December without winter gear. After lunch, he donned his overshoes and heavy parka. He knew that beyond the wall of white, the Hotel Pawnee stood across the street from the depot and in that fine hotel, the *Bull Rider Bar* enjoyed a statewide reputation for hospitality. He'd check out the action there.

Winston informed him that a rope had been strung from the door of the club car to the door of the depot. The depot not ten yards away could not be seen. The rope led him into a churning bank of whiteness. The near-gale-force wind out of the northwest threatened to blow him, "Dorothy style," not out of but over into Kansas. With the help of what a sailor would call a "lifeline," he successfully made his way into the depot waiting room.

The severe weather had made it impossible to heat the large, old nineteenth-century-style waiting room. Though unheated, the room gave immediate relief from the wind and the killing cold outside. He paused for a few moments to renew his acquaintance with this beautiful old high-ceilinged room. Fine snow was somehow finding its way through the many high windows. The snow wafting down from the high ceiling gave the silent room an eerie other-world dimension.

This venerable old depot had in its long life seen 10,000 and more moments of human drama. More than a few mail-order brides met their husbands-to-be for the first time here. Those brides stayed on to build lives and families. They pressed their husbands, then their sons and daughters, to build schools, churches and towns. When that was done, they pressed them to build cities and universities.

Hundreds of their young sons left through this room to fight in their country's wars. Wars have a way of not returning all of the young men they take. To each mother whose son did not come back, the missing lad would forever be the nineteen-year-old lad who had smiled and shyly embraced her as he said goodbye to her here in this room.

Thousands of World War II servicemen from all over the country hold special memories for this room and the large platform outside. Throughout the war years, women from North Platte and the surrounding small towns, farms and ranches (as far away as Broken Bow) supplied and served thousands of delicious meals and unknown numbers of cookies and donuts to several hundred traveling servicemen daily. The meals were free and were served with love, thanks, and most surely a host of silent prayers. Those prayers asked that each serviceman or woman that they fed would be allowed a safe return to home and family. Most of the women serving those meals had sons, daughters, husbands, uncles, aunts or lovers at some battle station in the outer world. Those servicemen and women were doing their best to bring the war to an end. The western Nebraska women who served up all of that delicious food were doing the same.

Out on Front Street, without the aid of a lifeline, the sailor managed to get safely across the street and into the friendly confines of the *Bull Rider Bar*. The bull to be ridden in that place was a leather and steel monster that, if you climbed aboard and inserted two-bits in the coin slot, would like to shake your eyebrows loose or, if you let go, throw you halfway across the room.

Filled with a wide mix of folks seeking refuge from the storm, the bar hummed with activity. The afternoon and evening were spent riding and slinging the bull. He swapped mostly "blizzard" and "storms at sea" stories with the many instant friends he found there.

Earlier in the small hours of the morning on that same third day of January 1949, another train, the *Los Angeles Limited*, had stopped at North Platte to take aboard a few passengers. After only a brief pause, she sped away into the night expecting to be in Cheyenne soon after dawn on her way to her namesake city in far-off Southern California.

Only a few miles west of North Platte, she ran headlong into a frightening change of weather. She had forced her way through hundreds of snowstorms in her many years of crossing the continental divide, but what she encountered this morning was not the usual winter storm. She ran into a storm with wind velocities and snow volume that few men on the eastern slope had ever before experienced. The storm would spread its death-dealing fury without mercy over broad reaches of the states of Wyoming, South Dakota and Nebraska. Its prolonged wrath would kill thousands of animals both wild and domestic. It would kill a hundred and more people as well.

The *Los Angeles Limited* knew nothing of all this. She only knew that her powerful headlamp could throw its light most of a mile down the track. Now suddenly she found that her light was being stopped only a few feet ahead of the engine. It was being blocked by an impenetrable wall of swirling snow. The snow was being driven by gusting, twisting, nearly gale-force winds. The temperature had plummeted to 26 degrees below zero.

There was no choice for the engineer but to dim his light and proceed at a fraction of his assigned speed. Running blind, he had no way to know whether the tracks even existed ahead of him. He understood clearly that this was no ordinary storm and that it was very important that he get his train over the grade ahead and into the safety offered by the Union Pacific yards at Cheyenne.

Because of his reduced speed and the rising grade, his engine soon had trouble dealing with the rock-hard drifts of snow that the shifting winds were building on the tracks. To get through some of the drifts required that he back up and hit the drift a second or third time. Hope was fading that he could bring his train into the railroad yards at Cheyenne.

The dispatchers in Cheyenne were aware of the need to give aid to the *Los Angeles Limited*. They sent a snowplow powered by three engines out to meet her. The snowplow soon found herself with zero visibility while bucking rock-hard drifts more than 20 feet deep. Facing the real possibility of stalling on the open prairie, the crew of the plow made the decision to stop at the hamlet of Hillsdale, Wyoming.

When the *Los Angeles Limited* reached Hillsdale, a decision was made that it was too dangerous to go further, even with the support of the multi-engine snowplow.

The high-plains road-crossing of Hillsdale had only a Union Pacific depot, a small market, a schoolhouse, a small church and three or four houses. It offered little security for the more than 200 people on the train, plus the crews of the train and the snowplow.

The population of 21 souls who lived in Hillsdale were themselves at risk in a blizzard as dangerous as this one. The electrical power supply had already been cut by the storm.

The powerful Los Angles Limited came to rest alongside the tiny Hillsdale Union Pacific Depot. She had sped past this humble building hundreds of times, each time giving it only a shrill blast from her whistle. Now she lay in its tiny lee like an exhausted dragon asking succor. She knew that lacking the external support that the major yard at Cheyenne could have provided, she would slowly but surely die here. Her sole hope in stopping was that, in so doing, her passengers and crew might be given a better chance to survive the storm. She would do her best to keep herself alive. She could keep the fires roaring under her boilers but while she lay here inert, the extreme cold would soon cause every exposed water and steam line that ran her length plus every greased bearing and moving part in her system to freeze up. The blowing snow would drift into all the sheltered voids up under her. In a few hours, she would be a solid block of steel, ice and frozen snow. In that same time, her great powers would have deserted her. She would then have lost all of her ability to keep her passengers and crew from joining her in a frozen death.

Her passenger list included all kinds of folks; families returning home after visiting with other family back East, businessmen and women back out on the road after the holiday break. There were cattle buyers, whiskey drummers, siding salesmen and servicemen, and also a large contingent of college students returning to classes.

Two bright young ladies in that age group were not returning to classes. They had just graduated from the Mountainside Hospital, School of Nursing at Montclair, New Jersey. Their names were Muriel and Mary Jane. The pretty green-eyed one with short, wavy blonde hair was Mary Jane Craig. Her lovely, blue-gray-eyed friend with curly brown hair was Muriel Teeling.

This was the first time either of them had ventured any farther west than a summer camp in the Pocono Mountains of eastern Pennsylvania. This train was to deliver them to Southern California. There in the California sunshine, they, along with other happy travelers, were to be feted with music, flowers and festive doings as they were welcomed aboard the flagship of the Matson Steamship Lines, the sleek and beautiful *S.S. Lurline.* After an expected picture-book voyage on the blue Pacific, the two young women were to take up positions as registered nurses at Queens Hospital in Honolulu.

For the most part, the clothes they had with them were the clothes they expected to wear in that perennially 72-degree paradise in the Central Pacific. Luckily, it was cold and snowing the day they boarded the train in New Jersey, so they were wearing light winter coats and overshoes. When the train stopped at Hillsdale, they were snugly abed in their private compartment.

At about seven a.m. on that third day of January, they awoke with their teeth chattering. They couldn't see anything out the window except a strange whiteness. A glass of water on their small table was frozen. They gathered up all the blankets they could find and together climbed into the lower bunk to try to get warm. They knew without being told that the train had stalled.

After a while, they got up and put on several layers of the warmest clothes they had. Breakfast in the elegant dining car was almost normal. The Steward and his crew did what they could to reassure everyone that everything would be all right.

Passing through the cars on their way back to their compartment, it became clear to them that the available heat was being sent to the chair cars where most of the older people and children were. The club car seemed also favored. It required no debate to decide to spend the day in the club car. They quickly made friends among the crowd of young people who gathered there. One young fellow from Omaha asked them if they played bridge. His name was Jack Moore. He was an ex-sailor and now law student returning to classes at the University of Montana. They spent the day making friends. They even played some bridge. The blizzard continued to rage outside.

The limited menu at dinner gave clear warning that food supplies were running low. This train was by now supposed to be nearing Los Angeles where it would be quickly refitted and restocked for its next trip east. It was dark and still snowing heavily when they finished dinner. As they passed through the cars on their way back to the club car, they found that some of the doors between the cars, once pushed open were refusing to close. This was allowing snow to drift into the cars.

When the heat failed in the club car at about eight p.m., the girls made their way to their compartment to go to bed. The porter had given them heavy woolen socks and an extra blanket apiece. They put all their blankets and their coats on the lower bunk and climbed in together. With their heads under the covers, they slept cuddled like a couple of hibernating bear cubs until nine a.m. on January 4. They got up and made ready to face the day as best they could with frozen plumbing. On their way to the dining car, they found that the floor and every horizontal surface inside the cars were coated with a half-inch layer of fine snow. There were hard drifts between the cars that had to be climbed over.

As they made their way along, their blue-gray and green eyes were about all that showed as they clutched blankets about themselves wintering Indian style. In one of the Pullman cars, a huge man they knew to be a cattle buyer stood in the door of his compartment. Under his wide-brimmed hat and graying hair, his friendly, weathered face was partially hidden behind a heavy, white mustache. He was holding a fifth of Scotch in his hand. His blue eyes asked them to pause a moment. "Good morning ladies. If ever I saw two lady Indians in need of a good belt of Irish whisky, I'm lookin' at 'em now." He turned to pick up a shot glass from the table in the compartment behind him. With a certain flourish, he filled the shot glass once, then again. The straight shot was a first for either girl. After the initial shock, they found that the fiery liquid had touched their lips like a puppy's warm kiss and had warmed their innards like a cup of hot cocoa.

Arriving at the dining car, they found that the blizzard had at last defeated its elegant spirit. The chief steward was now unshaven and looked ill. His normally handsome black face had a troubled gray look. The car was a shambles; everything was covered with a near inch-deep layer of sifted snow. With the steam lines from the engine frozen and all the batteries now dead, the crew had no way to do any cooking. The girls were each given a small dish of powdered eggs and two pieces of frozen bread. There was nothing to drink; they had only the memory of that imagined cup of hot cocoa. The heavy, bright silverware stuck to their lips threatening to tear their skin. They left the dining car hungry and for the first time they felt fear.

They couldn't see out of any window but they knew that it was still a blizzard outside; the temperature seemed stuck at twenty-six below. All systems on the train had shut down. Each girl was thinking, *"I'm glad Mother and Daddy don't know just how bad things are here."*

They felt some relief when they learned that the train crew was out in the blowing snow trying to break a trail to the unseen Hillsdale depot. The plan was to move everyone into the depot before night fell again. Miserable as conditions were on the train, some of the older people and mothers with young children were terrified at the thought of going outside to face the wind and the bitter cold. As the depot could not be seen through the storm, not everyone was convinced that it even existed.

As the train crew moved them out into the storm, many were crying hysterically but, it seemed, silently. Their human sounds were whisked away and buried beneath the whipping sounds of the drifting snow and the keening voices of the wind.

Two hundred and more people eventually spilled out of the now dead *Los Angeles Limited.* Jack Moore and his strong young friends guided and carried those less strong. No one was lost. All hands gained the shelter of the depot that did indeed exist at the end of the trail blazed by the train crew.

They found that the depot consisted of a waiting room, a baggage room and the three-room living quarters for the station master and his family. There were two coffee cups on the kitchen table and a glass half filled with milk; the milk in the glass was frozen. As on the train, snow had sifted in, covering everything. One had to wonder where the family was. Were they safe?

The building was immediately full to overflowing with the refugees. There was no water in the taps at the kitchen sink and the storm had cut the electricity. A coal-burning stove stood in each room. The stoves were soon burning warmly. The heat from the stoves plus the body heat of well over two hundred people soon had the upper part of the rooms unbearably hot while the floors remained stone cold and, of course, wet with the now-melted snow.

On the trip in from the train, snow was driven into everyone's clothes and hair by the force of the wind. With this snow now melting in the heat from the stoves, steam began to rise off everyone. The high humidity in the rooms made it difficult for many folks to breathe. The train crew brought all the blankets in from the train. Even with the blankets, conditions were not good for those who found it necessary to immediately lie down on the cold, wet floor.

The two young nurses, Muriel and Mary Jane, were the only ones present with any medical training. They were soon beset with fainting people. They went to work with gauze pads and smelling salts from a first aid kit they found on the absent Station Master's desk. They asked the conductor to have one window in each room opened a bit, and they insisted that smoking be allowed in only the baggage room.

An elderly man fainted dead away. They'd been drawn to him earlier because of the lovely child with him. It turned out that he was delivering the six-year-old child, his granddaughter, home to her family in Los Angeles. She had been visiting her grandparents in Chicago. Muriel was afraid he'd had a heart attack. They eventually got him to come around; he was having difficulty breathing but seemed to have no arm or chest pain so they were much relieved.

The Steward had salvaged 12 large cans of tomato soup from the train; these were emptied into a large kettle and placed on top of the stove in the waiting room. Muriel fed their elderly friend a cup of that precious soup; it seemed to revive him but did little to ease the fear in the eyes of the grandchild.

The storm had apparently caught the railroad family away from home. A small Christmas tree graced their living room, and a tiny new tricycle sat near it. An empty box with a picture of a china-faced doll with golden hair lay nearby. The doll had apparently gone visiting with its new little mother. A corner of the living room had been screened off to make a tiny bedroom for the girl-child who had received the doll and tricycle for Christmas. It was best not to think about where their host family might be.

Before night fell, the conductor found a stash of candles in a closet. In spite of the obvious fire danger, these candles were a godsend. They avoided the rash of panic attacks that would surely have occurred if the crush of human beings jammed in that space were required to spend the night in total darkness.

A lifeline was strung to a two-hole privy that stood 20 yards to the rear of the depot. After darkness fell, it was deemed too dangerous to allow people to go out to the privy alone. The college-student group soon organized themselves into necessary brigades. Jack Moore and others took charge of those efforts. They blocked a corner of the shipping room off with hanging blankets to create his and her "restrooms," each screened space contained three cold but quite receptive "honey buckets."

Guts had a lot to do with the choice of volunteer duty. The really brave ones took on the task of emptying the honey buckets at the outside privy. Others tended the fires and brought in buckets of snow to be melted for drinking water and for making coffee. The coffee was God-awful but life restoring. College freshmen were not allowed on either the honey bucket or the fresh water detail for fear they'd get the buckets mixed up.

Muriel and Mary Jane were on their feet the whole night. People were still fainting and severe colds were beginning to surface. A cacophony of throat noises and sneezes filled the rooms in the near darkness.

Grim as the situation was, friendships began to emerge. In the small hours of the morning, Muriel was at the kitchen sink washing coffee cups in melted snow water, when a young soldier offered to help. He said, "I've been noticin' all you're doin' an' I'm thinkin' you need a break." He pulled a bottle of wine out of a pocket of his G.I. field jacket. Let's find a couple of glasses an' check out the bouquet of this grape."

Muriel looked at the bottle and wondered how in the world that bottle of Gallo port could have possibly survived to be here in this place at this incredible time. She said, "That's the best offer I've had all day! I have two friends. May I ask them to join us?"

The young soldier replied, "Sure. You get 'em while I find four glasses." He rummaged in the kitchen wall cabinets while Muriel rounded up Jack and Mary Jane.

As a deadly blizzard raged in the darkness outside, four earnest young people from afar stood in a tiny candlelit kitchen in Wyoming. Engulfed in the sounds and smells of 200 and more people in four rooms trying to survive the night, these four young people stood with glasses in hand as expectantly as if they had stopped at an elite lounge on the Loop in Chicago to enjoy a glass of priceless sparkling burgundy.

The young soldier who had delivered that bottle of wine to this place offered the first toast, "I'm now AWOL exactly eight hours. Here's to the rifles in my execution squad. May they only pop and send out little American flags."

They all laughed and Muriel said, "May the *Coup de Grace-*officer's pistol do the same."

Jack offered, "Here's to new friendships, may they grow old."

Mary Jane, with moisture in her eyes said, "Here's to this moment, I know it will prove to be a special one for each of us. It will, I know, be a memory each of us will hold for the rest of our lives."

As they raised their glasses, the first light of the new day filtered through the frost on the window over the kitchen sink. They savored the grape. That Gallo port was indeed superior to any priceless burgundy being served anywhere under circumstances that were ordinary.

The special moment was short lived. A plea for help came from the baggage room. The girls put down their glasses and picked their way over sleeping people to find the person who was in trouble. Muriel hoped it would not be the elderly man with the pretty little granddaughter. It proved to be, instead a lady with two small children. She had not previously mentioned that she was pregnant. She was afraid that she'd had a labor pain. This, considering the impossibly crowded conditions, was a very heavy situation to deal with. They found a place for her to lie down and assured her that no matter what developed, everything would be all right. They silently prayed that this would be the case.

At daybreak of the new day, the storm abated but the temperature still hovered at 26 degrees below zero. As the sun tentatively showed his face, all of the older folks and most of the children were moved to the Hillsdale Church. Each person, if he or she were able, carried his or her own carryon luggage and blankets. The train crew, the college kids and some of the townsfolk helped those who needed assistance. At the church, as at the depot, there was no electricity, but gloriously there was tap water and functioning toilets. The honey-bucket brigade was disbanded with honors. Coal stoves that had been lit earlier provided priceless heat. The sifted-in snow had been swept from the floors so they were dry. All of the younger people were moved in the same manner to the nearby high school. Conditions there were much the same as at the church.

Late afternoon of that day just before dark, a low-flying Air National Guard C 47 dropped pallets of K-rations and bundles of blankets. A pallet of useless plug-in electric heaters struck the engine of the dead *Los Angeles Limited.* She fought back, by smashing the shipment to bits.

The move to the schoolhouse and church relieved the overcrowding and with that most of the immediate health problems. Muriel put the lady with the possible labor pain on actual "bed rest" and continued to hope for the best. She got others to care for the lady's two small children.

The reduction of the workload on the girls came just in time; Muriel in particular was showing signs of complete exhaustion. The Hillsdale high school coach, who had some first aid training, escorted her across the road to his house where his wife, Mildred, insisted that Muriel take a warm bath and go directly to bed. She was asleep the moment her head touched the pillow.

The dauntless Mary Jane spent a few hours asleep, wrapped in G.I. blankets on the floor at the schoolhouse then went over to tend to the folks at the church. The elderly man with the little granddaughter was there. Mary Jane was relieved to find that the better air in the church was making it easier for him to breathe.

Muriel slept until suppertime. The coach's wife had laid out a fresh blouse and sweater, plus underwear and socks for the sleeping girl. These things belonged to Mildred's daughter who was away at college. Muriel was appreciative of her host's thoughtfulness. Rested, fed and freshly clothed, she insisted on returning to the high school. The wind had died and the sky was clearing when she ventured outside. It was still very cold. The thermometer on the outside wall at the Coach's house read 28 degrees below zero.

After a supper of K-rations for all, the young crowd gathered in the music room at the schoolhouse. Muriel played the piano while everyone sang. Her repertoire was severely limited but no one seemed to notice. The group rendition of "On Top of Old Smoky" was the barnburner.

When things quieted down on the evening of the sixth of January 1949, Scotty, a young Wyoming cowboy and fellow passenger, asked the piano player to go for a walk. The snow under their feet made snapping sounds in the intense cold. They walked across the frozen drifts toward the depot. They wanted to pay their respects to the sad old *Los Angeles Limited.* They found her sprawled in the darkness like the frozen dead dragon that she was. Half buried by the drifts, her fiery breath stilled, she seemed to be waiting for more snow to complete the burial. The snow plow that had come to her aid had joined her in her frozen state. It too was nearly buried in snow and ice.

The depot was silent. No light came from the windows. Cold darkness prevailed at a small screened-off corner where a little girl had knelt at her bedside to say her prayers. There were no little-girl sounds in the room; she was not there to play with the tricycle that Santa Claus had brought for her.

To escape these thoughts, Muriel looked away to the sky. Stars without number were ablaze in the biggest and blackest sky she'd ever seen. One very bright, blue star especially caught her attention. It was Sirius. In his ancient wisdom, the all-seeing Dog Star knew that this lovely young lady would one day come to know him.

In Muriel's eyes, the stars were much the same ones she had seen in the skies over New Jersey, but here in this high country they had a brand new look. They were more plentiful, were brighter and sparkled more than any she'd seen before. They sparkled like the cupful of white diamonds she once saw a jeweler toss with a flourish onto a Louis the Fourteenth table covered with black velvet. This happened at Tiffany's in New York City. Her Aunt Millie had taken her there, probably to expose her to an aspect of the elite culture that her aunt was a part of in that great city.

Scotty broke the silence, "I apologize for the weather you've been seein' these past few days. Winter here in Wyoming is supposed to be more like what you're seein' here tonight. I think that storm some way slid down here out of Montana." Scotty continued, "We won't allow it to happen again soon."

Muriel shook off her melancholy. She smiled and thought, "*Scotty doesn't realize how funny he is.*" She laughed and said, "I accept your apology, Scotty. Your immigrant weather is awful but I must say your Wyoming sky is a thing of startling beauty."

Scotty said, "Shucks, out here you can get used to pretty stuff real easy."

As they turned to go back to the warm schoolhouse, they saw Jack and Mary Jane coming toward them. Muriel wondered if Jack would take responsibility for blizzards that slid out of Montana. She decided this was probably not the best time to ask. He and Mary Jane were absorbed in each other as they walked by under the brilliant Wyoming night sky.

Back in the schoolhouse, two guys from Idaho State asked Muriel and Scotty to play cards. The boys had been looking at a calendar on the wall. They said they were supposed to be playing basketball with their arch rival, Montana State, this very evening. After they played several hands of Gin, Muriel had won 80 cents.

Suddenly Jack Moore came running into the room. He announced, "A snow plow has come in from Cheyenne bringing five buses. They want to move everyone who will fit into the busses, down to Cheyenne this evening!"

Folks excitedly began preparing for the exodus. Muriel ran over to the church to check on the lady who had experienced possible labor pains; she seemed to be okay. Muriel and Mary Jane helped her and others who needed help to get on the buses.

On its way up to Hillsdale, the snowplow had bypassed 25 or more cars on the road. The grim task of digging those cars out and exposing their contents would fall to others at daybreak. Testifying to the sudden onset of the storm, most of the cars were well off the road. The drivers were very likely blinded by the sudden whiteout.

The bus ride down to Cheyenne was a rare and beautiful experience. The very cold night had the look and feel of moonlight but there was no moon. They were surrounded by a strange soft light created by starlight on the snow-covered land. All of the passengers, including Muriel and Mary Jane, were awe-struck by the sudden appearance of the rippling multicolored curtains of the aurora borealis. Appreciation for the striking beauty they were seeing in the northern sky was stronger than the heart-stopping fear that it can engender in some first-time observers.

Despite all of this beauty, Muriel and Mary Jane couldn't help wondering which of the half-buried cars they were passing might contain the little girl who is missing from her home in Hillsdale. They knew that if she should be in one of those cars, she would, in death still be holding closely her mom and dad and her new golden-haired, china-faced doll.

The headlights of the buses dutifully followed the long trail cleared by the snow plow. At Cheyenne, Scotty said goodbye. He would try to find a way out to his folk's ranch some 30 miles west of the city. At the "Eastern Slope Hotel," Jack Moore saw to it that the railroad would pay for hotel rooms for the refugees from the train. He and a young man from Laramie, Bill White, shared a room. Muriel, Mary Jane and Kay Brelin, a girl trying to get back to school at Scripps College at Claremont, California, jumped into the tub in their respective rooms. After a long hot soak, they each called home. This was the first word their folks had from them since they put their daughters on that train in New Jersey what seemed like an eon ago.

January 7 dawned beautifully in Cheyenne. The sky was cornflower blue and there was no wind. The temperature at ten degrees below zero seemed almost warm. Busses and trucks were arriving in town with baggage and the balance of the passengers from the *Los Angeles Limited.*

At eight a.m. Muriel showed up in the lobby, and then she, Bill White and Jack Moore walked over to the train station. The local paper had stories of the incredible size of the weather front; it had even snowed in Los Angeles! A picture taken from the air of the *Los Angeles Limited* showed her helplessly sad and alone. There was yet more to be sad about. As they feared, the Hillsdale Station Master, his wife and their five-year-old daughter were among those listed as dead in the storm. This sad news was eased by the fact that somehow they already knew. They learned from the Cheyenne station master that a local train was leaving at ten a.m. for Greely, Colorado. There they could catch a westbound train. They ran back to the hotel to get Mary Jane and Kay Brelin. They were the only ones from the *Los Angeles Limited* that had gotten up early enough to make that train. It got them into Greely at two p.m. There they at last had time to have their first complete meal. They dined at Sam's Café near the station.

The people back in Cheyenne, particularly the women, seemed to be almost in shock. They all had friends and family on remote ranches that had to be in danger; many had already been reported as missing. Which ones would be found dead?

The "blizzard of '49" transformed the sleepy, western town of Greeley, Colorado into a center for transcontinental railway service. The shock that showed on the people of Cheyenne was not evident here. Everyone was too busy! The frozen and buried trains on the main east/west line between North Platte, Nebraska, and Laramie, Wyoming, had rendered that line unusable. All westbound transcontinental traffic was being routed south and west from North Platte to Greeley on a freight-service line, then west and north on the same type line back to the main line at Green River, Wyoming.

These emergency conditions had brought about some interesting transformations. Bowlegged men who had until now ridden only cowponies, were now "railroaders." There was work aplenty to get things back to normal. Muriel was enchanted by one of those newly hired people. He said his name was "Smitty." He'd been hired as a redcap, carrying luggage for elders and talking to the refugee children. His bearded, friendly manner made his cowboy boots, leather chaps and wide-brimmed felt hat seem entirely ordinary in his new job. On the platforms, there were no prickly pear or Indian soap weed to ward off, but he said in his western drawl, "In this kinda' weather, I'd as soon go without ma' pants as to go without ma' chaps." A red bandana dropped from under his broad-brimmed hat to cover his ears and cheeks. It was tied under his chin next to a like colorful bandana tied around his neck.

In late afternoon, the sun disappeared and it began to snow again. The snow fell harmlessly; there were no vicious winds to drive it horizontally. Smitty said, "We c'n handle this kinda' snow real easy."

Word came that a train that had been held at North Platte during the storm would be coming through on its way to Los Angeles. It had put on extra Pullman cars so there would be plenty of berths for all those who wanted them. The train was the streamliner *City of Omaha,* she came through at seven p.m. The refugees who caught her found her to be a newer and fancier train, but they found her to have the same friendly atmosphere that made their old *Los Angeles Limited* so special. Muriel, Mary Jane and Kay Brelin slept well in their new Pullman berths. The chair cars were all full, so Jack Moore and Bill White had to hang out in the club car. Bill got off at Green River to go home.

Breakfast in the dining car was, if possible, even more elegant than their pre-blizzard experience on the *Los Angeles Limited.* Muriel and Mary Jane had breakfast with a blue-haired little lady who wanted to be called "Aunt Ruthie." When she quizzed them about their experience at Hillsdale, they talked readily about the small things, their distress over worrying their folks for so many days, and the problems with their messed-up schedule.

Aunt Ruthie said, "I'm just so sorry that you girls missed your boat to "Hawaya" but you know, I'm happy to tell you there's a nice young man on this train. He has a boat that's probably going that way. If you ask, I'm sure he'd love to just drop you off there. He took me to a wonderful movie in North Platte. He's just the nicest young man. You can probably find him in the club car. He stays there a lot drinkin' coffee and listenin' for news. I've told him that coffee's not good for him, but I'm happy to tell you, that's all he drinks."

After the Storm

Hillsdale, Wyoming Union Pacific crews, reclaiming the frozen Los Angeles Limited and the snow plow with its three engines that tried to rescue her. The snow plow ended up also a prisoner of the storm. – World Wide Photos

The two young nurses (left to right):
Muriel Teeling and Mary Jane Craig

Chuck Farritor, Chief Wheelman
U.S. Army Transportation Corps

Jack Moore, former Lt. J.G.
U.S. Navy

After breakfast the girls went back to their berths to get more rest. The night's sleep was great but it had just not been enough. They slept through lunch. That afternoon they looked around in the crowded club car to see if they could guess who the "nice young man" could be. Muriel spotted a young fellow who looked like he could be a sailor. Sure enough, there was a cup of coffee in his hand. She worked her way over and sat in an empty chair across the low table from him.

She said, "I think your coffee is cold."

Distracted from his study of a far mountain, he turned and said, "I can't tell you how many cups I let get away from me that way. May I get one for you? I must warn you, it has a bolt of lightning from the old sod in it."

"My father drinks Irish whiskey but not me; a glass of ice water would be wonderful."

Abandoning his interest in the far mountain, the young man went to the bar to freshen his drink and to get the requested glass of ice water.

When he got back from the bar, he set the glass of ice water in front of the new girl, then he said, "I could afford to buy drinks all day for a gal who only drinks ice water! I have ta' know your name."

Deferring his question, she said, "We have a mutual friend that says you have a boat that's going to Hawaii. My name is Muriel."

He looked at her for a long moment and said, "That's a beautiful name, I've never before met a girl named Muriel." She held his gaze for a moment then looked away.

He said, "My name is Chuck. I'm trying to figure who our mutual friend is. Whoever it is must be drinking something stronger than ice water. He or she should know that *boats* go to Catalina; a person with any smarts at all will take a *ship* to Hawaii,"

Muriel turned and said, "I appreciate that you like my name, but today I can do without a lecture in semantics, please excuse me." She stood up to leave.

The young man jumped up and put out his hand, "Please don't go, tell me about yourself. You must have come aboard last evening with the folks who were stalled on the train at Hillsdale. Can you tell me something of that?"

She sat down again; looking out the window at a far mountain of her own. She was absently toying with the ice cubes in her glass. The image of the frozen, half glass of milk that had belonged to a now dead little girl flashed again through her mind. When she turned, there were tears in her eyes. Quietly she said, "I can't talk about that just now." She turned to the window to gaze again at her own far mountain.

The young man made a guess and said, "An experience where death is a factor requires some time before you should expect to be able to talk about it. I'm waiting for time to pull a blanket over an image that I too am carrying in my head."

Muriel turned from the window, daubing at her eyes with a tiny handkerchief. She wanted to ask him to explain the loss he'd suffered, but the pain she saw in his eyes stopped her. She looked again at the far mountain. After a few moments, she turned, smiled at him and said, "I've changed my mind, tell me about the ships you sail on."

He seemed relieved. "Not much to tell. I've sailed on sea tugs, troop transports and hospital ships, then sometimes ammo and cargo ships. I'm presently assigned to the troopship *General McFall*. She's in for refitting in the Bay Area. She's been serving the troops in Japan and Korea. I wish what our mutual friend said was true, that I'd be going back to Hawaii. I love the Islands. Hawaii is the gentlest and most beautiful place on earth. Tell me about the circumstance that's sending you there?"

Her smile grew brighter still. She told him that she and her girlfriend were nurses trying to get to Honolulu to work there at Queen's Hospital.

Just as she finished speaking, a young couple came to their table, "Oh, Mary Jane and Jack! I want you to meet, oh my, I guess I don't know your full name."

The young man stood up and took Jack's hand. "Jack, my name's Chuck Farritor. Hi, Mary Jane, Muriel has told me about you. Won't you join us? What can I get for you to drink?"

Mary Jane said, "Thank you, we'd love to, but we can't stay. Jack's getting off at Salt Lake to catch a train north."

Jack said, "I'm glad to meet you, Chuck, I came to say goodbye to Muriel."

Muriel stood up and hugged Jack. She said, "Thank you Jack, we couldn't have made it through without you." She released him and sat down. She was crying. Jack stooped to kiss her on the forehead. As the young couple moved away toward the rear door of the club car, Mary Jane held tightly to Jack's arm. The train was slowing to enter the station at Salt Lake City. Muriel had again found a mountain outside the window to study. She daubed at her eyes with her tiny handkerchief.

It was obvious to Chuck that those three young people had been through a thing heavy enough to cause some serious bonding. They sat in silence. He joined Muriel in looking at her far mountain.

At the station in Salt Lake City, they saw a family gathering to greet a little blue-haired lady who got off the train. Chuck asked Muriel, "Is that our mutual friend?"

Muriel said, "You're right, that's Aunt Ruthie. How'd you guess?" She tapped on the window and waved. Aunt Ruthie smiled happily at them and waved back.

Chuck said, "I have to tell you, to help her kill time, I took that little charmer to a movie in North Platte. It was a rough slog through the storm getting to the theater but she was game. It was a double feature, "The Oxbow Incident" and another completely forgettable thing with Jose Iturbi at the piano and Eleanor Powell dancing. I don't believe she saw the "Oxbow Incident" at all; it was too grim for her. She loved the musical though, didn't miss a thing, told everyone on the train all about it."

Muriel said, "She's such a gentle soul. I wish I'd had more time to talk with her."

South of Salt Lake, the train zipped along through beautiful, snow-covered, mountain-rimmed valleys. At sundown, the sunset was so spectacular that almost everyone aboard saw it as a message of assurance that the storm was at last truly over.

January 8, 1949, a Friday, found the *City of Omaha* dashing across the hot California deserts. After climbing through a final pass, she dropped into the Los Angeles basin. As the train glided westward along the base of the snow-covered San Gabriel Mountains, she stopped at the small college town of Claremont to let Kay Brelin and others off. Her next stop would be the beautiful Union Pacific Station in the City of the Angels.

They said their goodbyes. Chuck wished them well and said, "Hope to see you in Honolulu!" The train slowed and stopped in the station. When the doors opened, a flood of humanity spilled out onto the platform like beans out of a bag. Muriel and Mary Jane, wrestling with their carry-on luggage, found their way to a payphone and stopped there.

In the midst of the fleeing horde, just before he dashed down the stairs to the tunnel that led to the station, Chuck turned and looked back. What he saw stopped him short. The two pretty girls were standing on the now vacant platform in front of an idle payphone. They looked like they were either out of change or out of people to call.

What the hell, considering he was running a week late now, what was he hurrying for? He would go back to see what could be done to get them off of that station platform. It turned out that they were hoping the person who was to meet them when they were scheduled to arrive in L.A. a week ago would somehow be there to meet them today. That poor guy was probably scanning the out-of-town obituaries in the Times, expecting to find their names there.

Muriel's dad, an executive at Manhattan/Raybestos of Passaic, New Jersey, had arranged for his company's Southern California representative, a Mr. Carlton Houser, to meet the girls at the train. Mr. Houser was to shepherd them from the train to the place where they would board the "S.S. Lurline." The girls had called the number they had for Mr. Houser. There was no answer. Either, poor Mr. Houser, fearing reprisals from Passaic over a botched job had committed Hari Kari, or he had decided, "To hell with it, I'm keeping my weekend date in Palm Springs with my girlfriend!" Whatever the case, Mr. Houser seemed to be out of the picture.

Chuck suggested a call to Matson Lines to possibly find space on another of their ships. The Matson line people said it would be five days before their cargo/passenger ship the *Hawaian Farmer* would be sailing for Honolulu. That didn't seem to offer an immediate solution. They picked up their things and went to the baggage area in the station. They were harboring doubts but were hoping to find their checked bags there. Almost incredibly everything was there and intact. The "cowboy railroaders" had worked a miracle. Those bags had somehow been snatched from the frozen bowels of the dead "*Los Angeles Limited*" and delivered to the baggage counter in Los Angeles to coincide with their owners' arrival there. An amazing feat indeed!

As nothing was likely to be resolved until Monday morning, it occurred to Chuck that the next order of business was to get these two young ladies off the street. He loaded them, bag and baggage, into a taxi and took them to a conservative business hotel in the city, the Hotel Alexandria. He checked them in there and suggested that they call home for some advice on how to get the rest of the way to the Islands.

The reason Chuck had come through L.A. on his way back to his ship in the Bay Area was to visit his sister Ann and her family. They lived in a suburb south of the city. He gave the girls his sister's phone number, then caught the red train to his sister's house. He'd stay overnight, then catch a train north to his shipping-out station, which was the Oakland Army Base across the bay from San Francisco.

He was stretched out on the couch in his sister's living room, listening to the UCLA/Stanford basketball game on the radio. It was, as always, a battle. With six seconds to play, the score was tied at 63. It was UCLA's ball out of bounds at mid court. He heard the phone ring and was glad it had nothing to do with him.

When his sister appeared at his elbow, his attention was focused on the action picture being painted by the voice on the radio. His sister said, "Look at me! It's some girl named Muriel; she says she and Mary Jane would like to go see Hollywood."

He said, "Yah', I didn't tell you about her." He turned his attention back to the radio. Several voices were shouting at once, the game was over. He had no idea what had happened in the final seconds.

He stood up and went to the phone in the kitchen. He said, "Muriel, don't tell me the hotel is on fire and you guys have to get out!"

The perfectly composed voice on the phone said, "Now don't be silly, we've both taken heavenly baths and we've called home. We now know what we're going to do; we're going to fly to Honolulu. The only question is what are we going to do tonight?"

Putting off her question, Chuck asked, "If you guys had the radio on, is there any chance you can tell me whether UCLA just might have won the game?"

Muriel said, "My goodness, what is a UCLA?"

He said, "I'd rather not have to explain that right now. Tell you what, now that I'm on my feet, I'm practically on the train back to the city, see you in 45." There went the relaxed visit with his sister and her family!

They went to Hollywood. After the mandatory rubberneck walk on the boulevard looking for movie stars and to see the busy marquees, they went dancing at Earl Carroll's famous Theatre/Restaurant. They danced among a smattering of real-life Hollywood stars and starlets. They tried their best to act like this was something they did every Saturday night.

A good-looking marine asked Chuck if he could ask Mary Jane to dance. Chuck said, "It's OK with me, marine. Her name is Mary Jane. Why don't you ask her?" He did and they did. On the dance floor, Muriel reached out and touched Rod Cameron. Chuck and "Rod" tried not to notice. The two young couples had a fun evening at "Earl Carroll's." Their evening in Hollywood ended with the marine getting on a bus back to his base at El Toro. They took a taxi back to the Hotel Alexandria, and for Chuck, the red train south to the suburbs.

It was six a.m. when the red train delivered Chuck back to his sister's house. Her husband, Bart, was just leaving for his usual Sunday morning round of golf. After a few hours of sleep on the couch, Chuck said goodbye to his sister and her beautiful young daughter, Jean Rae, then took the red train back to the city. He met the girls for supper at "Cliftons," a unique eatery in downtown L.A. After prolonged goodbyes there, the girls went back to their hotel by taxi, and Chuck stumbled aboard the "Lark," the night train to the Bay Area. He would sleep the night through in a chair car. Nothing, absolutely nothing, would disturb him. He would be back to his ship come Monday morning.

After his service on the good ship *U.S.A.T. Kincaid,* Chuck was delighted when he had again been assigned to the

U.S.A.T. General McFall. On Arrival in Oakland, he found that the *McFall* had just moved from the shipyard to a pier at the army base. The crew were working on the ship but had still not moved back aboard.

He reported to Mr. Wilson, the first officer. Considering the fact that he was a week late in getting back to his ship, he was a bit apprehensive. Mr. Wilson looked up from his paperwork and said, "Well I'll be damned! Chief, we've been getting news stories about a lot of cows and folks being dead in that storm up there in Nebraska and Wyoming, we were afraid maybe you was dead among 'em." He got out of his chair and came around his desk. Instead of a chewing out for being late, he gave the young sailor a bear hug. After the greeting, Mr. Wilson said, "Chief, we'll have a new skipper this trip. Captain Neilson's father died; he's back in Maine burying him now. His dad was a tough old bird and a great sea captain. Did you know that he was with Bartlett on the 'Roosevelt' when they delivered Peary to the North Pole?"

Chuck sensed Mr. Wilson's genuine sorrow at the passing of another colorful old, canvas sailor. He said, "Mr. Wilson, I'm sorry to hear of Captain Neilson's loss, thanks for telling me. If anyone is looking for me, sir, I'll be on the flying bridge."

His job as Chief Wheelman gave him the responsibility of caring for the bridge and its equipment. After the stay in the shipyard, he knew that a lot of things would be needing attention.

The girls found that the next "Pan Pacific Clipper" to Honolulu and beyond would fly out of San Francisco on Monday morning. They arrived in San Francisco by air on Sunday at eight p.m. Muriel's dad had called the Northern California representative for the Manhattan Raybestos

Company. That fine gentleman had arranged the flight and booked a room for them at the Saint Francis Hotel on Union Square. They found this hotel and their room several notches upscale from their digs at the Alexandria in Los Angeles.

When they got settled in at their beautiful eighth-floor room, it was about ten p.m. Using a mother-of-pearl inlaid bedside phone, Muriel dialed a number that Chuck had given her. It was his best guess as to where he might be. The ringing phone was a payphone on the wall in a kind of sterile holding tank at the Oakland Army Base, a place where "on the bricks sailors" could flop. Most of the crew of the *McFall* were there while their ship was in dry dock. A ship's carpenter off another ship who had just come in the front door, several sheets to the wind, answered the phone. After a few minutes of confused conversation, he left the receiver hanging on its cord while he staggered down the hallway banging on doors. He'd open each door and yell in his west Texas best. "They's ah' broad ona' phone, lookin' fer some 'cluck' named Chuck." (This is a cleaned-up version of his message.)

Eventually, the named "cluck" climbed out of a deep sleep and his warm sack. Standing in his skivvies in the half-light of a barren corridor, his bare feet doing their best to deal with the cold tile floor, he put the receiver to his ear. He could hear two girls talking. He said, "Muriel, you're going to tell me that your plane had to land on Catalina and you'd like to go dancing at the casino in Avalon."

The answer came back as sweet as sugar cane. "Not quite, Mr. Wise Guy. We found that we had to come to San Francisco to fly to Hawaii. We're at the Saint Francis Hotel. We don't fly out 'til tomorrow. We were just wondering?" There was a short silence, time for a male reality check.

Then Chuck said. "I have no idea what time it is, but if you two will promise to stay out of trouble 'til I can get there, I'll take you to what has to be a very late supper."

At number 9, Fishermen's Wharf, they had fresh jumbo prawns fried in butter at $1.10 a plate. A chilled bottle of Chablis was theirs for a $1.20. Then a walk and two cable car rides took them to the top of the city's seventh hill where the Mark Hopkins Hotel stands in unique splendor. The revolving nightclub at the "Top of the Mark" overlooks the world. As the large room with its exterior walls of glass turned on its axis, they could see the Bay Bridge, the City, the Golden Gate Bridge, the North and East Bay and Treasure Island. The booth they found themselves in was in the "corner of tears," the spot where tradition has it that wives and sweethearts gather for mutual comfort as they weep for their husbands or lovers as they sail out through the Golden Gate. Chuck said, "I expect you gals to be right here weeping as I'm sailing out through that gate come Thursday morning."

They laughed and said in unison, "Fat chance!"

At four a.m. they took a taxi to The Shadows, a beautiful night spot on a lesser hill near Coit Tower. The maitre d' took it in stride when they ordered breakfast. Over coffee, scrambled eggs and hash browns they again said goodbye. Chuck then put the girls in a taxi back to the Saint Francis, while he jumped on a cable car, then a streetcar down Market Street to the electric train that took him back across the Bay Bridge to the *General McFall* She was now tied up at the Oakland Army Base and would soon be loaded and ready to sail.

The *McFall* would sail this time to Korea, then through the Strait of Malacca and Suez to Europe. There she would bring another load of Displaced Persons out of Germany, taking them to South America.

To pick up the bodies after the train wreck that was Hitler's Germany was a monstrous task. People in numbers almost beyond count had been forced to find refuge in the Displaced Person Camps of Europe. They were held in the camps until some country agreed to accept them. Chuck had made one of those D.P. mercy trips before, delivering the D.P.s to South American countries.

The generous countries of South America took the D.P.s as they were. All were mentally and physically brutalized. Many had trouble making it up the gangway to board the ship. Some were carried, barely alive, down the gangway and delivered into the arms of the South American people. Those who had not survived the trip were buried at sea.

At sea, the dead were delivered each day to a volunteer detail of the ship's crew. Those men of the sea did what must be done. Chuck had regularly served on those details. The dead were people of all ages. Their spirit had seen them through countless impossible battles of survival under the Nazis. Now with their guard down, in the kind hands of their rescuers, their spirits had quietly surrendered to the accumulated damage that had been done to their bodies. The young American sailors respectfully delivered them to the sea. Like the wonderful people of South America, the sea also accepted them as they were. It quietly and gently folded itself over them.

Chuck went aboard the *McFall* at 0800 hours. After reporting to the on-duty watch officer, he went up to the flying bridge; he planned to air out the signal flags. Those flags and pennants were stored in two deep canvas-covered steel tubs, one tub on either side of the flying bridge. The flags were each suspended independently on rails in the tubs.

Just as he expected, the flags were damp and showing mold on some of the bottom ends. He started the colorful task of stringing them up on the halyards. These were the same halyards that he and his friend Eddie Boone had replaced with new material, when not all that long ago they had repainted this foremast.

The flags and pennants would dry out and be renewed as they flew in the warm, morning sunshine. By the chance placing of the flags, it was possible to spell out some unintended message. It did, indeed happen sometimes. He'd keep watch and head off any smart-ass comments from other ships' signalmen. He got a pair of watch binoculars out of their weatherproof storage cabinet. As he scanned the other ships berthed at the piers, he noticed particularly a small clean freighter tied up across the slip from the *McFall*.

The freighter had shed her wartime gray and was sporting the new peacetime colors. The hull was black with the superstructure buff and white. The familiar Army Transportation Corps logo, the winged wheel, was missing from her stack. It had been replaced with the first letters of the new name for the service *M.S.T.S.* (Military Sea Transport Service). She literally sparkled in her new coat of paint. Most ships of that design were named for seaman's knots. This one was called the *Clove Hitch*. As he watched, a man climbed the ladder to her flying-bridge and walked forward to look down over the cargo area. Damned if Chuck didn't recognize that walk. It was the walk of a man on skis. This man had been the first officer on a large sea tug. Chuck had sailed twice with him. They were delivering tows from Seattle to points west in the Aleutian Islands. His name was Jan Butts, a fun guy and a good deck officer. Chuck was within hailing distance, but to get his attention, he trained a signal lamp on him and blinked out a disrespectful greeting. The light got Butts to turn and look up toward the bridge of the *McFall*. As the message developed, he raised a fist and shouted, "Ok, wise guy, if you'll come on down here I'll either break your nose or make you eat our cook's cookin' for lunch."

Chuck killed the lamp and stepped out from behind it. He shouted his name across and down, then shouted, "Mr. Butts, what'er ya' doin' in California?"

Jan Butts shouted back, "I'm happy to tell you, my fine young friend, I'm Skipper of this little beauty an' we're headed out to Hawaii."

Chuck shouted back, "Were you serious about threatening me with your cook's cookin' for lunch?"

The answer came back, "See you at noon, an' I'll be considerin' whether or not I should go ahead and break your nose when ya' get here."

Chuck slid the notes from Captain Butts of the *Clove Hitch* and First Officer Wilson of the *McFall* across the counter at the base personnel office, and a pretty WAC clerk picked them up. Her khaki shirt and field scarf dutifully tried to hide the generous twin evidences of her womanhood. After checking with a trim, frosty female with sergeant stripes, the especially gifted young WAC was soon pounding out new orders in quadruplicate. Her typewriter was an ancient, olive-drab, Underwood.

The Chief Wheelman of the *General McFall* took a pay cut and put his Chief Wheelman rating in storage. Freighters don't use that rating. When the *M.S.T.S. Clove Hitch* sailed for the Islands two weeks later, Chuck was aboard as the Able Seaman on the "four to eight" bridge watch.

The great engines of the Hawaiian Clipper droned tirelessly over a seemingly endless expanse of blue Pacific waters. Her four enormous propellers caught and reflected the rays of the sun as they ate their way through the thin cold air. This "Clipper" carried a capacity load of mail and passengers.

Among the 45 passengers aboard were two fugitives from the *Los Angeles Limited.*

Muriel and Mary Jane were thrilled at the prospect of arriving in Honolulu after only a nine-hour flight. The pilot announced over the public address system, "We'll be arriving at five p.m. local time. Don't forget to reset your watches. The weather in Honolulu is beautiful and the temperature is 76 degrees."

Those two girls had in recent days climbed over hard-packed snow in the doorway of their Pullman car and felt the responsibility and utter exhaustion of caring for over 200 frightened people in four rooms through a long winter day and night. They had withstood the blast of 70-mile-an-hour blizzard winds on their faces.

They felt they knew personally a little girl who had frozen to death in the storm. Muriel and Mary Jane were indeed ready for a weather report like that.

The two fugitives from that deadly storm in Wyoming were emotionally overcome in an inexplicable way on landing in the complete peace and beauty of Hawaii. They felt the ambient softness in the air and the delicate fragrance of the plumeria leis that were placed around their necks. They felt deeply the gentleness of the Hawaiian welcoming ceremony. For reasons they couldn't explain, they found themselves sobbing in each other's arms. Those two young storm survivors found the welcome to be uniquely personal and restoring.

After the ceremony, when they had regained their composure, they made a call to Queen's Hospital. A van was sent to take them to "Sherman House," a lovely old mansion up on Nuuanu Avenue. Sherman House had for many years served as a nurse's quarters for the hospital.

The next morning when they reported to the hospital, they found themselves to be celebrities. Word had gotten out about their valiant work and ordeal in the Wyoming storm. Reporters from the Honolulu Advertiser waited to interview them and to take pictures. The write-up in the paper brought calls from several "Mountainside grads" who were now living in the Islands. Those kindly women wanted to befriend them and do what they could to welcome them to Hawaii.

The girls dropped easily into a happy routine of work at the hospital. They enjoyed many parties and double dates. The old grads and people at the hospital arranged the dates. They spent one Sunday in a Jeep, touring Honolulu and Pearl Harbor with two handsome marines. The experience was educational but the Jeep ride was bone shattering. They declined when the marines, who were nice but dull guys, called again.

They quickly began to think of themselves as veteran "Islanders." They felt perfectly comfortable apologizing for the weather when it rained all day. January 28 was one of those rainy days. Far worse than the rain, they each got a typhoid booster shot that day, which left them one-winged. In the mail that day, Mary Jane found a letter from Jack Moore. For Mary Jane, the sun immediately came out in all of its tropical warmth and splendor, and the pain from the typhoid shot went away. Enclosed in the letter was Jack's frat pin.

After graduating from the School of Law at the University of Montana, Jack would stay in that state. He'd been offered a job at a law firm in Cut Bank, a small but important town up quite close to the Canadian border. He suggested that Mary Jane come home to Montana in September so she could get a job there and they could start making wedding plans.

Mary Jane would happily do all of that!

The girls had just gotten home from work on February 3, when one of the other nurses in the house answered the phone in the hallway. The girl came to Muriel's room with the message that there was a guy on the phone who wanted to speak to "the lovely Muriel." She went to the phone thinking this guy must be some kind of nut. She had to adjust her thinking only slightly. It was Chuck. He said he'd managed the impossible; he'd gotten transferred to a freight/service vessel that would be plying the Islands for a few months. The reason he'd requested the transfer was that he needed to pick up a half dozen shirts that he'd left last year at a laundry on Hotel Street. He was, at this moment, in the bar at the Alexander Young Hotel. He was happily hugging his bundle of long lost shirts. Would she care to join him in the hugging? She would and did. They left the shirts with the barkeep and took a taxi to the Royal Hawaiian Hotel at Waikiki.

There on its stunningly beautiful, palm-studded patio under a spectacular Hawaiian moon, they danced to the music of a small band. A saxophone sighed and spoke quietly. Its sweet voice seemed to speak to them alone.

Just beyond the moonlit beach, the beautiful Pacific was softly caressing the island shore. Its gentle sounds were in tones that only lovers truly understand. Chuck and Muriel were beginning to understand its song.

The next day, a Sunday, Chuck and a shipmate, Rod Toomy, picked up the girls at the hospital; the girls were coming off of a split shift at noon. The guys, off for the day, had rented the old Ford convertible from the man in the Uncle Sam suit at the lot on Hotel Street. Rod was a junior engineer on the *Clove Hitch* and a nice guy. He understood that Mary Jane was in love with some guy in the states. That was okay, he'd just come along for laughs. Rod always provided a ton of them.

They drove out beyond Palea Point and stopped to climb on the rocks around the "Blow Hole." They watched as pressure generated by swells in the sea forced water through natural underground tubes far up onto the rocks of the shore. The seawater is forced periodically out through a hole in the rocks, creating a surprisingly powerful geyser. In their enthusiastic inspection of the phenomenon, they managed to get soaked to the skin. Not a problem. Their light cotton clothes would be dry in a few minutes.

Back on the road they headed on around to the windward side of the island. When the "I'm hungry" calls from the girls got to be too much, they stopped at a lovely Island restaurant and had dinner.

The old Ford labored on the steep climb up the windward side of the Pali. They ran into a sudden rain squall at the crest. They weren't able to get the rag top in place before the sudden squall got them soaked for the second time on their day's trip. This time they got a break. The fresh warm rainwater washed away the salt that the earlier sea drenching had left on them.

They managed to get the girls home shortly before midnight, avoiding a problem with the housemother at Sherman House. She was very uncomfortable when any of her girls were out past midnight with sailors.

The next day, Monday, Muriel was switched from "days" to the "three to eleven" shift. Chuck sat on the front steps of the hospital quietly waiting for her when she got off duty. They walked to the bar at the Alexander Young Hotel. They had a beer and talked 'til near morning. The heavily loaded *Clove Hitch* was leaving for Seattle at noon. The folks at the "AY" bar, who all knew them by now, helped them say goodbye.

Chuck put Muriel in a taxi to Sherman House, then walked down to the pier where his ship lay ready to go to sea.

On March 4, Muriel found a teddy bear in her mail. The bear came from Seattle with a note from Chuck. Then on March 28, Muriel got a phone call. The *Clove Hitch* was tied up out in the boondocks on the windward side of the island, unloading her cargo of ordinance there. On the 30th, she docked in Honolulu and a small bouquet of flowers came to Sherman House for Muriel.

The following Saturday, Chuck had a special invitation to a native family luau. He rented the same old Ford and picked up Muriel and Mary Jane. They drove out beyond Barbers Point to Nanakuli where the family lived.

When their hosts found that the girls were nurses at Queen's Hospital, they were treated as royalty. The girls didn't admit to not being familiar with the case, but they were delighted to find that the doctors and nurses at Queen's were recently credited with saving the life of a member of that native family.

The festive meal was delicious. It included a large pig wrapped in banana leaves and roasted in the classic Hawaiian way, buried in the sand beneath a huge bonfire. The traditional music and dancing were fun and wonderful.

The guests at the luau were absolutely charmed by an old uncle, a native storyteller. He told his stories while sitting cross-legged on a woven-grass mat. His brown skin and dark eyes caught and reflected the dancing, golden light from the tiki lamps. He told of how the world was born. It was a beautiful and uncomplicated story. He told an exciting tale of a long sea voyage that his people had made when the world was young, and he spoke of many gods. His gods were sometimes in the mountains, other times in the sea and sometimes they lived among the people. Those gods were never vengeful but were always loving and kind to all things. The gods were especially devoted to Mother Earth. His gods had learned to stay clear of the ill-tempered missionary God who sat on his golden throne in the sky and seemed always to be looking for trouble.

Tears often came to the old man's eyes and to the eyes of his listeners as he quietly told his stories. From the Christian missionaries, he and his people had learned a new way to do sex, which was a good thing. The missionary folks also tried to teach the people that their angry God had created the heavens and the earth. That part of their teaching made no sense. To avoid creating hard feelings, they pretended to believe the story.

Chuck and the girls thanked the host family for a wonderful evening then drove back to the city. They dropped Mary Jane at Sherman House, then Chuck and Muriel drove on up Nuuanu Avenue to the Pali. They had a special place on the Pali where they liked to park the old Ford. At that spot, it seemed, they could look out over the whole world.

Also from that spot, Chuck could greet his old friends in the night sky. He would say to them in his mind's voice, *"Look Capella and Sirius, look Rigel, see my Muriel! Isn't she the pretty one?"*

Sirius, the Dog Star, politely said nothing. If he could verbalize, he would've said, "Shucks, lad, I already know that young lady. I met her one winter evening on a frozen high plain in Wyoming. Since then I've been watching over her for you and the family."

This night, they had no sooner parked than the sparkling lights of Honolulu and the sky were taken away by a swirling, buffeting, tropical rainsquall. The storm tugged at the cloth top of the old convertible, but as always before, it successfully resisted being torn away. Snug in their nest, with banshee winds crying in the night and water cascading out of the sky, they talked. They talked little of the future;

the future seemed a distant mountain, a mountain too far away for them to see let alone make plans for climbing.

When the storm had spent its fury, the lights of Honolulu and the sky reappeared. The Island moon shone again in all its gentle splendor. Perhaps there was a lesson there. When the uncertainties of the present have passed, perhaps there will come a quiet time when plans for the future can spawn. For now, they were content to just hold each other close. Music from "Carousel" and the new musical "South Pacific" flowed softly from the car radio. It was 0200 hours when Muriel let herself in at Sherman House. The housemother didn't meet her at the door, but she must have been in a tizzy.

The next evening, when Muriel got off work at eleven, Chuck was again waiting on the front steps of the hospital. They had dinner in the Marine Room at the Royal Hawaiian. No time for stargazing this night. Chuck dropped Muriel off at Sherman House, then left the car with the man in the Uncle Sam suit. He was back aboard his ship well before she sailed at 0600 hours. The *Clove Hitch* would sail to Hilo on the big island, then to Wake Island and back to Honolulu. The cargo she was taking aboard was ticketed for San Francisco. She eventually arrived back in Honolulu on a Friday night. She was due to sail for California on Sunday.

Saturday morning, Chuck rented the Ford again. They went for a drive up Tantalus Road, absolutely the most beautiful drive in the whole world. Every turn in the road presented a new and different vista of sun and flower-filled fields with occasional glimpses of the sea, all backed by soft green mountains that quietly projected themselves into faultless blue skies.

Then the little Ford took them out Diamond Head Road through Hawaii Kai to Koko Head. They climbed down the rocks to the Pacific at a tiny tide pool beach. The Pacific

Ocean stretched unbroken, away to infinity. It, in fact, stretched away to that far place where it met and mixed with the icy waters of Antarctica.

They took off their sandals and waded into the warm seawater. Muriel made a project of finding and watching small sea-things in the teeming tide pools. Eventually she returned to the large, flat rock where Chuck sat watching her. They sat there in each other's arms until the sun dropped into the sea. They were hearing the quiet sounds that the sea was making. As on that night at the Royal Hawaiian at Waikiki, it was singing to them in notes that they had now come to clearly understand.

In the long twilight, they drove back downtown to Kau Kau Korner. There they had Kau Burgers and malts. They took the faithful old Ford back to the man in the Uncle Sam suit and walked to the AY-Bar. They found their usual spot in the corner booth where they would say goodbye. Friends joined them for a few moments, then moved on as others came by. The jukebox, in muffled tones, tried its best to find the right song to blend with or ease their pain of parting.

Men have gone down to the sea since they discovered that a wooden hull would move on the sea if they put up a mast to capture the wind in a canvas sail. As they left home for ever farther away parts of the world, most of them left girls or wives in some version of "a corner of tears." In all those years of seafaring, nothing had changed.

Eventually the cabbie they had called appeared at the door. They got up and followed him outside. After one last long kiss, Muriel got into the cab. Chuck closed the door and paid the cabbie. His eyes followed the cab until it made the turn uphill onto Nuuanu Avenue.

He hadn't seen it coming at all, this thing that had happened to him. He knew now that he was in love with this girl.

Admitting to himself that he was in love was a strange new thing. It was wonderfully exciting but he was suddenly beset with doubt; he felt a new and great vulnerability. How could he expect to hold a beautiful girl like Muriel for the long haul? The circles she traveled in were peopled by accomplished young and old men. Most of them of course were on the make and most possessed levels of influence, skill and education that were off his radar screen. He understood the depth of his love for her, but he had no way to know the depth of her feelings for him.

Wrapped in a cloud of gloom, he sat down on a bench at a bus stop on a now all-but-deserted Hotel Street. Leaning back he looked to the night sky. Grabbing for a mental lifeline, he looked for the Dog Star. The gentle blue giant was right where he should be, at 17 degrees south.

The cool blue presence of the Dog Star reminded him that his grandmother Annie, a lovely girl from a well-settled eastern family, had picked up and gone with his grandfather to raise a family in a house made of sod on a lonely western prairie. In a few moments, the disquieting pain in his upper chest quietly went away.

His mind was now free to think easy thoughts. He got up and walked toward the pier where his ship lay in the shadow of the old pineapple-shaped water tower.

The *M.S.T.S. Clove Hitch* would sail at 0600 hours. The rumor had been confirmed that she was scheduled to return to her Alaska run. Chuck had left no laundry in Ketchikan or Dutch Harbor so he'd say goodbye to Captain Butts and his great little ship.

With the *General McFall* now serving the troops in Europe, out of the Port of New York, she'd very likely be in New York when Muriel went home to New Jersey in December. He'd find a way to again get back to his old ship.

Mary Jane left the Islands in September. Jack Moore met her at the train in Cut Bank, Montana. On May 19, 1950, among a host of new friends, they were married.

As the *Clove Hitch* made her way to San Francisco, Chuck had no way to know that clouds of war were forming in Korea and the plan he'd made to rejoin the *McFall* would be changed under the weight of events. He also had no way to know that he had an appointment in Samaria to survive. His appointment was not in a biblical desert, it would instead be in Korea, in and under the cold gray waters of the Bay of Inchon.

Like his parents and grandparents before him, he would confidently follow the path ahead, guided as always by faith in his God and the gentle blue light of the Dog Star.

The future would, in its own time, quietly reveal itself.

-✱-

Story Twelve

Apra Harbor Jingle

The jack-staff on the bow of the *M.S.T.S. General Ross* stood foolishly defiant against the low green mountain that lay dead ahead. "Right five degrees rudder." The order came from the young naval officer assigned to pilot duty at this U.S. military installation on Guam in the Western Pacific. It's required of harbors the world over that each maintain a skilled staff who can safely guide ships into and out of that harbor. In 1950, Guam's Apra Harbor had become an important hub for the American forces. It became especially important in the effort to fight the war in Korea.

The order from the pilot was executed by the young chief wheelman. It was the chief's duty to steer the ship into and out of each port-of-call. The pilot was standing with the captain on the port wing of the bridge. With the engines of the giant gray troop carrier at "slow-ahead," it took a long moment for the jack-staff to begin its glide away from the threatening green mountain. It swung slowly to the right until the perfectly timed order, "Rudder Amidships" allowed the jack-staff to come to rest on the center of the narrow channel to the open sea.

Ahead, to the west, past the green mountain on the left lay the flat blue infinity of the Philippine Sea. That sea's, not always pacific, waters stretch over the Philippine Trench to Samar, far beyond the horizon. "Steady as she goes." The pilot, now standing at the engine-room telegraph in the wheelhouse moved the handles of that device to "half-ahead." The surface water of the channel was rippling and roiling; the pilot knew the rudders and keel would need additional thrust from the screws to combat the currents whipping from side to side in the channel. Chief Wheelman Farritor could feel the added propeller thrust in the wheel as he made the necessary moves of the wheel to keep the ship on a course down the center of the blue/green road to the open sea. For a ship as large as the *Ross*, the channel was little more than wide enough. As she made her way out of Apra Harbor, the side of the mountain that dropped almost vertically to the sea was interestingly nigh to the portside running light.

With the ship safely through the channel and past the outer buoy, the chief's duty was complete. He announced the ship's heading in degrees on the gyrocompass to the officer of the watch and to Watch Wheelman Burns, who had been standing at his elbow since the ship left the dock. Burns repeated the course, stepped to the wheel and locked his eyes on the gyrocompass.

Off duty now, Chief Wheelman Farritor walked out of the wheelhouse onto the port wing. He then walked up the ladder to the flying bridge. He moved to the area of what had been the port side gun-tub over the port wing of the bridge (all the guns had been removed from American freighters and troopships at the close of World War II). He looked to the west; he was just in time for the show. The sun had, as seemed to be its habit, paused for a moment on the horizon. The chief never tired of watching the performance put on by Apollo as the tropical twilight brought finis to his reign in the sky. Though he knows full well that his plunge into the night is inevitable, Apollo always bitterly resists relinquishing his power over the sky and the sea. In the last few moments before he loses the battle, he fires off weapons he hasn't used all day. He causes the western sky to ignite with an orange flame that quickly sets fire to the sea beneath it. The seabirds flying in the burnished light seem unaware that they fly on wings feathered with gold.

Thanked and dismissed by the captain, the young navy pilot left the bridge and repaired to the pilot ladder, which had been dropped over the gunwale on the main deck. As he debarked into the pilot-pickup boat, he knew that he'd be late for supper with his mestiza, she with the long flowing black hair and the soft red lips, she who filled the island nights with rapture for him. He hoped that she would not again be withholding, vexed by his lateness.

On the starboard wing of the bridge, the officer of the watch, Mr. Harris, stood talking to his friend, Cargo Officer Toller. Mr. Harris called out over his shoulder to Wheelman Burns, "Bring her around to 315 degrees, gyro." This would be the first leg of several course changes designed to take the ship on a loop safely around the island of Guam and on to the northeast. The order as given by Mr. Harris was delivered dangerously incorrect, and failing to keep a forward watch during the course change was an unforgivable breech of good seamanship.

Above on the flying bridge, Chief Wheelman Farritor was transfixed by the spectacle of a furiously flaming thunderhead in the northern sky. The white folds of it had burst into a red-orange flame. The flames somehow did not consume it. White caps that leapt out of the sea beneath it were transformed into tongues of fire. These tongues of fire seemed to be seeking the freedom that flight could bring to them in their father Apollo's realm. Then suddenly the color and the flames dissolved. Apollo's fury was spent. He had surrendered to the gentle tropical twilight and dropped into the sea

The spell the chief was under was shattered by a sudden realization that the ship was not swinging right toward the northwest like it was expected to do; instead she was turning to the left. He guessed immediately what had happened. Wheelman Burns had been given the order for a major course change without being given a rudder direction. With his eyes only on the gyroscope he had been unfairly saddled with a decision, to go right or to go left to the new course. He had made the wrong decision. Anger at Mr. Harris, who had given the incomplete course change order, would come later; right now it was the safety of the ship that mattered. She was turning directly into the same green mountain she had flirted with as she came out of the harbor.

With the mountain beginning to loom on the port beam, the chief ran to the ladder that led down to the bridge deck; he rode the handrails down the ten-foot flight. At the bottom, the momentum of his descent dashed him to his hands and knees. Without getting to his feet, he quick-crawled to where he could get his head in the open door to the wheelhouse. Shouting as he crawled, he called for Wheelman Burns to spin the wheel to hard right. Burns pulled his eyes from the gyroscope, looking to where the shouting was coming from, his eyes shot past the figure of his friend kneeling in the doorway. A mountain that was frighteningly close was clearly in view through the open door to the port wing; he immediately spun the wheel to hard right. The officer of the watch, Harris, still involved in conversation with his friend, Mr. Toller, on the starboard wing, heard the shouting. Harris stepped to the wheelhouse door and, looking through and out the port side door, saw the approaching mountain that Burns had seen. Harris ran to the wheel, grabbed Wheelman Burns by the shirt to cast him aside. The shirt ripped and came off the young man's back. Finding the wheel already in the hard-right position, Harris stood out of place and impotent. Burns, stricken and shirtless, stood his ground nearby.

The captain, responding to the shouting, came running out of the chart-room aft of the bridge. He and Second Officer Simms had been there charting the course to Honolulu. Understanding the situation at once, the captain ran to the engine-room telegraph. The indicator was in the full ahead position. He shouted to the Second Officer to sound "General Alarm" then yanked the handle of the telegraph to the stop position then immediately back to full ahead. He did this twice. This is the universal signal to the engine room that a ship-endangering emergency exists. It's called full ahead with a jingle.

The engineering officer at the controls in the engine room knows that the ship's survival might depend on the engine producing power far beyond the normal use level. The increased thrust delivered against the rudder in the hard over position can, under some conditions, turn the ship almost on its axis. In this case where the ship was running at full ahead, a quick course change is not possible. The forward momentum of its great tonnage is a force not soon redirected.

Under the dramatically increased RPM's of the engines delivered directly onto the rudders, the *Ross* began immediately to shudder from stem to stern. The shuddering increased to the point where things were flying off shelves and counters in the galley and mess areas. Living quarters were beginning to look like the chaos found in a dime store after a California earthquake.

The ship's crew and the troops in the holds responded to the alarm bell which was the signal for "abandon ship stations." Having arrived at their assigned station, each could only stand by in his or her life jacket hoping that the ship could save herself.

The nature of the threat to the ship was obvious to everyone on deck; the ones below could only wonder. The waiting period can be but a matter of a few minutes; she will either deliver herself to the safety of the open sea or crash onto rocks that will destroy her hull. She would then slide off the rocks and sink in the very deep water at the base of the mountain.

The captain stood by the engine room telegraph, his face as white as the seawater being churned up by his ship's thrashing screws. He had restored Wheelman Burns to his post at the wheel. The shirtless Burns was openly crying. His muscular, suntanned shoulders shook as his strong hands gripped the wheel. The sound of his sobbing went unheard, lost among the greater noises from the shaking that filled the ship. Mr. Harris wandered to the outboard end of the port wing where, leaning over the dodger, he could do nothing but watch the deadly approach of the rocks. The chief wheelman and the second officer were standing by at the captain's elbow, this being their normal "abandon ship station."

The swing to the left eased. The captain, seeing this, immediately ordered the wheel, "Hard left." Then a second desperate time of waiting ensued. All the while the ship continued to shudder monstrously as though in a death throe. The task now was to stop the momentum of her swing to the right; if it continued, she would most likely strike the rocks with her port quarter or stern.

The ship was pitching and rolling in a sea made rough by her desperately laboring screws. The troops standing by in their lifejackets were thinking, "Holy Jesus, we're safely on our way home, an' this damn ship is gonna' explode or somethin'!" After a very short time, that seemed endless, the swing to the right stopped.

The captain immediately ordered, "Wheel amidships," then yanked the telegraph to the stop position, then back to "full ahead." The ship stopped shuddering and a strange heavy silence filled her. She settled quickly into a smooth escape course to the west. As she fled toward the open sea, the wake from her great churning screws threw seawater onto the rocks that had threatened her life.

With the ship again beyond the outer buoy, the captain ordered a stand-down from abandon ship stations. He then put his hand on the bare shoulder of the tearstained watch wheelman and said, "Well done, Wheelman Burns; now right ten degrees rudder, steady her on three-one-five degrees gyro." With the ship safely steaming to the northwest, the captain joined Mr. Harris and Mr. Simms who were on the port wing "Mr. Harris, please report to the first officer. You will advise him that I have relieved you of your duties here on the bridge." With Mr. Harris gone, the captain turned to the second officer, "Mr. Simms, please go below to grab some supper; then report back here to relieve me as officer of this watch."

The captain went to the phone in the wheelhouse and called the chief engineering officer. "Mr. Olson, I thank you, sir. Your engines saved the ship today. Please check them carefully for damage and report back to me. Thank you again."

Out of the way on the starboard wing, Chief Wheelman Farritor stood by at the captain's request. As he was watching the sea ahead of the jack staff on the bow, gentle swells were rolling away to the horizon. The twilight sky had given way to the night, and the night sky was busy gathering its full complement of stars. He found his family's friend the Dog Star. He was right on station at 17 degrees south. The Dog Star was proudly holding aloft his ancient blue lamp for all to see.

The captain appeared at his elbow. "Chief Farritor, I thank you for your help in our effort to dodge that bullet today. I and the *Ross* are most certainly in your debt."

Looking into the captain's eyes in the near darkness, the chief said, "Sir, it was you who saved this ship today. I know I speak for the crew when I say 'thank you,' Captain." Sensing that the conversation was complete, the chief said, "Good Night, sir." He turned and went below.

The captain stood alone on the wing of his bridge, his eyes searching the dark horizon and the gently rolling swells that lay in the path of the onrushing prow of his ship. Second Officer Simms would be reporting soon to relieve him.

Before going to his quarters, the chief wheelman went to the crew's mess. He had missed supper, so he put a piece of bread in the toaster and made a cup of cocoa. A kid he knew from the black gang came in for a cup of coffee. In the days of coal-fired steam, the men who worked in the engine room soon took on the color of the dust from the coal. They were called, and thought of, as the black gang. Present-day ships' engine rooms are as bright and clean as a suburban housewife's kitchen, but the black gang name is still used, perhaps a tribute to those generations of engine-room sailors who earned the name.

The engine room sailor asked, "Chief, what the hell was goin' on up there?"

Spreading peanut butter on his toast, the chief said, "It's a complicated story, Danny. You guys sure shook the crap out of everybody while you were saving our butts! I'm bushed Danny, can we talk about it tomorrow?" He took his toast and mug of cocoa with him as he left.

The duty mess-steward called after him, "Chief, don't forget to bring that mug back."

Without turning, he said, "I hear you, Stan, goodnight, and thanks"

He climbed a ladder, then stepped through the open watertight door out into the night. The cabin he shared with the chief bosun was located outboard on the main deck. He stopped outside the open door to the cabin. "Boats" was busy straightening out the mess in the well-shook-up room. Each of his movements was punctuated by an outburst of randomly selected but sincerely intended swear words. Choosing to wait out that storm, the young chief turned and walked to the ship's rail to finish his toast and cocoa.

In the moonlight he could see dimly the Island of Guam falling away on the starboard quarter. The lamp on the control tower at the U.S. Air Force base on the high north end of the island blinked its measured message to the world. As he stood at the rail some 35 feet above the sea, he could see flying fishes playing in the roiling disturbance alongside the ship. The winged fish were illuminated by and silhouetted against the ghostly phosphorescent light embodied in the disturbed warm seawater. He wondered, as he had wondered several times before, whether he would ever be here to see again this part of God's remarkable world.

Suddenly he was dead tired. The storm in the cabin seemed to be easing, so he turned to go inside. Even if the rampage continued, it wouldn't matter; he'd close the curtain in front of his bunk and be asleep in a minute. He would sleep well, knowing that the great ship was safely back at sea. She was running at full speed on a course east by north, riding easily before a westerly trade and rolling gently on a sea swell out of the north.

The troops in the holds were anxious to get home. They had talked all those months about seeing that Golden Gate again. It would be only a few days from the time they debarked at Fort Mason that they would be at home with their families. Most of them were, however, delighted to hear that the ship would be stopping in Honolulu for two days. A day at the beach at Waikiki and a night in the bars on Hotel Street would give them experiences that would be easy to talk about when they got home. That'd give them more time to think through the stuff they'd done and seen in that hell-hole of anger, fear and exhaustion that was Korea. A lot of that stuff was not all that easy to think on, let alone talk about.

The chief wheelman had his own reasons to look forward to the stop in Honolulu. He wanted to see again that pretty nurse named Muriel at Queen's Hospital. He worried, after all these months, was Muriel still his girl? Had her busy life moved her on to someone new? That thought brought a scary pain to his upper chest. He put those thoughts aside.

On another matter, of one thing he was absolutely certain. He wouldn't go near the bar on Hotel Street where lovely ladies painted on black velvet dwell on its walls in well-lighted glory. If the red-haired girl that his friend Eddie Boone had fallen in love with had been sold and was not there, he didn't want to know it. He wanted, at least in his mind, to know that she would be there for his now dead friend to love, always.

He'd rent that same old Ford from the guy in the Uncle Sam suit on Hotel Street then drive up Nuuanu Avenue to Sherman House where Muriel lived. He'd park the old convertible under the ancient trees and sit on the front steps to wait for her to come home from work.

The kindly but suspicious housemother would check him out from behind the white lace curtains overlooking the broad front lanai. She had seen him before but he was sure that to her all sailors looked alike, and where her girls were concerned, their intentions were always suspect.

Remembering that cool shady lanai at Sherman House delivered to him the heavenly aroma from the bowers of plumeria that graced that lovely spot. In his mind that exotic but gentle tropical scent battled for a moment, then was overpowered by the ignoble odor from the broken bottle of shaving lotion that filled the cabin.

He was thinking of asking the captain to allow him some extra time ashore in Honolulu. As his mind struggled to find the best way to voice the request, sleep overcame him.

On a Friday at noon, the *M.S.T.S. General Ross* tied up at a commercial pier in downtown Honolulu. As Chief Wheelman Farritor was securing things in the wheelhouse, the captain hooked his finger at him and walked out onto the port wing of the bridge. The chief finished putting the dust cover on the gyrocompass, then quickly followed the skipper out of the wheelhouse. The captain stood looking out toward the City of Honolulu. He turned to face the young man and spoke quietly. "Chief, the first officer agrees with me that we owe you a couple of days off here in Honolulu. We'll see you back here an hour before sailing time. We sail at noon come Sunday." With a quiet smile on his face, the captain turned and went back into the wheelhouse. Chuck was immediately glad of two things: first, that he hadn't asked for the time off, and second, he was glad that First Officer Wilson and the captain knew of his friendship with that pretty nurse at Queen's Hospital. One afternoon at the Royal Hawaiian the last time they were here in Honolulu, he had introduced her to them.

Chuck figured that Muriel was probably still on the "three to eleven" shift, so he had some time to kill. When he got ashore, he first dropped in to say hello to his friends at the AY Bar at the Alexander Young Hotel, then he went to the car rental lot where the man in the Uncle Sam suit was in charge. The familiar old Ford convertible was already rented out, but he could have a sleek black Pontiac ragtop for the same price. On his way out to Waikiki, he pulled over to pick up a half dozen hitch-hiking soldiers from the *Ross*. They piled in, and he delivered them to the beach.

For himself, he had something other than the beach in mind. He parked and went into the half acre expanse of potted palms and colorful Batik-covered tables at the famous Royal Hawaiian Hotel Bar. He sat alone at a familiar table. A waitress that he didn't know smiled at him when he ordered a Gelded Barbarian Mai Tai. The other chair at the table was empty but in his mind's eye he could clearly see in the dim light, the broad smile and blue eyes of his good friend Eddie Boone. If Eddie was in fact there, he'd be enjoying a Gelded Barbarian and telling Chuck a new funny story.

The new waitress, lovely in her pale-green sarong, noted the sadness in the eyes of the young chief who drank his Gelded Barbarian alone and in silence. It was a sadness she often saw in the eyes of young men who came to sit for a time alone in this seldom-quiet place. She knew these men were drawn here despite or because of memories that haunt their young minds.

Driving back downtown in the long soft twilight, Chuck tooled the sleek Pontiac slowly up Nuuanu Avenue to Sherman House. He parked under the ancient trees in the front yard of the old mansion. Helen O'Connel was singing, *When the Deep Purple Falls over Sleepy Garden Walls* on the car radio. It was a song he had first heard as the family gathered in the light of kerosene lamps around the Zenith battery-powered radio to listen to the Saturday night "Hit Parade." In that old ranch-house kitchen, the radio sat atop the wooden cabinet of the icebox. Blackie, the ancient family housecat, usually lounged atop the radio. Her tail often twitched in time to the music. She liked the music fine, but there is no question, what she loved most about the radio was the warmth generated by the large, softly glowing vacuum tubes within the radio's wooden cabinet.

He waited for the song to finish, then cut the ignition and got out of the car. He crossed the yard through the gathering darkness and went up the five or six steps to the broad front lanai, standing there in the soft light from the elaborate old light fixture hanging by a chain over the front door. The heavenly scent from nearby bowers of plumeria surrounded him. The scent somehow fed his uncertainty and at the same time gave him comfort. He stood waiting, hoping for a return of the heaven he was in when he was last here.

Out on Nuuanu Avenue, the engine and gears of an old Dodge van growled and complained as the van climbed the steep grade from Queen's Hospital. They seemed much relieved when the driver made the turn onto the level lane that led to Sherman House. The brakes squeaked and the engine died quietly as it stopped in front of the steps to the wide front lanai.

The last nurse to climb out of the old van was a tall pretty girl. Just off duty, she was still in her white nurse's uniform with her nurse's cap pinned to her curly brown hair. When she turned to go up the steps, she saw Chuck. Her face lit up, then she squealed and ran up the steps to him. Chuck's fears vanished. He put out his arms and moved to meet her. Muriel was still his girl!

★★★★★★★★★★

-*-

Story Thirteen

At Last a Morning Calm

No one had to be told to run; the laborers dropped their tools and fled. The truck driver was out of his truck and gone. The backhoe operator instantly killed the diesel engine. In the sudden silence, there was only the deadly sound of gas escaping from an old, uncharted and now-broken gas line.

From his position by his pickup truck thirty feet away, the tall builder saw the operator jump from the seat of the backhoe onto the pavement. The moment he landed he was silhouetted against a cloud of flame. The operator half ran and was half propelled toward him by the outward force from the exploding gas. His mouth was open in a silent scream. The builder turned to his pickup for an old blanket he kept behind the seat. When he turned with it in hand, he found the operator lying at his feet. His clothes were afire, and silence had released the scream. The operator's scream spoke of fear and pain as only a human scream can. The old blanket snuffed the scream along with the fire. Only mewing, small animal sounds now came from under the blanket. Kneeling to comfort the young man, the builder had heard those sounds before. The reborn memory of those sounds put him into a chill, and on this warm California morning his whole body began to shake.

Secondary explosions came from within the burning backhoe and the bobtail truck. Suddenly he found himself and the operator being dragged farther away from the explosions and fire. The laborers had come back to help. One man said, "Chuck, gi'me your keys so's I kin move your pickup."

In the new, safer location the builder placed his face near the operator's pained one. He kept talking to the boy and doing the things he knew to do to try to keep him from going into shock before the emergency medical people could arrive. The builder was himself in his own state of shock. His mind had returned to a death scene from another time. His whole body shook as though he were terribly cold. He knelt over the suffering operator but he was somehow with a young sailor. The once smoothly suntanned face of that sailor was now the uneven color of lightly toasted bread. The lad's blue eyes were open but unfocused, and small mewing sounds came from him. Numbingly cold seawater lapped at his ears and chin. The water seemed to be trying to wash away the trickle of blood coming from a corner of the young sailor's mouth. His outstretched arms lay motionless on the surface of the cold dark water.

In the ambulance the medics looked at the builder only after they had done all they could for the critically burned backhoe operator. At the hospital, the young man was treated, then transferred to a special burn center in the West Valley. There he would get the care that would make him whole again. After treating the builder's minor burns, the staff doctor, puzzled by the episode of apparent hypothermia, began plying him with questions. After awhile, the doctor said, "Mr. Farritor, I'm no shrink, but I'm guessing that you need to free your mind of whatever ghost is lurking there." The builder recalled long ago being told essentially the same thing by a doctor who was in fact a shrink and could have been this young doctor's father or grandfather. He chose not to commit to this medic either, but he had made a decision. He would talk about it. After all these years he would tell the story.

In the years following the Second Great War, the Super Powers were at peace in the midst of what they chose to call a cold war. In the years of our Lord 1950 and 1951, good men were dying in a vicious and ugly little war. The only thing cold about the war in that place was the wind that blew for six months of the year off the Siberian steppes. It blew with a frigid breath that killed. When the season for the cold wind died, a new season came on with a wind that bore heat. The source of that killing hot wind could only be the doors of hell.

Death became subjective for the weary men who fought in that place. As they slogged their way up those ugly mountains or warily crossed frozen or fast-flowing rivers, they came to understand an awful truth. Death had a tradable value. Its coming would bring rest and with it relief from the stench that lay on that land. The stench was of human excrement, human waste spread copiously on that land by a thousand and more generations of Koreans.

Now added to the mix of smells in that place was the smell, like no other, of bright red human blood, blood that turned dark as it cooled and soaked quietly into that ancient and exhausted soil. To the men who bled and died there amid the screaming sounds of war, the meanest cut of all was that the natives called this land "The Land of the Morning Calm."

At a pier in the Netherlands the ship *M.S.T.S. General Ross* lay shrouded in darkness. In the year of our Lord 1950 there was no enemy near to do her harm. Habit, however, led her to seek safety in vigilance among the night's shadows.

It was five a.m. The sailor on watch at the bow struck two bells and called the bridge, "Able Seaman Frank Quinn on bow watch, all is well. Tell my relief to bring foul weather gear; he's gonna need it." He returned the phone to its weatherproof cabinet at the base of the jack staff. Fine drops of rain were falling from the lowering sky.

Amidships, on the starboard side, the young man on watch on the quarter deck (the area at the gangway), stood tall in his dark blue uniform. His chief wheelman's cap bore the emblem of the United States Military Sea Transport Service. His ship, a massive gray troop carrier, was tied up at a Dutch pier awaiting another contingent of her load.

The ship's lines to the dock lay slack. She was being held tightly against the pier by a sharp wind off the North Sea. The pads on the edge of the concrete pier gave off human-like groans as the side of the great ship pressed against them.

The chief wheelman was in his raingear. That equipment would ward off the heavier rain that came with the dawn. The watch officer who shared the duty at the gangway had, early on, taken up a position in a sheltered corner. He stood at parade rest, asleep on his feet. The young chief wondered if the watch officer was aware that only mules are supposed to be able to lock their knees and sleep standing up.

The bosun's mate approached the quarter deck from aft with two sailors. Boats spoke softly "Chief, we're gonna bring in the rat-guards and single up. We'll be quiet so's we won't wake your friend up."

The chief wheelman also spoke softly "I hear you, Boats. If you guys are planning to dash off the pier to that bar across the street, have a Dutch-Irish coffee for me." Their extended mission clear, the rat-guard party scampered down the gangway.

The young chief stood idly, trying to make sense of the Dutch lettering painted on the wall of the warehouse on the pier. The section of the wall he was watching suddenly became rolling doors that moved to the side until they had created a 40-foot-wide opening. Within the well-lit warehouse, under a Belgian national flag, a sharp military band had placed itself well back out of range of the now heavily falling rain. The leader raised his baton to begin a marathon montage of the music that had, for a thousand and more years, sent young Europeans off to war.

Far away to the right, at the upper end of the pier, a smudge of camouflaged movement became a battalion of Belgian soldiers in battle gear. They marched by company, four abreast, unmindful of the driving rain. The music from within the warehouse muted the sounds made by the marching column. As it neared the area of the great ship's gangway, the command halted. Orders were shouted in French by a grizzled sergeant. The first company proceeded in single file up the gangway and into the ship. The command moved forward, and the taut boarding process continued. The action was unaffected by the rain or the music emanating from within the warehouse. The Belgian national ensign hung on its staff, limp and dry. That ensign went unseen by the boarding troops. It served only the musicians who brought it to this place.

This was the second load of United Nations troops this ship would deliver into the firestorm that was raging in Korea. That firestorm would consume many of these young men as it had many of those she had delivered there earlier.

When the last of the boarding soldiers had disappeared into the ship and the quiet rattle of arms was stilled, the military band moved out of sight within the warehouse. The harbor pilot came up the gangway, and the now-awake watch officer escorted him to the captain on the bridge.

The rat-guard party came back aboard with the large metal rat guards. A few far-from-sober crewmen made it up the gangway just before the gangway was removed by a Dutch long-shore crew. With the quarter deck area secured, the young chief quickly walked up the several ladders to the bridge. As he did so, he had a lot of things on his mind. First there was the problem of no time to change into a fresh uniform. He knew this would be a problem for the new captain. The former captain, while being no pushover, was much more accepting of circumstance. The raingear the chief had been wearing kept the rain off, but the required creases had vanished from his pant legs and coat sleeves. He guessed that he'd be reminded of that shortcoming by this Captain who, it was rumored, had his skivvies ironed and his socks pressed.

What was most on his mind were the circumstances of this deadly Korean War. The war, remarkably, seemed to be some kind of ugly secret that not everyone knew about. The media, in total denial of what was really happening, called it a police action. When Chuck was home for Christmas, most of the people he talked to seemed confused as to whether Korea was a country or a nasty social disease.

His family knew the truth of it. His older brother, a Marine, had survived the battle at Pusan, the landing at Inchon, and the nightmare at the Chosin Reservoir. His outfit had advanced over a mountain range into a high valley. At daylight one morning they found the surrounding hills no longer white with snow; the hills were now a dozen shades of brown. A part of one American Marine division was surrounded by several full armies of well-equipped Chinese soldiers. That Marine unit survived by "advancing to the rear." They fought their way back over the ugly range of mountains they had just crossed, back to the seacoast at Hungnam. They carried their dead and wounded out with them. They were evacuated from that place by "*M.S.T.S.*" and U.S. Navy ships. Those American Marines would fight again another day. They were now locked in a death struggle near the 38th parallel with the new enemy, the Chinese.

The pathetic truth was that the war should have been over last October. MacArthur's poorly trained, Japan-based troops had been thrown into the fray when the North Koreans swarmed across the 38th parallel to attack and overwhelm the

South Korean army. MacArthur's troops, too, were no match for the well-trained forces from North Korea. The Americans retreated to a small perimeter around the southern coast city of Pusan. The arrival of U.S. Marines and other properly trained forces from the United States and the United Nations secured the Pusan perimeter. Then to the complete surprise of the North Koreans the, U.S. Marines went to sea and landed at Inchon just south of the 38th parallel, far behind the North Korean lines.

Afraid of being cut off and captured, the North Korean army literally fled back across the border, the 38th parallel. Orders from the United Nations were to drive the invaders from South Korea. Their mission was complete; the war should have been over!

It turned out that General Douglass MacArthur was not content with clearing the North Koreans out of South Korea. "Dugout Doug" wanted to, "Poke a stick in the eye of the Chinese communists." With that in mind, he sent American and United Nations troops into North Korea, headed for the Chinese border at the Yalu River.

This action got America and the United Nations into a land war with China, on China's doorstep. Anyone with good sense had to know that this was a war that would cost us dearly.

In the mountains of North Korea, only a few miles from their homes, the Chinese soldiers felt as though they were, in fact, defending their homeland. They were defending it from these strange troops that had come from halfway around the world to threaten them. With the aid of their overwhelming numbers, they battled the American and U.N. troops to a draw.

Eventually MacArthur was relieved of his command by President Harry S. Truman. Most of the 54,000 American deaths occurred after MacArthur's petulant and unwise crossing of the 38th parallel.

MacArthur would spend his dotage giving speeches, written by others, condemning President Truman and explaining his, MacArthur's, actions and inactions. MacArthur's myths were accepted as gospel by most of the press and a cult of Doug's followers. As promised in the words of an old army barracks ballad that the General was known to quote, he eventually "faded away."

Due to MacArthur's miscalculations, the whole United States Eighth Army had been caught strung out on a two-lane road up the west coast of the Korean peninsula.

One morning, using the brilliant tactic of the Carthaginian, Hannibal, the Chinese destroyed the hundreds of bridges on that coast road, then with mortar and artillery fire, virtually wiped out that American army. Each isolated American unit valiantly expended its ammunition, then spiked its guns, and those who could, escaped back to the south afoot. All of this, as in the first century B.C., Hannibal had caught and destroyed a full Roman army, which was strung out on a similar road. Catching the Romans marching through a heavily wooded area along the shore of a great freshwater lake, Hannibal suddenly struck them broadside with all of his forces. The Romans who were not killed in the initial powerful assault were pushed into the lake to drown.

You have to wonder where Doug's head was. America spent time and money training him to know better. The American Eighth Army had to be rebuilt from scratch by General Ridgeway, the competent general whom President Truman appointed to replace the tragic figure that MacArthur had become.

What had gotten the young chief to thinking about the war was the music from that sheltered band. It bothered him that the band had held itself apart from the reality of the driving rain and the clanking of weapons. Those weapons were being carried by other young men, some of whom would very likely soon die. The band's action seemed symbolic of what the world was doing.

Before he entered the wheelhouse, he paused on the sheltered wing of the bridge. The deck of a large, now unused, gun-tub above on the flying bridge provided that shelter. He proceeded to remove his raingear, at the same time doing what he could to encourage the creases to return to the legs and sleeves of his uniform. He then slid open the door and stepped inside the wheelhouse.

The bridge of a great ship always presents the atmosphere of a quiet chapel where the Holy of Holies is kept. However, during that hour when the ship is preparing to go to sea, should a pilgrim wander in to pray, he would very likely be trampled underfoot without having been noticed. Skilled people move quickly but silently about, doing the things that must be done to see to the ship's wellbeing when she has forsaken the harbor and returned to the place where she was designed to spend her life, the open sea.

The chief wheelman reported to the officer of the watch, then moved to his station at the wheel. He let his hands be warmed and his mind soothed by gently stroking the marvelous wood in the great ship's steering wheel.

When wooden ships were exchanged for iron ones, men who were to go down to the sea on those iron ships pleaded that the steering wheel of the new ships would always be made of wood. They understood, as do all men who go to sea, that the sea is an unforgiving yet holy place. A ship made only of iron is without a soul; it is in the wooden wheel that the ship's soul dwells.

When the last mooring line to the pier was let go, two Dutch tugs nuzzled at the ship's cloud-gray side to aid its passage out of the crowded harbor. The telegraph to the engine room brought her great engines to life.

The chief wheelman repeated and executed the orders to the wheel from the pilot. The jack staff on the bow moved slowly away from the straight-lined things on the shore and continued to swing slowly until it came to rest where only the soft, curved lines of the sea were visible. The *M.S.T.S. General Ross* moved quietly out of that busy harbor. She soon came to a place where the land ended and the sea and the sky prevailed.

The moment the Dutch pilot disembarked onto the pilot-pickup boat beyond the sea wall, the new captain slammed the telegraph to full speed ahead. Everyone knew that the engineers below would ignore his theatrics. They would bring the engines to full speed in good time. Those engines were like fine horses; there would be no casual use of the whip.

The weather front that had clouded the morning had moved on to the east. The skies over the North Sea and the Eastern North Atlantic had been washed sparklingly clear.

The sea, under a brilliant sun, was a busy heaving carpet of blue and white. The blue was a mirror of the sky. The white consisted of feathery whitecaps as bright as the wings of a gull. Bursting onto the open sea like a lioness released from a cage, the great ship eagerly plunged her prow into the rolling sea swells. Chief Wheelman Farritor executed the order from the captain to bring her to the left a full 60 degrees. Southwest by south was the first of a thousand and more courses the great ship would follow to carefully deliver her young soldier passengers back onto dry land. She could not know that the land she would deliver them to would be infinitely foreign and hostile to them.

Prompted by the watch officer, the watch wheelman, standing at the chief's elbow, reported crisply, "Chief, I am prepared to take the wheel." The chief announced the assigned course in degrees on the gyrocompass, heard the number repeated back to him, then he stepped away and his relief took his place at the wheel.

As his eyes adjusted from their lock on the gyrocompass, he saw what he was expecting. The "Old Man" (the captain) was hooking a finger at him "Chief Farritor, come with me, I must speak to you."

When they stepped through the door onto the starboard wing of the bridge, able seaman Frank Quinn, the young sailor on lookout watch, pulled his pea-coat collar up over his ears and stared with great intensity at the empty horizon. With the "Old Man" anywhere near, he wanted only to be invisible.

The captain delivered his "pressing" message to the young chief in his natural voice, a voice that could be heard a league upwind in a full gale. The captain then went back into the wheelhouse. He would hook his finger at selected others, all of those whose creases or actions he found wanting.

The chief collected his rain gear, then went over and gave his friend Frank Quinn a quick jab in the ribs. Without taking his eyes from the horizon, the startled Frank delivered some well-chosen words, words that, among other things, brought into serious question the human lineage of his attacker. The chief bent over laughing. When Frank was aroused, he displayed moments of poetic brilliance. The young chief then lingered silently on watch with his friend.

A lone seagull shared the beauty of the morning with them. The gull watched them intently as it skillfully kept pace about ten feet above and 20 feet outboard from where the two friends stood at Frank's lookout post on the starboard wing of that great ship's bridge.

Standing in the brilliant morning sunlight with his friend, the young chief was thinking that he was just where he wanted to be at this moment in his life. He knew there was a whole other life waiting for him, but for now he was pleased with things just as they were. It was not just that he was with good friends; this somehow even included the neatly pressed new captain. There was more. He loved the ever-changing face of the sea and the unbroken sweep of the sky, that proactive sky that covers all with a gentle beauty while harboring powers that will kill without mercy the unwitting and the unprepared.

Creating that sky was no mean task even for God. A human must study the sky to appreciate its complexity. Having made that study, the newly found wisdom will advise him to file away all that he's learned so that he may just see and enjoy the sky's beauty. Perhaps a gift from his Grandmother Annie, the young chief wheelman saw beauty in that big sky where others saw only boredom or a host of things to fear.

He knew the rippling, overwhelming colors of the aurora as it fills the sky around and below Polaris. He knew the gentle blue brilliance of the Dog Star Sirius, the golden haired lass Capella, and the delicate beauty of the Southern Cross. He knew them and a sky full of their friends, and he loved them all.

The beauty of the sea and sky was food only for the soul. Chuck's body clock reminded him that if he didn't get a move on, he'd miss out on breakfast. He picked up his rain gear, gently cuffed his friend's shoulder, then turned and went below.

Chuck was unaware that this would be his and Frank's last voyage. It was not for him to know that this time, in the "Land of the Morning Calm," a great harm lay in wait for the two of them.

The enormous glass front doors to the Staten Island Marine Hospital barred his way. Through the glass, the broad steps and front walk led his eyes away to the skyline of Manhattan looming silently beyond the dark waters of New York Harbor. The young chief wheelman waited. He had decided to let someone exit ahead of him; he was unsure that he had the strength to push open the heavy glass door. A pretty young lady absorbed in her own thoughts approached. The high heels of her stylish pumps clicked with that uniquely female sound as she crossed the marble floor of the lobby. With a brief accusing glance his way, she pushed the door open. Ignoring her unspoken accusation, he quietly moved through behind her before the door could close.

The sound of the door closing sent a shudder through his body. He was dressed warmly; so the shudder had nothing to do with the chill of the day. Alarmed at his body's reaction, he turned to go back inside but decided he couldn't pull the door open. The gaunt young man in the mirror of the closed glass door stood uncertainly looking at himself. His face was drawn and pale. The heavy leather and steel brace that bracketed his upper body caused him to stand awkwardly. His clothes fit badly; they looked much too big for him. They actually belonged to a person who was suntanned and weighed 70 pounds more than the pale young man who looked back at him from the glass. Also mirrored in the door was the skyline of the city across the harbor behind him. Somehow the view of that skyline allowed him to refocus and remind himself of the firm decision he had made. Today was the day that he was going to go out again into the world. His doctors had told him two weeks ago that he could go out on pass. From day to day he had put off going.

He was admittedly reluctant to give up the protected world of the hospital. As someone pushed the door open and came out, the images mirrored in the great glass door flew away.

He made no attempt to go back into the hospital through the slowly closing door. Before the mirrored images came back he had turned and started the difficult passage down the steps. His resolve and those steps would lead him to the skyline across the harbor where that outside world lay. At the stop in front of the hospital he boarded a bus to the ferry terminal. His mind toyed with the idea of catching a ferry to Manhattan, to go there and get gloriously drunk in the marble canyons of that fabled place. Instead he boarded a ferry to Brooklyn, as he had planned.

Pulling himself upward with his hands on the handrails, he laboriously climbed the ladder to the upper deck of the ferryboat. He wanted to check on something that some of the ship's crew had told him about when they visited him in the hospital. Looking at the low Brooklyn skyline, he could see exactly what they had been telling him about. When the crew of the *Ross* had earlier passed through the Verrazano Narrows on their way out to Korea, the rooftops of Brooklyn had cut a clean line. Now every rooftop had rigs that looked like pieces of bedsprings showing against the sky. He knew it all had to do with the new thing they called television. He'd caught a glimpse of one in a bar at the ferry terminal. On the small green screen a craggy-faced senator from Kentucky was grilling, not too successfully, a tough-looking dock worker foreman from the New Jersey waterfront. The folks in the bar were clearly in sympathy with the longshoreman, though most knew that the guy was probably as crooked as a dog's hind leg.

Ashore in Brooklyn he caught the Bay Ridge bus. He had made this trip before; Frank Quinn had twice invited him home for a weekend. The large Quinn family was very close and, like his own family, much aware of its Irish heritage. This day the bus ride was probably quite ordinary, but for him it was a monstrous ordeal. His body consciously negotiated each and every bump in the pavement. A lurch by the bus would leave him ashen-faced and sweating. He could feel the sweat working its way out of his crew cut hair, down his forehead and down the back of his neck. After an interminable time he heard the bus driver call out the name of the street where he knew he should get off. He began to plan carefully how he could best stand up and make his way to the rear door. His thought process was interrupted by a voice from the seat behind. The voice said, "Mister, it's wintertime. Why are you sweating?" He wanted to turn and smash his fist into the face of the speaker. He sat motionless for a moment, then turned slowly. It was a small, well-dressed boy with simple curiosity showing in his eyes. Embarrassed at his anger, he said nothing. He got to his feet and moved toward the door. He deliberately held the door open so the driver couldn't close it on him as he gingerly stepped down to the curb.

He was across the street from the large old house he knew to be the Quinn home. Suddenly he felt complete exhaustion. To counter a feeling that he must lie down on the sidewalk, he draped himself over a nearby mailbox. After a few minutes in that position, the overwhelming need to lie down passed. In his exhausted state he began again to doubt whether what he was doing was right. After all these months, could it be that the last thing the Quinn family needed was for one of Frank's friends to show up to renew their grief? Why should he, of all people, be there, he, the guy who was responsible for Frank's safety? This torment was not a new thing; his mind had been wrestling with this question all these months. He had always felt an obligation to go see the Quinn family, but he had never arrived at a way to handle it. How could he talk about Frank's death with them when it was not possible for him to even think about it?

There was a small neighborhood park near the bus stop. He abandoned his supporting mailbox and made his way into the park. Spying a drinking fountain, he remembered his two-hour pill. He fished one of the ugly purple things out of the box and downed it with a gulp of water. (Luckily the supply to the fountain had not yet been shut off for the winter.) He then eased himself onto a nearby park bench, adjusting as he did so the formidable body-brace that held his upper body rigid.

He had sought help early on. He had requested an appointment with the hospital chaplain to ask for guidance on how to handle his feelings of guilt and anger. At the appointed hour, stooped over in his gooney-bird body cast and dragging his left leg, he pushed his four-wheeled walker into the chaplain's office. The priest glanced up at him but continued with a telephone conversation. Draped over his walker, he waited for the conversation to end. The priest was voicing firm disapproval of a movie that was scheduled to be shown in the hospital day room. After a long and exhausting wait, the young man found it not possible to remain upright any longer. It was necessary to gather his strength and push himself out of the holy man's office. He had to get someplace where he could lie down. As he left, the priest again glanced up at him but continued with his telephone lecture. It was abundantly clear to the young chief that he was alone with his indecision, his guilt and his anger.

Since the day in that basement corridor when he had managed to convert his fear to anger, the anger seemed often to take the bit in its teeth. Moments of anger would reappear time and again. Here, sitting on this park bench, he knew again the anger he had felt on the ferryboat as it maneuvered to stay clear of a new Italian luxury liner entering the harbor. The foreign ship was being met by a flotilla of fireboats. They were blowing whistles and ringing bells while throwing dramatic patterns of water high into the air. His mind compared the welcome being given these strangers to what happens when an American troopship comes in with its band of exhausted young Americans home from a war that no one but them seemed to know about.

Incoming troopships were met by Army or Navy tugs, which would quietly escort them to a remote pier. That pier was always remote enough so that the long lines of olive-drab or gray buses or ambulances wouldn't offend or inconvenience the public.

The bench he had chosen to sit on had a picture-book view. It overlooked the choppy waters of the Verrazano Narrows and the tree-covered hills of Staten Island beyond. The deciduous trees on the hills of Staten Island were showing fall colors; there were enough evergreen trees in the mix to give the hills an overall green yet golden look. The beauty of the spot seemed to do little to ease his troubled mind. He looked at his watch. He had been out in the world for two hours and 20 minutes now. It occurred to him that he had spent most of that time either sweating in pain or being angry, probably not what his doctors had in mind for him when they suggested the outing. He stood up, adjusted his massive steel and leather body brace, and walked a few paces. He paused, and after a moment or two, returned to the bench. He made the necessary adjustments with his body brace so he could sit down again. He had to concentrate on whether or not to go in to see the Quinn family. Leaning his head back, he closed his eyes. *Perhaps if he went over it again in his mind he'd know what to do?*

The deep blue expanse of the Yellow Sea was busily dotted with whitecaps. The troop carrier *M.S.T.S. General Ross*, with her load of U.S., Dutch, Belgian, Greek, and Turkish troops faced into a fresh north wind. She was cutting easily through a crossing swell, only occasionally dipping her bow to a point where the speed of the ship and the wind combined to cause spray to whip over her bow.

The mountains of Korea dominated the horizon on the starboard beam. Chuck Farritor, the chief wheelman, didn't have to stand wheel watches at sea, so he was on the flying bridge practicing his navigation. The watch navigators tolerated ignorance as long as the ignorant one kept his mouth shut and kept his body out of the way. The chief dealt easily with both of those demands.

He'd bought his sextant at a pawnshop in San Francisco. It was, he knew, his badge of acceptance by the watch navigators. As each navigating officer first saw the instrument he wanted to take it in his hands to get its "feel." It was made in England by Heath, a company that had been making fine instruments for a very long time. The watch navigators were stuck with using government-issue "Mark II" sextants. The Mark IIs were adequate but they didn't have the classy feel that the old "Heath" had. He knew that the month's pay he'd invested in his Heath was money well spent.

Able seaman Frank Quinn was on lookout watch on the starboard wing of the flying bridge. Frank called out to his friend, "Chief, too bad you weren't our navigator out of Suez. You could've run us safely onto a beach in the Carlsberg Ridge. You know what, Chuck? I've got a bad feeling about this place, this time."

The would-be navigator's mind was involved with his task and what Frank had said didn't register. He got his "noon shot" and flipped Frank a grin and a Brooklyn cabbie's middle-finger salute. He then departed for the chart room below. In the chart room aft of the wheelhouse he'd work out his version of the ship's noon position. Lately he'd improved his technique to where he seldom, any more, placed the ship on a mountainside.

At Inchon harbor the next morning in the uncertain light before dawn, the captain was maneuvering the ship onto its assigned anchorage spot. The order for full port rudder came to the young chief through the speaker tube from the flying bridge where the captain had the conn. The powerful thrust of the screws on the rudders sent a heavy vibration through the mass of the ship. After 90 seconds or so, the order came to ease the rudder. He repeated the order into the speaker tube and spun the wheel to amidships. The telegraph to the engine room, operated by the captain at the repeater on the flying bridge, flipped to the stop position. The vibration died.

There was a moment of absolute stillness, then the disorganized clatter of the anchor chains whipping through the hawse pipes could be heard. When the chains had played out and were stopped off, the stillness that returned was soon broken by the sound of shouts and clanging as the deck crew loosed the chains that had held the deck cargo in place.

The *Ross* had stopped at Guam to take on a deck load of World War II, Quad-50s. The Quad-50s were clumsy looking, half-tracked, tank-like vehicles that could, despite their looks, cover rough terrain with surprising speed. Each one carried four old-style 50-caliber machine guns. These guns never jammed. They would fire every time a trigger was squeezed.

The Chinese had brought a new element to the war, an element that in Asian warfare was not new. In a tactic that was centuries old, the Chinese were frequently charging the U.N. lines under the cover of darkness with 1,000-man walls of screaming fury. Most carried the extremely effective old "Tommy Gun," the rapid-firing weapon made famous by the Dick Tracy comic strip in the 1930s. The U.S. had given these weapons to Chang Ki Sheck's forces. When Chang was defeated, he lost them to the Communists. It was hoped that the nightmare tactic of the thousand man charges could be stopped cold by the ugly Quad-50's.

The anchor chains had barely stretched taut when a self-propelled crane-barge came along the ship's starboard side and an army tug placed a flat barge on the port beam. The

297

ship's gangway was lowered onto the portside barge. The gangway was immediately filled with debarking troops. They double-timed across the barge and jumped into the first of a line of Navy "LCIs" (Landing Craft Infantry) that had appeared out of the morning fog. As soon as each LCI was loaded, it departed with a hollow roar back into the fog bank.

Sea watches were maintained, but all topside hands were ordered to work the deck cargo. Chief Farritor put dustcovers on the equipment on the bridge. Before he left the wheelhouse to help work the cargo, he stole a moment to, just one more time, allow his hands to caress the precious hardwood of the ship's wheel. As always before, a feeling of wellbeing came to him. He wished he could somehow bottle the ancient spirit in that wheel. He'd carry it in a flask on his hip and sip from it, as other men sip whisky or gin.

All of the action endemic to running the great ship had left the bridge and gone elsewhere. The bridge was again as silent as a chapel. He reluctantly ended his stolen moment at the wheel and moved toward the door. As often happened when he was alone on the silent bridge, he felt the urge to make the sign of the cross as he passed through the door to the wing of the bridge. Father Keller's teachings were largely forgotten, however vestiges of its disciplines had been, it seemed, lodged securely in his being. He smiled to himself at this thought.

He put on his heavy coat as he hurried down the starboard ladders to the main deck. There he would join in the labor of unloading the deck cargo.

It was soon apparent that the self-propelled crane was not entirely adequate to handle the heavy Quad-50s. The crane's task was to lift the Quad-50s off the main deck of the ship, across itself, then set them down safely on the barge that was tied along its own outboard side. Because of its lack of adequate height, the crane had great difficulty controlling the load when it first made the pick. The lifted Quad-50 did a lot of banging around, threatening to damage itself, other Quad-50s, and the ship. A technique was soon devised that seemed to work. The ship's cargo booms were rigged to allow the cable from each of the pair of booms to act as draglines to restrain the lift from opposite sides. With this improved technique, the unloading operation proceeded slowly and carefully.

The cold wind continued to freshen until it had begun to cause trouble with keeping the crane and its cargo-barge in place. The upwind hawser, the one securing the crane to a point on the great ship's foredeck, began to show signs of failure. Four sailors and the young chief wheelman set out to double the failing line. The hawser that held the crane-barge in place came through a port in the bulwark, then onto a set of bollards in the area of the present unloading operation.

To better see the full length of the troubled line, the chief took a position standing atop the bollard where the failing hawser was made fast. The new hawser was fed out through the port in the bulwark then tied to a heaving line that the crew of the crane-barge had thrown onto the foredeck of the *Ross*. With their heaving line the crew of the crane-barge pulled the hawser to where it could be made fast to a cleat on the foredeck of the crane-barge. The chief watched as his crew took the new line to the bow-winch, pulled it taut, then stopped it off and figure-eighted it over another set of bollards.

Frank Quinn was one of the sailors in his work party. When they finished making the new line fast, Frank leaned over the bulwark to view the results of their handiwork. Frank said, "Damn! Chief, that's fine seamanship!" It was said in jest, but there was a quiet pride in the saying.

Suddenly, warning shouts came from all sides. The chief turned to see a Quad-50,which had moments before been slowly lifting from its place on the deck ten yards away. It was now coming at him like a massive bullet, and it was little more than an arm's length away. He didn't want to be crushed between the bulwark and the flying Quad-50. There was no time to examine options. He threw himself backward over the side of the ship.

Lying on his back in midair, he had a momentary view of the stricken face of the cargo officer. Mr. Toller was staring at him in disbelief. Because some piece of the portside rigging had snapped, disaster had come to the *Ross.* Chuck hoped he wouldn't land on the steel deck of the crane-barge 40 feet below. He knew there was little chance of surviving a fall like that.

It seemed such an unlikely thing to be happening. How could it be that his life would end here today? It came to him that he might soon know the answer to the big question. What happens when you die? His curiosity was stronger than any fear. He felt only disappointment that he would not be there to see the rest of his life unfold.

As he fell, the advice given his survival class by the old chief bosun's mate at Sheepshead Bay came to his mind. "Make jumpin' off y'r ship the last thing ya' do, 'cause 'twill most likely be just that." He chased the image of the old bosun from his mind; he wanted to make room for someone else.

The new image was that of a tall girl with curly brown hair. Her blue-gray eyes laughed a lot. The picture of her in his mind was as he had seen her last. She was surrounded by beauty in blue pedal-pushers and a sleeveless white blouse. They were standing on the front deck at Sherman House on a hillside high above Honolulu. She was smiling. As he kissed her, he wished the scent of the plumeria in her hair could somehow come away with him. His allotted time in heaven had expired so he turned and got into his waiting taxi. The taxi would take him to his ship.

Suddenly his body was struck a violent blow from head to toe. His view of the high gray wall of the ship blurred and it became gray all around him.

He knew he had somehow missed landing on the deck of the crane. Landing on his back in the water had painfully knocked the wind from his lungs, and on landing he had somehow bit the inside of his left cheek. It hurt like hell and he figured it would soon be bleeding. Incredibly he was still alive!

He held his nose with one hand and kept his mouth tightly shut as he plummeted deep in the water. Survival training had taught him that he must keep the water from getting into his lungs until the air trapped in his clothes could bring him back to the surface.

First he must find his way out of the oppressive blackness he was in. The blackness seemed to be smothering him and holding him captive; the momentary period of captivity in a world of feathery darkness seemed an eternity. Eventually he came to realize that the great cloud of blackness lurking over him was the flat underside of the crane-barge. It was eerily coated with a fuzzy, dark marine growth. There was a feeling of great weariness over his lower body and he knew his mouth was filling with blood. It was scary but he managed to spit the blood into the sea without allowing seawater in. With one arm he worked his way out of the darkness under the crane barge toward the light. When he came into the light he popped to the surface. With the air and the light came the cold. The cold was an all-encompassing thing; it caused him to shake uncontrollably, making it very difficult to keep his head above water. The return of the air made him aware of heavy pains in his lungs and lower back. He was surprised to see Frank Quinn a few yards away lying on his back in the water.

The triangle of gray water they were in was closed off on two sides by walls of gray painted steel. The wind seemed to be pushing the two sailors into the point where the two steel walls came crunching together like the molars of some hungry giant. In the midst of his struggle to keep on the surface, he shouted to Frank to warn him of this new danger.

Frank's blue eyes were calm and he seemed to be trying to say something. The sound that came out of him was only the mewing sounds that a small animal might make. There was the look of a child on his face. Chuck could see that his friend Frank was badly hurt. The cold seawater seemed to want to help; it lapped gently over Frank's chin seemingly trying to wash away the blood that came quietly from a corner of his mouth. A dark cloud was forming in the water around Frank. The undistinguished gray of it was being transformed into a regal purplish cloud.

The crew of the crane appeared on the deck above them. They were shouting advice and throwing life jackets onto the water. One of them, wearing a life jacket, jumped in and landed near Frank, causing a cascade of pink sea water.

Struggling to get to one of the floating lifejackets, the young chief went under again. This brought on another battle for survival. The air that had been trapped in his clothes had apparently escaped. His boots and heavy winter clothes were now dead weights pulling him under. He held his breath and used both arms to fight his way upward toward the life jacket that he could still see floating on the surface. Despite his desperate efforts the jacket kept moving farther away. Then he was still. It wasn't that he had made a decision to give up; his arms simply quit working. As he slowly dropped away from the light, he still fought to keep the seawater out of his lungs. Just as a terrifying darkness began to surround him, a woven steel cable with an eye spliced at its end, came down right in front of him. He thrust his arms through the eye and yanked on the cable with a strength that he didn't know he still had. He wanted the sailor/fisherman on the upper end to know he had a bite. Like an old boot on a catfish hook, he felt himself being pulled upward away from the darkness. On the surface, the sailor in the life jacket helped him into a meat basket (a wire stretcher) and he was lifted onto the deck of the crane-barge.

The deck crew of the *Ross* had swung a cargo boom out over the deck of the crane-barge; Frank, in his wire stretcher, was already being lifted onto the foredeck of the great ship. In turn, the young chief was lifted aboard. As he swung upward, he again looked directly into the eyes of the cargo officer who was still at his post. The man's suntanned face was somehow the same odd color Frank's had been as he lay in the cold, gray water. It was the uneven color of lightly toasted white bread.

His training and his instincts told him that Frank was by now dead. Knowing it and accepting it were not the same. How could a neat guy like Frank be dead? Ugly as this place is, why would it pick out a good kid like Frank and kill him?

He recalled his easy acceptance of his own impending death as he plunged toward the deck of the crane-barge. Why was it then impossible to accept the fact that Frank had been killed? The violent shaking from the cold overpowered him again and his thoughts blurred.

A day later, flat on his back in sick bay with his legs in traction, he was told he had suffered severe injuries to his lower spine. The backside of his arms, legs and body plus the left side of his face were black and blue. He was told of Frank Quinn's death. The caterpillar-track of the Quad 50, grazing the bulwark, had in a scissors action, all but clipped Frank's body in two.

No one was blaming him for Frank's death. They didn't have to; he knew well enough whose fault it was. Why hadn't he taken better care of his crew? His guilt was a physical thing, it had a shape and a size and a color. His image of it was clear; it was an angry-looking encapsulated yellow boil. It lurked in a dark space behind his heart.

There was another factor; the silent tears that wet the flat pillow on either side of his head were shed in fear. No one was telling him that he would stand and walk again. Because of their silence, he assumed that he would not.

The first officer and the captain plus several of his friends came to see him in sickbay; however, as he came more and more under the influence of the painkilling drugs, conversation with anyone was impossible. His world became that which he could see on the backside of his eyelids. Frighteningly real, full-color nightmares galloped through his mind. The nightmares seemed to make those terror-filled runs on frantic schedules of their own making.

The ship's doctor mostly just pulled at his beard when he came by on his daily rounds. On one of his beard-pulling visits, the doctor asked his patient to sign a release. That piece of paper would allow the doctor to transfer his patient to the hospital at Clark Field in the Philippines. Even in his drugged condition, the young chief recoiled at that plan.

A good friend of his had suffered a broken leg in a man-overboard drill on a ship on the South China Sea and was transferred from his ship to the hospital at Clark Field. Beyond the terrible heat and the horror of ants and bedbugs in his full leg cast, the bottom line to the stories he told about that place was that in the end, they amputated his leg. Word was out that Civil War medicine was state of the art at Clark Field. The captain overruled the doctor on the issue. For better or worse, the young chief would stay with his ship until it reached New York.

Time warped for him in the incandescent-lit world of the sickbay. Without the sea and the sky to guide his life, days became meaningless as units of time. Perceptions in his drug-altered world were confusing. Inexplicably, he gained a heightened feel for the vibrations the ship produced. He knew when she was in a following sea, crossing sea swells, or cutting into oncoming waves. Without knowing the time of day, he knew when the midnight-to-four watch turned her to a crosswind course to allow the engine-room crew to blow the soot from her stacks.

It seemed that he slept all of the time and that he slept not at all. He watched in disbelief as his left leg atrophied to a point where it seemed a thing apart from his body. Beyond moving his arms, his life was without motion except that which his mind generated. Fear was the bench upon which everything rested. The fear that brought mind paralysis the most was fear of the future. Those recurring nightmares in color seemed to be absolute reality.

There was one thought pattern that provided escape from those deep canyons of fear. He consciously developed an alternate avenue of thought. It was into a memory world that involved a tall, pretty girl with laughing blue-gray eyes. He had dated this girl in the best of all times and in the most beautiful of all places, the Hawaii of the late 1940s.

They had played in the surf, sunned on the clean white beaches and explored Oahu in a remarkably durable old rented Ford convertible. The incredible vistas at every turn of the road raised goose bumps, as did Vaughn Monroe's record of "Ghost Riders in the Sky" on the radio.

They returned many times to the Pali, a sharp ridge from which they could overlook the world. Near there, on the windward side of the Pali, a waterfall had fallen skyward from the beginning of time. They learned of this in a story told one evening at a luau by a native storyteller. That ridge which was high above the city of Honolulu was subject to sudden attacks in the night by tropical rainsqualls. They held each other tight during those wild storms. As the squalls spent their fury, the wind tugged at the canvas top of the old Ford. On the car radio, Ezio Pinza coolly sang *Some Enchanted Evening*. He crooned the lyrics, seemingly unaware of the possibility of the convertible's top being ripped off by the banshee winds and his voice being drowned in the torrential downpour. When each storm passed, the island moon regained its magic. Its soft light found and touched them anew. The moon seemed always to be totally unaware of the storm's noisy passing.

Their love had been innocent, yet now in his fantasy he knew every dip and swell on her firm young body. The creativity of his imagination surprised him. This combination of memory and fantasy gave him precious moments during which fear and its terrible hand-maidens, the color nightmares, were held at bay.

The *M.S.T.S. General Ross* renegotiated the South China Sea, the Strait of Malacca, and the Indian Ocean. As usual she stopped at Colombo, Ceylon (Sri Lanka), to replenish her fuel and supplies. She especially needed fresh water. Her desalination boilers could extract but a fraction of the drinking water needed daily by her heavy human load.

On the Indian Ocean, she passed over Frank Quinn's mythical beaches on the underwater range of mountains called the Carlsberg Ridge. Beyond the Suez Canal, at ports in Turkey, Greece and Holland, she delivered fewer young men than she had taken from those shores. Some of the young men were whole and some were not. They were all marked in that unmistakable way that wars mark young men. The same could be said for the young Americans that she delivered back to the port of New York. There were no crowds to greet them just as there were no crowds to see them off when they were sent out to fight that ugly little war.

After a 40-day voyage from Korea on a bright Sunday morning, the *Ross,* with the aid of two army tugs, docked quietly at a pier on the west side of lower Manhattan. The *Ross* and all who were aboard her were glad to be home.

Navy medics carried the young chief's gurney down the gangway to the dock. As the gurney rolled into position to be loaded onto a waiting gray ambulance, members of the ship's crew shouted their goodbyes to him from the foredeck and the bridge of the great ship. Because his eyes were unaccustomed to the bright sunlight, he couldn't see who the shouters were. He slipped his arm from under the strap of the gurney and waved in their direction.

Leaving the lower west side with its young patient, the battered old ambulance took the Holland Tunnel to New Jersey, then down the Jersey shore behind the Statue of Liberty to the Bayonne Bridge. It delivered him to the Staten Island Marine Hospital at 0900 hours on that Sunday morning. The driver rolled his patient's gurney across the unloading dock and into a well-lit basement corridor. He then pushed the button on the wall that was there to announce the arrival of a new patient. Before he left, the gray-haired ambulance driver took the young patient's hand in his and said, "God bless you, young man. Welcome home." The patient was surprised at the effect of the words. The man's simple kindness brought quick tears to his eyes.

Chuck lay in that basement corridor strapped to his gurney from the time of his arrival at 0900 hours until 1700 hours of that day. Strangely enough, healing began for him there in that unlikely place.

By lifting his head with his arms he could see a clock on the wall down the corridor half way to where the corridor made a turn. He was surprised to see another occupied gurney perhaps a quarter of the way to the clock. The occupant of that gurney screamed often and loudly. The language of screams is universal, but when words accompanied the scream, they were in a language the young chief couldn't understand. That patient was apparently mad as hell at being lost in the bowels of a hospital and he wanted to let the world know how he felt about it. Unfortunately, the world he was addressing was only eight feet high, eight feet wide and perhaps thirty yards long. Their world ended at the point where the corridor turned and disappeared. Only his fellow corridor dweller heard his screams.

As the hours wore on, Chuck's fear and hunger grew and he was cold. He dozed off in mid afternoon and one of his reoccurring color nightmares came to him. It was the one with the "old men on the porch." He again recognized himself as one of the old men in the high-backed wooden wheelchairs. When he awoke he was, as always after that nightmare, in a cold sweat. This time he grabbed onto the memory that he knew had set the stage for the nightmare. With some difficulty, he forced his mind to play out the story.

In his mind he went again with his father and his brothers to the Custer County Poor Farm. They were there to visit one of his dead grandfather's old cowboy friends. He saw again the large two-story house at the end of a long lane off a county road in Dale Valley. He saw the old men lined up on the screened front porch in large, wooden wheelchairs. Grandpa's old friend and some of the others, the one's whose eyes were clear and sharp, were quiet and seemed angry.

On the way home, the boy asked his father about that. His dad said, "Seems to me they've got good reason to be angry." He seemed about to let it go at that, but decided to say more. "Those old boys sit there in a kind of pain that you've no way to understand. Most every joint in their bodies is swollen and red with rhumatiz and as long as they live there's nothing that's ever gonna make that pain go away. For a lifetime of Nebraska winters, with few warm clothes like we have to wear, each one of those old guys took care of herds of cattle out in weather that'd make a polar bear hunt cover. Come summer they'd be, it seemed, knee deep in rattlesnakes while putting up the hay that'd keep those same cows alive when winter came again."

"They'd work those cattle pretty much like we do, but their circumstances were a lot grimmer. They'd ride pell-mell after those half-wild, contrary-minded critters, maybe breaking a collarbone after taking a flying header when their horse broke a leg stepping into a prairie-dog hole. He'd find another horse an' tolerate the pain while the broken-collarbone mended itself. He dasn't take time off. If he didn't work, he didn't eat. On Saturday nights in town there'd be bar fights. They'd sometimes fight over a woman, or maybe fight because they each knew they'd never have a woman of their own. All their lives, they and their friends loved either the Union or the Reb flag. They loved that flag and their friends absolutely and unconditionally. The one and only thing they really want now is to rejoin their friends. There's no chance now of gettin' snake-bit, no drunks to fight with, and no late spring blizzards to get caught in. They all know that pneumonia (they call it new-mo-nee) is the only friend they have. Each one of 'em is wait'n the day when that quiet friend will come to take'm to the place where their friends are. Yah, lad. They've got plenty of cause to be angry. As a matter of fact, that anger is the one good thing they've got goin' for 'em."

With the relived story done, the young man lay stunned. In the mental retelling of that familiar story he had come upon a truth that had been eluding him. The message was suddenly absolutely clear: Engulfed in fear, a man has only fear. Starting right now, just as the clear-eyed old men had done, he would convert his fear to anger. If he embraced anger, he knew that he would never again suffer a fear-driven nightmare.

Fear was behind him. He was going to walk again or kick a hole in the wall with his one good leg. Wait a minute, how the hell could he do that? The image of a one-legged man kicking a hole in a wall made him laugh out loud. He realized suddenly, this was the first laugh he'd had since laughing at something someone in his work party had said the morning before Frank was killed. Wanting to do something to declare his new freedom and taking a cue from his corridor partner, he shouted out all of the swear words he knew in English, German, Tagalog, and Gaelic. The man on the other gurney joined in.

He lifted his head with his arms to get a better look at his corridor comrade. He still couldn't see the man very well, but when his eyes moved beyond the other gurney, suddenly, as though the thing had appeared by magic, he spotted a payphone beyond the clock, down near where the corridor turned.

By reaching out, he could just manage to grasp the corridor handrail. He pulled the gurney toward it then proceeded to pull himself along the wall toward the phone. As he moved past the other gurney, the man said something to him.

It was incomprehensible, but he looked like he was saying, "Where the hell you think you're a goin'?"

It took most of an hour for him to get to the phone. He had some change in a coin purse under his pillow. His hands were shaking badly from the drugs and from sheer exhaustion. Two dimes dropped to the deck and were lost. He finally managed to get one into the coin slot. An operator's voice came to his ear. In a voice as firm as he could make it, he said, "Operator, please give me a police dispatcher."

The police dispatcher who took the call listened to him for a moment then interrupted him to say, "I'm transferring you to my supervisor."

A moment later a woman with a strong, clear voice came on the line, "This is Officer Breen. How can I help?"

"Miss Breen, I'm a sailor. I may sound like I'm drunk but I'm not. It's the pain medicine they've been feeding me in sickbay. My tongue feels like it has a woolen sock on it. I'm in the basement of the Staten Island Marine Hospital. I was delivered here this morning off a troopship from Korea. There's another guy on a gurney here with me. We're hurt an' I don't think anyone in the hospital knows we're here." He was out of breath, and unable to continue.

The firm official tone was missing when Miss Breen next spoke. "You're just in from Korea? Mother of God, you poor boy! My brother was killed in a battle at some river there." Her voice trailed off.

"I'm sorry Miss Breen. I wish there was something I could say that'd ease your pain." She seemed to be waiting for him to continue. "Miss Breen, I don't know how it could happen but me an' this other guy have been strapped to our gurneys here since morning. The other guy don't speak English but he growls and screams a lot."

Miss Breen found her voice, "You poor boy, how old are you? I can tell that you're hurt! Mother of God! How could they just lose you in the basement? Those bastards, I'll jerk their chains till their eyes cross." Some of the official tone came back into Miss Breen's voice, she said, "Now first thing, I want you to look at the number on the phone you're on. Read it to me very carefully, I have to call you back." He had trouble with the numbers as she suspected he would. After several tries she seemed to think he had it right. He was so exhausted he had trouble getting the receiver back on the hook. When the phone rang, in a minute or two, it startled him. It was the first ring of a phone he'd heard in months.

When Chuck got the receiver back to his ear, he could hear Miss Breen raising hell with someone. He assumed it to be the folks upstairs in the hospital. When she came back on the line she had changed again, she was near tears, and she wanted to talk about her brother. "He looked so beautiful in his uniform. He accepted a commission in the Army Corps of Engineers. He loved the Hudson River Valley. He knew that something had to be done about the polluters. Most of the fish were dead and trees on the banks were dying. The beauty of the river would soon be gone. Its beauty would exist only on the paintings in the galleries on Park Place."

"They promised Danny that he could make a difference on the River." After a pause, she continued, "You know, I haven't been able to talk to anyone about his death. My friends don't seem to know that we're in a war. Instead of allowing him to do the environmental work that they had promised him, they shipped him out with an infantry outfit. Its name was a joke, the outfit had no horses but it was called the First Cavalry. His company was defending a line along some nothing river in that nothing country. One of his friends wrote me that Danny took a terrible wound to his chest. My God, how can that be? Why is our beautiful, caring Danny dead? His life went for nothing! Why? Why?" Her voice trailed off into sobs.

It seemed incredible to the young man that literally the first person he talked to here at home was asking another version of the same questions he'd been asking. He knew there was nothing he could say to this grieving lady that would be adequate, so he just cried with her. As though on cue, the man on the other gurney gave out with one of his very best screams.

The scream was still reverberating in the corridor when two teams of medics burst through a door beyond the turn. The team that came to Chuck's gurney was led by a young nurse with soft brown eyes. He said to her, "I have a cop on the phone, her name is Miss Breen."

The nurse with the soft brown eyes took the receiver from his ear and spoke her name into the phone. From the look of compassion on her face it was apparent that Miss Breen had not regained her official tone. After a little while she said, "We'll do right by them, Officer Breen. Thank you for your help." Then she gently returned the phone to its hook. She said, "Sailor, you seem to be able to make good friends even while lost in a basement. And I must say, you do know how to raise hell to get things done, don't you?"

As the team organized itself around him, the nurse with the soft brown eyes quickly read the chart that was hanging from a hook on his gurney. As the gurney rolled, she kept her cool hand on his forehead. She said, "Chief Farritor, I can't tell you how sorry we are that this crazy thing happened, but I want you to know that you're in good hands here. You will walk out of here, I promise you that!"

The young chief needed to hear that. He momentarily placed his hand over the cool one that was on his forehead. His voice broke as he said, "Thank you."

With his mind more at ease, he was thinking of Officer Breen. He felt as though he knew her and her brother personally. He was visualizing Danny's death. Danny, an environmentally schooled Cavalryman who had been given no horse, lay on his back in a dusty field. He was looking into an evening sky. The sky was filled with the same stars he had studied and loved as a boy in upstate New York. He knew he was dying. He was thankful that he was not dying alone. The familiar stars and his God were there with him. Bright red blood pumped through his hands as he held them over the hole in his chest. Danny didn't see his blood turn dark and soak into the dust of a Korean field, a field that smelled of human waste. He didn't see the North Korean soldiers splash across the river and run past without looking twice at the dead American. The American lay on his back with a sky full of stars reflecting from his unseeing eyes. The young peasant soldiers saw only a dead enemy; they saw naught a young engineer who had joined the American army to defend his beloved Hudson River Valley from industrial polluters.

Chuck's thoughts were jogged back to the present. A postman was cutting across the park headed directly for the park bench on which he sat. The postman had a shock of silvery-white hair and was bent under the weight of the mailbag he carried. As he neared the bench he slid the bag from his shoulder, then sat down.

"Lord, 'tis good to get tat 'ting off me back. Would ye believe me, lad, tat I've wore out a half dozen of tose bags in me t'irty years delivering mail ta folks here on ta Ridge?" Looking at the bag accusatively, he said, "Faith, I'm tinkin' tis ta' bag tat's here ta do **me** in. Do ye know lad? I was about y'r age when I came t'ru tose narrows in steerage on a ship from ta auld sod." In the midst of telling his story the old Irishman turned to look at his bench-mate.

What he saw made a change in him. After a few moments of silence, with his eyes on the tree-covered hills of Staten Island beyond the narrows, the old Irishman spoke softly, "One day, I expect tere will be a bridge across tose narrows. What a grand sight 'twill be! 'Twill be built by smart young fellas' like ye, young man." An innate wisdom told the old postman that it was important for this emotionally wounded young man to get on with the rest of his life. After a few more minutes of silent rest he stood up. As he did so he reached over and softly wiped the tears from the young man's cheeks. "Ye've got a lot o good days comin' lad. I know ta' good Lord'll see ta makin' 'tings right fer ye. Trust in him lad. Will ye do tat fer me? Will ye now?" The young man answered him only with his eyes.

Re-shouldering the heavy mailbag, the postman turned to retrace his steps across the park. He was ready to resume his task of delivering mail to the folks on the ridge.

Well after "lights out" in the ward, Chuck got quietly out of bed and padded out into the darkened corridor. The corridors were off limits to patients after lights out. To get past the nurse's station without getting caught took very precise timing. Actually it was a snap these nights. It had been a real challenge when he was stooped over in his gooney-bird plaster cast and pushing his four-wheeled walker. Things were further complicated by the fact that he was more or less dragging his left leg. He had in fact gotten caught many times. Even so, once he was ambulatory he missed very few nights visiting his friends in the night sky. His viewing point was the solarium at the west end of the wing.

When he got to the solarium, he went first to the north windows to view the incredible array of manmade lights in the Manhattan skyline. That sight was without equal anywhere in the world. To the west across the Kill Van Kull, the cities and small towns of New Jersey glowed softly in the darkness. Farther west the eroded remnants of the once mighty Pocono Mountains slept peacefully in the night's shadows.

Exciting as those views were, they fell short of the views to be found in the night sky. Each section of the sky displayed its own prized jewels. He paid his respects to the golden-haired lass Capella and to his and his grandmother's friend, the Dog Star. He always returned lastly to the west windows. It was there, far beyond the sleeping Pocono Mountains that his past and future lay.

Reflecting this night on the recent past, he recalled his visit with the Quinn family. It had gone better than he had ever hoped it would. He was not asked about Frank's death. They wanted only to share loving memories of their son and brother and to express gratitude to a friend who would come to share his memories of Frank with them. After the visit with Frank's family, the image of the ugly encapsulated yellow boil in the dark cavity behind his heart quietly went away. He knew he was not totally free of guilt, but the pain of it was gone.

He was feeling stronger every day. No longer on the ugly purple pills, he was standing tall and walking with only a slight hitch in his left leg. One of the requirements for release from the hospital was a heavy session with the staff shrink. The word was that you came out of that encounter with your mind looking like an orange after a bout with a mechanical juicer. His feelings of guilt in Frank's death would surely come up in that session but after that he could lock it all away in the back of his mind forever.

The girl with laughing blue-gray eyes no longer showed up in frustrated dreams of fantasy. Muriel Teeling's curly brown hair and laughing eyes were these days, never far from his waking thoughts. He was feeling so confident about the future that he had asked her to marry him. Having completed her contract with Queen's Hospital in Honolulu, she was now at home with her family in New Jersey.

Plans were complete. After a grand wedding at her parent's home with his Uncle Will and Aunt Ruby present, they would honeymoon in Havana and on the Florida Keys. They would then pack their clothes, books, wedding presents and dreams into an ex-army jeep trailer that they would hook to their new Studebaker starlight coupe. With thousands of other young couples from across the country who were doing the same thing, they would migrate to California. Before he left New York, he'd somehow find Officer Breen. He'd thank her for much more than rescuing him from a basement corridor all those months ago.

He would again take the ferry to Brooklyn and the bus to Bay Ridge. He would say goodbye to the Quinn family and he would wait on a park bench for an old Irish postman who came there daily to rest: he who delivered mail to the folks on Bay Ridge and words of wisdom and comfort to exhausted young ex-sailors. Chuck would ask the old Irishman to finish telling his story and he'd let him know that he would not be one of the young men who would help build the Verrazano Narrows Bridge. He had other plans.

Unlike his grandmother before him who feared that if she went too far west, the Dog Star would be unable to find her, the young ex-sailor knew, with certainty, that he would find the gentle blue giant in the California winter sky.

The first rays of the morning sun warmed and fed the flowers and greenery that made up the view from his study window. The air would soon be alive with the many birds that traded daily at the feeder near the vine-covered wall. The birds traded their songs and the sunlit flash of their bright colors for the food they found there. All of that would start later. These first rays of the sun had arrived to gently arouse the garden from its overnight rest. Retired now after 43 years of building schools and homes, Chuck turned from the window. Sitting again in his chair, he looked at his computer screen. He was done with telling the story and he felt a sense of relief that touched his soul. He was reminded of the feeling that came to him after his visit with the Quinn family. He recalled the moment when he realized that the encapsulated yellow boil lodged in a dark space behind his heart had gone away. This new feeling of relief was an extension of that one. Telling it to the computer seemed to be enough. He hesitated for several long moments before he made the moves to start the printer. With the printer busy making its unique clucking sounds, he stood up and moved again to the window. A pretty lady with blue-gray eyes came into the room. She joined him in watching the birds that had gathered at the feeder. Her once curly brown hair was now softly waved and touched with gray. She was wearing a white clinic coat. She would soon be off to her volunteer work as a Red Cross nurse at the local senior center. As they stood and watched the show being put on by their busy and colorful winged guests, she put her arm around his waist and leaned her head against his chest. He had at long last found a complete and genuine morning calm.

★★★★★★★★★★

Story Fourteen

Royalty in the Early Morning

A steady rain fell quietly on the rambling stables at Santa Anita racetrack. In the predawn darkness of a Saturday morning, the silence within the stable was broken occasionally by a gentle clinking of halter rings. The tall, powerful thoroughbreds were already awake and moving about in their stalls. They moved on manicured hooves that made no more sound than that of a dropped handkerchief in this quiet realm of power and royalty.

As the small hours of the morning grew larger, four visitors arrived at the guarded door of the stable. The guard nodded in recognition and allowed them in. Adapting to the silent darkness, they settled into their accustomed out-of-the-way observation spots. Chuck Farritor, a builder taking a rainy day off, was one of those quiet visitors. The regal animals in this stable were seemingly quite unlike the horses he loved as a boy. Those cowponies were strong and smart. Their sturdy legs could, when asked to do so, plant and stop a running steer when he came to the end of a throw rope that was looped around a saddle horn. Chuck knew well the two indispensable features shared by these thoroughbreds and any good cowpony. Those features were a huge heart and intelligent eyes. Those eyes are a clear window into that big heart.

Soon the trainers, grooms, workout jockeys, and stable hands arrived. They, too, seemed to fall into the quiet spell created by the silent thoroughbreds. The newcomers' greetings to one another were brief and subdued.

A trainer listened to a small radio behind the closed door of a tack room being used as an office. The voice on the radio spoke self-importantly of an upper-level low and of continued rain in the San Gabriel Valley.

The grooms and stable hands quietly commenced their endless tasks. Maids and minions to their regal charges, they knew and appreciated fully that blood from the likes of "Bold Ruler," "Secretariat" and "Man-O-War" flows in the veins of these often impatient and petty, but ever royal, scions of those equine kings.

A shaft of florescent light spilled out onto the stable's center aisle. The light came from the open door of the brightly lit room where the exercise jocks were quietly dressing for the morning workouts. Their work shirts were a wild collection of color. This riot of color was soon subjugated by olive-drab waterproof jackets with hoods. Their jean-covered legs were thrust into heavy, colorful knee-length socks, the tops of which folded down to create a rain-blocking grommet at the top of their boots.

As the gray dawn broke, the regal athletes were led out into the rain where they would, with varying degrees of success, do the things their riders and trainers asked them to do. They were willed on in their efforts by silent, stopwatch-holding trainers and visitors who hung over the track-rail, unmindful of the spattering mud as each horse and rider flashed by.

After the morning workouts, the visitors took off their raingear and cleaned up as best they could. They gathered as usual for breakfast at Benny's over on Huntington Drive. They didn't spend a lot of money there, but Benny was always tolerant of them. He understood the thing that made them get out at three o'clock in the morning. He understood that they were a kind of square "groupie" species, a species that is compelled to come out to see the "stars" of the thoroughbred world when those stars come to town. Over several cups of coffee, they swapped stories about horses they know or knew, and then they parted to go home to work on their "honey do" lists.

Later in the morning the vast parking lots at Santa Anita filled with automobiles large and small. Mammoth diesel buses from cities as far away as San Diego discharged their human cargos onto the tarmac. The cargo, in high-heeled pumps or shiny dress shoes, scampered to the shelter of the covered grandstands. At post time, they peered through a variety of binoculars. Most looked at horses they knew only by the names they saw printed on the program.

Though the quality of their audience has deteriorated, the thoroughbreds, when called upon again to go out into the rain, will valiantly try to do on that muddy track all that their riders asked of them. Their breeding will allow them to do no less.

On that day, as happens much too often, the magic broke in one of those fine-boned legs, and a mercy bullet found its mark in a regal forehead. The diesel bus folks likely made note of it on their programs by rubbing out the dead athlete's name.

The silent visitors who shared the quiet of that final early morning with the now-dead thoroughbred learned of the tragedy when they opened the sports section of their Sunday papers. Whether the dead athlete be stud or filly, they rejoiced in the memory of the beauty that was while they grieve for the loss of the joy and beauty of what might have been.

Their silent grief was tempered by the knowledge that the dead athlete has gone to a place where the blue sky is cloudless and the abundant grass on the meadow is green and invitingly tender.

They know that the likes of "Bold Ruler," "Secretariat" and "Man-O-War" would be there in that lush valley to greet the newcomer. The newcomer's once-shattered leg will again be whole. Thick mane will be flying from that proudly bowed neck as the newcomer trots briskly across the broad valley to meet the royal welcoming committee.

The silent visitors each know; this is a knowledge they share but must not talk about. No one, not even Benny, would understand.

Story Fifteen

Legacy

The engine labored quietly as their camper-truck climbed a narrow winding road to the Coconino Plateau. Patsy Cline, John Denver, Joan Baez and others were singing their songs on an all-night radio station out of Tempe, Arizona.

A father and his son Timothy listened to the radio in appreciative silence. Chuck, the father, marveled at the fact that Tim seemed to like the same kind of music he liked. Most of Tim's friends were caught up in a messy new kind of music that was hard for most older folks to recognize as music at all. Tim's wisdom or tolerance, whichever it was, made his dad love and appreciate the lad all the more.

As they listened, the night's darkness faded and gave way to an overcast new day. With the new dawn in place, a gentle rain began to fall. As the truck climbed higher on the mountain, the rain changed to a heavy, wet snow. The wipers did their best to keep two fan-shaped areas clear on the windshield. The morning news interrupted the music on the radio. The war in Vietnam dominated the news. With the war in its eighth and bloodiest year yet, the newscaster did what he could to make sense of the ongoing disaster in that faraway place. Chuck wondered anew why it wasn't clear to everyone that the right thing to do was to admit that our being at war in that country was a mistake. The only way to correct that mistake was to just get the hell out.

The truck engine's sound became less labored as the grade leveled off. As far as they could see through the still-falling snow, the road led across a brown and aqua-green desert. That desert was being transformed this morning into a great, still, uneven ocean of white. Because they had been this way before, the father and son knew the road they were on would take them to the south edge of Arizona's Grand Canyon. The virgin whiteness of the road eventually ended at a snowy parking lot near the great abyss they were seeking.

Leaving their pickup truck in a silent and otherwise deserted area, they made their way out onto a point of rock that dramatically overhangs the south bank of that great canyon.

The snow clouds were dark and so low it seemed they could reach up and touch them. Through the falling snow they could see deeply into that ancient canyon as it slept in silent shadows at their feet. The cloud cover seemed intact; yet as they watched in amazement, a great shaft of golden sunlight pierced the clouds and plunged through the falling snow to the blue and silver path of the Colorado River far below.

The sun's rays, reflecting off the mirror of each snowflake, lit that great canyon as bright as if it were high noon on a clear day. The view through the falling snow had the effect of giving that ancient canyon with its massive rock forms a feeling of infinite space, ethereal and mystical.

An awesome silence pressed itself on the two visitors. This great silence somehow became another dimension to the primal scene that lay before them. The golden shaft of sunlight lingered for what seemed a millennium. Its golden fingers found their way into the flowing river and into every nook and cranny of that storied canyon. Then suddenly it abandoned the colorful rocks and the blue river. The shaft of golden sunlight seemed, with great deliberation, to climb the snowflakes out of the canyon. Then it leaped back into and through the low, dark clouds overhead.

The father and son were spellbound, the father at this incredible interaction between terrain and weather. He came to know that his son saw it another way. The silence that had been a powerful part of what they had just seen held them transfixed. To avoid breaking the spell, they made no sound as they moved away from the great canyon's edge.

Tim was the first to speak. "You know what, Dad? God did that painting. He did it just for us." It took some moments for the father to make the adjustment to the mental plane that the boy was on. Suddenly it became clear to him that here in a snowstorm on an Arizona mountain a lad of 14 years was offering him a lesson in art and in faith.

As he matured and grew to manhood, Tim painted in remarkable dimensions of his own. Several folks in Beverly Hills and Westwood cherish the wall murals that grace their expensive homes. Those wall paintings are a legacy to life from a young man whose life was taken from him, his family and his friends much too soon. A new-age cancer brought Tim home to die in a room that had been his for a good part of his life.

His family prays to understand one day the why of it all. They pray to be able to understand that "why" as clearly as Tim understood a painting done in thundering silence on a miles-wide canvas – a painting that God chose to do, one day, for a boy and his dad.

Tim's ashes are interred in Claremont's Oak Park Cemetery. His high school friends installed a bench near his grave. The bench is inscribed with colorful and precious words authored by his loving Aunt Eileen, "TIM, THE STARS, CLOUDS AND SUNSETS ARE NOW YOURS TO PAINT." A few years after Tim's death, the children from *Oakmont*, the grammar school he attended, planted a magnolia tree near his grave. Those children knew of Tim from quiet stories that their gifted teacher, Olivia Ellis, had told them. The children named that beautiful flowering tree "Tim's Champion."

★ ★ ★ ★ ★ ★ ★ ★ ★ ★

-✶-

Story Sixteen

The Beauty of the Coming Night

Saturdays allowed Chuck the luxury of time for a second cup of coffee on their east-facing veranda. He watched the first rays of the day's sun strike and bounce off the snow on the top of the San Gabriel Mountains. The morning air was as cool and clear as the sparkling water that flows from springs on those mountains.

Today would be another great day. Later this afternoon he would have some friends in; they'd watch the University of Nebraska/UCLA football game together. Chuck was a faithful UCLA fan. His support for the Bruins wavered only once in a blue moon when, in a nonconference game, they'd play the University of Nebraska. This was one of those "blue moon" years! He probably will be the only one in the group rooting for the Big Red of Nebraska!

He figured he'd have plenty of time to do the one chore that needed to be done today. He had to go into the city to rescue his pickup truck from its place of nervous rest on a Los Angeles street. Its engine had blown the night before; he had abandoned the truck there and caught a ride home. This morning the towing company advised him that he had to be there when they made the hookup. He'd concluded that if he had to go there, he'd just as well tow the pickup to the yard himself. He'd use his camper truck and a tow dolly.

Before leaving on his errand, he looked in on his wife Muriel. She looked so at peace in her sleep, he decided not to risk waking her with a goodbye kiss.

As usual on a Saturday morning, traffic on both Interstate 10 and the Harbor Freeway was light. He took an off-ramp to the mean street in South Central where his pickup truck rested.

Miraculously her tires and chrome wheels had survived the night. She sat looking at him, almost indignantly, as she awaited rescue.

With the winch on his camper truck he eased the front wheels of the ailing vehicle up onto the tow dolly. He then took care to wipe up the engine oil that had bled onto the street from her fractured innards.

Getting underway, he maneuvered the little train up onto the north-bound Harbor Freeway and was soon again passing the sparkling new buildings of downtown Los Angeles. Each high-rise was busy singing its own song in the clear morning sunlight. He caught a glimpse of a high-rise on Bunker Hill that he had helped build.

After he closed down his own construction business at age 62, he had just gotten used to sitting on his veranda in his rocking chair when he got a call to go to work for a major builder out of Sacramento. He worked for that fine company as a construction superintendent on many large projects in Southern California. He had retired again at age 75.

Well onto the eastbound I-10 Freeway, he became aware of the sound of a chain dragging. He pulled over and stopped on the shoulder of the freeway adjacent to the sound barrier wall. He noticed the yellow emergency callbox on the wall near where he climbed out of his truck. The phone was awaiting its next chance to perform a function of service or mercy.

An 18-wheeler roared by in the outside lane of the freeway. A colorful logo on its great white box announced that it was from Mankato, Minnesota. There were snow chains hanging from its underside. He didn't envy that driver his wintertime crossing of the country. The man from Mankato's first trials would come very soon as he crossed California's snowbound Sierra Nevada.

Chuck climbed out and moved along the side of the camper truck next to the sound-barrier wall . He stepped between his vehicles and over the trailer tongue. As he did so, it occurred to him that his old pickup truck looked a little silly as she sat there on the dolly with her nose in the air. He felt a twinge of sadness knowing that, though she looked great, her 270,000 miles dictated a reality. Now with her major engine troubles, the time had come when the right thing to do was to put the proverbial pistol to her temple and set her free. He visualized the Willie and Joe cartoon from World War II where the G.I. artist, Bill Malden, had the often challenged pair of dogfaces delivering the coup de grace to their mortally wounded Jeep. He stooped to pick up the chain that had come loose and was dragging on the pavement.

The sound that suddenly changed the morning was not the bark of Willie's government-issue 45. It was instead a violent, roaring, screeching explosion of sound.

He knew he was spinning in the air. His eyes focused for some fraction of a second on the back of his towing vehicle. He knew that the bright red splotch he saw on that white aluminum wall was his own blood!

Then Chuck knew he was no longer spinning and the sound he could hear was the deep sound of silence. He knew he was not breathing. He was in a quiet place; a darkened sky seemed to be all around him. It was good to be resting. The need to keep moving had lost the power it had always held over him.

Then something warned him that he would surely die if he didn't start breathing. The short-sleeved shirt he was wearing allowed him to see that his left arm was broken. The bone wasn't protruding through the skin but midway between the elbow and the wrist, an ugly bruise glared at him and the normal bone alignment was out of whack. He pushed on the pavement with the other arm to rise to his knees. His neck was extended and his mouth was open like a range bull in the act of bellowing. No sound came from him. A deadly silence continued to fill his ears.

He began to comprehend that something had hit the outboard wheel of the tow dolly. The dolly's left fender lay near him; the fender had a tire track across it. He thought it strange that he had only socks on his feet. He wondered what had become of his boots. Then, accompanied by deep, sharp pains in his chest, air came into his lungs. He was suddenly totally exhausted. He dropped onto his right side near the wall.

With a partial awareness of what had happened to him here on the shoulder of the I-10 freeway, there came to him the memory of another brush with death. It was long ago in Korea in the cold gray waters of the Bay of Inchon. He thought of the wonderful Dr. Moser B. Taylor who had restored his life by rebuilding his lower spine. It was too much to think of that masterpiece of repair being ruined here today, smashed like a teacup under the heel of a vandal's boot. He drove that thought away. He would think about his wife, Muriel, their fine son, Tim, their lovely daughter, Cathy, and their bright grandson, Mark.

Paramedics appeared. He knew they spoke to him; he saw their lips move. The lightning flashes of pain began to fade from the again-darkening sky. Then, though his eyes were open, he could no longer see. He was immersed in the silent darkness of shock. There was a seductive quality to the beauty and peacefulness of the darkness that surrounded him.

The darkness itself possessed a quiet power. It held him in a strange haven of nothingness. Somehow he had gotten outside of his body and saw himself bootless and inert, lying near the wall. A voice or a thought told him it would be good to stay in this quiet dark place where he was protected from pain.

He felt himself being pulled out of the inviting dark place where he had found freedom from pain. He was being drawn back into the chamber of pain by a force that was a part of the bootless body lying near the wall. That body, though bloodied and broken, would not let him go.

He heard a soft voice say his name. He became aware of a white ceiling, then a white wall and a nurse with brown hair. He couldn't read the name on her ID badge, but the badge clearly read Garfield Medical Center. He knew that hospital was in the city of Alhambra. His son, Tim, was born at Garfield. It was called Garfield Hospital in those days.

The nurse was watching a machine that had wires leading to him. She said, "Welcome, Mr. Farritor. You've been away but now, thank goodness, you're back. We knew you'd be worried about your back. X-rays have shown that miraculously there was no harm done to the repairs that were made to it. You do, however, have serious internal injuries that the doctor is worried about, and your left arm is broken." The nurse continued, "Your wife was here to see you. She went to the cafeteria for a short break. She'll be back soon."

He knew it was important to the nurse to know that he could see and hear her, but he hadn't the strength to try to speak. Her image faded. He dropped away from her reality. He was on his east-facing veranda.

The snow on the San Gabriels was painted a reddish gold by the sun that was now low in the western sky. He decided to sit for awhile and rest. He knew that Muriel would soon be joining him. They would, as they had done so many times before, together watch the light on the San Gabriels change from the present reddish gold to a soft purple, then to blackness. All of this as the sun dropped below the western horizon.

His family's friend, the Dog Star, would soon be popping into view. As always, that faithful star would be holding aloft his ancient blue lamp for all to see.

As he hoped she would, Muriel came to him on their east-facing veranda. Chuck took her in his arms. Her blue-gray eyes were smiling. He kissed her. They held each other close as the flamboyant colors on the mountain quietly gave way to blackness. Resting quietly in that blackness, they know, are the great mysteries and gentle beauties of the coming night.

Glossary

Belay
To tie or otherwise make fast a line to a pin or cleat.

Bolster
Heavy horizontal member on a wagon frame. It sits above each axel supporting the wagon box and holding the box in place.

Boondocks
Rough, remote area. Word borrowed from the Tagalog language.

Bollard
Very heavy cast-iron assembly consisting of two short posts bolted or welded to a ship's deck. Hawsers used for tying the ship to the dock are figure-eighted over the posts.

Bridge telegraph
Brass-handled device on the bridge connected to a like device in the engine room. Deck officer moved handles to a setting such as *full ahead*. This setting would be repeated on a like dial in the engine room. Officer in engine room moved a similar handle to acknowledge the order.

Bulkhead
Any wall on a ship.

Bulwark
Heavy solid railing designed to deflect rough seas, especially on the foredeck area of a ship.

COG
Connivance of the Government

Commission pennant	A long, very slim, red white and blue streamer that flies from the top of the main mast of every vessel commissioned to serve the United States.
Conn (the)	Virtual command of any vessel.
Crow's nest	On WWI and earlier ships, a small compartment above the yardarm on a ship's forward mast, which was only large enough for one man to stand in while on lookout watch. Many of these, so equipped, vessels were still in the fleet in WWII. The sailor in the crow's nest usually got a very rough ride. The advent of radar made the crow's nest lookout obsolete.
Dodger	An angled protection wall designed to block or divert seawater brought aboard by rough seas.
Dogface	WWII American soldier.
Dog robber	An orderly who directly serves the skipper, commanding officer or general, always a very dedicated individual. It is said that if it is something that the officer wants or needs and it is guarded by a mad dog, the orderly will, without delay or hesitation, arrange to steal it from the dog.
Flying bridge	That deck that is located directly above the wheelhouse. It is always exposed to the weather.

G.I.	WWII American Serviceman (short for government issue).
Gunwale	Pronounced gunnel. Railing of main deck, any boat or ship.
Gyro compass	A mechanical spinning disc device that has all but replaced the magnetic compass on large ships. There is great value in the device's ability to support multiple repeaters in places where they are needed, as on the wings of the bridge and on the flying bridge.
Hal	The scheming computer in the movie, "A Space Odyssey"
Incoming	Incoming mortar or artillery fire.
Jack staff	A short flagpole on the bow of any ship.
Jarhead	An American Marine.
Ladder	A pedestrian access to another level, may be at 90 degrees or any lesser degree from horizontal.
LCI	An armed, very durable motor craft used for landing troops onto a beach. It has a ramp at the bow that drops down.
Lifeline	Safety lines strung along the deck at hip height from bow to stern in rough weather and along spars on square-rigged sailing ships at all times.

Long ton	British Maritime term, greater than a standard ton, which is 2,000 pounds.
Meat wagon	An ambulance.
Mestiza	Western Pacific colloquialism; attractive, often mixed-blood native girl or woman.
Overhead	Ceiling in a shipboard room or cabin.
Pad eye	Cleat bolted or welded to a deck, mast or bulkhead designed to allow the attachment of a shackle or hook. Usually a part of the cargo tie-down system or ship's rigging.
Plimsol mark	An established pattern of marks at the waterline of a ship's hull. Provides plainly visible evidence of whether a ship is overloaded and riding too low in the water or whether it is riding too high and is in need of ballast. Created by maritime insurers, it is required on the hulls of most nation's ships.
Quarter deck	The area at the top of a docked ship's gangway.
Rat guards	Large, light metal disks that are designed to be placed around a ship's mooring lines, keeping rats from moving on the line from the pier onto the ship.
Small stuff	Rope or line smaller than 1 ¾ inches in circumference.

Swab-jockey	Deck sailor (Navy or Merchant Marine).
Thwart	Any object or part of a boat or ship lying at 90 degrees to the keel. A seat in a lifeboat that is at 90 degrees to the keel.
Wheelhouse	The center, enclosed part of the bridge deck that shelters the ship's operating and navigation equipment plus the ship's steering wheel. Also called pilothouse.
Wheelman	The ship's crewman whose job it is to steer the ship. He is under orders from the captain or deck-watch officer. Also called helmsman or quartermaster (old navy, master of the quarterdeck).
Yardarm	A sturdy, horizontal member running thwartship, it is located on the foremast about half to two thirds of the way to the top of the mast. The ship's signal flags or pennants are raised or lowered on halyards (lines) run threw small pulleys attached to the bottom of the yardarm.